PORTAL THIEF CHARLIE

THE DRAGON MAGE BOOK 6

SCOTT BARON

"When the going gets weird, the weird turn pro."
– Hunter S. Thompson

CHAPTER ONE

Blood trickled down the man's chin, staining his prison guard uniform with sticky crimson. Another violent blow to the face was followed by a fresh splash of the sanguine stuff making its way from his interior to his exterior and splattering on the wall beside him.

The guard didn't feel any pain, though. Not because he was so badly injured that he was oblivious to the damage being inflicted upon him, but, rather, because he wasn't a man at all. Not technically, at least.

He was a cyborg. A metal person with a meat exterior. And as such, he could simply have his processors turn off his external pain sensors at will.

It was quite effective at stopping the occasionally distracting sensations registered by his dermis, but on this occasion, it was just as useful at blocking him off from the punishment being inflicted upon him by his green-skinned charges.

"Please, I implore you to stop," he said to the Tslavar prisoner looming above him.

A piece of metal rent from a table was dripping blood as the alien stood staring unmercifully at the cyborg. The guard might not have been as breakable as others of this world, but he most certainly could bleed. And that was something the rioting Tslavars took great pleasure from.

The alien prisoners had been in custody several weeks now, stripped of their weapons, both conventional as well as magical, the latter being assisted by the magic-wielding people from the distant galaxy now residing on Earth.

It had been a bit strange for the guards, ensuring none of the Tslavars had those seemingly harmless little bands around their wrists. But it had been made very clear that those were not simply decorative, and the magic they held could be substantial.

But it was not a bit of magical trickery that had sparked the poor cyborg's current predicament, but, rather, subterfuge of a far more commonplace variety.

It hadn't been all that out of the ordinary. At least, so it had seemed when one of the prisoners suddenly appeared to be rather ill. It was likely the result of his digestive system reacting with Earth food he was not accustomed to, or so it would seem. And so it was that the hapless guard opened the containment cell to check on the ailing man.

His cellmates quickly subdued the cyborg, stripping him of keycard and restraints before releasing the other Tslavars held in their cell block. Within mere minutes, over a dozen of their comrades were freed from their cells.

"How long?" Cal asked the facility manager.

"It's been a little over an hour," the woman replied. "I fear that they have one of our men. Jonesy, is his name. New to us and just getting settled in when all of this happened."

"They took advantage of a weak link in the chain," Cal noted, his powerful AI mind processing all variables in a nanosecond. *"And they were quite efficient, it seems."*

"Yes, they were," the woman said. "And they must be incredibly strong to have overpowered him like that."

"No, I think not," Cal replied, the facility's files already

scanned and processed as they spoke. *"There were simply a greater number of them, and having learned some of the workings of the cell system, it appears they released additional forces by utilizing his access card. And this guard, I see, was a standard model, not designed for hands-on guard duties. That alone is a red flag, but he then further breached protocol by going to check on a prisoner prior to his backup arriving."*

"I'm sure he thought it was urgent."

"Undoubtedly. But even so, rules are in place for a reason, and now we must take more extraordinary measures to put a stop to this."

"What did you have in mind?" the manager asked. "My men are standing by."

"Oh, we will not be using your men," Cal replied. *"I have more specialized forces at my disposal. In fact, the best of them has just returned from their deep space survey this morning."*

"Oh," she said, "but won't they need to rest after their long journey?"

Cal let out a small chuckle. *"No, they will be fine. I'll have them to your facility within the hour."*

Thirty-seven minutes had passed when a small ship touched down just outside the facility, disgorging a trio of square-jawed men whose boots had only just barely hit the ground before they set off toward the building at double-time. Their ship dusted off as soon as they were clear of the door, all parties moving like a well-oiled machine.

The leader of the team, if you could call just three men that, was a dark-haired man with a few small scars and sparkling eyes. He was a rather stocky man. They all were. Specialists of some sort, the manager assumed. And highly skilled.

"Okay then, let's see the security cameras," the point man

said as they shouldered through the doors into the monitoring station.

"Oh, yes, of course," the manager replied, scurrying out of their way. "It's these cameras over here."

"How many hostiles we looking at?"

"I–I can't say for certain," she admitted. "But I would think at least fourteen, if not more."

The man absentmindedly rubbed the stubble on his chin, but for some reason, she thought it was more a conscious affectation than an actual mindless act. His eyes flitted between the screens a moment longer.

"There. Camera nine. Zoom in."

The image that enlarged on the screen was disturbing, even knowing the victim of the violence was able to survive it. But the poor cyborg. He'd been severely mutilated, his flesh covering sliced and torn from much of his body. And that same body had been bent and broken at weak points, lengths of metal used as makeshift levers and pry bars in the Tslavars' attempt to break him.

"Okay, then," the man growled. "That settles it. We don't play nice. Let's go. Buzz us in when we hit the main gate."

The trio headed off at a trot, the confused facility manager rushing close behind.

"But there are only three of you."

"Yeah. So?"

"But there are over a dozen of them!"

The man paused a moment and flashed her a wicked grin. "I know. It's not even a fair fight," he said, then continued on his way.

The manager didn't know what else to do but return to the monitoring station to watch from afar. The men were insane, that much was clear. Three of them against so many of the strong and violent aliens? It was madness to go in there unarmed.

4

"Hello, you green-skinned bastards," a voice called out with great confidence. Moments later three humans walked into the camera's field of view. "So, which one of you is in charge here?"

"I lead these men," one of the larger Tslavar prisoners said, striding toward the man. "And who are you, human? Come to give us something new to play with?"

The man merely smiled, watching the alien draw near. Then, with blinding speed, he punched him so hard you could almost feel the bones in his face break over the video screen.

The Tslavar flew back several feet, bouncing off the wall and falling to the ground in a heap. Whether he was dead or merely unconscious was anyone's guess. A cheerful little smile teased the man's lips.

"My name's Sergeant George Franklin, and I've come to chew bubblegum and kick ass." He looked at the stunned Tslavars, several of which were grabbing makeshift weapons. "And I'm all out of bubblegum," he added, finishing his favorite quote. Then, without further delay, he leapt into the fray.

Sergeant Franklin was right about one thing. It was most certainly not a fair fight. He and his men were obviously made of far sturdier stuff than any human—or cyborg, for that matter—and in mere minutes, every last Tslavar prisoner who had been freed from their cells lay bleeding and unconscious on the ground. His team quickly bound all of their hands, then walked away, leaving them without another thought.

"Sorry about the mess, ma'am," he said. "We'd help clean up, but it's been a long several months, and we've still gotta go debrief with Cal." They then headed outside for the ship that had just dropped down from the sky without her seeing him even send a signal.

Realization dawned on her. She'd just been in the presence of three of the men who had played such a large role in the Great War. Heroes, each of them.

"Cyborgs," she said with a knowing gasp. "*Those* cyborgs."

CHAPTER TWO

Weeks had passed since the forces of Earth, led by a group of time travelers and their magical dragon, had driven back not one but two alien invasions.

A rather frantic search and recall mission had managed to reach a good many of the planet's distant craft, long away on survey missions across the galaxy, and just in time to participate in the most recent battle to defend their home planet. And a good thing, that was. Without so many of those newly returned ships on the playing field, Earth very well might have fallen to the Tslavar-controlled Urok forces.

The green alien mercenaries had been clever in their planning, seizing upon the opportunity presented when they encountered a new race possessing formidable military might. A selective application of magical control collars to the rulers and military commanders had, quite quietly, rendered them impotent, forcing them to serve their new Tslavar masters.

And their masters wanted war.

War, and to reclaim the magical portal to their home galaxy. A portal the Earth's forces had somehow nestled safely within the sun, the burning orb's own powerful energy fueling the magic protecting the portal from destruction, while simultaneously assuring the fate of all who passed through from the other side.

Only two shimmer-cloaked ships had made it through before the portal was lowered into the sun, but with the new resources they had stumbled upon, the odds of retrieving the gateway to their fleet seemed better by the moment.

That is, until Charlie and his dragon stepped in once more. That surprise, along with two of their companions quite unexpectedly leveling up in both power and skill, had put a violent end to the Tslavar plans, but not before a massive and deadly battle broke out in the skies above Earth.

The newly returned fleet had gotten in the way of the Tslavar plans, and the Urok ships they had commandeered were no match for Earth's mightier forces. But that was only part of the plan.

The sun still contained the portal leading to the Tslavars' home galaxy, and if they could just retrieve it, their own mighty fleet would swoop through and crush their enemy with no remorse.

If they could pull it from the sun, that is. Something they seemed to lack the magical power to accomplish. That is, until they kidnapped the lone Ootaki in the entire galaxy.

Hunze had been found sprawled on the grassy bluff of her home, oblivious to the world, the result of her powerful assassin lover's magical attempt to gift her control of her own immense power, stored and ever growing in her golden hair. The effort had rendered them both unconscious, and as such, she was easy pickings for the startled, and thrilled Tslavar captain.

With such a treasure trove of Ootaki hair, it would be a cinch to pull the portal from the sun. And he might have succeeded, if the formerly weak woman hadn't woken before he attempted to take her hair.

Hunze had never been able to wield magic. It was an ironic

trait shared by all Ootaki. Ever the power source, but never the user. That is, until Bawb's arcane Wampeh Ghalian master assassin's spell changed all of that.

She had not only killed the mercenary crew with no effort, but she'd also utterly destroyed their ship, leaving herself floating in space, safely ensconced in a ball of soothing magic. Hunze was the first ever magic-wielding Ootaki, and with the skills her love had given her, she was more than just a spellcaster. She was a legitimate threat to any who dared attack her or her friends.

In addition to Hunze's new power, it seemed Charlie had also evolved further, his own magic tied to both Ara's and the Ootaki power Bawb possessed. But now that Bawb had shared with Hunze, Charlie had somehow been brought into that loop as well, and the magic within him grew accordingly.

With a single spell, he froze all of the adversaries, leaving their ships floating in space for Earth's forces to gather and restrain. It was the end of the Tslavar attack, but the beginning of a new alliance, for once the control collars were removed from the Urok leaders, they were finally free to engage in diplomacy, rather than war.

And from what Charlie had seen of the Urok fleet while they'd been pursuing and shooting at him, there was a good likelihood the sharing of technology between the races would be most beneficial.

In the weeks since that final hostility had taken place and the Tslavar aggressors were thrown in confinement, the people and AIs of the returning Earth fleet were clamoring for action. Yes, they had been victorious, but it was not just their planet or system that had been attacked, but their very galaxy.

That was unacceptable, and they wanted to take the fight to the enemy and end this once and for all.

And it seemed they might just get their wish.

The massive portal was going to stay active. There was

simply no way to disable it without its fail-safe spell triggering catastrophic destruction of the Earth's atmosphere. So, if it was going to remain an open door, they figured, why not use it themselves?

There was an entire new galaxy just on the other side of that massive portal. A galaxy that, while possessing those who wished harm on Earth and its people, also contained myriad other races Charlie knew wanted nothing more than to live their lives in peace.

New trade established between the galaxies would prove beneficial for all involved, and the merger of the magical realm with the technological one could possibly even lift both to levels of advancement never before imagined.

A general meeting of the AI and organic leaders from all the allied races discovered in the galaxy thus far was called, and Charlie and his friends were invited to speak as to the benefits and risks of such a venture.

At the end of several days of discussions, a vote was cast. And with it, the very first intergalactic battle force and trade fleet was commissioned. The mightiest of their warships would prepare for battle, ready to face whoever it was that was hell-bent on attacking Earth.

They would travel with the intent to open lines of communication and form new trade alliances with the mysterious alien races, but first the threat had to be dealt with. And from what they'd already seen, it would not be easy by any stretch of the imagination. For that reason, the biggest guns would go through after the scouting ships determined what they were looking at, and would hopefully put an end to the threat once and for all.

And in their wake, the massive trading fleets of the members of the alliance would follow, fanning across the systems, reaching out to the people of the new galaxy as countless explorers had done throughout history.

"Then it is agreed," Zed finally said at the end of the confab. "We're actually going to do this. Hot damn––now that's exciting!"

The mighty AI leader of the space fleet had been through a lot of crazy situations in his long life, but none remotely like what they were about to do. This was going to be a trip to another galaxy. And it would be accomplished not with warp drives, but with magic. If he weren't a computer, it might be enough to make his head spin.

CHAPTER THREE

"Are you sure this is a good idea?" Leila asked as she slipped into her favorite jacket––the one with the hidden pockets stuffed to capacity with spare magical weaponry.

"A *good* idea?" Charlie asked, likewise gearing up with all the powered accoutrements he could carry. "I don't know that I'd call it a *good* idea. But it's the right one. It's what we need to do."

Charlie had taken pretty much all of their most powerful devices from the vault, giving Leila the pick of the litter, while he merely supplemented his own rapidly growing magical powers with some choice pieces.

They were going to take a chance, and it could go either way, depending on what they found on the other side of that portal. It might be a clear shot, the hostile ships having cleared out after their gateway to this galaxy was so abruptly cut off by the flames of the sun.

Or they could emerge in the other galaxy to find it teeming with enemy craft, hell-bent on killing them all and subjugating their planet. So far as they knew, odds were about even.

"You sure you want to ride with Eddie and Rip?" he asked as

SCOTT BARON

Leila strapped a particularly deadly knife to the small of her back, concealed by her jacket.

"Yeah," she replied. "I'm going to take Baloo with. I think his nose might come in handy sniffing out trouble when we meet the locals."

"If we make landfall without any major issues, that is."

"Obviously," she said, leaning in for a quick kiss. "The point is, I can't very well take him with flying on Ara. I've got a space suit, but Baloo outgrew the one he traveled here in ages ago, so riding in a ship is the only option if I want to bring him, which I do."

The massive canine from that other galaxy would be going back home, in a sense, though he'd been taken from it when he was just a wee pup. But return he would, and as a fully grown beast of an animal. And one who would not allow anything to happen to his mama.

"I'm going to check in on Bob," Charlie said. "Make sure he and Hunze are good."

"Okay, I'll be here if you need me," Leila replied, continuing to pack for what promised to be one hell of an adventure no matter how it turned out.

Charlie walked the short distance to his friends' house and rang the door chime. He could have just reached out to Bob with his silent telepathy, courtesy of their magical bond through Ara, but Charlie thought it was nice to rely on old-fashioned courtesy once in a while.

"Yes, we are ready," Bawb said as soon as the door opened.

"I didn't even ask you if––"

"But I knew that which you were going to inquire," the assassin replied. "I merely thought I would save us some time."

Charlie chuckled. The Wampeh had changed a lot since he'd first met him. Not only had his whole deadly assassin demeanor lightened up a whole lot, largely due to his blossoming relationship with his Ootaki girlfriend, but he'd also taken to

12

displays of humor on occasion. Something that always amused Charlie coming from so dangerous a man.

"So, you okay with Hunze flying over with Kip and Dukaan?" Charlie asked as he stepped inside.

"Why wouldn't I be?" Bawb replied. "Hunze is now more than capable of defending herself from all manner of attack, as I know you've seen."

It was true, the neuro-stim transfer of a whole plethora of deadly spells had made her nearly as dangerous as Bawb, now that she finally had control of her own magic. And that was a good thing, as she'd be traveling with the decidedly non-magical team of Kip, the AI spacecraft, and his Chithiid pilot, Dukaan.

Having a magic user as powerful as Hunze flying with them was a huge boon for the pair. And even if they wouldn't admit it aloud, Hunze's presence aboard their ship put both of them at ease.

"So, Leila's all geared up and ready to go. She's taking Baloo with this time, though I still don't think that's such a good idea."

"Charlie, that animal will protect her with its life," Bawb said. "Yes, he is sometimes a bit of a handful, but she will be far safer with him than without. And though the Magus stone she wears around her neck will protect her from most harmful magic, it is not infallible. She's not a powerful magic user, and every bit of help she gets will do her well."

"I know, I know," Charlie said. "It's just, bringing Baloo along means she can't fly with us."

"I am aware, and I understand your concern, my friend. But believe me, she will be safe with that massive beast at her side."

He knew his friend was right, but he still worried about her. They'd been through a lot, and the fear of losing her was a regular visitor to the back of his mind.

"So, the ships are all prepped," Charlie said, switching subjects. "Everyone is pretty well upgraded, thanks to Cal's buddies."

"Yes, I have been following the progress of the retrofits," Bawb said. "Between the modified rail guns and new pulse cannons, I think this fleet shall prove quite formidable should we find ourselves in need of weaponry."

Bawb was certainly right about that. Not only were their ships and those of their friends sporting state-of-the-art gear now, but the rest of the fleet had been upgrading as well and were now preparing for combat, armed to the teeth.

"What about magic?" Charlie said. "I mean, yeah, these guys have firepower galore, but the fleet is still not truly prepared for magic. Not the real stuff, I mean."

While the fleet had upgraded their defensive spells tied in to their shielding arrays, only so much of a magical attack could be deflected or absorbed, and their even knowing how to adjust their defenses to compensate was still a recent development.

It was only thanks to Ara and Bawb's work with the captured Tslavar shimmer ship that they were finally able to formulate a better defensive shield spectrum for the non-magical ships in the fleet. Having that craft to study had at least allowed them to refine their methods, now that they could clearly determine exactly what their forces might be up against.

Cal and Sid were also busy running quantum analysis based on replays of every single attack their forces had faced since the Tslavars had first invaded their system. The massive computers linked minds and ran billions of simulations with that data, and, in the end, merged that knowledge with what Ara and her Wampeh friend had found.

It wasn't perfect by any stretch of the imagination, but they hoped it would be effective. And when facing an enemy wielding such powerful magic, every little bit helped.

Bawb wore the entirety of the Ootaki hair he possessed, tightly woven within his lightweight armored chestpiece, bursting with power from the system's sun. In addition to that, both of his armlets were securely strapped on, the integral konuses and Drookonus contained within fully charged and ready for action.

At his hip, a new, surprisingly plain-looking shock-resistant holster carried his massively powerful wand, the magic-imbued wood having grown stronger every day since its harvest, the strand of Ootaki hair within feeding it a constant stream of magical charge. To some, it was just a stick, but in Bawb's hands, it was one of the deadliest tools ever created.

Looking at his friend strapping on all of that kit, Charlie almost felt bad for any who might cross him. And that was without even considering damage he could do with the myriad other blades and weapons the assassin typically had secreted on his person.

"Has there been word from the remaining survey teams?" Bawb asked, securing the last of his gear.

"Nope, not yet," Charlie replied. "Ripley's aunt is still out, as are several other teams. But it looks like her folks are ready to fight, so that's something."

"Excellent. Her mother is a formidable woman," Bawb said. "I've seen her spar with Rika, and her skills are exceptional."

"Let's just hope she doesn't need to use them," Charlie replied. "How's Hunze holding up? This can't be easy for her."

"She's holding up fine," the golden-haired woman said with a grin as she walked in to join them.

Since taking control of the magic growing in her hair, Hunze had been transformed. She was still the gentle, loving woman they all knew and cared for, but there was something more as well. Something strong. Powerful.

Beneath that kind exterior lurked the magic and knowledge to kill with a glance without breaking a sweat. The skills of the Wampeh Ghalian. Bawb had broken his vow by sharing the secrets with her, but being in a different galaxy than his assassins' sect, he rationalized that the rules didn't apply here.

15

Back in his own galaxy, however, well, that would be a matter open for debate.

Hunze had tightly braided her hair, the flowing golden locks thick from atop her head, while the buzz-shaved undercut from where she'd shorn herself to give her power to Bawb was quickly growing back in. And with every inch of growth, her power increased.

The braid was carefully wrapped around her body, a protective jacket containing hidden shock plates and pockets masking its presence. And that was a wise thing, for she knew full well the value of her hair, and it would be a shame to have to kill people to protect it.

Charlie looked at the literal power couple and felt a surge of pride. These were his friends, and they were exceptional. And now, it was time to put their skills to the test.

"All right," he said. "We might as well get going. Ara's waiting at my place, and Kip should be by shortly to pick you up, Hunze."

Bawb tenderly kissed the Ootaki goodbye, then headed off with his friend to step into harm's way yet again. Only this time, they had backup. And a lot of it.

CHAPTER FOUR

"So, how exactly do you plan on doing this again?" Zed asked from his massive command ship parked just beyond the range of harm of the sun's blistering heat.

The tactical AI knew full well what the plan was. Hell, he'd helped come up with it when all of their resources were placed on the table. But he was one for repetition, not only for his own sake, but that of all the forces operating beneath him. In this case, that was *all* of them.

"Pretty simple, really," Charlie said, though the act of great magic would typically be anything but. "Ara, Bawb, and I will fly in close to the sun and retrieve the magical tether linking the *Asbrú* with the safe space outside the sun's plasma."

"And the portal to this other galaxy?" Zed asked, knowingly.

"It's being created by the Ootaki magic woven through the entirety of the ship," Charlie replied. "It's a big portal. *Huge*, actually, though possibly not big enough for you to fly through. I guess we'll have to see if we can increase its diameter to handle the largest of ships once we've safely secured the other side. Hadn't really thought about that. But that's another discussion for later."

SCOTT BARON

"It is," Zed replied. "Now, as you were saying?"

"Right. So we'll get the tether and cast the retrieval spell to pull it from the sun. It should take a pretty significant amount of magic, and normally it would have probably taken just about everything we have. But things have changed of late, so we'll probably be able to do it pretty easily, I wager."

"I am happy to help," Hunze chimed in over comms, safely tucked away in Kip's speedy little ship.

"Thanks, Hunze. Actually, if you can provide some additional protection from the sun for Kip, maybe you guys can get close enough to help give it a pull."

"Consider it done," she said, and Charlie could almost hear her smile over the comms.

Finally she felt useful for more than just the hair growing on her head, and her increased sense of self-worth was almost tangible. And this close to the sun, the burning orb's radiant power was supercharging her magic, along with Ara and Charlie's.

"I wonder if the sun has the same effect on the other side of the portal," Charlie mused silently to his linked friends.

"It only appears to affect Zomoki and Ootaki here, though the Drooks do appear to be very minorly influenced by it," Ara said. *"There are other suns in your galaxy that seem to have powers conducive to building force compatible with other types of beings from mine, but so far as I can tell, only the two species are so greatly charged by this particular sun."*

"Yeah, I guess that makes sense. Good thing the guys on the other side shot their wad of Ootaki hair when they sent the Asbrú *and opened that portal, or we'd be facing a mega-charged enemy,"* Charlie noted. *"As it is, it looks like we'll be the only ones able to pull power from it on the other side."*

"I hope you are correct," Bawb said. *"To have been powering our enemies' forces inadvertently with this sun's energy would be most regrettable."*

18

"You can say that again," Charlie agreed.

Zed relayed a series of commands to the dozens of ships hovering near the sun, adjusting their positions to best cover the area where the portal would emerge. They'd be ready. At least, as ready as they could be. All that remained now was for Charlie and his friends to do their little magic trick.

"So, are you ready?" Zed asked.

"Yeah. Sorry. Was just running through some things in my head," Charlie replied. "Okay, so we'll pull the portal free. You just have your ships all standing by, guns hot and ready."

"They are already hot and ready," Zed said with a chuckle. "They've had their proverbial fingers on the trigger since the moment we arrived here, in fact."

"I knew I liked you for a reason," Charlie said. "Okay, then let's get to it. Ara, when you're ready."

The mighty Zomoki did not hesitate or wait for further urging, quickly shifting her course and flying right toward the burning ball of plasma, basking in the power as she drew closer.

Hunze cast a protective spell for Kip, allowing the little ship to fly alongside her dragon friend. Just as Ara was absorbing the sun's energy, so too was Hunze topping off her magical tank with the intoxicating power all around her.

The fleet sat ready, just a little ways behind them, safely shielded from the sun's rays. Eddie was ready, Ripley and Leila anxiously waiting inside his hull. Baloo, however, was happily napping against the bulkhead, there being nothing of interest for him to smell or chase in the vacuum of space.

Rika and Jo were right beside him, standing by.

Rika could have cast a spell to protect the *Fujin* enough to fly closer, but she was still learning all the nuances of her strange magic, a mix of the power of this galaxy her magic-inked tattoos gave her and the spells of the other. Rika, wisely, thought it better not to risk burning up in a ball of molten metal until she really had her powers dialed in.

But if her friends needed her help, she'd ignore that self-imposed restraint entirely, risks be damned. She just hoped it wouldn't go that way. She was fond of not being burned alive, after all. Jo would be grateful as well, she mused.

All around them, the AI ships of the fleet sat ready, quietly chattering among themselves. Mal and her ship, the *Váli*, were there as well, flown by Captain Lars Harkaway and his pilot, Reggie. Two of the heroes of the Great War.

Also present were a rather quirky ship named Marty, flown by Ripley's cousin, as well as another unusual ship named Gus, who seemed a bit more chatty than most of the other AIs.

And countless others were there in the mix as well, all ready to fight, if need be.

The Chithiid had sent a large contingent of ships as well, theirs consisting of both Chithiid vessels, as well as captured Ra'az ones, the latter taken from their former masters after the war.

Even the Urok had committed a contingent of ships to the cause, eager for the opportunity to get some payback for the indignity leveled upon them by the green invaders from the other galaxy.

Charlie didn't even need to say anything, so powerful was his link with Ara and Bawb while so close to the sun. The three began casting as one, Hunze joining in moments later as she felt the tug of her bond with Bawb flare.

It was as Charlie had thought it might go, the massive portal pulling free from the depths of the sun's burning plasma even easier than he'd hoped it would. Together, it seemed, they had quite a bit of power. Far more than Charlie had expected.

"Okay, y'all," he said over comms. "Here it comes."

CHAPTER FIVE

The churning plasma of the sun's surface bulged and shifted. It looked almost as if a solar flare was about to burst forth. But what emerged from the molten orange was not something so mundane as a jet of liquid fire, but rather, a fully intact spaceship from hundreds of years ago, sent through time and space as a Trojan horse of sorts.

Little did its senders know that their gateway to conquest would become the portal to their demise, the flash of the sun's power incinerating much of the waiting fleet when it was dropped into the sun just as it activated. Only two shimmer-cloaked ships made it through before destruction fell upon the rest of the waiting invasion fleet.

Charlie and his friends had been the cause of their ruin, saving Earth from invasion by their actions. And now they were doing the opposite, pulling the portal back out of the sun. But this time they were ready.

"Okay, it's coming, guys," Charlie said over open comms.

Of course, the arrival of the portal from the depths of the sun was plain to see for all watching as the Ootaki hair-filled Trojan horse ship powering the portal pulled free.

At first, it just seemed like any old ship miraculously surviving the sun's heat had suddenly popped into view. But then the portal followed right behind it, and it was massive.

Untouched by the destructive force of the sun, the portal was a perfectly round opening, leading to another galaxy just as easily as stepping through a doorway. It was bigger than Charlie had remembered, and he was pretty sure even Zed's massive ship could squeeze through if he tried.

"Looks like the sun really did a number on the Ootaki hair powering it," Charlie said to his Zomoki and Wampeh friends.

"Yes, the spell is far stronger, and larger, than before," Ara noted. *"The Ootaki hair powering it could already do so indefinitely, but now it seems the proximity to the energy of the sun has expanded the spell's potential."*

Bawb studied the portal with great interest, squinting slightly at the seemingly empty space leading to the stars clearly seen on the other side. *"Something is not right,"* he said, leaning forward, staring intently.

"Hey, anyone see anything on their scans?" Charlie asked over comms. "Bob thinks something's up."

All of the fleet had their scanners fixed on the portal, but none registered a thing. But scans weren't the only thing covering the area. Hunze had been subtly casting a marking spell the whole time, creating an invisible film of reactive magic across the entire opening––a film that flashed to life as a half dozen shimmer-cloaked ships burst through from the other side, followed by ten larger, uncloaked vessels.

The shimmer ships sparkled as they flew, the marking spell making them easy to see despite their camouflage magic. It was a neat trick, though one the enemy would likely only fall for once. Nevertheless, it had done its job and the allied fleet surrounding the sun quickly locked their weapons upon them.

"Hail them," Celeste Harkaway said from the bridge of Zed's enormous command ship.

"I've been trying, Admiral," the AI replied. "There has been no response."

"Are you using the skree parameters we retrieved from the captured ship?"

"Yes," the AI said. "I've been sending on all known frequencies, both of this and the other galaxy, calling for surrender lest they be destroyed. They refuse to reply."

Admiral Harkaway studied the scene. A total of sixteen likely hostile ships, all sporting magical weaponry. And none of them responding to peaceful attempts at communication.

"Suggestions?" the admiral asked.

"I propose dropping the portal back into the sun while we deal with this," Zed replied.

"You hear that?" the admiral asked over comms. "Can you get it back in there quickly?"

"Already on it," Charlie replied, having begun the process as soon as the first ships burst through.

But they couldn't simply drop the thing into the sun. That would risk triggering the deadman switch that would cause a magical attack on Earth's atmosphere. No, they had to go somewhat slowly. But not so slowly that any more ships coming through wouldn't risk being incinerated if they weren't precise in their course plotting.

The invading forces, realizing they were about to be cut off, began firing wildly at the tech ships, heaving magic at them with all the force they could muster. But the ships had been well prepared for such an attack, and those precautions and modified shield settings saved them from any harm beyond a minor scuffing of their paint.

"Take them alive if you can. We need answers," Admiral Harkaway commanded.

The alien ships, however, seemed to have other plans.

They intensified their casting, firing off all manner of spells, including some that threw solid projectiles from the craft, much like a magical trebuchet, only in space, and with far more force.

The first of those attacks slammed into the nearest Earth ship, pushing through its shielding and driving into the ceramisteel of its hull. The craft maintained its integrity, but only just. Any further impact and it would void its atmosphere and crew into space.

"Cover that ship!" Charlie bellowed into the comms as Ara lit up its attacker with a plume of magical flames.

The ship was rocked by the force, tearing apart moments later and reducing to a melted ball of slag.

"How did you do that?" Charlie asked, shocked.

"We've been so close to the sun for so long, I guess I didn't realize how much it had powered me up," Ara replied.

Charlie watched as the melted debris floated through the portal just as it submerged into the sun, a silent warning of what awaited all who would dare attack his galaxy. It wasn't what they'd intended, but if it made the point, then so be it.

The rest of the fleet was making quick work of the invading vessels. The magic being deployed against the combined forces was simply no match for the might of their technology. Some ships broke apart and drifted into the sun, burning up and leaving nothing behind, while others maneuvered in a desperate attempt at avoiding the overwhelming firepower.

"Enough!" Charlie yelled, throwing his hands wide and casting the stasis spell as best he could.

It was something he'd been practicing ever since he unintentionally froze the entirety of the Urok and Tslavar forces so recently, his powers exponentially increased by his link to Hunze's hair, as well as Ara's power, all tied in to the sun.

He wasn't quite sure if it would work, and there was a good likelihood it might knock him out if he pushed too hard, but being this close to the sun, he felt confident the added boost of the solar power would not only help with the casting of the spell, but would also keep him from draining himself so dangerously low in the process.

It was a hit-and-miss type of spell, now that he was consciously attempting it, and only a handful of the alien ships ceased all activity, drifting in paralysis as his spell took hold. The others continued fighting as fiercely as ever, but it was clear to all that their magic was simply not sufficient against the tech superiority of this galaxy.

All but the most powerful casters would likely fail in the face of this fleet's power, but the poor remaining Tslavar ships had no way of warning those on the other side of the portal now that it had been dropped into the sun once again.

So, they did what any self-respecting bloodthirsty mercenaries would do. They made desperate, last-ditch suicide runs at any ships close enough for them to hit.

In short order, every non-frozen ship had been destroyed. The remaining ones were gathered up by the unified forces, their crews disarmed and placed in confinement before finally having the stasis spell removed.

Things definitely hadn't gone as they'd anticipated.

They'd expected to maybe encounter one or two scout ships with whom they could open lines of communication. But this? This was entirely different, and it meant that for Charlie and the leadership of the fleet, it was time to come up with a new plan.

CHAPTER SIX

"Well, *that* didn't go as planned," Charlie grumbled as he paced the large internal hangar deck of Zed's massive command ship.

Ara sat nearby, resting beside one of the other AI ships that had come in after the battle to debrief with the other key fleet commanders. Mal was her name, the mind running the *Váli*, and she and Ara were getting along quite well considering one was an artificially intelligent spaceship and the other was a several-thousand-year-old space dragon.

"To be fair, we didn't exactly think it would go smoothly," Ara said as her friend strode past her again.

"The Wise One is correct," Bawb added. "Given what we already knew of the forces gathered on the other side of the portal, it seemed highly likely that we would be facing some sort of unfriendly force."

"Yeah, but this was a bit excessive," Charlie said.

"Perhaps. But to expect Tslavar mercenaries to engage in peaceful negotiation could be considered folly by many," Bawb replied. "And please, stop pacing."

Charlie abruptly halted. "Admiral Harkaway, do we have any intel from the ones we captured?" he asked.

The tall, lithe woman ran her mechanical hand through her hair. She really was quite striking for an older woman, and certainly a force to be reckoned with. Having met her metal-legged war hero of a husband, Charlie could see why she and the *Váli*'s captain were a couple.

"Zed has tasked a team of interrogators to see what they might pry from our guests," she said. "But thus far they're pretty tight-lipped."

"As one would expect of Tslavars," Bawb noted.

"So I've been told," she said. "Which is why I have also asked that he subject a few of them to a modified neuro-stim process to see if we might overcome some of those stubborn tendencies of theirs."

"You're brainwashing them?" Charlie asked, more than a little surprised. "But that won't really help our cause. We need intel, not a blank slate."

"Not wiping," Zed's voice said in the echoing hangar. "That's not what neuro-stims do. We're merely adding a little bit of back channel suggestion to try to make them more receptive to being open with us."

Charlie was perplexed. "You what, now? I'm sorry, that doesn't make sense."

Zed chuckled. "I suppose it wouldn't. I must remind myself that though you're human, you aren't really from around these parts. Or time, to be precise."

Admiral Harkaway chuckled. "What Zed is trying to say is that while you're familiar now with the learning applications of the neuro-stim devices, you haven't been familiarized with some of its less used functions. You see, the neuro-stim can also be used as something of a misinformation device, though it's rarely been used as such."

"Meaning?"

"Meaning we have been attempting to map the Tslavar mind's psychophysiology. Once we understand that, perhaps we can implant a little bit of *exaggerated* intel about our fleet. Something that will make us seem so formidable that only a fool would dare attack us. It's only been a hypothetical up until this point—a little something Daisy and her AI buddies came up with a while back but never actually implemented."

"Too dangerous?" Bawb asked.

"No. The war ended," she replied. "In any case, it is just one of several options we are pursuing, and it might not even work."

"So what do we do in the meantime?" Charlie asked. "I mean, there are obviously ships on the other side, and hostile ones. We've got the advantage, though. Our tech seems to pretty effectively overwhelm their magic."

"It *was* a rather lopsided event," Ara agreed. "I would have expected a better showing from them. However, with the modifications we helped the vessels make to their defensive systems, their normally deadly magical attacks were largely impotent."

She was right. While they'd anticipated some sort of resistance on the other side, but really hadn't thought the invaders would push through to this galaxy so quickly. Not after they'd undoubtedly lost ships to the sun's flames when the portal was first blocked to them.

But through they had come, and looking for a fight.

"So, we've got the edge," Charlie said. "They weren't able to report back to the other side, meaning they don't know we can stop their attacks."

"Giving us a distinct advantage," Bawb added.

"Yeah. So while Zed and the other AIs are trying to break the Tslavar prisoners, we move ahead as planned. Or, a slightly modified version of the plan, anyway."

Admiral Harkaway slowly paced, thinking over the plan, considering their options.

"We will have to go through with weapons hot," she said. "And with defenses on high."

"Agreed," Zed said. "But I calculate our forces should be able to deter any enemy attack for a time. At least long enough to allow our ships to adjust strategy if needed."

"But what if there are too many?" Charlie asked. "Seems there may be more of them than we originally anticipated."

"Possible. But if so, we will have our ships simply warp away to the pre-designated rally point and regroup. Every ship has the same coordinates already locked into their guidance systems. A simple straight line shot, not too far but enough to give them some space to get clear and adjust plans."

"What of the portal?" Bawb asked. "If their forces are greater than expected and drive ours away, what is to keep them from passing through once more?"

"We'll only send a small group of ships the first wave," Admiral Harkaway said. "The bulk of the fleet will remain on this side of the portal at first. A cork to the bottle, as it were."

"May I suggest one more safety?" Ara interjected.

"Of course, Ara," Harkaway replied.

"I think we should arrange for the portal to drop back into the sun as soon as we pass through. That will keep whatever enemy there is from backtracking to this side."

"But you'll be trapped."

"Yes, but we can layer a series of spells on this side. Spells that will automatically pull the portal free for a short window in, say, twenty-four hours. Then it will again drop it back into the sun and repeat this cycle for, say, a week."

"And what if you miss the window of opportunity?" Zed asked. "Things happen in times of combat, after all."

"True, but we will also leave a longer-term spell in place. One that pulls the portal free on a weekly basis."

"And if you miss that too?"

"Then it will submerge into the sun permanently a month later," she replied. "Beyond that time frame, it would be safe to say we are not coming back."

"And the portal? It will still be active regardless," Zed noted.

A grim silence filled the air at the thought. Charlie finally broke it.

"If that happens," he said, "leave a guard near the sun and pray they never find a way through."

CHAPTER SEVEN

The neuro-stim process on the Tslavar minds wasn't proving nearly as effective as the AIs had hoped. It was frustrating, but not entirely unexpected. They were a completely new alien physiology, after all. And on top of that, they were hostilely uncooperative.

The combination resulted in near total failure.

"Well, with all that mapping, at least we know how their brains are built," Rika said from the comfort of the *Fujin's* cockpit, Jo at her side, as the other ships began to fall into formation. "Not that it'll make much of a difference when I shoot them in the head."

A smattering of laughter sounded over the open comms channels before their ships quickly silenced them.

"Okay, everyone, that's enough," Zed said with an amused chuckle. "Take your positions and power up your weapons. We're going to take the portal live in five minutes."

The dozens of ships that constituted the defensive force slowly slid into place next to one another, each spaced precisely so they could not only fire a blistering, overlapping barrage on any hostile ships that might attempt to pass through the portal, but also plotting escape and evasion coordinates so the seemingly interwoven ships could actually scatter if need be without hitting one another.

Charlie and Bawb were ready to go, sitting comfortably atop their Zomoki friend while they watched the others fall into position. Rika, Kip, and Eddie pulled up alongside the dragon, likewise ready to go, once the powerful spaceship backstop was ready.

"Leila, you good?" Charlie asked over a closed channel.

"I'm fine," she replied.

"Is Baloo behaving?"

"He's sleeping, Charlie. Relax."

"Right, right," Charlie said. "Okay, just checking."

"I'll be fine," she said. "Eddie's got a shimmer, and his shielding is greatly reinforced on top of that. So relax, okay?"

Charlie forced himself to take a breath, consciously lowering his heart rate as Ser Baruud had taught him in his intensive gladiator training all those years ago. Leila would be all right. And if Eddie and Ripley failed, he had no doubt Baloo would make quick work of anyone who should board that ship and try to harm her.

"Okay, you're right," he finally said. "See you on the other side, babe."

Meanwhile, the Wampeh assassin also seated atop the Zomoki was reaching out to his lady love over a different channel, though his was a far different tone of conversation.

"If any should threaten you, dispatch them with no hesitation," he instructed.

"Or we could just run away, Bawb," Hunze replied. "It doesn't always have to end in bloodshed, you know."

Bawb smiled to himself. Even with the powerful magic coursing through her now at her control, Hunze still remained the same gentle soul. Gentle, but changed since they'd first met.

For if it was called for, she would unleash magical fury the likes of which most had never before seen.

"Yes. Of course," he replied. "I just wish for you to remain safe."

"I know, love. And I will be. You know this."

"I do," he said, and at that moment, he realized he truly did. Hunze's power was immense. Far greater than his, even after she had gifted him half of her hair. But she was the power conduit. The generator. And with his selfless act, returning her power to her, she had become far more than he'd ever expected.

And she knew the ways of the Wampeh Ghalian.

"Two minutes," Zed called out over the fleet's comms. "Charlie, are you and your magical buddies ready to cast those spells?"

"We already have," he replied. "There's a series layered in place on a countdown, just as we discussed. Everything is set. All we need to do is cast the activation spell and we'll start the clocks."

"Great work," Zed said. "We'll have you and your friends in the first wave, along with the *Váli* and Marty, and their accompaniment of heavy cruisers. Should be enough to handle pretty much anything you run into over there."

"Which is greatly appreciated," Charlie said. "Just make sure the relay ship is ready to pull back and tell you guys what's going on over there. I can't say for sure, but I'm ninety-nine percent sure comms signals won't pass through from one galaxy to the other, even if the portal makes it look like it's just a few meters away."

"Yes, I know," Zed replied. "And *that* is a phenomenon I would really like to study at greater length once we've established a stable transit path. But for now, one mission at a time, eh?"

"Probably a good idea," Charlie said with a laugh.

"One minute," Zed broadcast. "And by the way, where is

Eddie? He's supposed to be traveling with your team in the first wave."

"Right here, Zed," Eddie replied.

"Right *where*, exactly?"

"Here. Oh, hang on a second," Eddie said as he dropped his shimmer cloak.

"Oh, shit. Didn't know you were there, Eddie," Zed said with a chuckle. "Damn, now that's an effective bit of camouflage. I wish we could outfit all our ships with that."

"Well, there are already a few stealth ships among us," Eddie replied. "This is just a different kind of stealth, is all."

"Yeah, the kind that's invisible to the eye as well as to scans," Zed noted.

Ara and her friends watched the chrono ticking down the seconds, the magic buzzing at the tip of their tongues, waiting to be cast.

"Okay, t-minus ten seconds," Zed informed the fleet. "Casters, do your thing."

Triggering the spells linked to the tether attached to the portal was a relatively simple spell, but Ara had insisted that all four of the power users cast at the same time, just to ensure a redundancy of magic should anything happen while they were on the other side. To be stuck there, unable to return, was simply not something any of them wished to have happen.

Eddie and Rip reactivated the shimmer spell, fading into invisibility as the portal began to pull out from the depths of the sun. Finally, it was free, and the first wave of ships pushed forward through the beckoning opening, emerging millions of light years away in an entirely different galaxy.

The tech ships hit the alien space with a rumble, their systems going haywire as soon as they cleared the portal. The magic users were also shaken, the change in ambient magic being so profound that it almost took Ara's breath away, though it was her native environment.

She'd been on Earth for so long, soaking in its restorative rays, that being back home, where the solar energies were so much less potent for her, was a shock to her system.

The ships quickly righted themselves, scrambling to adjust their equipment to handle the drastically unusual conditions of the space they'd arrived in. It was odd, and definitely not within normal parameters, but they'd made it through.

"Okay, everyone. Keep your eyes open," Charlie called out to their band of explorers.

"Yes, be aware," Ara said. "Danger may be lurking. Oh, and welcome to my galaxy."

CHAPTER EIGHT

Ara hadn't been kidding when she had said to be aware. There was debris all around the area where they'd exited the portal. Some chunks were small, merely bouncing off of the defensive shielding the ships sported, but others were massive. So large, in fact, that the group had to break formation to avoid impact.

Marty, the rather quirky AI ship and best friend of Ripley's cousin, and the *Váli* pushed ahead of the rest of their rear contingent, weapons hot as they kept an eye out for hostiles. But it was Kip who was the first to realize what the debris actually was.

"Hey, uh, guys?" the little ship said. "I think this was a fleet at one time."

Charlie and the others turned their attention not to the abstract idea of a giant field of floating hazards, but to the composition of that obstacle. The things that had at first looked like strange asteroids were indeed what Kip had noticed.

Ships. Dozens and dozens of them, all burned to a crisp, the materials that had once been their frames and skins all melted into blobs of slag. Only the few bits that had somehow cooled quickly as the sun's fiery blast hit them and drove them from the portal remained to identify their original forms.

"Holy shit," Rika gasped. "Did we do this?"

"I'm pretty sure we did," Charlie replied. "I mean, we didn't do it directly, but when we dropped the portal into the sun, these poor bastards must've been right up on it, waiting to come through. The blast of the sun's plasma would have incinerated them all damn near instantly."

Bawb studied the drifting wreckage as Ara carefully maneuvered farther from the portal. It wouldn't be lowered back into the sun for several minutes, and he was not one to spook easily, but the sheer volume of destruction around them made even the great Geist reconsider their present location.

"It would appear the fleet that had been awaiting the portal's activation was even larger than we'd hypothesized," the Wampeh assassin said. "If a force this size had made it through, even with all of its ships present, the Earth would almost certainly have fallen."

"But we've got some pretty amazing tech, Bob. I mean, rail guns and plasma cannons?" Charlie said.

"Yes, but the sheer number of craft whose remains we see here suggests a force that would have overwhelmed our defenses by numbers alone."

Charlie hated to admit it, but Bawb was right. Now that he realized they weren't among mere asteroids and space debris, he could see clearly that there weren't dozens of ships. There were hundreds. Earth would have fallen in mere days.

"Well, I guess we got double lucky, then," Charlie finally said. "Good thing we chose to use the sun to contain the portal, though, to be fair, that was just an in-the-moment thing, and we had no idea it would destroy the fleet on the other side."

Ara slowed her progress and looped back a moment toward the portal. "Do you feel that, Charlie? Bawb? Hunze?"

All of them opened their senses wide, reaching for whatever Ara was referring to.

"I do," Hunze said with a surprised gasp. "But how is that possible? We've passed through the portal. Nothing transmits from the other side."

Charlie felt it too, as did Bawb. The strong power of Earth's sun was actually transmitting itself through the portal, even when the device itself was not submerged in it. Mere proximity, it seemed, was enough.

"Well, that answers that question," Charlie said. "I guess if we need a top-off, we can always swing by the portal to recharge our batteries. But I have to wonder how it'll be when the portal is lowered back––"

One of the rear ships exploded in a magical fireball, torn to pieces by a violent attack that cut through its shielding as if it wasn't there.

"We're under attack! Weapons hot! Engage all visible targets!" Captain Harkaway shouted over the comms.

He didn't need to relay that command. Everyone had already taken it upon themselves to do precisely that, and a firefight was well underway as dozens of mid-sized alien ships swarmed from behind the floating wreckage of one of their larger ships.

"Ambush. Should have seen that coming," Charlie growled as another of their ships exploded, then went dark in the cold of space. "Come on, guys, use the modified shield settings!"

"We are, Charlie. They aren't working!" an AI ship replied before falling to the alien onslaught as the others had.

"The mods aren't working in this galaxy! Fall back through the portal!" Captain Harkaway commanded, his AI and pilot working together to avoid the attack, while spraying hot death into the enemy ships.

Their guns took out several, the craft's casters not yet knowing how to defend against this novel form of weaponry. At least in that regard, the fight was somewhat even.

Marty was the first to reach the portal, his overzealous pilot blasting a pursuing craft from the sky with a whooping holler. "Only one minute before the portal drops into the sun!" he called out. "Everyone get through now!"

The smaller ships spun and retreated as fast as they could, but most were caught by the deadly forces that were lying in wait. Eddie flashed through the portal and spun once on the other side, guns hot and ready for any who might follow. The *Váli* followed close behind, trailing a pair of alien gunships.

Those were targeted by the massive cannons waiting for them on the other side, tearing them to shreds the moment they passed through, leaving their debris drifting back through the portal to the magical galaxy.

"Everyone else is through," Rika called out as she spun and juked the *Fujin* in ways it shouldn't have been able to move, her magical tattoos glowing faintly as she called upon the power flowing within her to aid her flight.

"There's not enough time for us to make it," Eddie broadcast. "I've run the numbers, and there are too many of them between us and the portal to get through before it drops. And in twenty seconds there's gonna be a lot of fire around here."

Charlie realized the AI was right. Never question an AI about something like math. Computers tended to take that sort of thing personally.

"Okay, everyone emergency warp to the rally point coordinates and get the hell out of here," Charlie called out over open comms. "We can't fight this many, and this place is gonna be a giant fireball in a few seconds."

It was a backup plan they'd had in place but hadn't expected to need to use. A last hope effort if things really went tits up. And boy had they done precisely that.

Kip was the first to warp, spooling up his drive and vanishing in a crackling blue flash. Eddie and Rika followed seconds later, all locked in to the same coordinates.

Ara, however, as a magical being born in this galaxy, had no need of technology to make the trip, using her magic instead to jump away, leaving the alien forces behind to flee the blistering plume of burning plasma the portal was about to eject into space.

A second later, she exited her jump, right on target, as planned.

"Holy crap, that was close," Charlie said with a relieved sigh. "Nice flying, Ara."

"Yes, that was a magnificent display," Bawb agreed.

"Thank you. Thank you both," she replied, taking in their new environment. "But there seems to be a problem."

"Problem? What problem? We made it, didn't we?" Charlie said.

"Yes. *We* made it," she replied. "But where are the others?"

CHAPTER NINE

Charlie scanned the empty expanse of darkness around them. It was entirely possible their friends had simply gone unnoticed in all that empty space. But then again, it was possible something else was afoot.

His magical internal radar told him the truth of the matter far more clearly than his eyes or silent comms could.

"They're not here," Charlie said. "Not now, not recently, not at all. There's no trace of any of their magic."

Ara nodded in agreement. "I, too, do not smell anything. It would appear we have arrived here alone."

"But the location was locked into every one of their navigational systems, were they not?" Bawb asked.

"They were; however, something obviously went amiss."

"You can say that again," Charlie concurred. "Look at the navs array on Ara's harness."

Bawb leaned closer to examine what it was Charlie had noticed. The human engineer was far more adept at wielding technology, but the Wampeh had always been a quick study, and the computer operating the navigation system melded with Ara's harness was a relatively simple thing.

"This appears to be suffering some sort of malfunction," he noted, tapping on the machinery. Nothing changed.

"Our tech apparently does not like this galaxy," Charlie said. "So whatever advantage we had against their ships back on our side, over here in this part of space, we're the ones fighting with one arm tied behind our back."

"A fine training drill to develop one's non-dominant limb," Bawb said.

"What? Oh, come on, Bob, you know what I meant."

"Indeed, I do. I was just, how do you always say? 'Messing with you'?"

"Levity? At a time like this?" Charlie griped.

"I see no reason for panic," Bawb replied. "The others are all very competent, and together, with their magic and tech weaponry, they will pose a serious threat to any who would dare attack them."

Charlie realized that Bawb hadn't quite caught on to the minutia of the technical errors now plaguing their systems. "Bob, you do realize that *each* of the systems will be malfunctioning, right?"

"Of course. But I fail to see how that makes things any––"

"And each of them will be malfunctioning in their own, unique manner," Charlie continued, watching his friend for the moment of realization.

He couldn't entirely see Bawb's face through his spacesuit helmet at that angle, but the Wampeh's body language shifted ever so slightly as it hit him.

"Oh. They would have all warped to the wrong coordinates, but their individual navigations systems would have sent them to different places," the assassin finally said. "This is not good. Not good at all."

"No shit, dude. That means that each of those ships will be out there on their own. And worse yet, unless they can figure out how to somehow get some magic tied into their drive and navs systems to give them a modicum of stability, I don't even know if they'll be able to make it back to the portal in time for the next transit window."

Bawb felt the armlets snugly worn inside his space suit. The Drookonus covertly hidden within one could power a ship by magic quite easily, if only he could get it to them. One of them, anyway.

Eddie possessed not only a konus, but also a strand of Hunze's powerful hair, and Kip had likewise been given a konus by Charlie to help him defend himself from magical attacks.

"Hey, wasn't Kip warp-jumping with you before, Ara?" Charlie asked. "Why didn't they come with us?"

"We were not utilizing that technique, as that was being done to pursue a vessel only I could smell. In this instance, we all had the same coordinates, so we didn't think it was necessary."

"And Rika's just straight up on her own with no magical ship link at all."

He was entirely right about that. The *Fujin* wasn't a magical ship, but Rika possessed more than enough of that on her own to possibly help guide them, though her magic being powered by elements from the other galaxy could possibly prove troublesome. The thing was, they simply couldn't know. Not until they found them.

What they didn't know was where their friends had ended up. Or how to track them down, for that matter.

"How are we going to find the others?" Bawb asked. "Can we even get within communications range to perhaps reach out to them that way?"

"You know the limitations of Earth tech, Bob. If we're too far out, like in another system, for example, the message simply won't get there. But how about a long-range skree? We're in the right galaxy for one. Do you think we could maybe get our hands on one and try to send it to the portable Leila has in her gear?"

"She still carries that?"

"It's small, so I didn't see any harm in one more piece of kit that might come in handy," Charlie replied. "Plus, skrees don't draw the attention that comms units do in this galaxy. I know you've gotten used to our tech, but it's probably best if we only use magic from here on out."

"Obviously," Bawb said. "I was merely surprised that she had packed it in her gear. Leila has become rather adept at Earth technology, thanks in part to Rika's tutelage."

Charlie couldn't help but grin. It was true, Rika and Leila had become friends, and that meant his queen had a damn fine pilot and Earth native to help her train and become more comfortable with the strange technology that took the place of magic on his home planet.

"So? What do you think about my idea?"

"A skree?" Bawb replied. "The thought is valid, but I'm afraid sourcing a long-range skree with the power we require would be a bit of a challenge. To send vast distances, possibly multiple systems away? That's Council-level magic, and I fear it could be quite difficult for us to get our hands on any."

"Even our fun-loving friend Binsala?" Charlie asked with an amused chuckle.

"He is always ready to make an appearance, when warranted," Bawb replied of his oft-used disguise. "However, we must first place ourselves in a system possessing users of adequate power to even warrant one being present. This variety of skree is not commonplace, Charlie. And more than that, they almost always are found in the hands of those involved in nefarious deeds."

"Like a certain assassin I know?"

Bawb grinned. "Perhaps. But let us find a suitable system

first. *Then* we can talk about Binsala the trader making an appearance."

Ara flew a lazy loop, sniffing for any trace of their friends, but as the minutes stretched into hours, it became abundantly clear that their friends were not merely sidetracked on the way to the rendezvous point. They weren't coming at all.

"All right, then," the massive Zomoki finally said. "They do not appear to be heading to this system. I propose we jump to the next system over and search there. If there is no sign of them as we approach the twenty-four-hour mark, then we should return to the portal to see if they've headed back there to perhaps try to pass through during the brief window it will open for them."

"Sounds like a plan," Charlie said. "Let's just hope we find them, one way or another. I worry about them all out in this strange galaxy on their own."

CHAPTER TEN

"Uh, guys? Where is everyone?" Kip asked his companions as they exited warp.

The faint blue crackling had barely faded, but he'd already fired up his scanners, probing the area for the others.

"I am not reading them on any devices," Dukaan said. "What about you, Kip?"

"I wouldn't have asked you if I had, Dookie," the ship replied, a hint of stress in his ordinarily chipper tone. "I've run a full-spectrum analysis of the area, and I've got nothing. Comms are silent too. Hunze, can you feel anything?"

The Ootaki reached out with her power, feeling for Bawb and the other half of her magically charged hair he bore with him. Her magic would always find its twin, but at this particular moment, the connection was nowhere to be found.

"No, there is no sign of them here," she replied.

"You sure? Maybe you need to recharge a bit. I can get us closer to the sun if you like," Kip offered.

"That will not be necessary, Kip, though I appreciate the kind offer. I absorbed a very large amount of power before we left. Our proximity to the Earth's sun was almost overwhelming in its intensity, in fact."

"Oh, right. Then do you need me to get farther from the sun?" Kip inquired.

"No, that's not necessary, Kip. This white dwarf star does not appear to have any particular magic-enhancing properties at all. In fact, you'll be interested to know that most of the stars in my home galaxy do not. At least, not anywhere near the extent of those in yours."

"I didn't know that," Kip said. "You know that, Dookie?"

"I wish you would stop calling me that," Dukaan said with an exasperated sigh. "And yes, I did know that, Kip. Ara mentioned it to me just a few days ago, when we were planning this excursion through the portal."

"Well, you could have told me."

"You're a superpowered AI, as you so often like to remind me. I assumed you already knew," Dukaan snarked back.

"Gentlemen, can we please focus on the issue at hand?" Hunze requested. "It seems we have reached the designated rally point, but the others have failed to arrive. What are your thoughts?"

Kip had multiple ideas instantaneously, but he held his electronic tongue, opting to let his Chithiid friend posit his theory first. His way of smoothing over their little tiff.

Dukaan stroked his chin in thought a moment, looking at the scans for the system. "I do believe that with no trace of the others having ever arrived in this system, it is fair to say that in all likelihood they must have gotten turned around somehow. I would wager they have most likely returned to the area of our departure to attempt to regroup with the separated ships and choose a new rally destination."

"But the enemy––" Hunze started.

"Will be close to the portal, which is back in the sun by now,"

Kip said. "But if the others do what I'd expect them to do, they'll warp back and stay on the periphery. Eddie possesses a shimmer, but the rest of us have to stay clear of the bad guys. Fortunately, all we need is the briefest comms contact and we can share new coordinates and warp right back out of there, ASAP."

"Why wouldn't they simply reset and warp here?" Hunze asked. "If they already have this location in their files, it seems the most efficient option."

"Yeah, but when things go wrong, we AIs tend to start from scratch," Kip noted. "Easier to negate possible problems by eliminating whatever chain it was that caused the failure in the first place. Luckily, we think a whole hell of a lot faster than you meat brains do," the AI said with a chuckle. "Uh, no offense."

Dukaan merely shook his head. Something he'd done frequently since partnering up with the strange computer mind powering this ship.

"Okay," Hunze said. "So that's the plan, then. We warp back to our original departure area near the portal and regain contact with the others. From there we can make a new warp jump to the new rally point where we can properly plan our next steps until the portal opens up for us again tomorrow."

"Sounds about right," Kip said. "So, you guys ready to go? No sense waiting around here, I think. If they haven't shown up by now, it's highly unlikely they will."

"I agree on this point," Dukaan said. "I, too, vote for the return warp option."

"Then we are unanimous," Hunze said. "Let's waste no further time. Our friends are waiting for us, and we have much to discuss."

Kip didn't need any time to prepare for the warp. In fact, while they had been discussing the option, he had already been spooling up his navs and priming his warp drive. He'd even plotted the exact amount of warp power he'd require to backtrack and drop them just outside the range of the alien ships they'd encountered before fleeing the system.

"Okay, hang on. Here we go," he said.

A second later all that remained of them in that solar system was a faint blue crackling in the space they'd just been occupying.

"Uh, guys?" Kip said as they exited warp. "You seeing this?"

"Of course we are, Kip," Dukaan grumbled. "We are not back at the portal."

"But I did the math. I'm good at math, Dookie. Tell her. This is what I do."

Kip seemed to be having a momentary existential crisis, his very core skills being called into question. This couldn't be right. It simply could not happen.

"It is his strong suit, actually," Dukaan said, hoping to calm his AI friend. "I have no idea what went wrong."

"I'll tell you what went wrong," Kip said. "We wound up in the wrong freakin' solar system is what went wrong."

"But I thought you were simply retracing our path," Hunze said, confused. "There should have been no room for error."

"That's the problem," Kip replied, more than a hint of panic in his voice. "There *was* no room for error. And the warp triggered exactly as intended, only it took us somewhere totally different."

"The navs, then?" Dukaan asked.

"Navs, warp, all of it," Kip said, forcing himself to calm down. "From what I can tell, something in this galaxy is making all of our drive systems act funky."

"Which means what, exactly?" Hunze asked.

"Which means the others didn't warp to the wrong rally point. *We* did. And now we just warped somewhere else. Somewhere else that is also the completely wrong place."

A sinking feeling hit the stomachs of the two flesh bodies aboard the AI ship, and if Kip had anything that was the electronic equivalent, it was experiencing the same sense of dread.

"Guys, this is not good," Hunze finally said, breaking the long silence. "We're going to need a plan."

CHAPTER ELEVEN

Eddie hit the gas and flew a quick loop of the immediate area the moment he emerged from warp, not knowing if the subtly crackling blue remnants of his warp signature were shielded by the shimmer magic cloaking his hull or not.

In any case, better safe than sorry was his motto, and so they hustled away from their arrival point to double back when they'd ensured all was safe and secure. It was then, as they approached the point of their initial arrival once more, that they noticed something odd.

They were alone.

"Huh, I wonder where they are," Ripley said as she pored over Eddie's scan readouts. "I'm not seeing them nearby. You think they ran into trouble and had to make a quick getaway?"

"Nah, not likely," Eddie said. "Check out the power signature readings. No residual energy from warp engines anywhere around us. Just that big, beautiful yellow dwarf star," he said of the system's radiant solar center.

It was a rather lovely solar system, surprisingly similar to the one they'd left behind, though with a few more planets than back home. One of them seemed to have a fair amount of space traffic moving to and from it. A civilized world, and advanced at that. And judging by all the ships coming and going, quite popular.

But that could also spell trouble for interlopers from another galaxy flying in a ship that simply wouldn't fit in, so they decided it was best to stay well clear of that world, at least for the time being. Once they'd circled back with their friends, *then* they would decide whether or not to even approach that beckoning planet.

"So it's just magic out here, then?" Ripley asked as she flipped through the spectrums on her scanning array one more time. "Not a trace of warp engines anywhere?"

"Nope. We're looking at the same readouts, Rip. We're the only warp engine in this solar system."

"What does this mean?" Leila asked, subconsciously clutching her Magus stone.

"It probably just means the others had some sort of drive system problem, is all," Ripley said. "I bet Ara and the guys got here first, saw that we were the only ship that made it to the rendezvous spot, and doubled back to find the others. I know it's what I'd do. Hey, do you think we should double back too? They might need a hand."

"No, Rip, let the dragon do her thing. It's a magical galaxy, and I'm sure she's far more adept at maneuvering around it than we are."

"Yeah, true. But what do we do now, then? I mean, do we just sit around and wait?"

"It kinda sucks, but yeah, I think that's what we've gotta do," Eddie replied. "I'll find us a safe spot to get us out of any possible shipping lanes––or whatever they have in this galaxy. Wouldn't want us being plowed into by some poor bastard who can't see the invisible ship now, would we?"

"That we would not," the teen agreed with a laugh. "You good with this, Leila?"

The olive-skinned woman loosened her grip on the potent, deep green magical stone hanging around her neck. It hadn't flared up in the slightest. Whatever was happening, she was in no immediate danger. At least, not of the magical variety.

"Yes, I think I'm fine with that plan," she said, letting out the breath she hadn't realized she'd been holding.

Eddie pivoted around, though in space there really is no up or down, and began searching for somewhere they might tuck away to wait for their friends but also observe the comings and goings from that strange planet so tantalizingly close by.

The AI ship and his teenage friend were of the same mind after mere minutes of flight, each coming to the same idea independently, yet together.

"Hey, guys?"

"Yeah, Rip?" Eddie said.

"I was thinking. I mean, we've got our comms setup wide open, and these magic ships don't operate on any of our frequencies, so we really don't have to filter out any chatter or other distractions."

"What are you getting at, Ripley?" Leila asked.

"Well, I just thought, why not be productive while we wait? I mean, with our shimmer, we can get pretty close to that planet without being seen. All we need to do is steer clear of the flight lanes, which all seem pretty well defined now that I get a chance to really look at them. What do you think, Eddie?"

The AI had been running analyses of the flight patterns as well, and had already laid out what he believed to be the safest routes should they feel like taking a little look-see.

"I don't see anything wrong with that. Do you, Leila? We'll still be a safe distance above the planet, but we can probably gather a fair bit of intelligence for the gang before they get back from retrieving the others."

Leila might have been unsure of the young ship and his teenage pilot at one point in her life, but having survived multiple alien encounters with them now, she had a deep confidence in their abilities, no matter how unusual they might sometimes behave.

And she wasn't alone in that assessment. Charlie, Bawb, Hunze, and even Ara had all said that despite their age and relative inexperience, Ripley and Eddie were a rock-solid team that they were honored to have flying with them. And with Ripley's uncle Cal providing them some of the more choice toys from the planet's experimental arsenal, they were also one of the best armed ships in the entire fleet, for their size.

"Okay, let's do it," Leila said, sinking into her seat and looking out the ship's window.

She was home again. Home in her own galaxy. It was a strange feeling, knowing that the stars she was looking at were the same she'd stared at as a girl, only they were now hundreds of years older, courtesy of some rather surprising time travel mishaps. They were older, but they looked exactly the same. Stars were funny like that. People, however, were not.

In that regard, she could never go home. Not to the one she'd left when she fled with Charlie so recently, but also so very long ago. Staring at the planet as they drew nearer, she couldn't help but wonder how things had changed in the galaxy in her absence.

Soon enough, she would find out.

CHAPTER TWELVE

The blue supergiant at the center of the system was a massive ball of energy, burning at over twenty thousand degrees Kelvin. That little factoid from her early days of spaceship pilot training flashed into Rika's head as she took the *Fujin* into a slow spin, surveying the unusual solar system she and Jo had arrived in.

Despite the ship's shielding, as well as the below-freezing temperatures of the vacuum just on the other side of the shatterproof glass windows, the blue light felt almost oppressive. Hot. Heavy. As if its energy was pushing down on them despite all of the protective measures in place.

Rika knew that wasn't possible. The ship's shielding had been strong to begin with, but when Cal and Zed began the upgrade process of her new baby, they'd gotten a little carried away in their excitement. As a result, the *Fujin* was far more heavily shielded and armed than a ship its size would normally be.

But something was still wrong, and it wasn't just the strange blue sun blaring down on them from the center of its orbiting worlds.

"I can't see the others anywhere. You feel them with that

magic stuff?" Jo asked as she flipped through comms frequencies, to no avail.

"No. Nothing. We're on our own here," Rika replied. "Something went wrong."

"Obviously."

"But what? The ship seems to be functioning smoothly. And the others, while dodging incoming alien fire, were still undamaged from what I could see before we warped." Rika paused in thought. "You did fix the warp core, didn't you? You said it needed a few tweaks, and it'd be––"

"Of course I did. Who do you think you're asking?" Jo shot back.

"Well, things got busy, so it could have slipped in the shuffle."

"I'm a cyborg, Rika. I don't sleep, and I sure as hell don't just forget items on my task manager. One of the benefits of having a processor for a mind. We're not subject to the little glitches you meat people have."

"Except when you melt down," Rika snarked at her.

"Well, obviously. But that's insanely rare, and hasn't happened since before the Great War. Nowadays everyone's been upgraded and is running in tip-top condition. So don't pin this on my perfectly amazing mind, thank you very much."

Despite the stress, Rika couldn't help but let out a little laugh, her mirth spreading to her cyborg companion. Soon both were sharing a hearty chuckle.

"Oh, thank you. I needed that," Rika said, wiping the tears of amusement from her eyes. "Okay, so we're in the dark here as to what happened, but your repairs *obviously* weren't the issue."

"Thank you for acknowledging that."

"You're welcome. And seeing as how you've got such an amazing AI brain up in there, how about you use it to figure out what actually did go wrong while I refine our scans?"

"On it," Jo replied, immediately running a basic data analysis internally as she replayed the readings from their systems from the time they passed through the portal into this galaxy to their present predicament after warping to the blue giant system.

She was unusual in her methodology, utilizing both her internal AI systems, but also tying in to the ship's logs as well, comparing them for any sign of anomalies. None jumped out at her, however. Everything *seemed* to be normal. Then she had an idea.

Jo pulled up the visuals from the external recording apparatus and began mapping out bright dots in the sky as frames flew by on the monitors.

"What are you doing, Jo?"

"Had an idea," she replied. "I'm running the recordings back and using the visual data to create a corresponding map of sorts based on those inputs, then cross-referencing them with the coordinates of our plotted rally point warp."

"Okay, so kind of like making a new star chart."

"Right. Only not quite. We just didn't have the time to properly get one put together, seeing as those alien bastards jumped us pretty much right after we got here."

The mapping on the screen continued to flash by, the space battle taking place on the screens quickly blotted out by a grid of the newly logged stars as Jo compiled the data from all of the combined recordings.

It took several minutes to parse the data from so many recording angles, and the heat of battle also made the images unusable in several instances. But for the most part they were sound. Finally, the flashing images faded, replaced by one incredibly dense map of the stars from their point of arrival.

"So, that's it, huh?" Rika said. "That's a lot of stars."

"Yeah, it's a pretty dense galaxy," Jo agreed. "At least from where we popped through the portal. But here's the kicker. I plotted our course based on the coordinates we'd all been given prior to crossing over. The rally point was a fixed location that should have been a safe spot to regroup, regardless of other factors."

"Right, that's the whole point of it."

"Exactly. But this is where we were supposed to go," Jo said, zooming the map on a bright yellow dot in the sky.

"But that star's a yellow dwarf," Rika said, staring intently at the screen. "We were supposed to meet in a system with a yellow sun."

"Yup," Jo replied. "And this one is blue. So, I assume you see the problem here."

Rika shook her head as the reality of the situation became crystal clear. "We're in the wrong place," she said. "And I honestly have no idea how to get us back to the right one."

CHAPTER THIRTEEN

Not quite a day had passed since the motley group of Earth ships and their dragon friend had passed through the portal between galaxies, and as of yet, they had been unable to reconnect. Eddie and his passengers weren't terribly concerned, though. If it came down to it, they'd simply warp back to the portal when it was scheduled to open and join up with the others there.

The thought was that if things went terribly wrong and they were split up, that would be the sure-thing rally point of last resort. They were all dialed in on Earth chronos, so regardless of the length of days or nights in whatever system they were in, the countdown would always be tied to Earth time.

While the alien ships would surely be there as well, the flames of the sun blazing through the portal would keep them quite clear. Meanwhile, the returning Earth ships knew precisely when it would be safe to approach, giving them a huge tactical advantage.

None wanted to use that final option to rejoin the others, but if things truly did go south, there really was no other choice. But in the meantime, Leila figured there was no harm in gathering a bit of news on her galaxy, seeing as she was home for the first time in centuries, courtesy of the mind-bending issues of time travel.

"I'll be fine," she said as Eddie invisibly set down on the outskirts of the bustling city they'd determined to be the hub of pretty much everything on this world.

It was a gleaming example of modern culture, clean and bright, a sprawling metropolis with many impressive buildings, their floating gardens magically suspended alongside the magic-buttressed towers.

Power users lived here, that much was clear. And unless Leila was mistaken, they were potent ones at that.

"You sure you don't want me to come with?" Ripley asked. "You know I've been practicing my casting, and I'd be happy to cover your six."

"Cover my six? Have you been talking with Zed again?" Eddie asked with a chuckle. "I know how much he loves all that military jargon."

"Hey, Uncle Zed's running the fleet. He's *supposed* to use military jargon," Ripley shot back with a smirk. "Anyway, it'd be cool to actually go run around on an alien planet. I mean, one with a real civilization. No offense to the Kalamani, but their spears and stuff weren't very impressive for meeting an entirely new alien race."

Leila understood where the teen was coming from. She herself had spent her whole life working Visla Maktan's grounds, never once even daring to think she might one day see another world, let alone become a spacefaring alien queen with a dragon for a friend. But life's funny like that sometimes, and here she was.

"The thing is, Rip, you're human. And that's not a bad thing, but you don't look enough like any species from our galaxy to go unnoticed. You'd *probably* be able to slip by without an issue, but given how tenuous our situation is right now, I think it's better if

I do a little reconnaissance on my own. I'm from this galaxy. I'll blend right in."

"She's right, you know," Eddie agreed.

"Yeah, but look how cool this place is!" Ripley griped.

She was right. Compared to the last alien world they'd seen—back in their own galaxy, no less—this was like the difference between a rocket ship and a skateboard. There was simply no comparison.

"Look, Rip, once we meet up with the others, we'll have safety in numbers enough to maybe do a little exploring," Eddie said.

Grudgingly, the teen agreed to put her little exploration on hold, but not before making it clear that Leila had better at least bring her a souvenir when they came back to pick her up.

"Okay, listen," Eddie said, serious for a change. "We've got about three hours before the portal opens again. Rip and I will jump back to the portal's system with the shimmer engaged and reconnect when the others show up and bring them back here to regroup. It's not really ideal, but given our options and no comms contact with them, I guess it's the best we've got for now. Sound good?"

"Don't worry about me," Leila said, scratching her massive beast behind his ears. "I've got Baloo with me. I'll be fine."

Her good boy whuffed a contented snort of agreement. He'd grown utterly massive since arriving on Earth, but now he was back in his own galaxy for the first time since he was a mere pup. Leila was looking forward to seeing how he reacted to the novel sights and smells.

Fortunately, he'd calmed down slightly since his truly rambunctious puppy days, though he was still very much a pup—just one that weighed a few hundred pounds and could kill a man with a single bite if he wished. But Mama would not approve of that sort of behavior, so Baloo kept his hunting to animals rather than people.

But if someone raised a hand toward Leila? Heaven help them.

"Okay, all clear," Eddie said a minute later when he'd ensured no one was nearby. "See you back here in a few hours. We'll hit you up over comms when we're back with the others."

"Thanks, Eddie. I'll see you guys soon," Leila replied, stepping out the door of the shimmer-cloaked ship and into the welcoming glow of this new world's yellow sun. "Come on, Baloo. Time to go exploring!"

The giant furball bounded out of the ship, seeming to appear out of nowhere, should anyone have been watching. But Eddie, for all his quirky ways, was sound in his AI skills. No prying eyes were observing. Leila and her pup were deposited on the planet's surface without anyone being the wiser.

A light breeze blew her hair as Eddie took to the skies once more, his invisible form heading for space, where he would then warp back to where they'd originated to join up with the others and find out why exactly they had failed to meet them at the rendezvous point.

With a blade hidden under her clothes in the small of her back, a powerful konus on her wrist, and a spring in her step, Leila strode toward the bustling city before her, alert as she reconnoitered the area, while also excited to see what wonders it might hold.

Though she had spent her entire life as an animal keeper slave on Visla Yoral Maktan's massive estate, Leila had encountered a great many different species over her years of service there. As one of the most powerful vislas in the Council of Twenty, Visla Maktan frequently entertained guests from all over the known systems.

It was this familiarity that would now serve Leila well as she took mental note of the various races represented on this world. Obviously, it was a base of power for some person, or persons, but she was less concerned with that at the moment than what other species might be lurking in the city.

She hadn't seen any of the nasty mercenary types she'd often observed accompanying their masters when they visited Visla Maktan's estate, but that didn't mean there weren't any here. She would have to be alert. Alert, but also letting herself enjoy the city just a little. For once, she could simply blend in.

For the first time in quite a while, the woman with the hint of green peeking through her olive-tanned skin was not a minority.

"Excuse me," she said to a blue-skinned Bantoon selling roasted nuts of some sort from a little kiosk. "Can you please tell me the way to the main marketplace?"

The man's eyestalks pivoted to look at the lovely woman who had stopped to speak with him, the rest of him following, leaning close with a warm smile. It was only when he'd leaned past the edge of the window that he noticed the huge canine at her side and quickly retreated within his kiosk.

"Just down this main thoroughfare a bit," he said, pointing at the wide road angling off from where they stood. "You'll turn left when you see the floating fountain of Haranna. From there, it is only a few minutes farther."

"Thank you," Leila said, turning toward the marketplace. She paused and turned back to the blue-skinned man. "By the way, can you tell me the name of this planet?"

"The planet?" he asked, confused. "But surely you know where you are."

"Oh, yes, of course. But I've been traveling so much and jumping between systems, the names get jumbled sometimes," she replied, not sure if her excuse would fly.

Her story seemed to work. There were so many wealthy and powerful beings passing through this world in a steady stream that this wouldn't be the first time an exhausted traveler had lost track of where they'd woken up––typically aboard a massive vessel that had cost more than the combined earnings most of the residents would see in their lifetimes.

"Of course," the man said, putting on a false smile, hiding his disdain for the über-wealthy as best he could. "You are on the great planet of Slafara."

"And the city?"

A strange look crossed the man's face, but his smile somehow stayed in place. "You are in Visla Nikora Palmarian's realm. The capital city of Palmar."

"Ah, of course," Leila replied with the warmest smile she could manage. "Silly of me. I've been traveling so long, it must be taking its toll."

"Yes, of course," the vendor said.

"Thank you for your assistance," she replied with a cheerful grin and headed off to gather what intel she could. And if that meant exploring an amazing new city and scoring a souvenir for Ripley in the process? Well, she would just have to make that sacrifice.

CHAPTER FOURTEEN

Ara had flown a tireless search for the better part of a day while Charlie and Bawb reached out with their own magic, as well as scanning with the Earth tech mounted to her flight harness. All three were exhausted from the effort.

They'd passed through not just the adjacent system in hopes of finding their friends, but also two other solar systems in the general vicinity. It was a lot of space to cover, especially while pushing their senses to the limit, but the need was pressing.

Normally, tracking Earth craft was a very difficult proposition, and that was still the case now. However, as this was the first time that warp drive technology was used in this galaxy, Ara had posited it might be possible to sniff them out against the background noise of magical interference.

Essentially, the rarity of the traces would be what made them visible. But where they had arrived lacked any of that. It was a no-go.

They searched and searched, circling planets and moons, probing asteroid fields, and even venturing near the suns of several systems. All to no avail.

There was always the option to continue their pattern,

spreading out farther and farther as they cast their searching net, but it was a big galaxy, and it was becoming quite clear that their friends could be anywhere in it. A ship-sized needle in a galaxy-sized haystack.

"I think it's about time we move on to Plan B. Or Plan C. Or whatever the hell letter we're down to now," Charlie said. *"You guys agree?"*

It wasn't what they'd wanted to do, but with all three of their friends' ships still missing, there really wasn't a better option any of them could think of.

"I believe Charlie is correct in his assertion," Bawb said. *"Much as I had hoped we would find them merely slightly off course, I fear something else has happened here."*

"Yes, I share this concern," Ara said. *"So, then. It appears plan whatever it shall be. Secure yourselves. I will jump us back to the general vicinity of the portal momentarily."*

"Just not too close," Charlie said. *"It doesn't pull out of the sun for several hours according to the chrono. We wouldn't want to accidentally get scorched."*

"I am quite capable of protecting you both from the sun's force, reduced as it is through the relatively small opening of the portal," Ara said.

And she could, as the dangerous energy itself would fuel her defensive spells. But there was more they had to be wary of as well.

"I'm also a teensy bit concerned about the whole alien-armada-wanting-to-kill-us thing," Charlie added. *"So, yeah. It'd be great not to jump in too close to them, if you don't mind."*

Ara didn't dignify that with a response, but, rather, jumped clear across that part of the galaxy, right back to where they'd come from.

She arrived a few planets out from the burning eye of the portal, which was quite clearly visible in the inky depth of space despite the distance. They were well clear of not just the flaming plasma, but the enemy ships as well, Charlie was pleased to note. Now all they had to do was find a safe place a little closer to the portal and wait.

If everything went as they hoped, the others would have the same idea and enact the last-resort protocol, returning to the portal just as it was scheduled to clear from the sun. They could then pass through as a team, regrouping on the other side, safe under the protection of the fleet of heavily armed ships.

But Ara was lacking the convenient shimmer protection that Eddie possessed, so flying close would require much care and a lot of patience. As such, she took her time as she flew from her arrival point, slowly picking her way through the floating debris of the system, closing in on her intended waiting place one small step at a time.

It was tedious, to say the least, but it allowed her to move undetected, and that was paramount. It also gave Charlie time to run a few scans on the other craft in the system as they drew closer.

They had just neared the edge of the area where they'd all made their emergency escape from when Charlie sensed it. Or smelled it. Whatever it was his ever-evolving magic was doing these days. And Ara smelled it too. Even Bawb could feel traces with the help of the Ootaki hair wrapped around him.

"Shit. What happened?" Charlie wondered. "This is totally wrong."

And about that, he was totally right.

There were traces of jumbled warp tech energy from their friends' hasty escapes, but it was not at all what they were expecting to find.

"I do not understand," Bawb said. "This is not the normal feel of warp power."

"No, it isn't," Charlie said. "Something is all kinds of messed up here. You smell that, Ara? Like, the warp field was leaking all over the place."

67

"I do," the Zomoki noted.

Charlie realized pretty quickly what had happened, he was just having a hard time letting himself believe it.

"This galaxy. It interferes with certain types of Earth tech," he finally said. *"I never ran into this problem when I crashed here, since the ship was wrecked, and I was just using really basic med scanners and stuff. And hell, we didn't have warp tech back then. But now? I bet anything flying under warp power will have all kinds of issues. And that means warp travel is out of the question, at least without magical guidance."*

"But Eddie not only has a konus built into his airframe, but also possesses a strand of Hunze's hair," Bawb pointed out. *"If any ship could maneuver out here, he's the one."*

The Wampeh had a good point when Charlie thought about it. If Eddie had figured out a way to use his built-in magical tools to help guide his flight, then it was possible he might be able to control his trajectory. At least, somewhat. Kind of like steering a crashing car while pumping the brakes––not total control, but enough to hopefully not hit a tree.

Charlie checked the chrono on Ara's harness. They'd been back in this galaxy for just over twenty-one hours.

"We've got three hours until the portal opens again," he said. *"So I propose we find a safe spot to hide and wait and see if Eddie—or any of them—make it back here to try to reconnect."*

"And if they don't?" Ara asked.

A feeling of grim doubt filled Charlie's chest. *"Then we'll be having a very long search on our hands."*

CHAPTER FIFTEEN

The streets of Palmar were wide and clean, the city itself a reflection of the will of the powerful visla who oversaw it. Vendors' stalls were arranged along the perimeter of the wider avenues, while floating conveyances traveled smoothly down the center of the roadways.

Leila walked tall and confident, partly because she actually was both tall and confident, but also because she had her massive canine at her side, helping clear the way.

It wasn't that Baloo was threatening anyone in particular––though one small quadruped pet did catch his attention, until Mama's sharp words quelled any thoughts of chasing and eating it––it was that his mere presence made anyone with half a brain think twice about getting too close to his companion.

Of course, she had been practicing not only her fighting techniques under Rika's tutelage, but had also been honing her magic-casting skills with the help of all of her casting friends, each of whom had their own unique skillset. And with the rather strong, yet unassuming konus she wore on her wrist, she felt comfortable she could handle most problems that might come her way.

But her goal here was to be subtle. Or as subtle as one could be when walking with Baloo at their side. In any case, she was gathering intelligence, making note of infrastructure and the city layout, as well as any other significant details of anything that might prove useful to her associates when they returned to fetch her.

After a good bit of walking, however, she felt her mind wandering, just as her feet were, her thoughts drifting to the strange reality she had returned to. Her own galaxy, but not. For everyone she had ever known and loved in this place was long dead.

The thought of her father dying alone in his hut while she was living in a time either before he was born or long after he was gone, depending on how you looked at it, was a sobering one. And for a moment, the bright and cheerful glow of this new world was just a little bit dimmer for it.

"Leave me alone!" a teenage girl's voice cut through the air, snapping Leila from her thoughts.

"She said, hands off!" another joined in.

Something was afoot. Someone was harassing a pair of teenagers. She knew she had to remain incognito, but there was simply no way Leila could just walk by. She needed to be low-key, but she figured she could at least reduce the degree of the confrontation a bit.

"Baloo, I want you to sit and stay here," she ordered her companion. "You hear me? *Stay*."

The great hound looked at her with a slightly hurt look in his eyes, for he understood full well what she wanted, and he wasn't happy about it. But Leila was Mama, and he always did what Mama said.

"Good boy, Baloo," she said, scratching his head before striding through the crowd to where the voices had rung out from.

What she saw made her stomach clench up. A half dozen Tslavar boys had surrounded a pair of girls, pulling at the parcels in their arms. One of them, she noted, had a slightly yellow tint to her skin, but her hair was an odd, mousy brown color.

The other was a tall girl whose skin was the lightest shade of violet, her eyes a deep purple that contrasted with her orange hair. The dark rings under her eyes betrayed her weakened state as readily as any doctor's report could, as did the slight tremor in her arms as she clutched her belongings.

"Come on, you can afford it," one of the Tslavar youths said, reaching for her parcel. "Give it up!"

"Leave me alone!" she shouted, though the exclamation came out far fainter than she'd hoped.

"Why is it always the damn Tslavars?" Leila grumbled as she strode purposefully toward the boy she assumed was the leader of the pack.

She was glad she'd had Baloo stay behind at the corner. It would have been bad form, not to mention drawn a lot of unwanted attention, if her pet had killed a handful of teenagers for the crime of merely being assholes.

"What do you think you're doing?" Leila said, putting her tall form between the girl and her harasser.

"What's it to you, half-breed?" the boy said.

A spark of something flashed inside of her, and a bit of steely will straightened her defiant spine even further.

"What did you call me?" Leila replied, an icy anger beginning to grow in her chest.

"You heard me. Half-breed!" he repeated with a sneer.

Leila found herself consciously restraining herself from the violence Rika had trained her to call upon in a flash if need be. She caught her impulse, reining it in, controlling it. She felt the anger begin to fade. Calm and cool was the way to handle this.

At that moment, one of the Tslavar's friends made the ill-fated decision to try to use the distraction to steal whatever it was the girl was clinging to so fiercely. He darted forward, hands grabbing for purchase, when Leila moved entirely on instinct.

The boy stumbled backward, unsure what exactly had just happened, other than the fact that his nose was suddenly bleeding and he felt rather lightheaded. Leila turned her attention to the other Tslavar youths, her anger back, and with a vengeance.

True to their nature, rather than do the smart thing and just walk away, the boys pulled weapons from their pockets. A rather pathetic slaap for one, a few knives, and what appeared to be a fairly unimpressive konus.

"You don't want to do that," Leila said. "Just take your friend and leave."

"You're lucky I don't hit girls," the apparent ringleader said.

"Yes," Leila replied with dripping sarcasm. "I'm *so* fortunate."

"You didn't let me finish," the boy continued. "I said *I* don't hit girls. But Alara here does."

A stocky Tslavar girl shouldered past the boys and forewent the formality of taunts and threats, opting instead for a direct and immediate attack.

Leila jumped aside, narrowly avoiding a meaty fist as it whistled through the air. The girl was strong, and she had obviously spent plenty of time fighting, judging by her willingness to engage. But she lacked a few things Leila had in abundance. Most crucially, in this moment, was speed. Speed, and actual tactical fight training.

Leila drew upon her sparring sessions with Rika and snapped out a quick series of kicks, first to the Tslavar girl's leg, deadening the nerve just above the knee, then hopping upward, striking her ribs and chin in quick succession.

Alara stumbled backward, startled by her opponent's tactic,

and was pulling a wicked blade from the sheath on her hip when a well-placed spinning kick to the temple laid her out for a nice, long nap on the dusty ground.

The boys couldn't believe what they'd just seen. Couldn't, or didn't want to. In either case, Tslavar honor was at stake, and they all rushed to attack at once.

Leila didn't want to hurt them, and she didn't want to cause any more of a scene than she already had, but neither did she wish to be murdered by a bunch of well-armed teenagers.

She dodged and weaved the flashing blades as she called up a series of spells that were some of Charlie's favorites. The boys stumbled backward when the pungent smell of feces filled their noses. It wasn't the most elegant of spells, but it bought her the space she needed to mask her casting abilities as she fought.

Leila quickly cast stun spell after stun spell, timed to land simultaneously with the punches and kicks she was dealing out to her attackers. It wasn't the prettiest of fights, but as Bawb often said, it was not the grace of the fight that ultimately mattered, only the results. And the result was a pile of unconscious Tslavars, and Leila standing over them without a scratch on her.

"I'm sorry about that," she said to the teens. "Are you okay?"

The violet-skinned girl's friend stepped in front of her. "Who are you? What do you want from Kara?"

"Want? I don't want anything," Leila replied. "I'm trying to help. I just heard the sound of you girls being attacked and couldn't stand by while that happened."

"They wouldn't have done anything," the violet girl, apparently named Kara, said meekly. "They know who my father is, so they wouldn't have actually hurt us. All they wanted were my Narakas cakes. I should have just given them to them. I can always get more."

"No, Kara. You can't let them steal from you. Next time we'll have to take Bahnjoh with us. Or you could tell your father. He'll make sure they––"

"You know I can't do that. It's not worth the hassle, Vee. And besides, if I do, he'll just have Grundsch start following me around every day again. You remember what that was like."

The yellow-skinned girl shuddered at the thought. "Yeah, that wasn't very much fun."

"No, not at all," Kara agreed.

A piercing shriek made all three of them spin around.

Baloo was standing there, a low growl in his throat. He had a Tslavar man's arm held firmly in his mouth. A mouth that could have just as easily torn the arm clean off. The deadly blade fell from the would-be assailant's hand as the beast bit down a little harder.

Leila walked over and picked up the knife. "You were going to stab me in the back? Why, you little shit! That's cowardly! What would your Tslavar elders say?" she shot at him with disdain. "Okay, Baloo, you can let him go. I think he has somewhere else he's supposed to be right now. Isn't that right?"

The man didn't utter a word, but just turned and ran as fast as his feet would carry him.

"I told you to stay," Leila said, turning back to Baloo.

The canine let out a tiny whine. He knew he'd disobeyed Mama.

"Oh, you. That's okay. You're a good boy, Baloo," she said, letting him off the hook with a warm ear scratch.

"This is your animal?" Vee asked, cautiously approaching the furry beast, her standoffish vibe fading at the sight of him.

"Yeah, his name's Baloo. You can pet him if you like. He only bites assholes."

Vee snickered at that. "Hello, Baloo," she said, stroking his coat. "Kara, check this out. He's almost as big as Bahnjoh."

The violet-skinned girl cautiously made her way over to the

contented hound, gently caressing the fur on his back. "He's so soft," she said, surprised.

"Yeah, well, you should see him after he gets back from playing out in the woods sometime. Mud head to tail, I tell ya," Leila said with a laugh. "I'm Leila by the way."

"I'm Visanya," Vee said.

"And I'm Karasalia," Kara added. "Karasalia Palmarian."

"Palmarian? Like the guy the city is named after?" Leila asked.

"Yeah. My dad."

"Whoa," Leila said, realizing she'd quite possibly just stumbled upon the greatest source of intelligence on the entire planet. "Well, since you're obviously a bit shaken up, and since some idiotic people seem to want to harass you for some reason, let me and Baloo at least walk you guys home."

"Oh, you don't have to do that," Kara said. "Really, we should be able to come to the market without problems."

"You'd think," Vee said. "But obviously that's not the case. Kamar and his buddies are the same assholes they were when we were kids."

"You can say that again," Kara said, a little smile curving her lips upward.

"Okay. They're assholes," Vee repeated with a chuckle.

Leila had a good feeling about these two. Whatever issues Kara's father might have, his daughter seemed to be a good kid.

"Come on, Baloo and I will accompany you. Just consider yourselves our tour guide."

"You're not from Palmar?" Vee asked.

"Nope. Just arrived today and don't know the first thing about this place."

Kara warmed a bit at the opportunity to repay their interesting new friend. "Well, if you put it that way, then I suppose it's okay. We're heading over there," she said, gesturing toward the ritzy part of town. "Me and Vee will gladly fill you in on our home while we walk. It's the least we can do."

"Wonderful. Lead the way," Leila said, following her unlikely new friends, while scoping out everything in sight as they walked. "I'm looking forward to learning all about your beautiful city."

CHAPTER SIXTEEN

The walk through the city was a far more relaxing experience for the teens now that they had a badass new friend and her intimidating beast as companions. Whether they wanted to admit it or not, Kara and Vee were rather enjoying the stares they were drawing.

For once, it was an agreeable sort of attention.

"Uh, are we going *there*?" Leila asked as the girls made a beeline for the most opulent of the gleaming towers, its dozens of surrounding gardens floating alongside the building every few levels, levitating on a magical cushion.

"Yeah, that's home," Kara said.

While Leila had grown up on Visla Maktan's sprawling estate, it seemed that Visla Palmarian's domicile was vertical rather than horizontal, though the myriad hovering outdoor spaces gave it nearly as much land as Leila's father had tended back when she was a girl.

This visla was obviously a man of not only great power, but also considerable wealth to be able to afford such a home. The buildings nearby were nice, make no mistake, but this was simply magnificent, towering high above all the others.

They approached a guarded entryway, where a dozen armed men stood at attention.

"Denna Palmarian. Welcome home," the head of the guard said, using her honorific title as a lady of the Palmarian house.

"Thanks, Shozzy," the teen replied, striding into the foyer.

"The beast stays here," the guard said as Leila and Baloo followed.

"It's okay, Shozzy, they're with me."

"But your father––"

"It's fine. I'll deal with him if he has a problem with it."

"Very well," he said, stepping aside. "But do keep your beast in check."

Leila didn't dignify that with a reply, opting to silently follow the teens onto a wide, opalescent disc.

"Which floor do you live on?" Leila asked as they activated the spell powering the elevation platform.

"Floor?" the teen replied, confused. "What do you mean?"

"I mean, which level is your family's."

"Oh, I see," Kara said, blushing a deeper violet. "Uh, we don't really have a level."

"What she means is, her dad owns the whole place," Vee clarified.

"Wow," Leila managed to say. "And I thought the estates in Malibu were palatial."

The girls gave her a funny look.

"Maliboo?" Vee asked.

"Home," Leila replied.

Up and up they went, the disc powered by an invisible magical force raising it high above the city. From this vantage point you could see everything, and despite being brought up surrounded by nature, Leila had to admit, in its own way, it really was a beautiful place.

The platform gradually slowed as they neared the upper floors, stopping just below the top.

"C'mon, this way," Kara said, leading the way.

Leila followed the teen and her friend as they traipsed through the incredible home as if it were nothing special. But the teen had grown up in it, so Leila supposed it really was nothing special to her. We grow to the size of our containers, Leila's father had once said. Apparently, that held true to people as well as plants.

An enormous alien the likes of which Leila had never seen strode into the corridor. It was male, she thought, and had only four fingers per giant hand. The musculature it possessed was impressive, to say the least. Impressive, and intimidating. Then she saw the golden band firmly clasped around its neck.

A control collar. The huge being couldn't harm them if it wanted to. Leila breathed a silent sigh of relief.

"Where have you been, Denna Palmarian? I heard there was an incident in the marketplace," he said, noting the signs of a scuffle on her clothing and parcel. "What happened? Tell me. Are you harmed? Who is in need of killing?"

"No one, Grundsch. And you know how Father feels about you returning to your violent ways. You're better than that," Kara replied.

"But you were not to go to the marketplace alone. Your father says I am to protect you. And if I am not present, Bahnjoh should be at your side for any such outing, at the very least."

"I'm fine, really."

"But you could have been harmed."

"But I was not. Leila here helped us with our problem."

Leila gave a little wave. "Excuse me," she said. "But I've never seen your species before, yet for some reason you seem strangely familiar. I just can't place it."

"I am Ra'az Hok," Grundsch answered. "The last of my race, so far as I know." He fixed a hard stare on the newcomer. "But how do you know of my kind?" he asked with a menacing curiosity. Then he shifted his gaze to Baloo. The canine stared right back, not flinching in the slightest.

A clacking sound echoed out across the space as a massive six-foot-long beast that resembled a huge dog, but with a thickened hide beneath its fur and giant teeth walked into the room, its claws reverberating off the floor with every step.

The Graizenhund was as big as Baloo, if not a little bigger. And he was tough.

"Stay, Baloo," Leila commanded.

"Bahnjoh, be good," Kara warned the beast, but it had already focused its attention on Baloo, the two circling one another like a pair of apex predators hovering over a kill.

Then, despite their masters' orders, the two giant beasts lunged at one another, spinning in the air as their snapping jaws and pinwheeling legs morphed into a whirling mass of fur and teeth.

As quickly as it started, the melee abruptly ceased, the two breaking apart, once more going back to their menacing circling, sniffing each other with great interest.

"Oh, this is not good. What do we do?" Vee asked, looking at Leila and her friend.

"I honestly have no idea," Leila replied.

Both canines growled low, staring intently at one another. Then suddenly, without warning, Baloo's tail began to wag, and he bounced high in the air. Bahnjoh, startlingly, did the same, his tail likewise flapping side to side. The two then took off running, chasing each other around the entire level.

Grundsch let out a deep chuckle. "It appears they have each discovered a new friend," he said.

"Wild," Leila murmured, breathing a sigh of relief. "It's not every day Baloo finds someone he can roughhouse with."

"The same can be said for Bahnjoh," Grundsch noted, then returned his focus to his young mistress. "Now come, Denna Palmarian. Your father awaits you."

CHAPTER SEVENTEEN

The power in the room was tangible, even for a barely powered woman like Leila. Visla Palmarian was so strong he simply leaked excess magic from his body like others might sweat.

Leila quickly tucked her Magus stone into her shirt. She didn't think it would flare up, giving away its magical secret, but she knew just how powerful it truly was, as well as the great lengths some power users would go to in order to acquire one.

It was strange, the realization that such a massively powerful man had such a weak child for his offspring. It hardly seemed possible, but Kara's sickly body hardly held any traces of magic that she could sense. She was a visla's daughter, but compared to him, she was a speck of sand on the beach, while he was a towering wave.

"You're looking well, Father. I'm glad to see your strength retur—"

"Silence, child," he commanded. "My eyes on the street have told me of your foolishness, Karasalia," he said, chiding his teenager. "Whatever inspired you to act in so careless a manner?"

"I'm sorry Father. Me and Vee––"

"Visanya and I."

"Yes, sorry. Visanya and I, we were just going to the marketplace to pick up some Narakas cakes. We thought it would be a nice treat."

"A nice treat that put you in harm's way," her father grumbled. His eyes flicked to the Ra'az servant. "And you, Grundsch. Why were you not with her?"

"Apologies, Visla. I was unaware the denna had departed."

"And the beast?"

"He was here, in the tower, Visla," the enormous man quietly replied.

Visla Palmarian stared at him a moment, his displeasure clear, but so, too, was the fact that this was not Grundsch's fault. Not this time, at least.

Leila noticed something odd in the power wafting from the visla. As if it was reduced somehow. As if his strength wasn't entirely present, though it was still leaking off of him, if that made any sense.

Were her friends there with her to back her up, she might even have been brazen enough to inquire about his unusual gift, but Leila decided this was most definitely not an opportune moment for such queries.

"And this must be the ferocious woman I've heard about," he said, turning his attention suddenly to Leila. "Step forward. Let me see you."

Leila approached the visla, stopping just in front of him. "I am called Leila, Visla. I was just walking down the street admiring your city when I heard a commotion."

"And you stepped in to help my daughter and her friend, despite being outnumbered."

"Well, they seemed to need assistance, and I know how to fight a little, so I thought I would see what I could do to help."

"Fight a little," the visla said with a laugh. "Oh, my dear, I've heard what you did to the Tslavar rapscallions. I think it is safe to say you know how to fight more than just a little. Who trained you?"

"Just a few friends."

"You must have talented friends if they imparted these skills to you."

"Yeah, I guess so," she said, feeling a momentary swell of pride in her man. "One used to be a gladiator, actually," she said, before remembering not only where she was, but when.

"Oh? There are so few systems that still allow gladiatorial combat these days. Ah, to have been alive during the peak of the tournaments. Now that must have been an era," he said, a far-off look in his eyes. "But that is an entirely different discussion."

"Father, is Mareh back yet?" Kara interjected.

"Her stepmother," he clarified for their guest. "No, Daughter, your dear stepmother is still with her friends. I expect she'll be back soon enough, though."

"Mareh's great," Kara informed Leila. "She's really smart, though she's always off visiting her friends in distant systems. I'm trying to convince her to take me with her someday, but she keeps saying maybe when I'm older."

"And with good reason. You know how she is. A socialite, my wife, as evidenced by her most recent voyage. Apparently, she double booked obligations without realizing it. Can you imagine?" the visla said with mock horror. "Having to rush off at a moment's notice, all for a silly social engagement? What's a woman to do?"

"Don't make fun," Kara said. "You know it's part of the reason you adore her so."

A warm smile wormed its way onto the visla's face, and in that moment Leila could see that yes, indeed, he was thoroughly smitten with his wife.

"Well, I think I've made my concerns clear," he said, shifting his thoughts back to his daughter. "Do not do it again. Am I understood?"

"Yes, Father."

"Good. Now, why don't you go show our new friend the grounds? And for heaven's sake, offer her something to eat. You are a visla's daughter. Decorum and hospitality are cornerstones of our reign here."

Leila followed Kara and Vee out of the visla's chambers and onto a hovering bridge that led to one of the uppermost floating gardens. It was spectacular to behold, and at this altitude, there was no shade from the other buildings to block the sun's nourishing rays.

"That'll be all, Grundsch. I'm home now. You don't have to follow me around within the tower walls, you know," Kara said, dismissing the Ra'az guard.

He responded with a mere grunt and a nod, then lumbered off to wherever it was he went when she was not around.

"I can't help but think I know his species from somewhere," Leila mused. "I just can't place it."

"Grundsch is one of a kind," Kara said. "So's Bahnjoh. They were both found in a crashed ship when I was just a little girl. The craft had been horribly damaged from what I've heard, and all of the other crew were dead. All but Grundsch. He was taken from the ship and healed, but it was nearly three months before he regained consciousness."

"And what of the animal?"

"Bahnjoh? His mother was pregnant with him when they crashed. The rest of the litter died, but he was a tough little guy, and somehow, he survived."

The story reminded Leila of her acquisition of Baloo, a tiny pup taken from his mother far too young. Only her nurturing and care had kept him alive in those early, vulnerable days. Hard to believe when you saw the massive beast he had grown to become.

They walked a loop of the garden as Kara and Vee told the stories of growing up in the visla's household. The two had met at a very young age, and though Vee's adoptive parents were only a lower-ranking emmik mother and entirely unpowered father, Visla Palmarian nevertheless approved of the friendship, and the two had been together ever since.

As for Kara, it turned out her real mother, a beautiful woman and powerful visla in her own right, named Azaraella, had died when she was still a young girl. It was a difficult time for her father, the next several years, but the fates finally smiled upon him when he met a most caring and wonderful woman named Mareh, while giving in to his young daughter's plea that he take her to a social event.

It had been love at first sight, and following a quick courtship, the two were wed. This was much to his daughter's delight, as Mareh was, while an older woman, of course, almost like a big sister that Kara had never had. And as Kara's health took a turn for the worse as she grew, Mareh stayed by her side, a constant source of loving support.

All in all, Kara and Vee seemed like good kids, and Leila hoped they'd get to meet Ripley when her friends returned. She had a feeling they'd all get along swimmingly, though the Earth girl's ways might shock a few of the more stodgy of the house's staff.

They had walked a long loop and were about to re-enter the tower from one of the servants' recreation decks on the far side of the building, when Leila noticed something unusual about the wall. Something that didn't seem to belong there at all.

"Uh, what *is* that?" she asked, pointing to the dusty gray handle sticking out of the wall at waist height.

"Oh, that. It's the heretic's sword," Kara replied, as if that were a normal thing to say.

"Heretic? I'm sorry, I don't follow."

"An assassin Father captured when they came to kill him.

They were sneaking in through the servants' chambers when Father fell upon them. It was odd, though. At first, his spells didn't seem to work as planned, though they did stun the attacker. But as he cast a powerful stun spell, they drove their sword deep into this wall, just as the spell knocked them to the ground."

"But no one has thought to take it out? Seems an odd thing to leave impaled like that," Leila said.

"No one can," Kara replied. "Oh, everyone's tried. We even had a sort of party one time, where Father held a contest to see if anyone could remove it. He said whoever could pull it free would receive a small estate and honorary title, if you can believe that."

"So what happened?"

"Well, they all failed, obviously," the teen said.

"So, what happened to the assassin?" Leila asked, subconsciously squeezing her Magus stone as she gingerly placed her hand on the sword's pale grip.

"Oh, she's locked in the highest cell in the tower."

"Highest? Not in a dungeon?"

"Oh, no. Father says it's much harder to escape from high places than low ones."

Leila heard the girl talking, but her focus was nearly entirely on the weapon lodged in the wall in front of her. Something about it was speaking to her. As if it was reaching out.

Kara and Vee shared a knowing look as they watched their new friend tighten her grip on the handle and pull with all her might.

The sword did not budge at all.

"You felt it, didn't you?" Vee asked.

"I... Yes. What is it?"

"No one knows, but everyone who grabs it has felt that strange tug. The heretic won't tell us anything, though, so I guess we may never know."

Leila pondered what that could possibly mean, then glanced out at the lowering sun. A lot of time had passed. Too much time. She checked her comms, hiding the device with her body so as to avoid any questions about the tech-magic device.

No sign of Eddie and Rip.

This was not good. This was not good at all.

CHAPTER EIGHTEEN

"We're so screwed," Ripley said as she once again flipped through the scanners, surveying the solar system for any sign of where their friends were. Or where *they* were, for that matter.

They'd made over a dozen jumps in the hours since they'd left Leila to gather intel, and none had gone quite as expected. The first was thought to have been an anomaly—merely a miscalculation that took them off course. Only when they had again arrived at an unintended point in space did they realize something was very wrong.

They tried to backtrack, to return to what they had initially assumed was the correct rally point system, but even that was apparently not an option, as their warp drive seemed to be sending them places they had not plotted out.

"How are we going to get to the others?" Ripley moaned. "And what about Leila? She's stuck on some planet, and we don't even know how to get back to it. Holy hell, this is bad," the teen said, slumping even lower in her seat.

"It's this galaxy, Rip," Eddie said. "Don't blame yourself, and don't blame me. There was no way we coulda known it'd be like this."

His words were true, but they didn't relieve his young friend's stress. The clock was ticking, and what had started as a simple backtrack to a rendezvous point had become a desperate search for any sign of their friends.

"We've got to find a way back, Eddie. I mean, we're both magic users now. So if the warp drive is really that messed up, we can just magic ourselves there, right?"

"We're not Drooks, Rip. We don't have the right kind of magic to propel and guide the ship."

"But we've got Hunze's hair. That's gotta be good for something."

Eddie thought a moment, which for an AI meant he ran over a million scenarios through his digital head. "Hmm, you know what? I wonder..."

"Wonder what?"

"If there's actually something we could do using the stuff Bawb installed, and Hunze's hair. What spells do we have at our disposal that might help us dial in our course?"

"Well, there's not much specifically for that," Ripley replied. "But we did have that tracking spell from back when the Tslavars first made a run at Earth, but I don't know if that––"

"Ooh, yes! That's the one!" Eddie exclaimed. "Think about it, Rip. We were using it to track Ara's magic, at least as best we could. But we've gotten better since then."

"Yeah, but––"

"But nothing. We've got a way to track our way back to the portal."

"I'm not following, Eddie."

"The sun, Rip. Don't you see? That's the only spot in the whole galaxy that emits that kind of power, and we have more than enough history with our own sun to be able to tweak the spell to hone in on it. And, bonus, it emits magic. I mean, we couldn't perceive it before Ara and them showed up, but now that we're dialed in with a strand of Hunze's hair, it should act like a compass of sorts."

Ripley realized what Eddie was saying. "And the sun is our north."

"Exactly."

"Can we do it, you think?"

"If we start casting, I think we'll know soon enough," Eddie replied. "You good to try this?"

"Hell yeah!" the teen replied, her spirits suddenly improving.

It took only a few minutes for the duo to get their magic dialed in to the strand of supercharged Ootaki hair melded to the konus in Eddie's frame. And once they achieved that, a course was clear.

Well, clear*ish*. The signal was incredibly faint, but that pinpoint of Earth's sun's energy was the lone spot in the entire galaxy that type of energy existed, and Hunze's hair was drawn to it like a moth to a flame. In conjunction with the spell they'd previously used to track Ara's magic in pursuit of the flame-marked Tslavars, it looked like this might actually work.

Using the magic to hopscotch across systems with their malfunctioning warp system, Eddie managed to get them close enough to their destination to continue in close without another warp. The portal would open in just minutes. All they had to do was get in position and the others would hopefully show up.

But there was just one problem.

"Eddie?"

"Yeah, Rip?"

"They don't have magic," Ripley realized. "How will they find their way back?"

"Kip has a konus. Charlie installed it. And Rika's straight up bristling with the stuff."

"Yeah, but none of that is Ootaki magic. It won't guide them here."

Ripley was right. While the others did indeed have access to magic, it wasn't the variety they'd need to find the portal again. They were just as lost as Eddie and Ripley had been, only they lacked the compass to find their way back.

"We'll figure something out," Eddie said, his AI mind racing for options but finding none he liked. "In the meantime, we can't just sit here and mope. We've got resources. We're shimmer cloaked, so at the very least, we can do a little sneak around and see exactly how big this enemy fleet is. Find out what we're up against. Then, when we finally meet up with the others––"

"*If* we meet up with them."

"No, *when* we meet up with them. It'll work out, Rip. I know it."

She had to admire his confidence, but it was something she simply couldn't share. Things were bad, and hope was perhaps not entirely lost, but it was certainly running on fumes. But he was right about one thing. At least there was something they could do in the meantime.

It wasn't a plan Ripley was happy about, but it was action. And action was better than doing nothing.

"Okay, Eddie. Take us in."

CHAPTER NINETEEN

A massive, floating graveyard of burned-out wreckage.

That's what Eddie and his young friend faced as they slowly picked through the obstacles on their way toward the flaming eye of the portal, the sun's plasma still spewing forth like a deadly geyser no one dared go near. The bodies of the crews of those ruined ships had been reduced to less than ash in an instant, but the remains of the varied craft had survived in one form or another, for the most part.

The intense heat of the sun had warped and melted them into mostly unrecognizable forms, but knowing what to look for now, Eddie and Rip could easily discern that the floating hunks of fused materials were actually asteroid-looking wrecks, torched by the sun's heat. The final resting place of thousands of unfortunate souls.

The bits that hadn't been reduced to space dust and scattered among the stars, at least.

"Eddie, look at them all," Ripley gasped as they slowly edged through the debris field, shimmer cloak fully engaged. "So many wrecks. We must have taken out over half their fleet. There are hundreds of them."

"Or less, but just broken into pieces," Eddie noted. "Still, yes. That's a *lot* of destroyed ships. And do you see the remaining fleet hiding out just past them?"

"How can I miss them?" Ripley asked as she flashed the scanner across the ships lurking in the dark, waiting for whatever new victim might eventually come through the portal. "And I still don't have any signs of the others on any of the scanners."

"With all the interference from the enemy fleet, the wreckage, and the sun, not to mention the issues with this galaxy screwing with our systems, it's not surprising."

"Yeah, I know. But I thought there'd at least be something."

"Well, the portal is going to pull clear and open in barely one minute," Eddie noted. "If they're here, we'll know soon enough."

Ara, Charlie, and Bawb actually *were* there, but the unusually dense nature of the shattered moon they had taken refuge behind was unexpectedly blocking their tech-based communications systems. And Leila was the only one with a skree, so far as Charlie knew. And she wasn't responding to it.

So Eddie and Rip moved close to the portal and waited, unaware just how close their Zomoki friend and her passengers actually were.

"Nothing on comms," Eddie noted as the chrono ticked down to the final seconds of the countdown. "The portal should clear in five seconds, Rip. It looks like we're alone."

"Well, shit," she grumbled.

The flaming plasma started to recede right on schedule as the portal began to pull free from the sun's embrace.

"Here we go," Eddie said, maneuvering closer as the heat diminished. "Comms are wide open and hailing. If the others made it back, now's their chance. The portal's only gonna stay open a few minutes."

"Then keep your ears open," Ripley replied.

"You know it."

The burning eye in the sky faded, but Eddie was already on his way toward the portal before it had begun to shift, relying on his chrono and foreknowledge to get a jump on any enemy ships that might have the same idea. He was nearly there when a familiar shape emerged from the other side.

"It's the *Váli*!" Ripley exclaimed. "Uncle Lars! We're here!" she blurted over her comms.

"Ripley? Oh, thank God you're okay," a concerned woman's voice replied. "Where are you?"

"Mom?"

"We're both here, Ripley," a man's voice replied. "We don't see you."

"Dad? We're still cloaked. But, you both came? All the way to another galaxy?"

"You're goddamn right we did. No one shoots at our daughter and gets away with it," her mother replied. "But the goddamn portal closed before we could get you. We've been waiting on the other side, worried sick."

"I'm okay, Mom, but the others are still out there, and there's a whole mess of bad guys out there just past the debris."

"Captain Harkaway told us. But listen, Ripley, there's no time for us to kick all of their asses right now, and we don't know if they're listening in, so get your scrawny butt through the portal, and quick."

"Mom, the comms are still safe. They don't know how to tap into them yet. At least, I don't think they've figured it out."

"Don't know, don't care. The important thing is to get you safe."

Timing was everything, and the enemy fleet chose that moment to begin casting their spells from the distance as they rushed from their safe hiding spot toward the newly opened portal.

Mal, the *Váli*'s AI, and Reggie, the ship's pilot, unleashed a fierce barrage with not only her rail guns and plasma cannons, but also a novel creation Zed had given them for their retrieval mission. A scatter missile.

It was very, very unconventional, and quite primitive in design, essentially like an old-timey fireworks display, only the blast of glistening stars the explosive projectiles released were themselves micro-explosives, drifting like a tiny minefield.

It wouldn't cause any real damage to the ships that flew into them, but it would give them reason to hesitate, and that was what anyone trying to make it back through the portal would need. A distraction.

"Dammit, Ripley, listen to your mother. Get your ass through the portal, and now!" her father ordered.

"But, Dad––"

"No 'but, Dad,' Rip. Move it. Eddie, you hear me? Get my daughter out of here."

"But the others are still out there! We can't leave them! And Leila! She's all alone!" Ripley pleaded.

"It sucks, I get it, but we'll come back later, I promise. This isn't leaving, this is regrouping. But right now, you have to move. We've only got a minute, here!" her father replied.

Ripley was torn, but Eddie knew better than to argue with her parents. That couple had helped save the world in the Great War. Instrumental in the victory, in fact. They had clout. And pulled strings. And pulled the strings of the people who pulled the strings. Basically, they were not people on whose bad side you wanted to find yourself.

"Okay, Rip. We're going through," he said, spinning and heading straight for the portal. "We're on our way, but I'm keeping the shimmer engaged. Don't want to drop it anywhere the enemy can see," he broadcast. "We'll go visible the moment we hit the other side."

"Good call, Eddie. We need every surprise we've got," Captain Harkaway said over comms. "We'll be right behind you when the portal closes in thirty seconds."

A loud, staticky squelch sounded over the comms channel, interrupting their connection just before Eddie crossed over.

Reggie and Mal ignored it, continuing to strafe the advancing enemy fleet with everything they had until an orange glow began to fill the portal. They then spun around and crossed back over to their own galaxy as the gateway once more sank into the sun, blocking the enemy from any form of pursuit.

CHAPTER TWENTY

Three pairs of eyes had watched from a distance as the *Váli* fired off its final volley of weapons fire and darted through the portal back to their own galaxy. Things had not gone exactly as they'd expected.

"Well, hell," Charlie grumbled. "That's just fucking great."

Ara was floating quietly in space a safe distance from the conflict, her two passengers as perplexed as she was at the turn of events. Despite the comms array she had built into her harness, they had utterly failed to reach their comrades.

"That appeared to be Captain Harkaway's ship," Ara noted. "And they seem to have received a few novel new weapons upgrades."

"Indeed. But they did not appear to hear our communications broadcast," Bawb noted.

"No shit, dude. And we could only barely hear theirs, and garbled at that. This is a total clusterfuck."

"In some regards, but from what we were able to hear from their side of the conversation, it does seem that at least Eddie was present, and he was able to return to the other side of the portal," Ara said.

Charlie had to admit, she was probably right. "Yeah, he must've been shimmer cloaked, and far in the distance, so no chance we'd have seen him. But yeah, based on the limited snippets of their comms exchange we did manage to catch, that seems to be the case."

Unfortunately, they were working with an incomplete set of facts, having only heard small bits of the interaction. The shattered celestial materials floating around the system were messing with their comms. That was something they'd need to address for their fleet's future attempts to bring the fight to this galaxy. If there was a future attempt, that is.

Ara abruptly flinched as a wave of magic washed across the area. Charlie felt it too, and even Bawb reacted, his Ootaki hair picking up traces of the force and transmitting it to its wearer.

"We must jump. Now!" Ara said.

"What?" Charlie managed to ask as Ara jumped away without further hesitation.

They arrived in a distant system with a dozen gaseous planets orbiting a blue supergiant. The strange power emanating from the sun made Charlie almost swoon from the unusual sensation. Whether that was a good or a bad thing, he wasn't quite certain.

"What just happened, Ara?" he asked.

"There was a power user there," she replied. *"Incredible power. A visla. Maybe even stronger. For that reason, I took us to this place. A system that interferes with most magic."*

"I can feel it," Charlie said. *"It's not the most pleasant of sensation."*

"Nor for me, but I felt it was a safe precaution to take. I've not been to this system in many, many years, but necessity dictated this destination."

"But hang on. You said stronger. What's stronger than a visla? I didn't think there was anything like that," Charlie asked.

"I do not know, Charlie. But whatever that was, its power is immense."

"So it looks like we're up against far more than we expected," Charlie said. *"At least Leila was with Eddie and Rip. She'll be safe back on the other side of the portal. The others, though, we'll need to find, and soon."*

"Hunze can more than take care of herself against most threats now," Bawb said. *"And while I am obviously still concerned for her safety, I am far less so than during previous encounters."*

"And Rika, too," Ara added. *"Her power is quite strong, and also from the other galaxy. I don't know how that would play out against a caster from this one, but there is a possibility it could work in our favor."*

"Yeah, but we'll have to find her first, if we want to find out," Charlie said. *"There's a lot more going on than we thought, and if there's a power user that strong then we've gotta be dealing with the Council of Twenty yet again. Dammit, I thought we were finally done with those bastards."*

"Apparently not," Bawb replied. *"And we are now fighting in the dark, so to speak."*

Bawb was right. They'd come through expecting some sort of armed encounter, but both the ferocity and potency of their opponents proved to be far greater than any had anticipated. And this was *after* what seemed to be roughly half of their fleet had been destroyed.

If the invading force had succeeded in their plan and come through the portal en masse, Earth, and their entire galaxy, would surely have fallen.

"You guys know what this means, right?" Charlie asked.

"I'm afraid I do," Bawb replied. *"Sourcing a long-range skree is now a lesser concern. Even if we rejoin our friends, we simply cannot return through the portal now. Not without first gathering intelligence as to what, and whom, we are dealing with on this side. To send any*

further ships through into this conflict without knowing what we are up against would be sheer folly."

"Exactly," Ara agreed. *"We must travel to hubs of activity and quietly inquire. Gather intelligence. See what we may learn of this new threat."*

"You know what we need, don't you, Bob?"

The Wampeh sighed and shook his head.

Charlie grinned. Yes, his friend knew exactly what he was thinking. *"Bob, my dear friend, I think it's time our friend Binsala paid a visit."*

Binsala the trader was one of the assassin's most effective intelligence-gathering personas. A good-natured man with a penchant for alcohol and festivities. The sort of man no one ever expected any sort of violence or subterfuge from.

Precisely the impression the master assassin intended, and a good many had fallen under those seemingly innocent hands over the years.

"Binsala the trader is always glad to engage in commerce in this most wonderful system," Bawb said, his body shifting into a loose posture to match his drunken slur. "And if we make new friends in the process,

"You're way too good at that, man. It's almost creepy," Charlie said with a little chuckle.

Though he couldn't see inside his friend's space helmet, he was one hundred percent sure the Wampeh was smiling.

CHAPTER TWENTY-ONE

Ara felt an odd pang of nostalgia at the sight of the trio of ringed gas giants they passed as they flew toward the warmer climes of the system's central planets. The beautiful red dwarf sun cast off less heat than its yellow and white brethren by nearly half, so only the most inner of the twenty worlds orbiting it were habitable.

But of those, the planet Dinastra had long been a shining beacon of magical power. And with good reason. It was one of the major seats of Council power for nearly seven hundred years. And that was *before* the mighty Zomoki had leapt forward in time.

Of course, her last visit to this particular place had been under less than hospitable circumstances. She had been resting on one of the hottest of the inner worlds, recovering from laying a small clutch of eggs on a distant world known only to her and one other. A place where they did their part to continue their species.

But Zomoki weren't pack animals, and their young were space ready when they hatched. From there, it was up to them to make their way in the worlds, their innate magical powers––if they were fortunate enough to have been born with any, for it was a crapshoot as far as who, if any, possessed those abilities–– would be instinctive to them.

In time, they'd learn more advanced magic. Akin to the way other species crawled, then walked, before they ever ran. So it was for Zomoki.

But after this particular birthing she had been pursued by a band of Tslavar traders who just so happened to be restocking their ship in the system, when, by utter luck, the newest member of their crew happened to catch a glimpse of the red Zomoki as she went to land on the small, hot inner planet.

His sharp eyes had earned him much praise, and after quickly completing their resupply, the Tslavars made quick time for Ara's resting place, seeking to capture the weakened and valuable creature for sale to the arenas.

She had escaped that time, though the battle and subsequent use of magic required to jump clear had nearly killed her, weakened as she was. And yet, despite all of that, she still had a soft spot for this place that had––prior to that one incident––always been a comfortable, safe refuge, despite the Council of Twenty's presence.

"It's beautiful, Wise One," Bawb said over comms, giving in to the need to say it aloud despite their internal link.

"Yes, it rather is, I think," she agreed. "I've spent many a cycle in this system over the centuries, and it has always proven to be a welcoming haven. Of course, the worlds are under Council control, and I never ventured too close to their commerce hubs."

"Makes sense," Charlie said. "Wouldn't want to ruin a good thing getting Council goons trying to capture you constantly."

"Indeed. But come. I shall take you as close to the central cities as I dare. You and Bawb––I mean, *Binsala the trader*–– should have little trouble arranging a conveyance to take you the rest of the way."

"Yes, I do believe our drunken friend is quite adept at making friends and securing transit. Isn't that right, *Binsala*?" Charlie joked.

"You laugh now, but your feet will thank me as we ride into town in comfort," the Wampeh said with a chuckle.

Ara shifted her course, avoiding the busy cargo and transit lanes orbiting the two main planets. They could have opted for one of the ones either closer or farther from the sun, but the heat and cold, respectively, would have made for an unpleasant visit for her friends. Not to mention the comfortable worlds were where the Council of Twenty had set up their seat of power.

The Zomoki tucked herself small as they neared the atmosphere. "Hold on firmly. I am going to make a somewhat hasty entry into the atmosphere to limit our vulnerability at the exosphere."

"Got it," Charlie replied. "I'm good. You, Bob?"

"Strapped in and ready," he said.

"Then here we go."

Ara's magic easily countered the buffeting winds and heat of reentry, simultaneously masking their arrival by limiting the temperature differential between herself and the surrounding atmosphere. The result was only the slightest of flashes of light as she pierced into the planet's skies. After that, she was just a tiny speck, unnoted by any.

"Wow, check that out," Charlie said as they descended and grew closer to civilization.

"The cities look different," she noted as she made her descent. "But after several hundred years from when we first jumped away to your planet's past, I suppose that is to be expected."

"Yeah, things change, especially over centuries," he agreed. "I'm just glad we wound up back in the future instead of stuck a few thousand years ago, ya know?"

"I believe we are all in agreement with you on that point," Bawb interjected.

A few minutes of flight time later, Ara had successfully avoided the craft in the immediate area, managing to swoop in low between some hills to deposit her friends close to a commerce area.

The duo quickly stripped off their space suits and donned what they hoped was still at least somewhat fashionable alien attire, then said their farewells and made their way to the nearest trading establishment to procure a ride to the city center proper. It was there they would then set out to find the most useful Council lackey, whom they would ply with alcohol as they extracted all of the information they could.

It was a relatively short walk, and Charlie and Binsala were both relatively hungry when they stepped inside the selected venue. They still needed a ride to the city proper, of course, but a little sustenance along the way wouldn't hurt. And Bawb still had coin from this galaxy, though it was of a very old vintage. He hoped it would spend just like it always had.

Their money was welcome, fortunately, and Charlie and Bawb made quick work of finding a group of merchants heading to the capital after dinner. Stumbling upon a fellow trader seemed like quite a wonderful bit of luck. Even more so when Binsala showed a few of the wares he had to offer on this occasion.

"You must take these to Mratani the Broker," a merchant named Cremortz said. "He only deals with antiquities such as these. May I?" he asked.

"Of course, my friend," Bawb said with a warm smile. "Binsala the trader is always glad to show his wares."

Cremortz picked up a somewhat small enchanted pendant from the collection of goods Bawb had laid out to show his new friends. "This is exquisite," he said.

Bawb didn't think so. It was decent craftsmanship, and the enchantment was sound, but there were far finer examples out there.

"Where did you acquire such an ancient piece?" Cremortz asked, holding it up to the light for a better look.

"You know as well as I, a trader never reveals his sources," Bawb said with a cheerfully disarming laugh.

Charlie had to hand it to him. When he did his Binsala routine, all traces of the deadly and stoic Wampeh assassin vanished. If anyone even tried to suggest the jovial, unthreatening man at their table was the deadliest man in over thirty systems, they'd have been laughed out of the establishment.

"I must have this," Cremortz said, his mind shifting from admiration to business. "I will offer you thirty for it."

"My friend, you know as well as I what this piece is worth," Bawb replied, having absolutely no idea of its value, seeing as he was hundreds of years out of date on his pricing knowledge.

But Bawb had a trick, one used by merchants galaxy wide. He would simply let his clients haggle with themselves.

"Well, yes," Cremortz said. "But for a *friend*, I'm sure we could come to an arrangement."

"A friend, yes," Bawb replied. "But we have only just met. However, I enjoy your company, Cremortz, and you are a most excellent conversationalist, so I'll tell you what. Offer me a fair price, along with a ride to the city center after we finish our meal, and you will have a deal."

"A fair price, you say? But what do you consider a fair price?"

Bawb leveled his cheerful gaze on the man. "You and I both know what is fair, my friend. So make your offer, and let us be on our way to see the sights of this marvelous city."

Cremortz sized up his new friend and made a decision. Bawb had no idea if the sum he had accepted was excessive or just enough, but he knew people's nature well enough to be certain it was not underpaid.

The men finished their meal and gathered their things, then stepped out into the night, their destination, the city center proper.

CHAPTER TWENTY-TWO

The city center was a bustling hive of nightlife that Charlie got the distinct impression would be still be going strong until the sun was high in the sky come morning. In other words, his kind of city. The kind he'd visited on occasion while running with his dear friend Marban and their merry band of space pirates.

But now he was in such a place for a different reason. *Nefarious* reasons. Well, a different kind of nefarious reason. Piracy was fairly straightforward nefarious, after all. Tonight, however, they were infiltrating the Council of Twenty's ranks and gathering all the intel they could, then smuggling it back out to their waiting comrades on the other side of the portal.

With the right information, they could adjust their shielding and attack formations to handle the armada that stood in their fleet's way. All they needed was to carefully slide into the good graces of the right, careless Council officer.

"Here you are, my friends," Cremortz said, slowing his floating conveyance as they approached what appeared to be one of the busiest hubs in the city. "Center of town, just as you requested."

Bawb was stone-sober, but he played up the drunken trader

with such skill that had Charlie not know for a fact he had cast a particularly unusual and rare spell on himself that evening––one that took liquids from his mouth and deposited them twenty meters away––he would have sworn Binsala the trader was drunk as a skunk.

"Thank you, Cremortz! You truly are a good friend, indeed," Bawb said as he slid from their ride onto seemingly unsteady legs.

"Whoa, there. Are you all right, Binsala? Perhaps you would prefer I take you to your lodging to sleep it off for a bit."

"Nonsense! I am fine! Fit and ready to conquer the night!" Bawb said with an exaggerated hiccup.

"He'll be all right," Charlie interjected. "One thing about Binsala, he can hold an amazing amount of liquor."

"As I have seen," Cremortz said with a laugh. "Well then, my friends. I shall leave you to your evening. But do see Mratani the broker in the morning. He will be most interested in what you have to offer. And be sure to tell him Cremortz sent you."

"Of course," Charlie said. "And thank you again for the ride."

"It was my pleasure. And part of our deal as well," the man said, patting the pocket that now contained his new treasure.

Their merchant friend was about to depart when Bawb stumbled back to the floating conveyance and leaned drunkenly on his new friend. "Tell me, Cremortz. I've had some less than savory experiences with Council representatives. It would probably be wise if I did all I could to avoid them. Could you point out where they tend to congregate?"

A confused look crossed Cremortz's face. "Did you say *Council* representatives? As in the Council of Twenty?"

Bawb nodded in the loose-necked manner only the drunk could manage.

"But there hasn't been a Council presence in this system for ages. Not for hundreds of years, in fact."

Bawb and Charlie hid their shock well, but internally, they were churning with confusion.

"Bawb, I'm sure Ara was right about this system," Charlie said with their silent connection.

"I agree," Bawb replied. *"But something strange is afoot. And we must get to the bottom of it immediately."*

The Wampeh turned his bleary eyes to Cremortz and belched. "Waitaminute," he slurred. "I thought this was a Council stronghold. I was told this was one of their main planets in the region."

"Then you were told wrong, my friend. I mean, this *was* a Council planet, but that was back before the Earthman revolution."

"I'm sorry, the what?" Charlie blurted.

"Very funny, Charlie," their new friend said. "Everyone knows about the Earthman revolution."

"We're not from around here," Charlie replied, not knowing what else to say.

Cremortz gave him a funny look. "But it was galactic. Nearly all of the Council strongholds were overthrown in the revolution. Surely you haven't been confining your trades to just the few remaining Council strongholds?"

"I'm afraid we have," Bawb replied. "Lucrative contracts keep us there normally. This is the first time we've ever ventured so far out."

"Good save," Charlie commended his friend silently.

"Thank you. But we must find out more of this revolution. If the Council is essentially no more, then who was attacking our forces?"

"One way to find out, I suppose." Charlie sent to his friend as he turned once more to Cremortz. "Tell me something. How exactly did an organization as powerful as the Council wind up being overthrown? I mean, on the worlds we frequent, they still rule with a pretty firm grip."

"All an illusion of power, my friends. Their back was broken when an internal power struggle led to the destruction of the great world of Tolemac. It is said to have been one of the gleaming beacons of art and culture, and also one of the few formidable worlds that was free of Council influence. That is, until the Council unleashed a great magic and ended Tolemac, and all its millions of citizens, in a terrible instant. *That* was what started the revolution. The spark that took down an empire."

"But why the Earthman revolution?" Charlie asked.

"You really don't know, do you?"

"Hence my asking you," Charlie replied. "Please, humor us."

"Well, it was one of the old vislas. One of the Maktans, as I recall. They seized control of a huge quantity of the Council's power during a particularly ill-advised pursuit of a lone Zomoki and the Earthman slave who had escaped with it. Apparently, the Earthman fought back against the visla and slew him in a great battle upon the Balamar Wastelands. Only, the visla had a child, and that child was more than a little bit mad. Worse, they possessed the same magic as their father and used it with far less restraint during the turmoil following the battle, managing to wrest a great quantity of Ootaki hair, along with other magical items, from the lesser casters in the Council who were present."

"It was theft, then?"

"Of a sort. The strongest of them, those who would have stopped the child's madness, were in distant systems. And as a result, she unleashed a weapon never intended for use."

"Which destroyed Tolemac," Charlie said, softly. "And all in pursuit of a lone Earthman."

"Yes."

"That's horrible," he said, the knot in his stomach twisting to Gordian proportions.

"Yes, but no," Cremortz said. "It was the spark, you see. Because of that one man's defiance, slavery was ended in a majority of civilized systems. And the Council was driven to the farthest, least powerful fringe systems of the known galaxy. It ushered in all of this," he said, gesturing at the magnificent city around them.

"Thank you, my friend. That was a magnificent story," Bawb said with a drunken slur. "But we are keeping you from your bed. Perhaps we will see you again tomorrow."

"I would like that indeed," the merchant replied. "Should your trading be light, reach out to me on skree and I shall see if I can be of service."

"Thank you, Cremortz. You are a good man," Charlie said, patting him on the back.

The merchant merely smiled and waved as he flew off into the night.

Charlie turned to his very sober friend.

"That was us, Bob. The battle at Tolemac."

"It was."

Both stood silent a long while. Finally, Charlie let out a low whistle.

"Holy shit, man. We started a revolution."

"I know, Charlie," his Wampeh friend replied. "And it would appear our side won."

CHAPTER TWENTY-THREE

The human and her cyborg wingman knew they were in trouble, but they were nevertheless doing all they could to rectify the situation. Rika was a take-no-shit kind of woman, and Jo—already a tough cookie in her own regard—had only become more so since partnering up with the magic-wielding human.

Their warp drive was fully functional and purring like a kitten. Unfortunately, they were in a universe devoid of felines, so the analogy didn't really lend much confidence to their situation. In fact, while all of their systems were functional, they now seemed to work in ways not entirely as designed. Like the warp, for instance.

They'd been trying to get back to the portal for well over twenty-four hours now, Jo's tireless cyborg mind not requiring sleep, and thus leaving her able to give Rika a few much-needed breaks for power naps.

Of course, the stubborn pilot wouldn't lay her head down for a proper rest. Not even with a highly competent AI at her side monitoring their ship. The thing was, she had a vague idea where the portal they'd arrived through was. Kind of like a little itch in the back of her consciousness that she couldn't quite scratch.

Jo postulated that it was likely the draw of the galaxy on the other side of the portal reaching out to the magical pigment that was now an integral part of Rika's flesh.

Rika would have joked that at this point she'd lost count of how many systems they'd warped to so far, but that wouldn't be accurate. Jo possessed an AI mind, a steel trap of data and information. And Rika was a highly trained pilot with a mind easily capable of keeping track of each attempt.

Thirty-seven.

That was how many systems they'd warped to in the day and a half since arriving in this strange galaxy. In most systems they visited, they would run a basic survey, quickly plotting out the worlds and moons, while also logging a map of the sky around them. After the first dozen warps, they had amassed a fairly functional, though basic, star chart. At least enough of one to give them the most basic idea where they were in the galaxy.

The warp was a total crapshoot, though. A crapshoot they could somewhat steer, but that was just as much hopeful thinking and guesswork as skill. But there was one thing they could control, for the most part. Distance.

The amount of energy the warp drive expended varied, the power sometimes launching them nearly half the full distance intended, but other times only moving them a quarter of the way. But it didn't overshoot. And that one saving grace allowed them to more accurately dial in their location, warp by warp, map by map.

Had they been warping greater distances than intended, the possibility of arriving far outside the area they'd been mapping would have been a very real likelihood. And if that happened, their carefully compiled star map would lose usefulness by many factors.

"We need to make planetfall," Rika finally said after their

thirty-eighth warp. "This is getting ridiculous already. We need intel. *Any* intel."

"Agreed," Jo said. "And perhaps we'll be able to source a proper star chart in the process. We've seen at least a few inhabited planets so far. Hopefully the next one we find is advanced enough to provide one."

"So it's settled. The next viable planet, we hop down and see what we can see," Rika said with a satisfied smile.

They were going to do *something*, and something was better than aimlessly flying around, *hoping* for progress. Sure, what they were already doing was technically something, but it felt like a roll of the dice every time, and this damn galaxy kept coming up with critical hits against them. It was time to talk to actual people and change the dynamic.

It took them five more systems before they finally arrived in the orbit of a warm but habitable world circling a dark sun, the majority of whose rays were just beyond ultraviolet. A black sun, Rika knew from her time as a powerful visla's slave.

Rare, powerful, and often dangerous. They'd have to be on their toes here, but the denizens of this world would almost certainly possess advanced star-mapping records.

They set the *Fujin* down at the city's landing site, knowing full well the attention the strange ship would draw. But there was little to do for it. They were offworlders and not from around these parts, which would be readily apparent the moment anyone got a good look at the human and the flesh-covered cyborg who looked like one.

They just hoped their completely novel ship would serve to bolster their air of mystery, which might buy them some leverage. People, no matter their origins, wanted to be associated with the interesting and exotic. And this pair certainly fit the bill.

The two women strapped on their weapons, both tech and magic, though the pulse pistols on their hips were hidden by their long coats. No need to draw *that* much attention for no reason, Rika reasoned.

They stepped into the airlock and sealed the ship behind them. Then Jo popped the external airlock door and they stepped out into the artificial light of the dark planet's magically illuminated streets.

"Well, it's breathable," Rika said, taking a deep breath of the warm air as she surveyed their surroundings. A handful of familiar species had come to see the strange new visitors on their floating conveyances. "And it's certainly an advanced planet," she added. "Right. Let's go see what we can get out of these people."

The solar energy pressed down on them like an invisible fog, only made of something far weightier than water mist. It was annoying to Jo, her dermal sensor readings having a hard time discerning what exactly was so off about their surroundings.

Rika, on the other hand, felt the power as well, but it didn't seem to bother her. In fact, she appeared to have a little spring in her step, though that might also have been from finally stepping out of the ship after so many hours of focused concentration as they warped to and fro.

The city itself was comprised of relatively low buildings. Squat structures that had few windows, if any, and were made of a dark, reflective material.

"That stuff probably shields them from the sun," Jo posited.

"Yeah, the lack of windows too," Rika noted. "It's like an Alaskan winter. Only artificial lighting. Man, it would drive me crazy living like that twenty-four-seven."

She had a point. The city did have the feel of a bustling nightlife, but given the lack of day and night, it could just as easily have been a busy morning rush on the streets. There was just no way to tell at a glance.

The population consisted almost entirely of pale variants of races Rika had encountered in her prior life as Malalia Maktan's slave. The lack of normal sunlight had faded the pigments of all who spent any length of time on this world, taking deep oranges to faint ones, and chocolate brown skin to pale cream.

There were even a few Wampeh present, though with her newfound magic, Rika could sense that they did not possess the inherent power her assassin friend did. It was probably a good thing, the way they were eyeing the newcomers like fresh meat. If there was a rumble, it wouldn't be a pretty sight, and Rika had no intentions of being anything but the victor.

They walked for several minutes, following the winding streets and alleyways deeper into the city center.

"You know where the ship is, right?" Rika asked.

Jo tapped her head with a finger. "Computer. Got it on lock down."

Rika chuckled. "I knew you did."

"Yeah, just testing me, I'm sure," Jo replied with a grin. "So, where do you want to start? I have a feeling star charts aren't cheap, and we've only got Earth stuff to trade with."

"Most of it will be novel enough to buy us some things, I'd wager," Rika replied. "And pretty much everywhere accepts magic as payment. Maybe I can power something in exchange for what we need."

"Is your power even compatible, though?"

"Good question," Rika said. "I hadn't thought about that. But you know what? I think we've earned ourselves a few minutes' respite, and that place over there smells like a restaurant, or at least a place that serves food. Come on, I'm freakin' hungry, and it's been a long day."

"Day and a half," Jo corrected.

"Right. So let's get a bite, *then* we'll go see what we can get out of the locals."

The two women stepped out of the sun's pulsing energy and into the well-lit establishment. It was a good thing, too, as, unbeknownst to Rika, her tattoos had begun to glow from the strange power all around them.

Inside, they discovered that it was indeed a restaurant, though more of a local dive, judging by the clientele. But at least the establishment was very well illuminated, and as the bright lights of the interior washed over their skin, an unexpected side effect was the glowing tattoos peeking out of Rika's top faded in the light.

The pair grabbed a quiet table at the far end of the room to plan their next steps. Across the restaurant, a handful of pale men watched the women with great interest. The apparent leader looked to his friends. With a little nod, he rose to his feet, crossing the space, the others in tow. He was going to greet the newcomers, and he had a feeling it would be a most interesting interaction.

CHAPTER TWENTY-FOUR

Rika had only just begun to feel the strain of their ordeal ease up the tiniest fraction as she melted into her seat. The smells of novel ingredients and spices being blended by skilled hands had imparted a welcoming and warm aroma to the entire establishment. It was like being hugged by your favorite foods without even having them in your belly yet.

Oh yes, she was going to eat well, for her stomach had just told her in no uncertain terms that it expected to be filled, and soon. Jo, on the other hand, did not actually need to eat. Her flesh was perfectly capable of sustaining itself from the nutrient-dense feed packet she carried inside her torso.

It was a simple thing, and only needed refilling on a roughly monthly basis, but if she exceeded that timeframe, there was always the option of simply eating food like her human companion did. And sometimes she chose to, enjoying the easy conversations they had over a meal. Tonight she would as well, just to keep up appearances on this strange world.

Fortunately, she didn't need to worry at all about what she ate. The digestive system hidden within her body was startlingly efficient at what it did, and, unlike the human she appeared to be, there would be no waste matter for the cyborg to process out after she ate. Her high-efficiency artificial digestive tract meant she never had to deal with the unpleasantries of certain human bodily functions.

A shadow fell across the table as a tall, slightly chubby Wampeh stood over the two women. Behind him, four friends of varying races stood nearby. While the others were not Wampehs, they were all nevertheless incredibly pale, obviously lifers from this planet, their pigmentation fully native.

"Why hello, ladies. Welcome to the Stricken Maiden," the Wampeh said. "I'm Jorall."

"The what?" Rika asked.

"My place of business," he replied. "And the best food in the system."

"Ah, gotcha," Jo said. "We were just about to try some of this legendary cuisine."

The cyborg had little actual interest in doing any such thing. At least, until it seemed diplomacy was in order. And in a restauranteur's place of business, the highest form of flattery was to partake of, and compliment, his culinary wares.

The man smiled, but there seemed to be a little something behind that smile that neither woman could put her finger on. He waved over the waiter and quickly instructed him what to bring out.

"Uh, we're sort of low on local currency," Rika said. "We wanted to first inquire about trading for our meal."

"Oh?" Jorall said, but not seeming terribly surprised. "And what do you offer in the way of trade? It is my establishment, after all, and you seem to be such charming women. I'm sure we can come to an arrangement."

Rika flashed a glance at Jo. Both were a bit skeeved out by the man, but if he was a business owner, and a fairly well known one at that, he might prove a valuable resource as they got their bearings on this planet.

"Well, I'm hesitant to part with it, but I have this tech-magic torch the likes of which you've never seen anywhere in the galaxy," she said, removing a small LED flashlight from one of her pockets.

It wasn't an important bit of equipment, and she'd only brought it along because she wondered what they'd do if suddenly the lights went out in this dark city. More importantly, they had a dozen of them back on the ship, so parting with it was of no consequence whatsoever.

However, in this galaxy, where such a device had never been seen, she was pretty confident she could trade it for the information they needed. She held it out on her palm, displaying it for those hovering around their table.

"A tube. And small at that. Is this some sort of container?" Jorall asked, picking up the offered device. "It feels odd. There is no magic in this."

"There is, but it is a most rare variety of power that very few ever have the fortune to witness," Rika said with a straight face. "Push the button there, and you will see what I am talking about."

Curious, the man held the flashlight at arm's length and pressed the button. An incredibly bright beam cut through the restaurant, the blinding flash causing one of the waitstaff to drop their tray with a crash.

Jorall quickly pressed the button again, shutting off the high-lumen barrage.

"What manner of thing is this? I felt no magic, yet it cast such a powerful light spell."

"Precisely. And that's what makes it so valuable. Valuable enough for our meal, I'd wager."

"Indeed, I believe I can happily accommodate your trade."

"Good. But one other thing," Rika added. "We also need a star map. Best one you've got."

"A map? I will gladly provide one. But surely your guidance spells will take you where you need to go."

"Yeah, normally they would, but we've been having some problems with them lately, so a map is the easier option," Jo chimed in. "You do have star maps, don't you?"

"Of course we do," Jorall said with a warm grin as he turned his new possession over in his hands, examining the cool metal casing that housed the silent magic that powered the device.

Little did he know it was just a simple battery doing the heavy lifting. With the ultra-high-efficiency LED bulb, it would last for hundreds of hours. But once it went dead, there would be no way of recharging it in this system. But Jo figured that what he didn't know wouldn't hurt him. And they'd be long gone by then anyway.

"You are obviously not from these parts," Jorall said.

"What gave us away? The flashlight?" Rika joked.

"Not this," he replied. "But your strange metal vessel. I was made aware of it upon your arrival. It is unlike any I, or any on this world, have ever seen."

"Like I said, we're not from around here," Rika replied.

"No. But craft of this type of construction have been seen before. A long, long time ago."

Rika stiffened slightly. There was only one ship he could possibly be talking about, and it was the one she'd crashed in when she first came to this galaxy. The *Asbrú*.

"You know, they say the man who started the revolution came to us in that vessel," he continued.

"The revolution?" Rika said, startled, before catching herself. "Of course. The revolution. The one that, uh, did that thing."

"Effectively ending the Council's rule, yes. We've all heard the stories, of course. The Earthman and his allies, and the giant metal man who fought alongside him, like a living statue, as he battled the Council's mighty ships and casters."

"Shit. You mean Charlie," Rika blurted.

"Of course. The one who started it all, as we all know."

They were interrupted as plates of steaming food were placed before them on the table.

"Please, enjoy with my compliments," Jorall said.

Rika wasted no time taking him up on the offer, the novel spices doing wondrous things on her tongue. Having the owner of the joint ordering for you meant your food came first, and at this moment, she was glad of it.

"So, this metal man," Rika said between bites. "I know about the revolution, obviously, but that part of the story is different where I come from. What did they teach you out here in this part of the galaxy?"

"Oh, there were many tales. The metal man fought valiantly, smiting many of the Council's men before being buried in the sands by a mighty spell."

"And you know all of this how, exactly?" Jo asked.

"Why, from the testimonials of the survivors, of course. They were quite detailed in their descriptions of the events, as the military tend to be."

Rika and Jo chewed their food, pondering what this might mean. If it was true that her old mech was not only intact, but might still be there, waiting for her to salvage it, then a trip to the Balamar Wastelands would most certainly be in order. That is, if they could find their way to those desolate plains.

"Jorall, can you get me a map to that planet specifically? The one where the Balamar Wastelands are?"

"It is a forbidden destination ever since the revolution. No one goes there anymore. No one."

"But I'm not asking you to take us there. Just that you get us a map that shows the way," Rika said.

"I'm sorry. I have the information, but that's simply not happening," he replied sharply.

Rika felt a surge of anger in her veins.

"What... what *is* that?" Jorall said, staring intently at her face.

"What is what?" she asked.

"It just, it looked as though the decorative markings around your eyes seemed to be illuminated from within for a moment."

"Oh, that," Jo interjected. "Yeah, the ink they used does that sometimes. Just a trick of the light, is all."

"Ah, I see," he replied, unconvinced.

"Look, we really need that map," Jo said. "Isn't there something you'd take in trade for it? Like Rika said, we're not looking for a guide, just a map."

Jorall looked at his men with a grin. They had been leering at the two women for some time now, their interest far less veiled than their boss's.

"Well, you do possess *one* thing I might be interested in," Jorall said, looking them up and down with a sleazy smile.

"Nope. Not a chance," Rika said, her appetite suddenly gone. "And if you think––"

An enormous man with rippling muscles disrupted her rant as he hurried past their table straight for the restrooms, tears streaming down his flushed face.

"Uh..." was all Rika could manage.

"He attempted the challenge," Jorall said with an amused smile. "And lost. We shall be taking possession of his conveyance, now. Hushteeno, go collect it, will you, please?"

The faintly red-skinned man––really more of a pink after a life in this system––nodded once and hurried out to gather their booty.

"Did he just lose his ride over an eating challenge?" Jo asked.

"Yes," Jorall replied nonchalantly. "There was something he wanted that I possess, and he was willing to wager his conveyance against it that he would succeed where so few ever have. The spice of the nasturian shrub is most painful, yet causes no physical harm, you see. So it is a fair challenge. Mind over matter. Yet to date, not even a full handful have ever succeeded."

Jo flashed a look at Rika. "Then I challenge you for the map," she blurted.

A grin slowly spread across Jorall's face. "And if I accept this challenge and you lose, you know what I claim as my prize," he said, looking between the two women. "From *both* of you."

"Don't do it, Jo! It's not worth it! And he probably doesn't even have the map to begin with," Rika said.

"Oh, I can have it on the table in front of you within minutes," Jorall shot back, eagerness in his eyes. "So, what shall it be?"

"Bring it on," Jo said, settling into her seat to face the challenge from which so few ever emerged successful. "We're in."

She noted Rika's hidden smirk. "Be careful, Jo," her friend said.

"Don't worry about me. I've got this," she said, then sat back to wait.

CHAPTER TWENTY-FIVE

The star map to the planet containing the Balamar Wastelands lay on the table, the veracity of its contents confirmed by an independent observer. Beside it was a platter of food, a pitcher of water, and a plate of bread. It was a relatively small platter, but then, looks could be deceiving.

Rika was not party to the challenge, not on the competitive portion, that is, but her curiosity had gotten the better of her and she'd taken the tiniest of tastes of the food on the plate in front of her friend. It looked somewhat like a hearty stew of sorts, and it was lacking the usual pungent smell one would associate with spicy foods.

However, one tiny taste and Rika found herself frantically grabbing for the large pitcher of water, hoping beyond hope it might extinguish the flame she was certain had sparked to life in her mouth.

"So...hot..." was all she managed to say between gulps of water, her face red with heat.

Jorall chuckled and adjusted his manhood in his trousers in a very overt manner. This was a wager he was sure to win, and when he did, he would take great pleasure in claiming his prize.

Rika was a sweating mess from just a taste, and they'd seen what had become of the enormous man who had bolted for the restroom and still not emerged. Whatever this Nasturian shrub was, Jo had a sneaking suspicion it was more than just a regular old run-of-the-mill organic irritant it produced. She had a pretty good feeling that there was some inherent magic compounding the effect.

"Bottoms up," Jo said, then scooped up a large portion of the stew with a piece of bread and popped it into her mouth.

Onlookers gasped at her cockiness. To start with so big a mouthful was ballsy. Most began with the smallest of tastes, trying to prepare themselves for the sensory onslaught from the meal.

But not Jo. No, she just went to town, scooping up bite after bite, never once reaching for the water on the table. She was more than halfway through the plate when Jorall began to feel his certainty of victory waver. Worse, a small crowd had gathered to watch the unfolding of the event. The cocksure proprietor was losing face.

"Are you sure you wouldn't like a drink to dull the pain?" he asked, attempting to break her concentration.

Jo simply smiled at him between bites. "Nah, I'm good. But thank you for the offer. And my compliments to the chef. Once you get over the heat, it's really quite tasty."

That set Jorall off. "Did Froozal make a weak batch? I'll have him beaten soundly," he said, tearing off a small piece of bread and dipping it in the sauce, then popping it in his mouth. The blistering heat hit him almost immediately, his pale skin flushing as the tiny morsel of Nasturian spice assailed his system.

But Jorall was proud. Proud, stubborn, and not about to show weakness in the face of this woman who was merrily eating the entire plate without so much as a bead of sweat on her brow.

No magic could negate the plant, of that he was certain. There was simply nothing to explain her immunity but a one-in-a-million fluke of her taste buds.

In that regard, he was correct, in a sense. Though not her taste buds, per se, but the underlying nervous system attached to them. The little buds were undoubtedly screaming with pain, feeling as if they were aflame in the bowels of hell itself, most likely. But Jo had one trick up her sleeve that no one else in this galaxy had.

She was a cyborg.

For her AI mind, it had been child's play simply turning off all pain receptors in her mouth, just as she would silence any other program she was not using at the moment. The result was a belly full of the spicy meal, but minus any of the distress it caused to all others.

And as the digestive system deep within her body was mechanical in nature, there was no stomach lining or intestinal tract to suffer further irritation by the meal as it digested.

Jo found herself out of bread, but the plate was essentially clean. Nevertheless, she didn't wish to lose on a technicality. And besides, the act of picking up the plate and literally licking it clean, then sucking the last remnants from her fingers, was one she greatly enjoyed. Especially as Jorall was still suffering the effects of his lone, tiny bite.

"Thanks!" Jo chirped, then let out a little burp. "That was really good. I'll have to come back and get the recipe from you. But for the moment, we've got things to do."

Jo swiped the map from the table as she and Rika got to their feet, carefully tucking it into a secure pocket. Then the two victorious women walked out into the darkness.

"That was interesting," Rika said. "Nicely done. I assume you turned off your pain receptors."

"Of course," Jo replied. "And nice acting. You almost had me convinced you really were concerned."

Rika grinned, though the lingering burn in her mouth made the act a bit uncomfortable. "Come on, we need to get back to the *Fujin*. Something tells me our welcome on this world is coming to an end."

The duo ducked down a side street off the main thoroughfare, following the internal map Jo had laid out as they made their way into town. They were on course, just via smaller, less-traveled streets and alleys, was all.

It was a tactic that would buy them a bit of anonymity. Unfortunately, it also provided less-than-savory types an opportunity.

"Oy! You hang on there," a voice growled from the shadows.

A half dozen men emerged from the dark patches in the alley not illuminated by the magical lighting, the red-faced Wampeh at the front. Jorall was obviously still in pain from the Nasturian, and he was now channeling that pain and anger at the women before him.

"You cheated," he growled. "And I think you owe me something."

"You saw her eat every last bite on the plate," Rika said, stepping in front of her friend. "And you even tasted it yourself. Your place, your food, your rules. Face it, Jorall, you lost, fair and square."

The Wampeh did not like being spoken to with anything but deference, and Rika's words very much rubbed him the wrong way. He was a man of importance here, and he would not be disrespected. Especially not in front of his men.

Jorall shoved Rika aside, moving for Jo. Or, he tried to, anyway. But Rika was no pushover, and the moment the man laid hands on her, all bets were off.

She tried to be gentle––or at least not outright shatter his arm––but that was the extent of her kindness. Jorall was sent flying back into his men, startled by both the woman's gall to actually fight back, as well as the efficiency with which she'd done so.

"Oh, you're going to regret that," he hissed.

"Not as much as you," Rika replied as he lunged at her.

A quick tussle sent him through the air once more, but this time with far more force. He slammed into the alley wall, nearly chipping the hard material with the impact. Rika spun on the others, ready for a fight, but Jorall's backup all shared the same look of terror as they scooped their boss from the ground and took off running.

"Huh, that was easier than I thought," Rika said.

"We have to get off this planet, and I mean *now*," Jo said with a worrisome urgency in her voice.

"But––"

"No buts, Rika."

"But I can handle them."

"Not looking like that you can't," Jo replied, pointing to one of the nearby reflective walls keeping the sun's radiation out.

Rika immediately saw what Jo was talking about. It might have been her magically enhanced vision, courtesy of the tattoos now glowing around her eyes. Or it might have simply been that it was so plain to see that anyone, powered or not, would be hard pressed not to notice the glowing woman in the alley.

Rika stared at her reflection a moment longer. Jorall had apparently pulled loose her shirt in the scuffle. Funny, she hadn't even noticed, but then, fighting is like that sometimes. The thing was, her tattoos had come alive, the normally almost invisible white ink glowing a dangerous purple hue that seemed to pulse with ill intent.

"Holy shit," she gasped, quickly pulling her top tight over the markings.

"Yeah, you said it," Jo replied. "This sun is totally messing with your power. And when you get angry you start to glow. It happened a little in the restaurant, but it was bright in there and

129

you were only annoyed. But out here? This shit's not right. We have no idea what this place is doing to your magic."

"I don't feel any different," Rika said.

"Yeah, but who knows what might have happened if you tried to cast. Hell, as amped up as you were, you might have even unleashed magic without even knowing. I don't think you could have thrown a full-grown Wampeh that far and that hard otherwise."

"But I didn't cast."

"Precisely my point. It just came out of you without you having to say a word."

"Almost like Charlie and Ara," Rika mused.

Jo appreciated her friend's newfound talents, and they'd certainly just gotten them out of a scrape, but she was also well aware that with the drastic shift in her powers, she might have very well killed them without even meaning to. Or killed Jorall and his men. Or both. Or even something far worse than that.

"We need to go, Rika. Off this planet and out of this system," Jo said.

"Right, right," Rika agreed, the glow around her eyes fading, but more due to her conscious efforts than a reduction of the power pulsing through her.

The two women bolted through the streets, not caring what people might say. Not now. Not with a star map safely in hand.

They raced on, dodging pedestrians as they pushed their pace. Jo was a cyborg, and she would never tire. Rika, however, was human, and humans could not maintain the pace she was moving for any length of time. Or so Jo had thought. But with the dangerous new power flowing through her, Rika was not an ordinary human, and as a result, they reached the *Fujin* in record time.

Jo hoped the exertion had let her friend burn off a little of that scary power she'd absorbed, but it didn't seem to be the case. Jo was none too thrilled at the idea of being stuck in the confines of a ship out in space with a ticking time bomb of magical powers. But there was no time to properly assess her friend's power, or her stability. They had to leave, and now.

Skipping the pre-flight, Rika powered up the ship and punched it, blasting them out into space in a ground-shaking liftoff. People would talk, obviously, and there was nothing to do for that. So the duo flew off into the inky black, leaving confusion and rumors in their wake.

CHAPTER TWENTY-SIX

Kip was beside himself. Not literally, though, as an AI, he could *technically* have his main processor unmounted and held next to his ship's physical form. But in this case, he was beside himself with worry. Worry that he and his friends might not ever find their way back to the portal and their fleet. Their home.

They'd been warping time after time for nearly two days now, and yet they were no closer to understanding why their drive systems weren't taking them back to the portal as intended.

A konus was melded to Kip's frame, an addition Charlie had placed there not too long ago to help provide the ship some extra protection against magical attacks. In theory, it should have been enough to help guide them back to where they came from. Only, sometimes theories don't play out exactly as expected.

Like this time.

Hunze didn't feel the draw of the tiny blip of the Earth's sun peeking through the portal light years away as the konus on Eddie had. Being attached to the living body generating and storing its magic, Hunze's hair reacted quite differently than strands that had been shorn off in that regard. And she hadn't had a tracking spell mounted to her as Eddie had.

But one thing had changed, in that now she was in control of her own power, sensing the subtle magic soaking in and filling her even more as they warped from system to system. The strength of the magic was a drop in an ocean compared to Earth's sun, but nevertheless, so many variants of power layering within her was a heady mix.

Hunze had considered gifting a strand to Kip, but, unfortunately, there was something about the little gunship that precluded him from a full grasp and control of magical casting. He was simply old. Old by AI standards, that is.

Eddie was actually young. As in, only a few months of proper independent thought and flight. As such, he still possessed a certain malleability of his mental architecture that rendered him flexible enough to successfully incorporate magical spellcasting into his core processes. For Eddie, casting had become as regular a thing as breathing for others.

But Kip, on the other hand, was not so fortunate. Make no mistake, he was still a very unusual and odd AI, but personality aside, his core processing parameters were more or less fixed, and as such, the konus welded into his ship acted more as an autonomous defense mechanism than a controllable magical device.

Hunze tried to help guide them as they warped from system to system, and had she been asked to perform the task a few months later she'd likely have been able to do so. But the ability to use magic was so new to her, and that particular trick was one she hadn't learned yet. In addition, the many skills that Bawb had transferred to her via their neuro-stim link were impressive and vast in their range, but he was an assassin of the Wampeh Ghalian first and foremost.

He specialized in the spells that were needed for that lifestyle, not those of a navigator, though he had given her some fairly advanced spacefaring navigation he'd found useful in tracking his quarry in the past.

But it was nothing like what they required to backtrack their way to a distant portal, all while dealing with malfunctioning warp technology from an entirely different galaxy.

Long and short of it, they were screwed. The only question remaining was exactly how screwed.

When the chrono had finally ticked off the second clearing of the portal without their being any closer to finding it, Hunze finally said what they were all thinking.

"We need help," she said. "We cannot continue to blindly fly about in hopes of stumbling upon the portal."

"She is correct," Dukaan said, rising from his seat and rolling his neck with a series of loud pops. "We've been at this for two days now and are no closer to success. Someone has to know how we can get back. We just need to find a person willing to help."

Kip, ever proud of his piloting prowess, had to admit she had a point. He'd tried every trick in the book, and then wrote a few new ones in the margins as well, but all had failed, and even the perpetually chipper AI was beginning to show signs of stress fatigue.

"Yeah, I know," Kip said. "And we've only got a few more days before the portal's spells will slip into a once weekly opportunity rather than daily. I think I speak for all of us when I say we don't want to be on this side when that happens."

"Obviously," Dukaan said. "Staying here any longer than is absolutely necessary would certainly not bode well for me, I am afraid."

"What do you mean?" Hunze asked. "You are safe aboard this ship, and with friends."

"Yes, but that is not what I was referring to," the four-armed man replied. "Tell me, Hunze. Have you ever seen one of my kind before?"

"Well, no. But I'm sure––"

"Have you ever even heard of my kind?" he interrupted. "For that matter, are there any quadripalmar beings in your galaxy, so far as you know?" he asked, holding up all four hands.

"Well..."

"Precisely my point. Anywhere we go, anywhere we seek supplies or refuge, my presence will risk our discovery."

"We don't care what people think about you, Dookie," Kip said. "Isn't that right, Hunze?"

"Of course not. You are our friend, first and foremost," she said. "However, I share his concern." She began absentmindedly twisting a strand of her long, golden hair. "It is easier to cover my hair than it is for him to hide his second pair of arms, but I am Ootaki, and we have long been hunted and captured for our hair. Treated as a thing. An asset. All it takes is the wrong person taking note and we'll be faced with capture and slavery all over again."

"Unless you magic the shit out of them," Kip suggested. "That'd probably work."

"Yes, but it would also place a huge amount of unnecessary pressure upon us. A spellcasting Ootaki? I'm the first ever, so far as I know. It would be spoken of across the systems, and with something like that, it's only a matter of time before this news would reach the wrong ears."

"So what do we do? We cannot simply stay out here, warping from place to place blindly," Dukaan said.

"No, we cannot," Hunze agreed. "We need information. Information and a bit of magical skill."

"And supplies," Kip added. "Not that I need food, but you guys will, and I wasn't exactly designed for long-haul space exploration on my own, you know? I mean, my replicators are pretty basic. All of my previous survey missions were always as part of a small group of ships, the larger ones resupplying the rest of us as we flew on. I don't need much, really, but Dookie would use up most of our supplies in less than a month. And there are two mouths to feed, now."

Both Hunze and Dukaan knew the oddball AI, while strange in his delivery, was spot on in his relaying of important facts. They simply *had* to make planetfall and resupply. And if they could acquire a means to help them reach their destination, all the better.

"Okay, you guys, hang on," Kip said. "The planets here all have unbreathable atmospheres. I'm just gonna pop on over to another system and see if we have any better luck."

"I shall cross my fingers, as Ripley says," Dukaan said, digits on all four of his hands crossing in silent hope.

"May we just find a habitable world," Hunze said from her seat.

Then, with a crackling blue flash, they were gone.

CHAPTER TWENTY-SEVEN

Ara had flown her friends to five different worlds as they followed up on tips and chased down leads, hoping to find someone, *anyone*, who might be able, and *willing* to part with some information about the mysterious visla pushing the buttons of the fleet that no one seemed to know about.

Or more accurately, those who did know were also clearly far too scared to so much as utter a word, or even give a knowing wink. Bawb had seen this behavior before, having been the cause of it on more than one occasion. People were scared. Scared because they'd been made very aware of what would happen to those who loosened their lips. The tactic was as old and tried as any, and it was effective.

The people's darting eyes when asked about the mystery fleet also made something else clear. They obviously believed they were being watched, and that any slip of the tongue would reach the ears of those whose paths they'd rather not cross.

The result was that after a couple of days of travel, schmoozing, and more than a few intense inquiries, all they knew about this mysterious visla was that they seemed to exist in rumor alone.

None would utter a name. No one had seen a thing.

"This is getting ridiculous," Charlie griped as he downed a bowl of stew, chock-full of whatever local plants and beasts the proprietor had rustled up that morning.

Bawb chewed in silence a moment, his jaw clenching, and not only from the food in his mouth. "We are going to have to change tactics," he said, finally. "This is an untenable situation otherwise."

"Agreed. So that's what, five strikes?" Charlie said.

"Strikes?"

"Baseball. I'll explain later. If we ever get back to Earth, that is. But basically, it means five tries and no love."

Bawb was familiar with Charlie's odd vernacular by now and got the gist. "That appears to be the case, though we do have one final lead to follow up on. I'm not sure how much credence I place in the ramblings of a man *that* drunk, but in my experience, inebriation does often lead to a certain willingness to part with information that one might otherwise be reluctant to share."

And share the man had done, though only once they'd stumbled drunkenly into the night and away from listening ears and prying eyes. Only then did their new friend spill a few key bits of information. It had been a few days since he had given up his secrets, and now it appeared they had no choice but to follow up on the words of the drunkard. It had been an interesting night, of that all were certain.

"It all started after the revolution, ya know?" the man had slurred as he slid against a wall, coming to rest on the ground. He looked around, realizing he was no longer standing, and actually seemed a little surprised to be seated, but that quickly passed when Bawb and Charlie plopped down beside him and offered another drink.

"What was that bit you were saying before?" Charlie asked. "The power grab?"

"Oh yeah, that. Well, it was hundreds of years ago, back when the revolution happened, but the stories are all pretty clear. Ya see, it was all turmoil and mayhem and chaos and...what's that other word for chaos?"

"Uh, chaos?"

"Yeah! That's it. It was chaos!" the drunk exclaimed. "But the Council, it didn't just go away without a fight or nothin'. Someone started a coup within. Stole all sorts of stuff. Things they'd been stockpiling for years. Seems someone had inside information and used it to loot the good stuff while they were all in disarray."

"But who was it?"

"Dunno. But they're long dead, that much I do know. But all that power they stole and hid, someone was bound to find it one day, now weren't they?"

"I guess so," Bawb replied, offering the man another drink with a friendly smile. "But do you really think that whoever it is running things now has all of that old magic?"

"Rumor has it," the man replied. "But don't take my word for it. Commander Yakatan said he once saw them first hand when they were taking possession of some Drooks from the shipyards."

"Oh? He actually saw them?"

"Well, he said he did. But I haven't seen Yakatan since—hell, where was that?"

Had Charlie and Bawb been in chairs, they'd have been on the edge of their seats. As it was, they played it as cool and disinterested as they could manage.

"What? Some shitty little dump of a planet, I bet," Charlie said, trying to spark the man's memory.

"Orvall," the man said.

"Orvall?" Bawb repeated. "The slave trading hub?"

"Where've you been? Hasn't been slave trading there for a hundred years," the man said.

"So they say. But we all know what happens in public and what happens in private are two entirely different things, am I right?" Bawb countered with a drunken hiccup and a belch.

Charlie had to hand it to him, he really did play the part well.

The drunk tapped his nose knowingly and gave Bawb a sly smile. "Oh, you know, don'tcha? Yeah, you do," he said, then tried to climb to his feet. "Where's the bar?" he slurred, falling back to the ground in a heap.

Charlie and Bawb shared a look and a quick nod of agreement. A second later the man was sound asleep, rendered that way by Charlie's little knock-out spell, silently cast just like Ara had taught him.

"Back to Ara," he said in a hush.

Bawb nodded and climbed to his feet. The two then stumbled off, acting drunk until they were well clear of the slumbering man. Ducking into a side alley, they quickly shrugged off the booze-soaked outerwear they'd acquired for the evening's recon and tossed it into a bin, then walked back to the main streets, heading for their waiting friend.

"Orvall?" Ara said with clear distaste when they relayed the information to her at her hiding spot outside of town atop a low hill where a copse of trees provided her adequate cover.

"Yes, Wise One, I am afraid so," Bawb replied. "Though it is apparently no longer an *overt* slaver hub."

"Nevertheless, I find this world abhorrent," Ara said. "But we have other leads to follow up on. Voyaging to Orvall will be our last resort. Agreed?"

Charlie and Bawb nodded their assent and began donning their space gear. They had five other worlds to visit first, and if they had any luck, they'd be well on their way to finding out exactly who their enemy really was before the day was over.

"You know, if this visla who stole so much from the Council did indeed have secret Council intelligence from the time of our final battle and Malalia's pursuit, then it is entirely possible they have all of her records prior to her disappearance as well," Bawb said. "And you know what that would mean."

Charlie did, and he didn't like it one bit. "It means they would know what she did all those years ago. It would mean they know there's another galaxy ripe for conquest, just a wormhole warp away. Or in this case, a portal jump away."

"And given what we've seen of the portal that now links both galaxies, as well as the sheer magnitude of Ootaki hair that was somehow acquired to power it, I think it is a very reasonable assumption that this visla knows full well what is on the other side," Ara said. "And they are coming for conquest."

Charlie settled into his seat atop his Zomoki friend's back and prepared for the hunt for more information. But Ara was right. It really did look like the recipient of all that stolen power also inherited something of equal value. The location and means to reach Earth.

"Shit," Charlie grumbled. "This is not good."

CHAPTER TWENTY-EIGHT

It had been a while, and Leila was concerned, but if you had to wait around, doing so in a visla's opulent estate wasn't a bad way to go about it.

Time had passed with no word from Eddie or Ripley. Too much time. Days, in fact, since the visla had to hurry off on some official business yet again. Despite the generous hospitality Visla Palmarian offered to the woman who saved his daughter from a degrading attack, Leila was very much ill at ease.

The portal would have cycled open and closed several times while she'd been stranded on this planet. If her friends didn't return for her soon, it would shift into a short run of weekly appearances before falling into the sun and sealing itself off for good.

If that happened, Leila would be forever trapped.

Away from her friends. Away from her new home. Away from her king.

She tried to distract herself from the growing feeling of dread by learning all she could of her galaxy since the time she'd so abruptly left all those hundreds of years prior. Fortunately, Kara was a wealth of information. Having grown up in the house of one as powerful as her father meant all the best tutors and instructors.

It was a strangely familiar scene, actually. One that reminded Leila of Visla Maktan and his despicable daughter, whom she had grown up alongside on his sprawling estate. The girls had been friends, of a sort, when they were young. But as they matured, Malalia Maktan quickly fell into her role as the next in line for her father's seat at the Council of Twenty.

But from what Leila had gathered, the Council itself had seemingly disbanded, scattered to the wind in the aftermath of a great revolution that turned the civilized systems on their heads. Of course, with every revolution and power vacuum created by it comes a new breed of individuals clamoring for control.

Kara couldn't say exactly who ran things these days, or from where, for that matter, but suffice to say, though the Council of Twenty was effectively reduced to a mere shadow of itself, whoever had seized the mantle––and magical assets––had created their own conglomerate. One that sounded as dangerous and connected as the Council had ever been.

Only this one was careful. Quiet. Secretive. Leila would have a lot more digging to do if she wanted to find any *real* answers. But that would have to wait.

"What are you doing?" Kara asked, breezing into the lounge area where Leila was yet again reviewing historic records from the visla's shelves.

The teen seemed to be gaining strength the last few days since her father had departed on his trip, and Leila was glad to see her with renewed energy.

"Oh, I'm just reading up on history, is all. I'm really fascinated with that sort of thing," she replied.

"No, not the records," Kara said. "*That.* The other thing in your hand. What is it? I've never seen anything like it."

Leila had been absentmindedly keying her comms as she read, hoping to receive a pingback from Eddie and Rip, but all she'd heard was static so far, with the exception of one garbled burst of noise that sounded nothing like her friends. So it was with alien magic and Earth tech. Occasionally, there would be the slightest of crossovers, but nothing functional.

She keyed the device off and offered it to the teen. "Here, see for yourself," she said as Kara examined the comms unit.

"What is it?"

"We call it a comms unit where I now live. It's basically a piece of tech that allows me to talk to my friends over long distances."

"Oh, like a skree."

"Yes, like a skree. Only different. It's hard to explain."

"So are they back yet? Your friends?"

"It would seem not," Leila replied. "I'm actually a bit worried about them. It's not like them to stay away for so long."

"Do you know where they went?"

"Well, yes and no. It's complicated," Leila said.

"Huh. Well, I hope you find them. Though I've been really enjoying our talks. It'll be sad to see you go just as we've become friends," Kara said.

"I'll come back to visit, don't you worry," Leila said. "And you've still got Visanya to keep you company."

"Yeah, but Vee and I have history. You and I are just getting to know each other. It's kind of refreshing, really."

Leila had noticed that the two girls had an interesting bond between them. Something more than mere best friends, it seemed, but she'd been hesitant to ask about it. Now, however, the opportunity presented itself organically.

"Kara?"

"Yeah?"

"I was wondering. It seems like you and Vee have a lot of affection and care between you."

"Ah, *that*," Kara said. "Well, Vee and I were an item briefly. It just sort of happened. I mean, we've known each other forever, and we're such good friends, so it just seemed natural."

"But it didn't last?"

"No, it didn't work out that way, so we're just friends again. After all, it's not worth losing one of your dearest friends over a failed romance, right?"

Leila was impressed by the teen's openness. "So, no boys, then?"

"Oh, I like them too. Really, it's all the same to me for the most part. I mean, bodies are just coverings for the person inside, after all, and that's the part that really matters."

"You're a surprising young woman," Leila said, taking the comms unit back. "And I really wish I could stick around with you, but I think it's time I headed out to try to find my friends."

"Do you have any idea where they are?"

"Well, they're off-world, and if I can pin down the location of a certain fleet of ships that would be in the system they were heading to, I should be able to figure where exactly they went."

"But you don't have a ship," Kara noted. "How are you going to get there? And how are you going to actually find them? It's a big galaxy, Leila."

"I'll figure something out," Leila replied, hoping she could. Of course, it was her secret hope that her Magus stone would step up when it realized she was in a bind and do *something* to help her. It had saved her in the past, and she had to wonder if it might once again.

"This is silly. My father has plenty of ships at his disposal. I'll have one of them take you to look for your friends. I'm sure he won't mind."

"Are you sure? That's a big expenditure of magic."

"Please. You've met my dad. He's got magic to spare," she said, a slight shadow falling across her demeanor for just an instant. "Funny, he gets all of that power and winds up with a daughter who can barely cast a spell."

Leila had seen it before in her Ootaki friend. A different circumstance, but nevertheless similar in a way. "Maybe you'll come into your own power eventually."

"I wish."

"Don't count yourself out yet," Leila said. "Hey, you know what? Why don't you come with me while I look for my friends? It'd be fun, and you and I could practice spells together while we travel."

"I'd love to, believe me, but my father is quite strict about my going anywhere in the city. Imagine how he'd be if I left the system while he was away. Of course, if my stepmother was here, she'd let me go, but she's still off with her friends, and without her giving the okay, none of the staff will let me go. They kind of fear my father a little, you know?"

"With his power, I can imagine," Leila said. "But he seems like such a nice man, especially for a visla."

"He is, but that doesn't mean he's not still intimidating. That much power kind of makes people nervous if they don't know him."

"I suppose I can understand that," Leila said, thinking of her Zomoki friend and those who feared her until they got to know her.

"Well, come on. Let's get you a ship," Kara said. "The sooner you find your friends, the better."

CHAPTER TWENTY-NINE

Captain Sandah had been in the service of the Palmarian family since he was a boy, steadily climbing the ranks aboard the various vessels utilized by the visla and his wife over the span of decades. He's been there for the birth of Karasalia, as he had been for the death of her mother. While not the most senior captain in the small fleet of vessels at the visla's disposal, he was one of the most respected and trusted.

For that reason, Kara selected the good captain to be the one to take her new friend to find her lost comrades. She knew her father would be minorly annoyed she had sent off one of his craft without his approval, but knowing it was helmed by a well-trusted servant of his house would put his mind at ease.

And besides, she hoped his skills would perhaps help her off-world visitor accomplish her task sooner rather than later, so she might return to spend more time at the estate. It was nice having company who wasn't trying to get something from her, due to who her father was.

Leila, for her part, truly enjoyed the clever young woman's company as well, though she still had reservations about her father. Leila had grown up on a visla's estate, and she knew full well just how deceiving looks could be, no matter how pleasant of airs were put forth.

"I do hope you are successful finding your friends," Kara said as they walked to the ship's berth on one of the several elevated landing platforms hovering atop her father's tower. "It would be great if you brought them back with you. We could even call up Vee and have an outing, all of us. It'd be fun showing them around."

"I think they would like that," Leila said with a warm smile. "But we do have a few things we really must address before we can enjoy a vacation like that, though I'm sure Baloo would love nothing more than to hurry back to play with Bahnjoh."

"Those two have been inseparable," Kara said, watching the two enormous animals chasing each other around the elevated deck. "I think it's done both of them good having someone to frolic with."

"I agree. It's just that Baloo's so big, no other canines want to play with him, it seems," Leila said.

"Same for Bahnjoh," Kara replied. "So if not for our sake, then let's promise to reunite for theirs. Deal?"

Leila smiled brightly and pulled the girl in for a tight hug. "Deal. I hope to see you far sooner than later, Kara."

"And I, you," she replied. "Fly safe!"

"It's Sandah who'll be doing the flying, but yes, I'll do my best," Leila said, turning to her furry companion. "Come on, Baloo! We're going!"

Baloo and Bahnjoh stopped their bouncing play, looking at Baloo's mama. It was time to go, they both knew despite not exactly speaking the language. The two nipped and licked each other one last time before Baloo trotted off to join Leila aboard the ship, letting out a little farewell howl as he boarded.

Bahnjoh, though not a naturally howling creature by nature, returned the call in kind as his new friend departed.

Everyone safely aboard, the ship then closed its doors and

silently lifted off into the sky, destination unknown, guided by the strange woman who had somehow received the visla's grace.

"Where exactly are we going?" Captain Sandah asked as they easily exited the atmosphere, thanks to their retinue of powerful Drooks.

"I'm not sure, exactly," Leila replied. "Hang on. I need to see if I can reach my friends now that we're in orbit."

She dug into her pocket and pulled out the comms unit, keying the device as she called to Eddie and Rip. As before, there was a tiny burst of static, but nothing more.

"Damn. Well, I had hoped it might work."

"An odd type of skree, I take it?" the captain asked, eyeing the strange tech-magic device.

"You could say that," she said, once more pocketing her comms. "So, it looks like we're doing it the hard way, then."

"Yes, you mentioned that prior to our departure, but what exactly is this hard way you speak of?"

"Well, you're a captain, right?"

"Obviously."

"And you're a captain for one of the most powerful vislas in any of the nearby systems, wouldn't you say?"

"Visla Palmarian is far more powerful than that. But yes, your general point is correct."

"Right. So as a captain for such a connected man, you probably have the ability to talk to other captains. To see if they've noticed anything unusual."

A curious look spread across Sandah's face. "Unusual how, exactly?"

"Well, that's the thing. You see, I'm pretty sure my friends went back to this system we were in before we warp––I mean, *jumped* to this one. But they've gone on without me, and without them I don't have any way of plotting a course to meet up with them, you see?"

"Ah, your navigation Drooks were aboard their vessel, and as they are tardy in their return, this leaves you with no means of plotting a course."

"Yes! Exactly!" Leila exclaimed.

"But what does this have to do with my position, or that of the visla?"

"You can make some inquiries. Send skrees out to see if anyone might have noticed, oh, a giant fleet of warships gathered around a graveyard of burned-out wrecks," Leila said, wondering how he'd take the request.

Surprisingly, Captain Sandah took it in stride. He'd worked under the visla long enough to know strange things often followed power users. And what his passenger had just described sounded like precisely the sort of thing some of them might get up to behind the backs of their comrades.

Of course, he didn't exactly want to go stepping on the toes of any emmiks or vislas, but as he was under the protection of the great Visla Palmarian himself, the risk would be minimal. And more than that, his passenger's quest actually sounded a bit fun.

"I will make inquiries, as you requested," he finally replied after a moment's thought. "Though I cannot guarantee the captains of any vessels in such an armada would respond directly, it is quite difficult to amass a fleet of any substantial size without someone taking note."

"Fantastic!" Leila chirped, her spirits the highest they'd been in days. "How long do you think it will take?"

"Oh, not long at all."

"Even better!"

"Yes, quite. It should take only a few days, I would think," Sandah said.

Leila felt her spirits shift from soaring to sinking. "Days?" she said, mentally calculating the next appearance of the portal.

Time was running out, and unless they moved fast, she'd have to wait an entire week for the portal to once again present itself as a passable link between galaxies. And her friends might need her sooner than that.

She took a deep breath, forcing herself to calm down. It would do no one any good if she freaked out now, especially in front of the captain, when he was so willing to do her bidding. No, she needed to play it cool. But how could she do that while aimlessly flying around in space?

Suddenly, an idea struck. There was one place she could be taken while they waited. And while it might not be where she wanted to go, being back in this galaxy, she was now offered a little bit of closure.

"Do you know the route to Visla Maktan's former home?" she asked.

"It is in our records, yes," Sandah replied. "But no one has lived there for centuries."

"I know," she replied, her mind already made up. "But I wish for you to take me there while we await your skree replies."

"As you wish," Captain Sandah said, then relayed the new course to his men.

Leila was going to make a detour. Not to where she wanted to go, but where she needed to.

For the first time in hundreds of years, Leila was going home.

CHAPTER THIRTY

Karasalia Palmarian was the lady of the house, at least while her stepmother was away on yet another of her frequent social trips, and as such, she was given the run of the place, including areas normally off limits to teenage girls. Her father would likely not have approved, but it was one little act of rebellion she could perform at home without really going against his rules.

As it was, there were times Kara simply wished she could just fly away to someplace new. Someplace where no one knew her as Visla Palmarian's daughter. Somewhere she could just be a normal person.

But she wasn't a normal person. Not in the eyes of the millions living around her, each well aware precisely who her father was. And so it passed that she spent far more time in the tower than she actually wanted. But if she was to be cooped up in the vast building, at least she could make the most of it, exploring every nook and cranny.

Eventually, she had found her few favorite spots, several of which were rather unlikely for a girl of her stature.

One such area was situated at the topmost reaches of the structure. Her father had long said it made more sense to keep dangerous prisoners far above ground, where escape would mean a long, yet brief, plunge to their death. It was there that she had discovered something about herself. A hidden talent.

While the prisoners were forced to serve their penances in silence, Kara's magic, while minimal, was so close in nature to her father's that she was actually able to effect one tiny little spell. Not perfectly, mind you, not by any stretch of the imagination. But this one spell she could at least make work. Somewhat, anyway.

"Are you awake?" she asked the narrow slot in the thick door to the cell that housed the worst of the worst. The heretic. The one who had tried to kill her father.

A rustling from the muted prisoner within let her know the answer to her query. She was awake, but unable to talk. Kara aimed to fix that. If she could.

"*Ifaran sprechio*," she quietly said, drawing upon the limited power within her.

Immediately, the sound of breathing shifted to muffled grunts.

"Okay, that didn't quite work," the teen grumbled, refocusing her energies for another try. "*Ifran sprechio*," she said once again, and this time a raspy voice emerged through the slot.

"Better," the voice said, then was silent once more.

That was the thing about countering her father's spell. It didn't really work for the most part. All Kara was able to do was provide a temporary glitch in the spell itself, and that was only because of her blood ties to the visla making her magic similar enough to cause the unusual effect. Still, it was something, and it allowed her to converse with the prisoners when she so wished it. Though the conversations were typically quite one-sided as the tweaked spell would now only let the prisoners speak in disjointed words most of the time.

The majority of the prisoners in the holding area had little to say of substance anyway, and their conversation was not missed

SCOTT BARON

in the least. The newcomer, however, was a different story. And her father's spell, it seemed, didn't quite affect her the same as the others for some reason. That made her different. And different was so rare in her regimented existence. Different was interesting.

"How are you today?" Kara asked through the tiny slot.

"Free. Stuck," the heretic said. "Must the key. Hidden in sight. Help. You," she said.

Kara had jotted down the strange woman's words, as had become her habit whenever she'd visit her. The unusual, prophesy-like utterances were confusing, but as she'd deciphered the first few, Kara realized this odd prisoner appeared to know things. Things she couldn't know. In fact, Kara was beginning to believe she might even be an actual soothsayer.

There were oracles, of course, and her father had access to all if he so desired. But those seemed to speak in contrived and measured words, all to create a desired impression, whereas the heretic spoke plain truth, albeit in a very halting manner.

"Help me?" Kara asked, reading back the woman's words. "How can you help *me*? Why do you think I need help? I'm Visla Nikora Palmarian's daughter, why should I need help?"

A rustling behind the door told her the woman was standing just on the other side of the thick barrier. Kara had long wondered why her father had insisted on constructing this part of the building so unusually. No clear windows, no observation panes. Just thick, heavy doors to cells formed by equally thick and heavy walls.

And the heretic was not a powered being, so far as she knew. Just a regular person who had made the very poor decision to target the most powerful visla in Lord knew how many systems. But Kara couldn't help but admire her, in a strange way.

To come barreling into their home, of all places, the residence of Visla Palmarian, and looking for a figh,t all while

154

lacking any magic weaponry at all aside from her unusual sword? Well, it was folly, for sure. But it was almost charming in its sheer brazenness.

"Help. Free. Uh. Fly away," the woman said in her magic-choked, grumbling voice.

Kara had often wished she could fly away, but how was it this strange soothsayer knew her most hidden wishes?

"Explain," the teen demanded. "How would you have me be free? How would I fly away?"

A long pause on the other side of the door left a heavy silence hanging in the air, the anticipation thick as the visla's daughter's ears strained for the heretic soothsayer's next words.

At long last, the woman cleared her throat and spoke. "Free, uh. Soar. Escape."

Kara almost stepped back at the words. Was she actually suggesting she knew a way for her to fly away? But what was this escape bit? Kara didn't want to escape, she was happy where she lived. At least for the most part.

Still, the words lingered in her head long after she had gone back down to the lower levels to meet up with Visanya for lunch. The soothsayer knew *something*. The tricky part was going to be figuring out exactly what that something was.

CHAPTER THIRTY-ONE

Captain Sandah was accommodating of his guest's request to make a little detour while he was awaiting word from the multiple skree messages he'd informed Leila he had sent inquiring of any large fleet being amassed anywhere in the known systems. It might take time, but unless those behind the machinations of that force were incredibly vigilant, someone somewhere was bound to have seen or heard something.

It was fun, in a way, being part of a little adventure with his unusual passenger, though exactly how long he could be away from the visla's estate he was unsure. He recognized his passenger as part Alatsav from the faint green hiding under her olive complexion. In fact, Captain Sandah was pretty sure she would return to a pale green entirely if she spent enough time away from pigment-changing solar rays.

But landfall was on the menu this day, and Leila and Baloo would be walking the sunny ruins of the once great Visla Maktan's estate in short order.

Sandah flew a slow loop around the grounds, taking in the overgrown landscape and crumbling buildings from the air.

"Are you sure this is where you wish to land?" the captain asked. "There hasn't been anyone here for a very long time."

"I know," Leila said, emotions welling in her chest at the sight of her former home. "This is definitely where I need to be."

Need. Not want. She'd finally said it out loud. After so hasty a departure, the visla and his goons hot on her trail, Leila was finally coming home.

Sandah put the ship down at the wide-open space of the former landing zone, the magic used to keep it free of growth still in place after all these years, though only a glimmer of what it had once been. Nevertheless, the greenery of the world had decided there were far easier places to take root. Places where spells weren't fighting them every step of the way.

The ship settled onto its cushion of magic just above the ground and opened the doors.

"Come on, Baloo," Leila said, stepping out into the familiar warmth of the planet's afternoon sun.

She took a deep breath, filling her nose with the smells of her childhood and her lungs with the restorative freshness of untouched nature. Baloo padded to her side and sniffed the breeze.

There were things out there, he could tell. Tasty things, from the smell of it. But his mama had other plans at the moment, so he would forego his hunt and stay by her side for the time being.

"I'll be back in a little bit," she called back to the captain. "I've got a skree if you need to reach me," she added.

"Very well. Just call if you need any assistance," he replied, then set to work assigning respite shifts for his crew to break off and enjoy a bit of the fresh air while they could. No telling how long they'd be in space before they had the chance again.

Leila and Baloo walked the estate, the familiar pathways long overgrown, replaced by animal trails, easily recognized by her sharp eyes. After all those years spent caring for Visla

157

Maktan's pets, it was still second nature to her, even after such a long absence and an entirely new life.

She made her way to the buildings, the magically protected stonework around the fountain long overgrown with algae and moss after the spells finally wore off. The walls had crumbled in some places, where they'd relied more on magic than construction prowess to create the structures, but all in all, they remained mostly intact. The little door to the kitchen, where Charlie used to spend so much of his time, she noted, was open.

"Come on," she said to her furry companion as she headed inside.

Kara had filled her in on the bits of history Visla Palmarian's records didn't cover in great detail. The girl had a fascination with the past, which was something of a boon for Leila as she researched the fate of her former home.

It seemed that Visla Maktan had suffered a terrible fate after the battle upon the sands of the Balamar Wasteland. The Council was spread thin at that moment, preparing to start hostile activities to give them just cause to claim new systems, and those systems' power, as their own in exchange for the Council's "protection."

But things had gone wrong. What should have been a decisive victory had flipped, leaving the visla mortally wounded, his ships in disarray, and one of the Council's most treasured power sources destroyed in the fighting, the lone Ootaki survivor lost to the wind.

Malalia Maktan, the visla's overzealous and cruel daughter, had stepped in and seized her father's seat at the Council table in the turmoil, and as the most powerful user present, she commandeered the collected resources the Council of Twenty had been preparing for their war and turned them instead on the pursuit of a pair of slaves and their Zomoki friend.

That part Leila knew all too well, for she was one of the escaped slaves atop Ara's back.

The destruction of Tolemac—which had triggered a time/space event that had thrown Charlie and his friends not only to another galaxy, but also back in time—had set off a powder keg of anger aimed squarely at the Council. Thanks to Malalia Maktan's brash move, a revolution began, and all because of a lone Earthman named Charlie.

The aftermath left Malalia persona-non-grata, though she still clung to her power through violence and subterfuge long enough to wrest control of enough Ootaki hair and other magical devices to make an attempt to pursue the escaped human.

It had become something of an obsession for her, and it had taken her a few years to do, but she finally succeeded in acquiring enough magic for her mad plan. Enough power to make her attempt. But *something* happened, though no one really knew what. All they did know was in the blink of an eye, Malalia Maktan was gone. And she never came back.

The servants on the estate had been unexpectedly set free of their slavery, the magic binding their collars fading quickly with the last blood heir to the Maktan line now abruptly gone. Many disbanded and fled the estate immediately, but others chose to remain, spending the rest of their days living as they had before, but this time as free people.

But even that eventually came to an end, and finally, the last of them was gone, leaving the formerly impressive estate to lie fallow for centuries, untouched and unvisited until this very day.

Leila exited the building. There was nothing for her there.

She turned for the familiar plot where the animal pens had been, arriving there in short order despite the overgrown paths. Traces of the enclosures remained, but most had fallen victim to time, nature reclaiming the stones and soil over the centuries.

Baloo, naturally, had found something to roll in that smelled quite interesting, and a small grin formed on Leila's lips at the thought that at least there hadn't been any fresh waste piled there in hundreds of years.

With some difficulty, Leila then turned from the animal pens and began walking toward the little cottage she'd been raised in. Her father's home.

In but a relatively short walk, she found herself standing before a humble stone marker beside a ramshackle yet sturdy little stone building, overgrown but still intact. Tears welled in her eyes as she stared at the ground. So simple a thing, a grave, yet it possessed such power. Memory. Love.

Hertzall had known he would never see his daughter again, and yet he had bade her flee without a second's hesitation, wanting for her the life she deserved, free from slavery and control. And once she had gone, he had stayed on, tending the land he'd known his whole life. But he'd ended his days a free man, and that knowledge at least warmed Leila's aching heart.

"You'd be proud of me, Father," she said softly. "I did good. Better, even. I was a queen. And Charlie? You remember him. Well, he was my king."

Baloo let out a little whuff, nuzzling his face into Leila's hand.

"Of course," she said, wiping the tears from her eyes. "How could I forget you? And this is Baloo," she said, scratching his ears. "He's a very good boy."

She stood there a while longer, deep in thought, then walked into the little stone cottage she knew so well. Memories came rushing back to her, flowing in of their own accord. And just this once, she let them. She looked around her former home. *Had it always been this small?* she wondered.

The hearth was still intact, a sturdy mass of stone that had warmed her chilled bones many a night. The last time she'd seen her father had been right in this spot.

"I wonder," she said to herself as she reached for the little stone she'd seen Hertzall remove when he'd gifted her with her mother's Magus stone.

With a little tug, the stone came free, the centuries of dust flaking off the seams. There, in the little hiding spot rested a small, sealed tube. With trembling hands, she reached in and retrieved it, opening the magically sealed cap for the first time in centuries.

She smiled to herself. Her father must have traded with one of the others who remained at the estate to cast the spell for him. He always was rather rubbish at anything not pertaining to trees and plants.

Leila tilted the tube and peered inside. There was a folded scrap of parchment, and a larger rolled up note inside, hermetically sealed all these years. A letter from her father. A letter to her. *Dearest Leila.*

It has been a long while since you were last here, and I admit I miss the sound of your voice and your smiling face regularly. But I am your father, and far more important is that you are making it out on your own. Without a collar. Free. Free to explore the galaxy as you see fit, and with whomever you should desire. Admittedly, I did not want to say anything at the time, but I really hope you got together with that nice alien boy you were running around with. I had a good feeling about him.

I am leaving this note for you in hopes that one day you return and remember. Remember where I'd hidden your mother's Magus stone all those years. For there was something I forgot to give you in all the rush, and that oversight has worried me for a great many years. Along with this letter, you will find a single spell. There is a blank space in the spell. It is for your name, and your name alone. With this, when it senses you are ready, the stone's power will be yours to command.

Now, it was your mother who was the one who carried the secrets of the Magus stone with her, so I'm afraid I cannot help you with the actual how *of how you use it. But you've always been the cleverest of girls, and I have no doubt you'll make a quick study.*

By the time you read this, I will be gone, but just know that I love you with all my heart, and I lived my days happy in the knowledge you were living the life I had always wanted for you. You've always made me so proud to be your father, and that's the best thing a man like me could ever hope for.

Love always,

Hertzall

Leila spent a long time sitting outside on the porch, salty tears rolling down her cheeks, Baloo silently at her side, a steady warmth resting against her. Leila cried, but on this occasion, they were not tears of sadness. Not entirely. More than anything, they were the cathartic tears of a warm memory and the closing of a most important chapter.

CHAPTER THIRTY-TWO

The bustling streets of the dingy planet with the weak white sun on which Hunze and Dukaan walked seemed strange and alien to them both. For one of them, it was because she had spent her entire life in slavery, rarely allowed anywhere remotely public, her hair too valuable an asset to permit even a modicum of freedom.

For the four-armed man at her side, however, it was a more literal circumstance. Dukaan truly *was* an alien on an alien world. A being not born of this galaxy, and thus, the only one of his kind ever to be seen in it.

They had come to this planet, this bustling city, as something of an act of desperation, though not quite a last resort. But Hunze and the others realized the needs weighing down on them as every day passed.

The need for food. The need for information. The need for help as they blindly warped around the galaxy.

The plan had been to land on the first advanced planet they came upon. Normally, that would have been an exceedingly difficult task in and of itself, seeing as there were hundreds of millions of solar systems in the galaxy, but less than a thousand known to be inhabited.

However, Hunze might not have possessed the skills needed to guide them to the portal, but she was bristling with power, and one thing she could do was vaguely sense the presence of manipulated magic in a general direction, much like a magnetized needle would point north. Only she was steering them toward civilization.

The question was, how civilized was the civilization?

They'd been at it for several days, the clock ticking down on their last two opportunities to reach the portal before it slipped into a weekly pattern, then sealed itself off entirely into the sun. The first inhabited system they came upon was an advanced one. Too advanced for their liking, in fact. That level of society typically meant Council control, so far as Hunze knew, and that was something they wanted to avoid.

They had made a preliminary survey and logged the system in their charts as best they could, given their constraints, then warped away, again searching for a civilized world. Only one a bit *less* civilized. One where they could safely obtain supplies. One where they could hopefully hire a magic-wielding navigator on the down-low.

"Are you sure about this place?" Dukaan asked as they stepped out onto the soil of the alien world. "It seems a rather rough world."

Hunze pulled her hood farther over her head, hiding her hair and all but a shadowy glimpse of her face. "We don't have a choice, Dukaan. Time is running low, and we are hopelessly lost."

The four-armed alien grunted his reluctant agreement. "Very well. We shall proceed. Stay close, and alert. I have been to places like this before. Not in this galaxy, obviously, but the feel is the same. We would do well to be wary as we progress."

"Yeah, this place kinda creeps me out," Kip said. "You guys

be careful out there, I don't want to have to go flying around on my own out here."

"Thank you for your concern," Dukaan said with a wry grin. "Now, let us waste no further time. We acquire food supplies, we inquire of a navigator capable of achieving what we require, then we depart. No deviation from this plan. Agreed?"

"Agreed," Hunze said.

"Very well," Dukaan said, strapping a pair of blades to his hips, along with two expanding clubs. Pulse weapons would draw too much attention, but these, he reasoned, were within acceptable parameters.

A weapon for each hand, as he'd been taught in the years after the Great War ended. Since he couldn't very well conceal his four arms or the eyes at the back of his head, he might as well make good use of them should the need arise. "Let us begin."

The unlikely duo had quickly walked a fair distance into the city. The vessel landing zone where Kip had touched down was public enough that no one would overtly attempt to steal the ship, though the distinctly non-magical vessel with just the faintest whiff of magic to it––thanks to its embedded konus–– was a curiosity that had drawn much attention since landing. Resting on the ground, no less. In a world where every other conveyance and ship rode on a cushion of magic.

Kip had most certainly been noticed, and his weapons systems were all hot and ready to go should the need arise. He just hoped his friends would return before anything like that became necessary.

It was interesting seeing so few control collars among the local population. Hunze paused and asked one of the collared servants why that was. The man seemed surprised to hear such a query, but gladly filled them in on the state of slavery in the civilized systems.

She was surprised to learn that there had been a rebellion, and with the dilution of the Council of Twenty's power, so, too, was there a drastic shift in the slave trade. In fact, only in the most backwater systems or the few still under sway of the last dregs of Council power, would you find them used.

"And why do you wear one, then?"

The man flashed a morbid smile. "Because this is one of those backwater systems," he replied, then hurried off to complete his chores before his owner returned.

It was all a lot to take in. A paradigm shift in the way things worked in this galaxy had occurred, and Hunze found herself wondering if perhaps her own people were finally free of the bonds of slavery.

As they passed a good-sized arena standing five levels high, with low, arched windows looking out upon the city, her musings were abruptly interrupted.

Horrible, shrieking cries filled the air, making the fine hairs on the back of the Ootaki woman's neck stand up. It was inarticulate. Primal. Yet it was familiar.

"Zomoki," she whispered to Dukaan, glancing at the gated doorways to the arena's ground-level viewing area. "They have Zomoki here."

"Keep walking," the Chithiid urged. "We are not here to rescue dragons, nor do I believe they will be nearly as friendly and accommodating as Ara is."

It was an accurate assessment, she realized, for Ara herself had said it. Most of her kind were not intelligent creatures like her, but rather, inarticulate beasts. And that someone had captured so many of them by the sound of it was not a heartening realization.

"We should seek another world to find answers on," Dukaan said, noting the rough men lingering around the arena eyeing the hooded newcomer and her four-armed friend. "We are drawing too much attention by our mere presence."

"You're right," Hunze said. "Let's return to the ship."

But it was too little too late.

Three drunk, scrappy-looking men had already peeled off from the spots on the arena wall where it had appeared that either the building was holding them up, or they it, and were heading straight for them.

"I shall handle this," Dukaan said, placing himself between his friend and their accosters.

The men didn't seem all that interested in the Chithiid, though his four arms were something of a novelty. But it was the cloaked figure behind him, the one with the clear shape of a woman beneath the material, that had caught their eye.

Dukaan knew they couldn't use force against the men without risking a far larger incident, so he tried to simply block them with his larger body. Unfortunately, there were three of them, and even drunk as they were, the numbers were in their favor, and one managed to stumble his way around the Chithiid long enough to lay a hand on Hunze's cloak.

Dukaan immediately pushed the man off, but not before he had pulled the hood from her head. Hunze quickly pulled the fabric back in place, but it was already too late. She'd been noticed by the sharp eyes of Emmik Hunstra, where he had been watching the scene from his private balcony on the uppermost level of the arena.

The rotund man was only a moderately powerful emmik, but on this world, that was enough. He ruled with a combination of bluster and violence, wielding his magic for personal gain and control.

The odd, multi-limbed man had initially caught his eye as he stood there taking in the sounds of his city after a particularly enthusiastic session with one of his favorite slaves. He hoped he hadn't been too rough on her, as the cost of a healer's magic was steep, and he was loathe to spend more than he had to.

That thought drifted from his mind as he watched the amusing antics of some of the local drunks accosting what were obviously newcomers to his world. Always good for a bit of entertainment, the rabble that gathered around the arena between bouts.

The tall one was actually pretty good, using his size and bulk to physically block the men, while avoiding an outright fight. Hunstra had to give credit where credit was due. But one of the trio had managed to circumvent him, going so far as to lay a hand on the woman's cloak.

Now it was getting interesting, Hunstra thought, leaning over the railing for a better look. But then his world turned upside down as the woman's hood was pulled away.

"It...it can't be," he gasped.

But Ootaki were unique in the galaxy, and though he'd only ever seen one under the watchful eye of the visla who owned it, there was no mistaking what was on his doorstep.

The emmik snatched up his skree and called to his henchmen below. "Durkhoz, there are two offworlders in front of the arena. A man and a woman. Capture them at all costs."

Down on the ground floor, the lanky man who headed up the emmik's personal goon squad leapt to his feet. "Immediately, Emmik!" he almost shouted into the skree. "It shall be done."

When the emmik wanted something as desperately as was clear from his tone, it behooved all to move as quickly and efficiently as possible, lest they face the petty tyrant's wrath.

Durkhoz's choice men were off strong-arming merchants and collecting taxes for the emmik that day, so only a handful of lesser men were available to him at the moment.

Still, there were only two in need of capturing, and one of the quarry was a woman, he reasoned. The five present would suffice.

"You five, with me," he commanded as he headed for the courtyard out in front of the arena.

The men jumped to their feet and followed as he raced off to capture his master's new prize.

"You two!" Emmik Hunstra called down from the balcony, buying his men time. "I would like to have a word with you."

CHAPTER THIRTY-THREE

There wasn't much blood, which Dukaan was grateful for. Had the men's noses erupted with more of the sanguine stuff, he'd have been left standing in the courtyard in front of the arena looking like a bloody mess, drawing even more attention to them than the little altercation already had.

As it was, a four-armed alien the likes of which no one in this galaxy had ever seen and his female companion were still more than enough to cause heads to turn. And now, it seemed, the fat man high above in the building had taken an interest in them as well.

That couldn't be good.

"We really should leave," Hunze said, a worried urgency in her voice.

"Agreed," Dukaan said, but by then it was too late.

Durkhoz had taken the precaution of sending three of his men sprinting to the perimeter of the courtyard so they could more efficiently block off the streets that fed into it, cutting off the newcomers' means of escape, while he and the two remaining of his men approached from the arena directly.

"We do not wish you any harm," Hunze said, locking eyes with the man as he drew near. "We just want to be on our way."

Durkhoz laughed at the harmless woman and her freak show friend. "Oh, you don't want to hurt me? Well, that's just fine, but it doesn't mean I won't hurt *you*," he said, a wicked grin on his face.

"Durkhoz, do not injure the girl," Emmik Hunstra called down from his balcony.

His thug was none too pleased with that, but he knew better than to ignore his master's commands. "And the other one?"

"Oh, you can rough him up as much as you like," Hunstra replied with an almost gleeful chuckle.

He was simply beside himself with excitement. The four-armed alien would be a wonderful addition to his collection, but the Ootaki? Oh, she would increase his hold on this world tenfold. Hunstra was already the most powerful magic user on the planet, but only by a little. With her hair in his possession, however, none would dare oppose him.

"You hear that? The emmik says we get to have a little fun with you," Durkhoz said as his men began slowly circling Dukaan and Hunze.

"Not the girl," Hunstra called down again. "The four-armed freak will be taken to the gladiator camps, but the Ootaki will be my plaything. Once I've shorn her, that is."

"That shall not be happening," Dukaan growled, pulling his clubs free, extending them to full length.

Hunze felt her cheeks go flush with anger. This wasn't just a mugging. This was an attempt to take their freedom. To enslave them. To debase them.

The rage-fueled magic surging through her body threatened to lash out at any moment, but Hunze looked around at the bystanders who had gathered to watch the free entertainment unfolding before them and had a realization.

She simply couldn't use her magic. Not now. Not now that

they knew she was an Ootaki. They couldn't afford to draw that kind of attention on themselves. If word of a magic-wielding Ootaki got out, well, she could only imagine what forces might be brought to bear in hunting them down.

"Enough time wasting. Get them, Durkhoz!" the emmik commanded.

That was all the ruffian needed to hear. He raced at the four-armed man, leaving the girl to his men. She was only a woman, after all, and not worthy of his attention. The odd alien, however, could prove an amusing opponent. He'd never fought a four-armed man before. This would be fun.

Or so he thought, until the full weight of one of Dukaan's clubs smashed into his ribs, knocking the wind out of him momentarily.

Two of his men swarmed Dukaan, giving the thug time to regain his breath. Surprising, this opponent was proving to be, he mused, smiling as more men came rushing from the arena doors. There were over a dozen now. This was going to get interesting.

Had it been a straight-up fight, Dukaan would likely have fallen, though he was a far more skilled fighter than his opponents had initially given him credit for. But there was another factor at play that none of the hired muscle seemed to take into consideration.

The girl.

As was so often the case, she was relegated to the place of helpless bystander in the minds of the swarming men. That is, until the lithe woman dove into the fray with the ferocity of one with a far different upbringing than hers. That of a Wampeh Ghalian, the myriad skills and techniques flowing through her as though she'd been using them her whole life.

And thanks to the neuro-stim procedure with her assassin lover, it essentially felt like she had, and she moved accordingly.

Refraining from using any magic, Hunze tore into the men

attacking her friend, disabling, but not outright killing, all who stood in her path. From high above, Emmik Hunstra saw what was happening with shock and awe.

"She is magnificent," he gasped, before realizing those were *his* men she was laying waste to.

His men were trained, and they were skilled, but this woman was somehow moving through them as though they were standing still. The realization dawned on him that despite their numbers, his men were going to lose, and badly.

Hunstra turned and sped from the room, moving as fast as his oversize frame would allow him, racing for the courtyard on the ground floor, where he himself would put a stop to this humiliating rout of his men.

He hurried for the stairs, taking them two at a time, his knees shouting at him for the abuse. He really had let himself go, he realized, putting on a bit too much weight, perhaps, since seizing control of the city.

It was a rare moment of introspection for him, soon joined with another revelation. The regret that he had placed his personal rooms on the uppermost floor, at the wrong angle, and too far from any action below to be properly able to affect the outcome with his magic.

Minutes later, winded and sweating, Emmik Hunstra finally reached the ground floor of the arena building. He'd have liked to pause to catch his breath, but there was no time for that. Lunging forward, a man on a mission, he made for the doors to the courtyard, shoving those in his path out of his way without a second thought.

Hunstra burst through the doors into the streets, his magic pulled up, stun spells ready on the tip of his tongue, but what he saw defused all of that in an instant. All that remained of the priceless woman and her companion were his unconscious men, broken and beaten where they lay in the street.

The only men still standing, in fact, were two of the drunken fools who had instigated the whole thing in the first place. It seemed they had not warranted nearly so fierce an attack as the others. Still, they were staggering around in confusion, though whether that was from inebriation or concussion was open to debate.

"Where did they go?" the emmik demanded, grabbing the nearest of the pair and pulling him in close.

The reek of alcohol wafted off the man, so potent it nearly made Hunstra's eyes water. How the man had not succumbed to his drink at this point was a marvel of his physiology, as he quite possibly had more alcohol in his veins than blood at this moment.

"Where?" the emmik repeated, slapping the man to get his attention.

The drunk's eyes cleared for a moment. Long enough to realize who it was who was manhandling him. *That* was enough to sober him up. At least enough to point across the courtyard in the direction the duo had fled.

"Toward the landing area," Hunstra realized, releasing the man from his grip.

He would send men to catch them before they could reach it, only the ones at his disposal at the moment were all unconscious at his feet. He had others stationed throughout the city, but given what had just happened, they would undoubtedly meet the same fate as this lot, if not worse.

So, they would observe from a distance, watching but not engaging. Keeping the emmik informed while he planned his next move.

Whispers filtered through the air, and though Hunstra couldn't hear the contents of the conversations, his imagination was filling in the blanks for him.

"Did you see that? Humiliated, he was," one might have been saying.

"He's getting weak. Losing his grip," another seemed to note.

Of course, he couldn't know what they were truly saying, but that didn't matter to a man like Emmik Hunstra. He had been made to lose face in front of his people. To look a fool. To appear weak.

There was only one thing to do to regain face. It would cost much coin. Far more than he would ever spend in normal circumstances. But this? The whispers filled his ears as he stormed back into the arena. *This* warranted it.

Hunstra took his time walking back to his offices, getting his anger under control as best he could. He then summoned a servant and handed him a sealed message, along with a magically protected parcel containing a hefty advance payment. The servant heard the destination and blanched, then pulled himself together and headed out to do his master's bidding.

Only then did Hunstra allow himself the slightest smile. The woman would be his, one way or another. The ball had been set in motion.

CHAPTER THIRTY-FOUR

Kip emerged from his very hasty warp with a crackling blue flash, his friends safely aboard, but only just.

"You had a bunch of friends following you, you know," he said to his passengers. "Like, the streets were full of people chasing you. I was watching on my scanners the whole time."

"Yes, we had more than a little trouble," Hunze admitted. "Fortunately, we were able to extricate ourselves without too much harm."

She was uninjured, her Wampeh Ghalian skills keeping her from harm. Dukaan, on the other hand, had sustained a few scrapes and bruises in the scuffle. Hunze gently applied a healing paste and bandages to the ones that seemed most in need, while her friend sat patiently in his seat.

"That was impressive back there," she said. "I'd never seen a Chithiid fight like that before. Very unconventional."

Dukaan smiled. "Yes, I have trained in a few styles that are not typical for my people."

"Dookie goes to an underground fight club," Kip chimed in. "He's one of the best, actually."

"Kip, please. It is unbecoming to brag," Dukaan said.

"But it's true. You can't deny facts. You're kinda really good at this stuff."

"What is this fight club you speak of?" Hunze asked, her curiosity piqued.

"It is a gathering of all who feel the need to air grievances, let off steam, or just learn to fight," the aching Chithiid replied as she wrapped the last bandage around his arm. "Originally it was a means for human and Chithiid survivors of the Great War to come to terms with their new reality. One where former enemies turned allies could test one another in a non-lethal setting. It was tense for a while, but a semi-friendly, yet aggressive, means to blow off steam proved to be a most welcome means for the more traumatized to overcome their issues."

"Yeah, it's pretty cool," Kip added. "And now that everyone is cool with each other, all that post-war tension is pretty much a thing of the past. But back in the early days, people got a bit excessive at times, if you know what I mean."

A faraway look flashed across Dukaan's face as he recalled the early days of their fights in a hidden space in Los Angeles's downtown area. "Yes, things were a bit tense," he agreed. "And a few of us, from both sides, may have taken to it a bit too much."

"Yeah. Tamara kicked your ass more than once, if I recall correctly," Kip said.

"She has a cybernetic limb."

"And you have four arms. Seems like a reasonable trade off," Kip shot back with an amused laugh. "Anyway, it helped you beat back the bad guys today, and that's what matters."

Dukaan turned to his seemingly harmless friend. "That was not me, Kip. I was overwhelmed. It was Hunze who put an end to the fighting."

"Oh, shit. Did you drop them with a big old spell?" Kip asked.

"No, that would have drawn far too much attention," she replied. "I merely used the skills Bawb had gifted me."

177

SCOTT BARON

"She took out nearly a dozen men in no time," Dukaan added. "It was astonishing. She saved my life, for certain."

"They weren't going to kill you, Dukaan. They just wanted you for a gladiator slave."

"A fate as foul as death, I feel," he said. "In any case, thank you. I owe you my freedom, and shall not forget this debt."

"We're in a really unusual situation," Hunze said. "We do what we must to survive. You do not owe me anything."

Rather than debate the issue, Dukaan simply let the issue go, but his own code of honor was quietly keeping score, and behind his cool façade, he knew he owed her one.

"So, new plan," Kip said. "We obviously need to find a different place to get help from. Preferably not such a nasty planet next time. You think you can help guide us to one, Hunze?"

"Seeing as how it appears the Council is no longer intact––at least not in any size or manner that might be of use to us––I believe we are going to have a harder time finding one who might be a guide. A person who might know where a massive fleet had gathered. This makes things difficult."

"But on the bright side, we can probably say that it's safe to land on the more advanced worlds now, right?" Kip asked.

"Yes, but only if we can find our way back with this faulty warp system," Dukaan noted. "Even knowing the location of our recent visits, reaching them may take some doing."

"Then we'd better get started," Hunze said. "We've lost this day. The portal will open and close before we can hope to reach it. That leaves us but one more attempt before it reverts to a longer interval."

"So, let's get to it, then," Kip said," powering up his warp drive. "You think you can focus on that planet we passed up on? The more civilized one? Just get me close, and I can take us in without warp from there. Charlie kind of supercharged my drive systems a bit."

Hunze focused her magic, tying in to the konus in Kip's frame, while reaching out to sense the traces of the world they'd flown near but bypassed in an overabundance of caution.

"I think I have it," she finally said. "Just use less warp than normal, I fear we may drastically overshoot otherwise."

"Got it," Kip replied. "Here we go."

A second later the little ship vanished, the crackling blue warp residue the only trace that it had ever been there. That, and the powerful magic-tracking beacon that had been quietly attached to Kip's hull when he'd made his hasty escape from Emmik Hunstra's world.

Had Hunze been less distracted she might have noticed the powerful spell as it was cast upon their ship. But she'd just brutalized a dozen men and was fleeing for her life, so it was only natural she would be a little preoccupied.

The caster had done as Emmik Hunstra had commanded. Stayed well out of sight and did not attempt to engage. All the unassuming woman had done was cast her most powerful tracker upon the craft as it lifted off. Most tended to let their guard down when they took to the skies, believing themselves safe, and this ship was no different.

It would take effort, and a very specialized sort of magic, but a person, the *right sort* of person, could now track Kip wherever he went, so long as they didn't cast a cleansing spell on their ship. And from what the caster had seen of the passengers, that sort of thing was not likely their usual protocol. So the tracker would stay in place, and one day, eventually, it would serve its purpose.

CHAPTER THIRTY-FIVE

It was rough going, but Kip had kept records as they flew, and the stars were consistently staying within the very rough parameters he'd been using for a rudimentary guidance system.

Of course, without Hunze focusing her significant power on the konus mounted within his frame, Kip would have stood a snowball's chance in hell of ever successfully reaching their target system. Even with her help, however, the galaxy's strange effect on warp technology made anything resembling controlled warp a joke.

The AI, for all his quirky behavior, was still a fairly advanced system, despite his humble origins as an artificially intelligent toaster. He'd been upgraded so many times since his initial transfer into a ship during the Great War that he was essentially the same as a full-fledged mid-tier AI.

That meant Kip still possessed all the processing power of his less unusual brethren, and he was using every last scrap of that capability to try to find a workaround to their warp drive issue. Unfortunately, their tech simply would not function in anything resembling a remotely predictable manner.

"I think this might work," the frustrated AI said as he

spooled up the warp drive yet again. "But hell, with our luck, it might just dump us out on the other side of the galaxy."

"Fortunately, even malfunctioning as it is, I do not believe the warp drive possesses the capability of so long a warp," Dukaan said.

"I was being hyperbolic, Dookie. Jeez, let a guy kvetch a little, okay?"

"My apologies, Kip. I sometimes forget how you enjoy a bit of self-pity."

"Self-pity? Dude, we're all screwed here! First our team gets their asses kicked at the portal—which is about to sink into the sun for a full week if we don't hurry this up. Then we warp to God knows where. And then we find out my warp system doesn't even work properly in this place."

"Yes, it is a difficult situation, but you are performing admirably. And despite the problems in your warp system, you are making good progress using what limited star charting we have at our disposal," Dukaan said.

"He's right," Hunze added. "And my magic is not used to this type of work, so it is partly my fault that we've not reached our target already. But I truly believe that with the right navigator aboard, their magic will be able to properly guide us to where we need to go."

"If we ever find a power user who also happens to know the location of this non-Council fleet," the AI griped.

"We can only try. Now, let's give it another go. I think we are close enough to the general region of that system that I can help our konus focus on that backtrace signal and get us somewhat close."

Hunze didn't wait for Kip's reply, but instead began focusing her considerable power on one of the spells Bawb had gifted her when the neuro-stim embedded within her his considerable knowledge of magic. It wasn't a navigation spell by any means, but it was a rather powerful tracking one.

Unfortunately, unlike the other spells of his she had been using, this one seemed to be having issues, as if the magic were experiencing interference that caused her trace of their former path to waver a bit. The result was they had made sixteen small jumps, hopscotching around the area she felt was the one they needed to reach.

The Konus welded to Kip's frame was flush with power, linking the ship to the Ootaki in a loop of magic.

"Okay, here we go again," Kip said, then engaged his warp.

They popped into existence a great distance away once more, but this time something was different.

"Holy shit! It worked!" Kip exclaimed as he scanned the planets around them.

Dukaan and Hunze looked at the long-range scans. He was right. Though the warp had deposited them at the far edges of the solar system, they had finally managed to warp back to the right system. And once they made their way to the bustling, modern planet close to the sun, they would begin seeking guidance in earnest once more.

Kip didn't bother attempting to land in a remote, hidden location, opting rather to set down right in the busiest hub he could locate. It was situated in the heart of one of the largest cities on the planet, from what their initial survey had told them, and it was there they felt they had the best chance of procuring not only the information they needed, but perhaps even the person they needed to help them guide their little ship home.

"Fully armed this time," Dukaan said, strapping a pair of pulse pistols to his hips. "If we are not dealing with this Council of Twenty you have spoken of, I think we should take whatever precautions necessary to defend ourselves, short of exposing your magic."

"I am okay with that," Hunze agreed, strapping on a pair of knives, tucking a variety of deadly implements into the hidden pockets she wore much in the manner Bawb had done so many times before.

His knowledge truly was flowing through her now that she found herself in a potentially dangerous situation, and that feeling connected her to him, despite the vast distance between them at that moment.

"Okay, let's begin. We've obviously been taken note of since we landed. I just hope that additional attention Kip is receiving will also bolster our reputation as something interesting and unique," Hunze said.

"Are we certain that is what we want?"

"Normally, no. But I'll tell you what, Dukaan, I believe, in this instance, we shall need to make a bit of a show if we wish to receive the information we require."

"Very well, then," he said, moving for the door. "Kip, we will have comms on at all times. Keep your weapons ready, and be prepared for a rapid liftoff should it be needed."

"Oh, you don't have to tell me after that last planet," Kip replied. "Just get what we need. I'll be ready."

With that the Chithiid and Ootaki strode out onto the new world in search of help. Help, and answers.

CHAPTER THIRTY-SIX

"Oh, you're back," Karasalia said as she rounded the corner, nearly running into her father.

"Yes, things were able to be resolved a bit quicker than anticipated," he replied, hugging his daughter and kissing her head.

Visla Palmarian's return home was unexpected, but a welcome surprise, and Kara hadn't even noticed his powerful ship when it landed on one of the floating platforms atop the building.

As it so happened, her stepmother had also just returned only the day prior, back from her socialite buzz about the systems. It was good timing, actually. Kara was feeling a little blue at having made, then lost, a new friend in such a short span.

"Don't worry, dear. I'm sure your new friend will visit again," Mareh had consoled her when she first saw her stepdaughter's distress upon returning home.

And Kara did hope Leila would be back. It was nice having someone to hang out with every day. But now, with both her father and stepmom home, at least there was less of that empty feeling to the estate. Sure, Vee would come over and they'd talk about life and their dreams of one day getting off of this planet and seeing the stars, but then she would go back to her own home, and the place just felt *empty*.

"Are you all right?" Visla Palmarian asked his daughter. "You're looking a bit paler than when I left."

"Just a little run down is all," the teen replied.

It was true, though. Her light violet skin was even paler than before, and the bags under her eyes seemed a bit more pronounced. Her father couldn't understand how the child of one of the most powerful vislas in ages could be so fragile. But life tended to work in mysterious ways, it seemed, and such was the luck of the genetic draw.

"Well, I will have Tulagda make your favorite meal tonight. That should perk you up a little."

"Thank you, Father."

"Dearest, when did you return?" Mareh asked, joining the pair in the hallway.

It was almost a sixth sense gift she had, always knowing when her family was together under one roof. In that, Mareh seemed almost like a nesting mama hen, keeping all of her chicks close and secure under her wings.

"I only just returned," the visla replied, tenderly kissing his wife.

After all those many years together, the passion she ignited in him was still readily apparent to all. And it was a good thing, for the visla needed someone to temper his power.

"So, how was business?" Mareh asked, breaking their embrace.

"Oh, fine. You know how it is. Just some complications that required a visla's oversight."

"Well, they were lucky to have you," she replied. "You're the most powerful visla I've ever met, and I'm sure having you there put everyone's mind at ease."

"Yes, I do hope so," he replied. "There have just been some...*things* that needed handling. And I fear I will have to return sooner than later, given the latest turns of events."

Kara was not happy to hear he'd be heading out again, and soon, likely, but her curiosity was piqued at what could possibly require his attendance so urgently.

"What were you doing out there, Father? Not anything dangerous, I hope."

The visla turned to his daughter, a wall of professional cool snapping into place for just an instant. A moment in which Kara saw the powerful, aloof man everyone else knew.

"You know I don't talk about that, Karasalia," he said flatly. Realizing his tone, he shifted to a warmer air. "But how are you, really? I do get worried about you, you know? You look so tired."

"Just a low-energy day," she replied.

"And your new friend? Where is Leila? I expected the two of you to be thick as thieves when I returned."

"Unfortunately, she had things she had to do. Her friends were late in returning, so I had Captain Sandah take her out to find them. I hope you don't mind."

At his daughter's words the air began to crackle with an invisible energy as the visla's anger flared in spite of himself.

"You did *what*? And without my approval?"

"But, Father, it's just for a few days, probably. Maybe a week."

"Dammit, Kara. I have men like Sandah on standby for a reason. My most trusted, most loyal of captains. The ones I can trust no matter what. He was to undertake a task for me upon my return, and now I come home to find my child has gone and sent him away. Just wonderful," he growled, the magic leaking off his body tangible in the air.

It was rare that her father got this way, but when he did, Kara knew better than to offer anything other than apologies. Excuses simply would not fly in his world. Not when he was this upset.

The perplexing thing was why something seemingly as

insignificant as sending a ship away for a few days would set him off so. But he was a visla, and the demands upon him were many. And Kara knew quite well the extent of just how much she *didn't* know about what he really did.

"I'm sorry," she said, eyes averted. "But he should be back soon. I meant no offense, Father. I was just trying to help Leila."

"And now I am without my––Why do I bother laying out plans if they will be spoiled so easily by a careless teen?"

The anger and frustration weren't going away, it seemed, but were bubbling to the surface. Whatever task he had planned for Sandah, it must've been quite important for him to react so strongly, and in front of his daughter no less. Usually, he was far more careful to keep her from his side when these incidents would happen.

Fortunately, Mareh was a good and loving wife, and she had ways of reducing his overflowing magical rage. But that was something Kara really didn't want to think about. As close as she and Mareh were, that was still her dad, after all, and that particular thought was kind of gross.

"Dear, Kara didn't know your plans for Sandah," Mareh said, stroking her husband's cheek, unafraid of his welling power. "And if Sandah had known he was to be tasked on a mission for you, I am certain he would not have left."

"Well––"

"You should be proud of your daughter, Nikora. She was trying to help her friend. And that was the least she could do, after the brave woman stood up for her when those terrible Tslavar boys harassed her."

"I really didn't mean to upset you, Father," Kara said, meekly. "I just wanted to do something nice for Leila."

"A shame your friend already left," Mareh said. "I'd have very much liked to have met her to offer my deepest thanks in person."

"But maybe she'll be back," Kara said.

"Yes, perhaps," the visla said, an odd look on his face. "Grundsch, there you are," he said as the large manservant and his hound padded in. "Is everything in order?"

"Yes, Visla. The grounds are secure."

This was interesting. Grundsch normally went about his duties silently. To have been summoned by her father so soon upon his return, something must have been afoot.

"Is something going on?" Kara asked.

"No. Nothing to worry yourself about, dear. Just a strange feeling is all. One can never be too cautious. A lesson you'd be wise to learn," he replied. "And Sandah, off world until who knows when."

"Let it go, dearest," Mareh chided as she put her arm around Kara's shoulders. "You're losing sight of what is truly important in your life. Now, Kara, tell me all about your new friend," she said, walking the girl away from her father. "Leila is such a pretty name. I want to hear all about her."

Mareh would handle him later. For now, it was time to catch up with her stepdaughter.

CHAPTER THIRTY-SEVEN

With a new day came a calmness of character in Visla Palmarian that Kara almost found unnerving. He was still upset over her sending Sandah off with Leila, but to see him shift so radically in the span of just one night? Well, she didn't want to think about whatever tricks her stepmother might have employed. But whatever she did, at least there was no magic seeping out of him in angry spurts.

In fact, the visla actually seemed a little bit tired. Worn out, you could even say.

She must have really done a number on him, Kara mused, instantly grossing herself out with the thought. The ball she had been making hover in front of her fell to the ground as she was distracted by the mental image.

"Karasalia, you're not focusing," her father said as the tenuous grip she had on her limited magic crumbled.

It was humiliating. She couldn't even keep a simple ball afloat in the air. The Hakanan Test. A child's spell that anyone with a modest amount of power could perform, and one that would help determine her place in the magical hierarchy when they came of age to undergo the Trials. And that was just what the visla used as her concentration exercise. Something of a touchstone he would throw in with the rest of their training to help ground his frustrated daughter.

She should have excelled at it. She should have passed the test years ago. She should have been able to keep the ball in the air and stable no matter what distractions were thrown at her. But she could not.

Yes, she knew all the spells he had taught her. She was a visla's daughter, after all, and the words flowed from her lips as easily as they did from his. But try as she might, Kara simply did not have her father's gifts.

Despite his rather low energy morning, the visla was apparently still harboring a bit of annoyance that he just couldn't seem to conceal. And Kara knew that it couldn't be about her poor magical abilities. He'd been trying to help her overcome her natural shortcomings for years. No, this was about her sending off a ship without his permission.

An overstepping of boundaries a man of his considerable power would be hard pressed to accept from anyone, even his own daughter.

"Father, are you okay?"

"Fine, Kara. Continue your practice. Again."

She cast the spell once more, lifting the ball off the floor with relative ease this time. She focused a tendril of power, willing it to keep the ball afloat, then shifted her attention back to her father.

"Are you sure you're all right? You seem upset still. I don't see why you're so angry about Sandah. He'll be back soon enough. And besides, you've got other trusted captains to run errands."

"I'm not discussing this with you," he said, curtly.

"But, Father!" The ball dropped again.

Visla Palmarian glared at his daughter. "Dammit, Kara! The business of a visla is not to be questioned by an impulsive child! Now do as you are told. Cast the spell," he growled, his anger bubbling ever so slightly beneath the surface, despite whatever miracle her stepmother had worked on him the night before.

Karasalia Palmarian was nothing if not her father's daughter, and his harsh words brought her own anger rising up, and far more potently than she ever would have expected. She cast the spell, hard, using all the power she could muster. But she didn't cast with finesse, and as a result the normally benign little ball began smashing into the walls, the artwork hanging on them, and just about anything else in its path as it flew about the room.

Shocked, Kara tried desperately to cancel her own spell, but to no avail. Finally, her father stepped in, just as the ball was about to career into a priceless sculpture that had been in the family for centuries.

Had she cast a killing spell, he might have been concerned, but blood ties tended to prevent those particular spells from being used against a relative. An odd quirk of magic that had kept more than one family from tearing itself apart. But destructive tantrum spells were another thing entirely, and they could do significant damage.

"*Incarus*," he said firmly, the spell cutting off the magical charge that had been powering the ball. It dropped harmlessly to the floor.

"You see? *This* is the problem. You cannot even cast the most simple levitation spell, let alone properly defend yourself. It is unbecoming the daughter of a visla to wallow with the unpowered commoners so. And you're almost of the age where the Hakanan Test is mandatory, and my daughter *cannot* fail. Your very placement in society is at stake."

"I'm sorry, Father. I'm trying. I've *been* trying. It's just, my power is inconsistent. It's stronger some days."

"Yet most days it is not," he shot back. "No, this settles it. I am having a new specially crafted konus made for you. A powerful one, worthy of my daughter. You know the spells by heart. Hopefully, with an adequately over-charged konus at your disposal, you will be able to at least present the *impression* of a powerful caster. But until then, you are not to leave this building, is that understood?"

"But--"

"No buts, Kara. You are defenseless and foolish, and the konus you've used to train with and overcome your shortcomings has been woefully inadequate. The Trials are coming, and you will use a disguised konus if you must. I shall speak with the master craftsmen on Goralis in the morning. They owe me many favors, so you will be placed at the top of the list. You will have your konus completed and delivered within two weeks."

One of the house servants poked his head into the room, though he seemed quite reluctant, given the tension in the air. "Visla, there is a certain *someone* here to see you?"

"Already? Damn. Show them to my private offices."

"I have already done so, Visla. They have been provided refreshment and merely await your arrival," he said, bowing out of the room

Visla Palmarian was clearly disturbed by the early arrival of his mystery guests. He turned, heading for his offices.

"But, Father, what about Vee? There's a performance tonight. We're supposed to meet--"

"You can skree your friend and tell her you will not be joining her," he shot back in a tone that made it very clear that particular conversation was over.

Kara was sulking on her favorite of the floating gardens when Mareh came upon her, a small tray of picnic foods in her hands.

"Mind if I join you?" she asked.

"Of course not," Kara replied.

"I heard what happened," her stepmother said. "I'm so sorry you had to see your father like that. I tried to calm him as best I could, but he is a tremendously powerful man, and sometimes there's just nothing for it."

"It's just unfair, is all," Kara said. "I mean, why now? I've always been able to come and go as I please."

"With Grundsch following close by," Mareh noted. "Only recently have you been heading out on your own, and it frightens him."

"Frightens? He's the most powerful visla in centuries. What's there to be frightened about?"

"You, dear. He's worried something will happen to you."

"But it's not fair. I just want to see Vee. We were going to go see the exhibition at the arena tonight."

Mareh gently rubbed her stepdaughter's shoulder. "He won't keep you locked up forever, you know. Trust me on this, every girl eventually has her freedom. Some a bit earlier than others, though," she said with a little snicker.

Kara looked at her with a conspiratorial grin. "Oh? Do tell."

"Well, if anyone asks, you never heard this from me, but when I was your age, you could say I was a bit of a handful."

"I can imagine."

"To tell the truth, I was really quite good at getting my way, and nothing could keep me from going where I wanted. In fact, my father didn't even realize I had once snuck out and stolen one of his ships for a night until I told him of it years later."

"Really?"

"Oh, yes. He was most certainly not amused," Mareh said, and both burst out in peals of laughter.

"What else?" Kara asked, her mood greatly improving by the second.

"I'll tell you about it someday," Mareh said. "Suffice to say, many of those little acts of defiance shaped me into who I am."

"Strong and cultured," Kara said.

"Cultured? I can credit my teachers for that, I suppose. But, I was not always the refined woman I am today," Mareh replied.

"And more than my family's tutors and rules, it was those adventures that really made a difference. But I shouldn't be telling you all of these things. I wouldn't want you to think less of me. Now, what else has gone on with your life while I was away?"

The conversation shifted to other topics. Boys, Vee, Kara's new friend, Leila, until finally, Mareh took her leave and headed back inside to check on her husband. Kara, however, remained outside a bit longer, taking in the fresh air while pondering what her stepmother had told her.

CHAPTER THIRTY-EIGHT

It was still relatively early, but the sun had set across Palmar, leaving the gleaming city awash in a magical glow of soothing power. The visla himself had seen to it when he first came to power that all of the main roads and thoroughfares were provided with illumination at no cost to the citizens, magical or otherwise.

Just one of the many projects he implemented to keep the people content. For while it was indeed an altruistic deed, he also realized full well that simple things like free lighting and well maintained waste disposal systems would give the city dwellers a sense of pride in their homes. And pride meant keeping them in order, which, in turn, led to a sense of ownership even where there was none.

It was a clever strategy, and one that had made Palmar one of the shining cities of the realm. It also let Visla Palmarian focus his energies on more important tasks, now that the commoners had been placated.

But every city has a seedy underbelly. Even one as seemingly refined as Palmar. And it was in those darker side streets and alleys that both the population's rabble as well as those simply wishing to pass unnoted would travel come nightfall. Waiting near the intersection of a bright footpath and one such alleyway, Visanya stood patiently, marking the time until her best friend was to meet her.

Karasalia had been grounded, essentially, though her father was unfamiliar with that Earth term. But the result of his edict was the same. His daughter was under no circumstances to leave the tower. He had made that quite clear.

Two weeks of what was essentially in-house confinement were what awaited the teen. And beginning on the eve of her planned outing, no less. Normally, she would have reluctantly accepted her fate, resigned to a boring few weeks with nothing to do but perhaps walk the gardens, play with Bahnjoh, and maybe try to make sense of the heretic's cryptic prophesies.

But this evening, something had changed.

Namely, Kara, good and obedient daughter, was nowhere to be found in the tower's walls.

She had felt an overwhelming urge to do something. Anything, but take her father's unfair command lying down. She wasn't a little girl anymore. She was nearly a woman, and it was high time she began being treated as such.

Her conversation with Mareh, and her stepmother's unexpected revelation of her disobedient youth, had lit a fire within her. The faint beginnings of a stubborn push back.

"Mareh turned out amazing for it," the teen rationalized as she made her way from the highest reaches of the tower to the subterranean footings of the building. "And Father loves her. So, really, this is justified. I'm actively striving to become more like the woman he respects and adores. Who wouldn't want that for their child?"

It was a tenuous bit of mental gymnastics at best, but with Vee waiting for her, and a fun evening they had been planning for weeks ahead of them, Kara found her ability to rationalize her way through the situation had reached new heights. But heights were not where she would be making her exit from.

She could see now quite clearly why her father placed the prisoners' cells atop the building. Even for the daughter of the visla himself, it would be near impossible to effect an unnoticed escape from such heights. In fact, if she were noticed, it would likely be because of her body plummeting from above.

No, it was a nearly impossible task to make her exit from atop the tower.

"How in the world did the heretic manage to make her entrance so high?" she found herself wondering as she took the little-used service lift down to the mezzanine level. She would have to ask about that when next she visited the would-be assassin. But for the moment, she needed to focus on her escape.

She rounded the corner heading to the back of the decorative sculptures, all facing the other way, toward the main space of the floor. She then passed through a wide archway leading to the delivery ramp that passed all the way down to the storage area underground.

No deliveries were taking place at night, which was why she had selected this route, and as such, the area was free of prying eyes. There were a few small magical wards in place, mounted along the corridor, but her bloodline allowed her free passage without triggering an alarm.

She didn't even need to attempt a bypass spell with her konus, tucked away within her sleeve.

The utilitarian service corridor allowed the visla to keep his tower in a state of perpetual readiness for whichever high-ranking emmiks or vislas might come to visit him at a moment's notice. Sometimes even less than that, for men and women of that type of power often did as they pleased, regardless of whom they might upset by their actions.

Fortunately, Visla Palmarian was an exceptionally intimidating force to be reckoned with, when he wanted to be, and while his guests were often some of the deadliest, most powerful people in the realm, they respected his abilities and authority in this place and dared not overstep.

Servants were to be summoned, not seen, and their labors performed out of sight. Kara smiled to herself as she made her way through the corridor toward the nondescript building just across the courtyard from her father's tower. She could see why her father refused to house any prisoner in a dungeon below ground. Though escape was highly unlikely, if they did somehow manage it, the same path she was using for her illicit egress would be at their disposal as well.

There would be numerous magical wards and locks to overcome, of course, but there was always that little possibility that one might just manage an escape. Like Kara had just managed, she thought as she stepped into the quiet storage space of her father's outbuilding.

Exiting cautiously onto the street, the hood of her nondescript overcloak pulled over her head to hide her from prying eyes, Kara began walking with a little spring in her step as she ducked down the adjacent alleyway she knew would loop her around to the agreed upon spot where her friend was waiting.

"That wasn't so difficult," she said, a feeling of cheerful accomplishment mingling with the adrenaline of disobeying her father. "I don't know why I hadn't done that before," she mused as she trotted off into the night.

CHAPTER THIRTY-NINE

Kara had been walking nearly ten minutes when she saw Vee's long brown hair, contrasting nicely with her pale, pale yellow skin, waiting for her a block up ahead. She waved at her friend as she passed beneath a light in the alleyway, hurrying her pace.

Vee waved back, but then a look of concern flashed across her face. Kara was alarmed, and rightly so. She spun to find four Tslavar bullies crowding around her, stepping out of the shadows they'd been lurking in.

"Where do you think you're going?" the larger of the group asked, menace in his voice.

"I'm just meeting my friend. She's right there. She can see you, you know."

"Yeah? And what of it? Weak little girl like you. Weak little girl like her," the Tslavar said.

Kara had initially thought these were the brothers or cousins of the boys, and girl, Leila had embarrassed in the street several days prior, come for a bit of payback. But then she realized she didn't recognize any of them.

"Look, you should really leave," she said, trying to channel some of her stepmother's inner strength.

But the spirit she showed only made the men laugh, and it was not a pretty sound.

"Oh, I don't think so," the man said. "No, I don't think so at all."

Things were going from bad to worse, and quickly. Kara flashed a look at Vee, who was desperately grabbing at a passerby, pointing toward the dark alleyway, but the Tslavar bullies were standing between Kara and the light, and all anyone would see was the backs of several rather large green men. Not the sort of thing just anyone goes and sticks their nose into. Not if they knew what was good for them.

"Leave now and I won't harm you," Kara said, calling upon the magic in her konus, making a few small pieces of refuse lying in the alley float menacingly behind her, as if ready to be launched as unlikely projectiles.

"*Incarus*," the Tslavar said, casually.

Her spell dissipated immediately, the items dropping once more to the ground.

"You actually thought you could scare us with a levitation spell? Oh, that's rich."

"You don't know what you're getting yourself into," Kara blurted, her growing fear outweighing her desire for anonymity. "You don't know who I am."

"Of course we do, *Denna Palmarian*," the Tslavar replied with a wicked grin.

It was at that moment that Kara realized this was not a random alleyway mugging, and she was not merely an unlucky passerby. The Tslavars grabbed her, shoving a rag in her mouth, not even bothering with a silencing spell as they dragged her back into the shadows.

This wasn't a mugging at all. It was a kidnapping.

. . .

A good ten minutes had passed by the time Visanya reached the visla's tower, tears streaking her face as she rushed inside.

"I'm sorry, miss, but the visla has ordered we not allow visitors in at this hour," the lead guard at the entrance said. "You'll have to see Denna Palmarian in the morning. Or perhaps you could reach her by skree, if you wish."

"No, you don't understand! Kara's been kidnapped!" the teen blurted.

A look of concern flashed across the guards' faces. If someone had snuck in on their watch and taken the visla's daughter, there would be hell to pay.

"I'll send one of my men to check on her," the man said, turning to relay the command.

"No, she wasn't taken from here. We were out in the streets, heading to a performance at the Krespi Theater, when some men took her."

"Men? What sort of men?" the guard asked, realizing now that far more was afoot than he'd originally thought.

"Tslavars, from what I could see. Four of them. They grabbed her. They took her!"

The guard swallowed hard. This was not a message anyone would want to relay to the visla, but time was of the essence, and any delay would result in more punishment than the men who had failed to protect his daughter would already receive.

"Come with me," he said, quickly ushering Visanya into the visla's private, express lift.

They flew straight to the top, her ears popping from the rapid shift in pressure. Vee had never been in Kara's dad's personal lift, and now she knew why. The man radiated power, so the forces it generated by such rapid an ascent were nothing for him to dispel, brushing them off like dust from his cloak.

For normal people, however, it felt akin to being shoved down into the ground by a giant hand as they rocketed skyward.

The pressure abruptly ceased seconds later as they reached the visla's private offices.

"Visla, I am sorry to bother you, but this young woman has disturbing news."

Visla Palmarian looked up from his papers, quickly sliding them into a drawer, out of sight.

"What is it, Visanya? Didn't Karasalia tell you? She's not to leave home until she––"

"She's been kidnapped!" Vee interrupted.

No one interrupted the visla. No one. But this news? His displeasure shifted from the foolish child who had dared do so to the realization of what she had just informed him.

"Kidnapped? From within *my* walls?" He glared at the guard, angry magic crackling across his skin as he rose from his desk. "How did this happen? Who let––?

Twice in as many minutes, he was interrupted again. "We were outside, sir. Kara was meeting me to go see a performance. They snatched her right off the street before I could do anything."

The force of the power rippling off the visla was enough to make even the guard feel his knees go wobbly, such was his anger. In fact, all of the staff for several levels felt his rage to varying degrees.

"Darling, what's the matter?" Mareh said, rushing into his office in only a robe, her hair still damp from the shower she'd been in moments before.

The visla was positively crackling with magic as his emotions flared. Mareh approached him carefully, then put a soothing hand on his shoulder, braving his wrath with the confidence of a wife.

Ever so slightly, his anger subsided. Or, at least the overt magic it caused did.

"They took her, Mareh," he said, gazing into her eyes with the pained look of a worried father. "Kara has been kidnapped."

"Kidnapped? But who would be so foolish to do such a thing?"

"Tslavars," he growled. "And when I find them, they will regret having ever been born."

"Have they made any ransom demands?" his wife asked.

"What?"

"Ransom. They wouldn't have taken her for no reason. She's a very valuable child, worth a lot, they must surely know."

"They will receive no ransom. Only pain and death," he growled.

"And rightly so, dearest. But for now, they are in the city somewhere. None could escape so quickly. So use your power. Shut down the transit hubs. Decree that no ships come or go. Lock this city down tight, and then let your best men do their job. You are their visla, yes, but you are in no state to be seen roaming the streets looking for our daughter," she said, gesturing at the magic sparking from his body.

It was moments like this that Visla Palmarian's esteem for his wife grew even greater. "You are right, love," he said, his magic coming under control a bit more. He glanced at the guard. "Send Grundsch out with Bahnjoh. If that beast cannot sniff her out, none can."

"Immediately, Visla," the man said.

Mareh looked at Visanya and the guard and subtly nodded for them to leave while the leaving was good. The two wisely heeded her and stepped quietly from the room.

The visla's wife then poured a stiff drink from one of the decanters on the table. "Drink this."

"I do not want a––"

"It was not a request," she said softly. The one person who could interrupt him with impunity.

He took the glass and did as she bade him, downing the contents in a single gulp, his eyes watering from the burn.

"Now, dearest, come sit with me a moment. You must control your emotions if you are to be of use to our daughter."

Mareh took him by the hand and led him to their bed chambers.

He would find Kara, bringing to bear his full fury and power, but not like this. He couldn't be seen in public in any state less than that of total control, and he knew it. And so he went with his wife, knowing her gentle touch would help restore him to a more rational state. But soon, very soon, his wrath would fall upon those who dared touch a hair on his child's head.

CHAPTER FORTY

Charlie and Bawb had been scouring the main cities and spaceports of Orvall for nearly the entire day, trying to pin down the elusive Commander Yakatan. It seemed the man had a penchant for changing locale as often as some changed their clothes, though on this world that might not be as often as one would think.

In any case, there had been more than a few challenges in their quest to locate the man, not the least of which were three separate mugging attempts by opportunist locals who took the unassuming duo as easy marks, not a dragon mage and a Wampeh assassin.

Those foolhardy souls quickly learned their lessons, but Charlie and Bawb asserted themselves without killing anyone or using enough magic to draw undue attention to themselves in the process. Violence was par for the course in the seedy streets of Orvall. High-tier magic, however, was not.

So the two hid their strengths, making the pummeling their attackers suffered appear to be no more than a mugging gone wrong.

It was actually one such incident that gave them the crucial bit of information needed to find their quarry.

"I didn't know!" the poor mugger said, writhing in pain from the wrist lock Charlie had put him in while Bawb dispatched his accomplice with a rather brutal kick to the head.

The man fell to the ground in a heap, unconscious but breathing.

His friend, however, didn't know that.

"Please, don't kill me!"

"You hear that, Bob? Don't kill me. After he comes at me with this shitty little knife," Charlie said, brandishing the man's own weapon in his face. "It's rude to attack people with knives. Come on, I want to hear you say it."

"Yes, yes. It's rude to attack people with knives," the man sputtered.

"That's more like it," Charlie said, satisfied, as he turned to his Wampeh friend. "So what do you think? Should we stick around here a bit longer, or head out for the next spaceport?"

"Yakatan's vessel must be here somewhere, but I fear we are soon going to be relegated to the smaller cities, and one of his stature would not likely be found in such."

At this the writhing man perked up. "You're looking for Yakatan? *Commander* Yakatan? I can take you to his ship. It's nearby."

"We were told the *Prahana* is not docked here," Bawb noted.

"Well, no. There's no *Prahana* here," the man agreed. "But Yakatan, he changes the name of his ship every so often. The *Prahana* became the *Ishkoval* about three months ago."

Charlie and Bawb shared a look. If this was true, then that would explain why the man had been so hard to track down. And anyone who would change not only location, but also the very name of their ship, was likely very averse to being located by strangers.

"It seems this unfortunate mugging has become your lucky

day," Charlie said, letting the man straighten up, though not fully releasing the grip on his wrist. "I'll make you an offer. If you take us to him, I won't break your arm. We'll just call this even. Does that sound fair to you?"

The hapless mugger nodded his fervent agreement.

"Good," Charlie said. "Lead the way."

It was a weaving maze of stalls and vendors, the narrow walkways cramped with all manner of spacefaring adventurers and the planetary denizens looking to trade with them. The route to the *Ishkoval* was circuitous, seeming to double back on itself more than once, though that was due to the multiple levels, which did not seem to follow any set pattern or road map.

By the time they finally reached the ship, Charlie was just about ready to break the man's arm for lying to them, but there it was, the *Ishkoval*, large as life. Actually, it was a bit larger than that. Charlie had expected a somewhat nondescript vessel, given the description of Yakatan's rather antisocial ways, but it seemed their quarry was one for hiding in plain sight. And what a sight it was.

"That's his ship?" Bawb said as they drew close. "Rather difficult to disguise, I'd think."

"He doesn't need to," their unlikely guide said. "No one on Orvall would dare meddle with Yakatan."

"Oh, he has a reputation, does he?" Charlie asked. "Then he sounds like precisely the man we need to speak with."

At long last Charlie released the poor man, sending him on his way, cradling his aching arm. He turned to his Wampeh friend. "So, shall we?"

"What exactly were you thinking?" Bawb replied.

"Front door, I think. It's not as though we've gone unnoticed, after all," he said, glancing up to the eyes watching from more than one of the craft's windows.

Bawb nodded his agreement, and the two men set out for the extended gangplank leading into the large craft.

"What business do you have here?" asked a burly man with thick legs and arms that sported wicked-looking, clawed hands.

"We've come to speak with Commander Yakatan," Charlie said.

"Never heard of him," the man replied.

"Oh? Well, I was told that Yakatan was a connected man, and one with a knack for trade. A man who knows an opportunity when he sees it. It would be a shame for him to miss out on the chance for trade unlike any he or anyone else on this hole of a planet has ever seen," Charlie said, channeling his old pirate days for extra swagger in his speech.

The guard did not kick them off the gangplank immediately, and Charlie knew they were as good as inside. Now it was merely a question of when.

"Look, if you'll just bring us to Yakatan, I'm sure he will reward you handsomely for being the bearer of so profitable a trading partner," Charlie continued.

"Oh, will I?" a booming voice said from behind them.

Charlie and Bawb turned, slowly, so as to not start a fight when they merely wished to talk.

"Commander Yakatan, I presume?" Charlie said.

"In the flesh," the man replied. He was somewhat smaller than his voice would make one assume. Sturdy and well-muscled, no doubt, but not much larger than the human and his Wampeh companion. "So, what's this I hear about some new trade opportunity?"

"We have access to things the like of which you've never seen," Charlie said.

"Never seen? Ha! Not likely," Yakatan said, walking up the gangplank and shouldering past them. "But come, let us take a look at your wares. Perhaps you may still possess some trinkets one of my wives might take pleasure in."

Charlie shrugged at Bawb, then followed the man inside. The Wampeh assassin quickly assessed the number of men, their weapons, and positions, all in a glance, then fell into step behind his friend.

There were a fair quantity of Yakatan's crew on hand, but he was quite confident they could take them if need be.

His senses turned up to eleven, the Wampeh assassin walked deeper into the trader's ship, his fingers gently resting on the holstered wand at his hip, ready for whatever may come. He just hoped none of that would be necessary.

CHAPTER FORTY-ONE

Deep into the depths of Commander Yakatan's vessel Charlie and Bawb had been led, a small contingent of dangerous men in front and behind them, boxing them in as they walked, not realizing the men they thought to be intimidated were far more dangerous than the lot of them combined.

"Why do you carry around a piece of wood?" one of the impromptu guards turned escorts asked, eyeing Bawb's wand poking out of its holster, ready to be deployed at a moment's notice.

"Oh, that," the Wampeh assassin said in his most nonchalant tone. "I suffer from a rather irritating skin condition, you see. Flaking, oozing sores. It's really not terribly pleasant," he said, enjoying watching the man try to create just a little bit more space between them. "This stick," he said, drawing his wand, careful not to accidentally discharge a spell and kill everyone on board the ship, "makes for a most wonderful back scratcher, you see," he said, then proceeded to reach over his shoulder and scratch his back with the most dangerous scratcher ever made.

"Huh, just seems an odd thing to carry around," the man said. "But if you're itchy, I guess whatever it takes, eh?"

"I'm glad you understand," Bawb said, re-holstering the weapon.

Charlie had heard the exchange but refrained from turning to watch, fearing any interest in the goings-on might tip off Commander Yakatan that something more than met the eye was afoot. The other men seemed rather slow of wit, but Yakatan had that look. The look of a man grabbing for power, wealth, whatever he could lay his fingers on. Those sort of men were never to be fully trusted.

At long last, they reached what appeared to be Yakatan's personal galley, complete with a long table suitable to feed not only himself, but his many wives as well. Rare tapestries were draped from the wall, the quality of which Charlie actually knew from his time living in Visla Maktan's estate.

Then there was the other artwork and select pieces of furniture. Yakatan, it seemed, was not only a man of means, but also of surprisingly good taste. And with a penchant for antiques. Charlie realized they had an ace in the hole if their initial proposal was met with reticence.

Most of their possessions, by the very fact that they had traveled through time carrying them, were antiques, and having left the past, skipping all those centuries of aging, they were in a condition never seen outside of museums.

"Sit," Yakatan said, gesturing to the long table. "Are you thirsty?"

"I *am* quite parched," Bawb said, knowing a drink with the trader was the most common and casual way to open the bargaining discussion.

And Bawb wasn't afraid of being poisoned, having many spells lingering about his person at all times for such petty attacks. But he didn't think Yakatan was the poisoning type. At least, not when there was an intriguing trade offer he had yet to learn the details of. In fact, he seemed very much like the poison-you-later type should a deal go south.

Large glasses of a ruby liquid were placed before them. Charlie knew the powerful beverage well from his time as a pirate.

"Ah, grogstram," he said with an eager grin, downing half the glass in a single draught.

Yakatan was surprised at the strange man's familiarity with, and fondness for, the rather hearty beverage. "I see you know your drink," he said.

"Oh, yes. Had many an *interesting* night thanks to grogstram," Charlie said with a chuckle.

"Hmm. And you two are proving to be most *interesting* guests. Now, let us cut to the chase. What is it you want, and what is this profitable trading opportunity you claim to be able to offer me in return?"

Charlie paused a moment, making sure to choose his words carefully. "What we want, is your help in the way of gathering intelligence. Things a man of your connections would have heard."

"Such as? I hear many things," Yakatan said.

"Such as, who, exactly, is the visla amassing an enormous fleet without anyone seeming to know about it?" Charlie asked bluntly. "And where might we find him?"

"Ah, that," Yakatan said, knowingly. "You sure you want to stick your noses into that business? It's a dangerous thing, venturing into a visla's world."

"We're certain," Bawb said, sipping from his glass. "And we will pay handsomely for this information. If you have it, that is."

"Oh, I can get you that information, no doubt. I know a man in this very city with what you seek. But it will cost you, and far more than the likes of you can possibly afford."

"I'd beg to differ," Charlie replied. "As we said earlier, we can make you a very wealthy man with our trade opportunity."

"And what is this trade that could offer such inordinate

profit?" the commander asked as he downed the rest of his grogstram and signaled for another.

"Something no one else has ever brought you," Charlie said. "Goods the likes of which no one in any of the known systems have ever seen."

"You sound like one of the hidden world seekers," Yakatan said with a laugh. "Always dreaming of fortune and glory as they search out planets that simply do not exist."

"Does this exist?" Charlie asked, tossing his comms unit onto the table.

The metal device looked utterly out of place in the magical confines of Yakatan's ship. Clunky, almost, yet there was something about it. An utterly alien feel that went beyond the inelegant design and lack of magic. No, this felt otherworldly.

The trader picked it up and turned it over in his hands, studying the unit, while not having the slightest idea what it was for. But he'd been in the game a good many years, and he'd never seen anything remotely like the device. And novel meant valuable.

"An unusual trinket," he said, downplaying his interest. "But there is no power in it, and I have seen far more pleasing designs from the junker shops down in the Lowers."

Charlie extended his hand for the comms unit. Yakatan placed it in his palm, curious what his guest might do with it.

"This is called a comms unit," Charlie said. "It is a device from a powerful, new world that has not yet been discovered by the Council. I mean, what's left of it, that is. Or anyone, for that matter. And I'm offering you the opportunity for first dibs. You'll be the very first trader to establish formal trade with this new partner. Think of the riches one with a corner on that market might amass. It could be quite substantial."

"Doesn't look terribly inspiring a trinket, if you ask me," Yakatan lied.

"Let me demonstrate," Charlie said, keying on the device. "Hey, Ara, you got your ears on?"

"Yes, I am listening, Charlie. But why are you using your comms device?"

"Just sitting here with our new friend Commander Yakatan. Wanted to demonstrate how the comms works, and it's not as interesting if I call Bob when he's right across the table here."

The Wampeh chuckled.

"Anyway, that's it. Just checking in. Hopefully we'll be done here soon. Commander Yakatan says he knows a man here who has the information we need."

"Excellent news. I shall be standing by."

Charlie switched off the comms. "See?"

Yakatan was not impressed. "So it's a skree."

"No, not a skree. Jeez, you just said it has no magic, right?"

"Well..."

"And yet we were able to talk to our friend a fair distance away with no magic and no interference from the ship's hull."

"Well..."

"And I know for a fact you've never seen tech-magic like this before. No one has. And this is just the tip of the iceberg."

"What is an iceberg?" the trader asked.

"It's a giant, floating––Oh, that's not important. What is important, is that we can make you wealthy," Charlie said, pausing to read the man.

Yakatan had a good poker face, he had to give him that. But Charlie had run with one of the most successful pirate crews in twenty systems, and he'd learned more than a little about reading a man in that time. And Yakatan was definitely interested.

Finally, Yakatan nodded his head. "I will accept your deal," he said, sliding the skree from its pouch on his hip.

"What are you doing?" Bawb asked.

"I need to call ahead to secure safe passage to see Mandoog."

"Mandoog?" Charlie asked.

"He runs this whole place. The big boss, ruling from his lair in the Lowers. The man we're looking for works for Mandoog. There's no deal with him if Mandoog doesn't agree first."

"Well, then. Let's go find this man with the information we seek and take him to get permission from this Mandoog person," Bawb said.

"Yeah," Charlie agreed. "Time's a wasting."

CHAPTER FORTY-TWO

Yakatan strapped on a pair of blades and slid a slaap into a pouch on his waist.

"You expecting trouble?" Charlie asked as they prepared to seek out the reclusive man with the knowledge they so desperately needed.

"I always expect trouble," Yakatan replied. "It's kept me alive this long."

"A wise philosophy," Bawb commented.

The Wampeh was well armed as well, though his devices were hidden in plain sight—a pair of konuses fused into his seemingly decorative armlets, and countless blades secreted on his person. And, of course, there was his wand. Nothing but a stick in the eyes of all they met, but if he were to wield it and unleash its full force, the destruction would be catastrophic.

As for his Ootaki hair, he felt it wise to leave that with Ara for safekeeping. He knew no one could take it from him, but seeing a Wampeh sporting enough magic to turn them to red mist might make men think twice about having anything to do with them.

"Okay, now we're going to have to head down six levels, then cross over the pit bridge before we go up to the top level across the port, so mind your step."

"That seems a rather circuitous route," Bawb noted.

"That's because it *is* a circuitous route. This fella, he spooks easy."

"I thought you said you were calling ahead," Charlie said.

"I did. But not to him. To my lookout, who's clearing our descent to Mandoog's place. As for this guy, well, we'll just have to catch him off guard and then drag him with us is all."

Suddenly Charlie wasn't as confident in their new friend as he'd been just minutes before. And even then, he was only moderately so. But the shifty fellow was their best chance in dozens of planets and even more cities. If Yakatan couldn't help, they didn't know whom to turn to next.

"Lead the way," Charlie said as he followed the trader down the gangplank and into the churning throng of people milling about twenty-four seven.

It was twenty minutes into their walk, just as they were cresting the steps to the top level that Charlie sensed something was wrong. They'd just made the rather malodorous descent to the lower levels that provided them trouble-free passage across much of the region before returning up top, but up here they were exposed.

"*You feel this?*" Charlie silently asked Bawb.

"*Yes. Be ready,*" the assassin replied.

Just moments later, a throng of attackers came at them from all sides, casting stun spells from a relatively safe distance, hoping to take them down without the messiness of an up-close fight.

"Bawb, two up high!" Charlie warned his friend.

Bawb spun and cast simultaneous defensive and offensive spells, negating the rather amateur attack, while blasting the two men who had sent the spells his way flying through the air into the wall. They slid to the ground, and would not be getting up for quite some time.

Commander Yakatan was casting smoothly and efficiently, knocking attackers back while keeping himself protected at all times. He wasn't landing any serious shots, but he was at least keeping from being captured.

And that's what Charlie thought this was. A kidnapping attempt. Someone had likely gotten word of the off-world traders with valuable goods and decided they wanted that trade route knowledge for themselves.

"Okay, this is getting stupid," Charlie growled as a thundering magical blast nearly knocked him from his feet. "Ara, you hear me?"

"Yes, Charlie."

"We've fallen under attack. You close by?"

"Not terribly. I've taken up shelter across the city in the outskirts. Why?"

"Might need you to do a flyby and clear off some of these pests."

"But I will be seen."

"Maybe. Just stay alert. If it gets bad, I'll call."

Charlie tucked the comms back into his pocket.

"So, what's Ara flying?" Yakatan asked. "Must be a pretty powerful craft if you want her to fly in for air support."

"Yeah, she *is* the air support," Charlie said with a laugh, then quickly redoubled his defensive casting as a trio of spells slammed into his magical shielding.

"She's what?"

"She's a Zomoki," Charlie said. "And her flames are no joke. So if it gets really bad and we call her in, stay close to us."

Yakatan's eyes went wide. "You possess a speaking Zomoki?"

"I wouldn't exactly say we possess––"

"How much for it?" Yakatan blurted, ignoring the fighting around them.

"Not open for discussion. She's our friend, not our slave," Charlie said.

"Everything is open for discussion, and a talking Zomoki? We could all retire wealthy men!"

"Goddamn slaver planet," Charlie grumbled, firing off a series of powerful magic blasts. Too powerful for the konus he was wearing, he realized. He just hoped no one had noticed he had been using his own power and not the device riding on his wrist.

The fighting ceased abruptly, the attackers turning and running away.

"I guess they had enough," Charlie said, though he wondered what had really just happened. "Hey, where's Yakatan?"

He and Bawb spun, searching the area. There, fifteen meters away, Yakatan was having words with one of their assailants. And not heated ones. *Conspiratorial* ones.

"Sonofa... Get him, Bob!" Charlie shouted, taking off at a run.

Yakatan saw him and quickly pulled his skree to call for backup. The magical device flew from his hand when a minorly enchanted blade whipped through the air, smashing it from his grasp.

Bawb had thrown it while at a full run, Charlie realized. That sort of precision was what had made him the most deadly assassin in, well, more systems than one would care to count.

Yakatan turned and bolted, heading toward the crowded marketplace. Bawb drew his wand and took aim, ready to reduce the traitorous man to a pulp, but then stopped, carefully resheathing the deadly implement.

"What are you doing, Bob?" Charlie asked.

"There were too many people around him to use it safely," he replied. "It appears we are now forced to pursue him on foot."

"Shit. Then come on!" Charlie said, taking off at a full run, hot on the heels of the backstabbing trader.

CHAPTER FORTY-THREE

Charlie's boots rang out loudly as they hit the landing of the level below, but he had forward momentum and simply tucked into an easy roll with the impact, dispersing the force and winding up on his feet.

He had used one of Ser Baruud's old tricks––one that was strikingly similar to the old Earth sport of parkour––in his extremely rapid descent in pursuit of Commander Yakatan as he fled deeper into the depths of Orvall's subterranean marketplace. It seemed certain things, such as efficient body movement, were not galactic, but universal.

Bawb was well versed in that, and many other, forms of physical prowess, and was keeping pace easily, more concerned with maintaining visual contact with the man darting through the crowd up ahead of them. He was barreling through them without a care, the Wampeh noted. And he was drawing attention. Too much attention.

The tight marketplace rumbled with an abrupt shift in air pressure. Charlie looked at Bawb as they ran, more than a little confused.

"Just a vessel departing," Bawb said, not even remotely winded by talking while running.

"A ship? Down here?"

"Many trading vessels that are here for longer term stays, or illicit trading, dock far below the surface on worlds such as this," his friend replied, shifting his shoulders and hips as he flew between two carts and a trio of vendors without missing a stride.

Charlie, on the other hand, while a very talented free runner, had nevertheless bumped more than a few people as they ran. And unlike Yakatan, who had quite a reputation, and thus something akin to rudeness immunity, Charlie was drawing angry glares as he went.

But they had more important things to do. They'd been set up by the commander, and on top of that, the bastard wanted to capture and sell their friend. As much as they knew he would almost certainly be unable to accomplish that feat, nevertheless, that could not be allowed to stand.

A gust of air greeted them as they descended yet another level, pursuing Yakatan deeper and deeper into the subterranean maze. This level was slightly less densely crowded, and up ahead, Charlie could see why.

The somewhat wider passageway opened out onto what appeared to be an open-air landing, and what was beyond that was nothing more than empty space for hundreds of meters. On the far other side Charlie saw some ships hovering, their gangplanks leading down to the market's trading hubs.

This was how the ships moved around underground. An enormous tunnel system hidden from view from the surface. Charlie was willing to bet there was a nondescript entrance up top, just big enough for a ship, that led into the vast chamber.

The drop would be enough to kill a man easily, but Yakatan didn't slow his pace, but, rather, increased it as he barreled right for the edge.

"What the hell is he doing?" Charlie asked. "Yakatan! Stop!"

he called out, but the man ignored him, leaping headfirst over the railing without hesitation.

A few seconds later, Charlie and Bawb reached the railing, sliding to a stop.

"What the hell did he do—–Oh, for fuck's sake," Charlie groaned, realizing he was going to have to jump off a perfectly good platform in a moment.

Bawb had already hurried back several steps and was running for the railing.

"Don't delay, Charlie," he said with a grin as he dove through the air past his friend, right into the open space.

Bawb didn't fall to his death, however. There was a series of fixed ropes used to tie off the docked vessels, keeping them steady as other ships shifted the air pressure around them, and he grabbed one mid-dive, as Yakatan had done, sliding down to the ship below, then running after the trader across its hull.

Ropes. It was such a simple, non-magical means to conserve Drook power that could otherwise be directed toward far more important things. Every little expenditure added up, after all. It was just, Charlie didn't expect anything so mundane at this point.

He took a few steps back and launched himself after the others, careful to cast a protective spell for his hands as he grabbed the line and slid down. No rope burns mid-pursuit. That wouldn't be fun and would make any hand-to-hand combat far more uncomfortable.

Bawb was in close pursuit of their prey, and Charlie was catching up to them both now that there weren't throngs of people in his way. Running as a hobby was paying off. Then he saw a familiar shape docked up ahead. The *Ishkoval*.

Yakatan had apparently contacted his ship before Bawb had destroyed his skree and had them reposition the craft, coming down below to meet him. It was still far across the docking space, but if he reached it, the fight would morph into something far less subtle. And far deadlier.

"*We've got to keep him from the ship!*" Charlie silently messaged his friend.

"*I see it,*" Bawb replied, drawing his wand mid-stride.

Charlie didn't think he'd risk hitting any bystanders, but then realized they were still atop a docked ship. Until they made it back to the landing, they were in a clear space.

Yakatan reached the edge of the craft and hurled himself through the air in a powerful leap, the man's surprisingly strong legs carrying him all the way across the deadly gap and onto the platform.

Unfortunately for him, Bawb had anticipated the move, and rather than running faster, the assassin had stopped in his tracks, using both hands to steady his wand as he forced his heart rate to lessen and his breathing to slow.

The thing about his wand was that it had a tendency to release a little more power than intended. Or a *lot* more, as the case often proved to be. It wasn't a flaw of the device itself, but rather a side effect of its unusual construction. The combination of the konus within its wooden shaft and the strand of supercharged Ootaki hair––along with the wood, rendered nearly unbreakably strong by the Balamar Waters Bawb had grown it with––made the whole thing akin to a race engine placed in a normal-looking vehicle. There was simply no low setting, and power *wanted* to be used.

Bawb took careful aim and unleashed a stasis spell, and not a weak one. The wand did the rest, ramping it up many fold as the power flew true, nearly all of the magic striking Yakatan mid-air.

He had made an impressive leap, but he hit the deck and collapsed, his body frozen in place. A few bystanders fell from the effects of the trace, residual magic that had gone astray, but Bawb was okay with that. It wasn't a killing spell, and as they'd only received a small portion of it, they would likely recover soon enough.

Yakatan, on the other hand, would remain quite firmly frozen in place.

Charlie slowed his run, allowing himself a moment to suck down a few massive lungfuls of air before calming his racing heart as his friend had done. By the time the two men scrambled down to claim their captive, neither looked remotely winded from the pursuit, which had taken them far deeper underground than he'd originally realized.

The planet had been a rebel stronghold during the rebellion, and Charlie could see why. With its myriad winding and hidden routes, it would have made a perfect foothold for rebel forces.

Charlie and Bawb walked over to their fallen prey. He was frozen in deep stasis, all right. *Really* deep, from what Charlie could tell.

"Overkill much?" he asked with a chuckle.

"The wand, it tends to get carried away," Bawb replied, the device already safely sheathed and benign in appearance. No one had seen him cast with it. Let them think he'd merely used his konus.

"Uh, Bob?" Charlie said, his hands dropping to the knife on his hip.

"Yes, I see them," the Wampeh replied, a pointy-toothed grin spreading across his face.

He'd been forced to fight and pursue, but had done so with great restraint. But in close quarters like this? Against the dozens of men slowly emerging from the crowd, surrounding them? Restraint would not be an option.

"Lower your weapons," a man who appeared to be the group's leader said. He was quite tall, with short, multi-colored braids of material woven into his hair. His shoulders were both broad and thick with dense muscle. In fact, his entire body seemed chiseled from stone rather than flesh. Charlie knew the race, he'd fought a few of them in his time as a gladiator.

The funny thing about the tough-looking ones was they still bled just as easily as anyone else. Only they just looked more impressive when they did so.

Charlie and Bawb didn't recognize him from Yakatan's crew. In fact, none of the men around them appeared to be from the trader's ship. This was something else.

"Not happening," Charlie said, knife now in hand and his tensed magic ready to uncoil.

"If you fight us, this could be messy," the man said, far too overconfident.

Bawb smiled, flashing his pointed teeth menacingly. "At this moment, I could do with a little messy," he said, his smile and the true nature of the Wampeh it revealed making the men step back a little from the man who could drain them of their power. If they had any, that is.

"This is your final opportunity to stand down," the leader said. "The great Mandoog does not offer second chances."

Charlie perked up. "Mandoog? You work for Mandoog? Hell, he's the man we're looking for," he said, sheathing his knife. "Well, then. Take us to your leader."

CHAPTER FORTY-FOUR

Charlie and Bawb followed the man with the braided hair. Quintz was his name, they learned, and he was one of Mandoog's captains. When word of a disturbance had reached their boss's ears, he'd sent him to quell the unrest. Much like a Mafioso in the old days of Earth, Mandoog––while definitely a dangerous man in his own right––kept the peace in his realm. With an iron fist, if need be.

Commander Yakatan was hoisted up and carried by Quintz's men, leaving Charlie and Bawb free to focus on the route taken and the number of men they might face. They hadn't been disarmed, but they could see why. It appeared nearly every person they passed this deep in the network of the Lowers was one of Mandoog's in one way or another.

After a good ten minutes of walking, they reached what appeared, for all intents and purposes, to be just another doorway. Only the magical wards and booby traps cast around it gave away that it was anything out of the ordinary.

Charlie could feel them with his magic. Normally Bawb would be able to as well, but as he was not wearing his Ootaki hair at the moment, he simply relied on Charlie to suss out any worrisome spells. Nothing threatening to them. Not at the moment, at least. So Charlie gave a little nod and followed Quintz inside.

The vast chamber beyond that innocuous door was really quite impressive, the quality of art and other artifacts on display making Yakatan's little collection pale by comparison. And as for that frozen man, he was dumped unceremoniously at the feet of the very rotund, yet also very powerful man sitting in what could almost be called a throne, though it was really just a gilded seat large enough to accommodate his substantial frame.

Golden robes covered the bald-headed, bronze-skinned man's bulging flesh, but it was clear enough that he enjoyed the finer things his station afforded him, and one such thing was food, apparently. But given the way his men averted their gaze in his presence, the power he wielded, though not magical in nature, was proportional, if not greater, than his physical mass.

Mandoog looked at the inert shape of Commander Yakatan and spat with disgust.

"Yakatan. I should have known," he said with a rumbling bass voice. He then turned his amber-eyed gaze to the newcomers. "But what of you two? Making quite a stir, from what I hear. And a Wampeh of your nature? Unusual in these parts."

"We are sorry to have disturbed you, Mandoog," Bawb said, taking the lead as his status as *that* sort of Wampeh seemed to give him clout. "We had negotiated a transaction with this man, but he attempted to double-cross us, his men attacking as we were to complete our deal. He then fled down here, likely thinking himself safe in the maze of the Lowers. I apologize sincerely for disturbing your realm."

Mandoog liked what he heard, and having a Wampeh of this rarity and power show any form of submission in front of his men would only enhance his clout. So far, this discussion was starting on the right footing.

"I can see your reasoning for your actions," Mandoog said. "And I accept your contrition. Now tell me, what exactly was it that this scum was attempting to swindle you for?"

Bawb didn't hesitate, even in front of all of Mandoog's men. There was no sense playing coy. Time was running out, and they had no choice.

"Yakatan was taking us to a man he said possessed information we need. Information about the fleet no one will talk about. The visla whose name none will say aloud," Bawb said.

"Oh?" Mandoog said, curiosity piqued. "And what were you willing to trade to speak with this man?"

"To open trade routes with an entirely new system, great Mandoog. One never before opened to commerce with any of the civilized systems," Bawb replied. "Exclusive. An opportunity to forge an entirely new commerce agreement with a new partner."

Mandoog studied the two men before him a moment. They appeared ordinary enough when they had arrived in his realm, that much he knew from his men, whose eyes were everywhere. But there was more to them than that. This intrigued him.

"I already know the answers you seek, and I can provide you that information," he finally said. "And at the same price Yakatan had offered."

"Fantastic. Then let us––"

"*But*" Mandoog interrupted, "this visla is very powerful. So powerful there is talk that none can stand before him in combat and survive."

"Not liking the sound of that, Bob," Charlie quietly said.

"Nor I. Though we've heard that of others in the past, have we not?"

"We will take our chances," Bawb finally replied.

"Not without the right weapon," Mandoog countered. "And I'll not risk being exposed for giving you this information unless you stand a chance of actually defeating him. And I happen to know of a powerful weapon that is purported to be able to defeat this particular visla should it but touch his skin."

"Then we shall acquire this weapon," Bawb said as though it were no big deal.

Mandoog laughed, amused at the man's confidence. "Oh, it is not so simple as that, I'm afraid. And the path to it is one none have been able to follow. But you are *motivated*, it would seem, so I'll make you this offer. Retrieve the ancient weapon, and I will give you the information you seek. With that power in hand, I will even join you and help you destroy them myself."

"Seems straightforward enough," Charlie said.

"The last who said that perished in the flames, just as all who tried before them have."

"Flames?" Charlie asked.

"You'll see," Mandoog said with a wry smile. "The directions are quite cryptic, yet there is no doubt as to their provenance."

"A riddle?" Bawb asked.

"Not exactly. But more of an impossible task. One I am hoping you are motivated enough to overcome," Mandoog said. "*Slafara flames kiss the ring, the guide, the map, to greet the king.*"

"Poetry?" Charlie asked, confused.

"Prophecy," Mandoog replied. "Do what none have been able and figure out how to retrieve what we seek, and my services are at your disposal."

Bawb nodded at Charlie. They had no choice.

"We shall undertake this task," he said.

"Good luck, my new friends. You'll need it."

Charlie and Bawb moved to haul Yakatan's inert form up between them.

"You may leave that traitor with me. My men will put him in storage pending your return," Mandoog said.

Charlie shrugged. "Works for me."

"And me," Bawb agreed, dropping Yakatan back to the

ground. "Thank you for this hospitality, Mandoog. We shall see you again soon, if all goes well."

"I will have one of my men show you to the surface. I assume you will find your way to your vessel without further aid."

"Thank you, Mandoog. That is correct," Bawb said.

Mandoog nodded to a lithe brown-skinned man with piercing silver eyes. "This way," the man said, leading them out into the winding maze of streets and tunnels.

The door closed behind them, leaving the human and his Wampeh friend to make the long trek back to the surface. Inside, Mandoog summoned his most powerful caster.

"Tinko, can you please undo this spell? Our poor Yakatan seems to have gotten himself into something of a bind," Mandoog said.

"Of course, Mandoog," the caster replied, summoning his power and focusing on the inert man on the ground. He strained and strained, but, it seemed, his magic couldn't put a dent in the spell Bawb's wand had cast.

"My apologies, Mandoog. I do not know how it is possible, but this spell is too strong for me to break. Far too strong."

Yet another unusual occurrence with these newcomers. They seemed to indeed be more than initially met the eye.

"Very well," Mandoog said. "Thank you for your efforts."

The caster left the way he came. His boss looked down on the frozen man lying before him.

"I'm sorry, my friend. It seems you're going to have to stay that way for the time being. At least until they return with my prize. And when they do, we shall be ready for them with all the magic at our disposal. We will take it from them and present it to the visla. After so many years of quiet, loyal service, I'm sure he will reward us handsomely for it."

CHAPTER FORTY-FIVE

Poor Kip was at a loss. The normally spunky AI ship had been directed and redirected to more than a few different locales on this world in the past few days, and each time his friends were braving unknown dangers, while all he could do was sit quietly on the landing pad and wait.

He had no choice. For the AI ship to make his consciousness known would be a big mistake. One that could force them to flee the entire planet, even.

It was tough going on Hunze and Dukaan as well. They'd missed the window for the portal and now would have to wait the remainder of the week until it reappeared. What had begun as a somewhat pressing urgency had become far more of a ticking clock, and they were well aware of that fact.

They'd quickly changed tactics from overtly asking if people knew of a large fleet forming in some distant system. The scared looks more than a few people gave them at those words told them more than enough. This was taboo. They'd have to be far more careful in sussing out what they needed.

Fortunately, they had finally managed to track down a well-connected trader, one who happened to also deal in black market items for his off-book clientele. It was that man who––after accepting a portable power wrench as payment, a device the likes of which he'd never seen in the galaxy––directed them to find a fellow named Olosnah. The smuggler captain was said to be more than a bit of a rascal, but one who could find them what they needed...for a price.

And what they needed was a very specialized caster. One who could pinpoint a location by magical signature alone, guiding a ship across the vast distances between systems unerringly. Hunze was unable to lock in to the magical signature of the portal's connection with Earth's sun, but one who specialized in that very niche skill should be able to do so without significant problems once they had the general location.

And that was the thing they didn't have. The portal could have been anywhere. For that reason, they needed information as well as navigational skill. And it seemed the smuggler could provide them with both.

They hoped.

If his knowledge of back channels and hush-hush goings-on was legit, he could be a most helpful ally indeed.

"Is this really the place?" Dukaan asked, eyeing the filthy exterior of the establishment. On an advanced world such as this, it stood out for its lack of sophistication. In fact, the little cantina seemed for all appearances to be a wretched hive of scum and villainy.

"We go where we were told," Hunze said, opening the door, releasing a wafting funk of smoke and sweat. "We simply do not have a choice at this point."

She stepped into the dimly lit interior, her Chithiid friend in tow, both hoping they'd end this day as they'd started. Namely without conflict.

Dukaan asked the bartender where he might find this Olosnah fellow. The woman gave him a questioning look. "Are you sure that's who you want to talk to? I know several other pilots who would be glad for the work, and at half the price."

"I appreciate your offer, but it is Olosnah we seek."

The bartender shrugged and pointed across the room to a light-blue-skinned man with his back to the wall and his feet on the table as he casually surveyed the room. He'd obviously seen the newcomers enter, just as he'd noted the bartender pointing him out.

Yet he stayed just as he was, his fingers gently tapping his leg. The fingers, however, had a thick konus riding on the wrist above them, and it was ready for action.

Hunze and Dukaan crossed through the crowd to his table.

"Are you Olosnah?" Dukaan asked.

"Depends. What do you want?"

"We have come to discuss a trade in exchange for information."

"No smuggling?"

"No, nothing of the sort. We are simply seeking knowledge, as well as one who can help us procure the services of a particularly unique navigator."

The blue man stroked his chin in thought a moment, looking over the unusual pair. The one with four arms was unlike any species he'd ever seen before. The woman at his side was barely visible under her hood, but he did think she had nicely shaped lips.

"And you can pay?"

"Handsomely, Mr. Olosnah," Dukaan replied.

"Call me Olo," he said. "And we really shouldn't talk here. The walls have eyes and ears, you know."

He rose from his seat, bumping into a burly ochre-skinned man with horned protrusions sprouting from the back of his head.

"Watch yourself!" the man grunted.

"What was that?" Olo asked, as if offended.

"I said watch where you step, you stupid––"

He didn't get any further, his sentence abruptly punctuated with a fierce right hook that sent him to the ground in a heap.

"Come on," Olo said, hurrying for the door.

Dukaan and Hunze didn't know what else to do but follow him.

"I thought you said we were being watched," Hunze hissed, clearly displeased at his drawing attention to them.

"Oh, we were, Princess, but we couldn't just get up and walk away. That would draw attention, seeing as you had only just arrived. That's why I created us a little diversion. You see, Azok there runs with a pretty unsavory group. It would only make sense I'd want to clear out after our little incident."

Dukaan smiled. "A misdirection. Most clever."

"Thanks. Now, let's go somewhere we can talk privately."

Olo's quarters were located in a surprisingly nice section of the city. The streets were clean, the buildings all gleaming and new. It was quite a dichotomy, the shift between his home and the less than reputable cantina he'd been frequenting.

They stepped inside, Olo first disarming an alarm and booby trap spell, which he reactivated the moment the door had closed behind them.

"You can never be too cautious," he said. "Please, have a seat. Make yourselves comfortable."

Dukaan and Hunze did just that, sinking down into the spotless chairs in his likewise pristine abode.

"So, you say all you want is information, eh? That, and a navigator?"

"Yes," Hunze said. "But a highly specialized one at that."

"Oh, I know the most skilled navigators in forty systems. But can you pay?"

She nodded.

"This might be the easiest job I've had in months. Now, what exactly is this other thing you need? Inside information on which cargo shipments are going to be targeted by pirates? Or perhaps the whereabouts of a wayward husband? Or wife? Whatever, I don't judge."

"We need to know in which system someone is amassing a secret fleet," Hunze said. "It is likely a visla at the helm. But that is all we know. None will talk about it."

The blue man went silent. "You realize what you're asking? How dangerous it is to even bring that up?"

"We've come to that realization," Dukaan noted.

Olo thought about it a moment. "What you're after is hard information to come by. And pricey. *Very* pricey. Now, if the Council was still running things, it would be fairly easy to get that intel you want. That sort of regimented structure always lends itself to back channels and graft. But they all but disbanded ages ago."

"So it is true? The Council is no more?" Hunze asked.

"Essentially," he replied. "Though you were right about the fleet. Everyone knows, but no one will talk about it. They have spies everywhere, you see. But yes, a massively powerful visla has been quietly consolidating power among systems for some time."

"So you know where this fleet currently is?" Dukaan asked.

"No. But I can find out. Mind you, it won't be easy, and it sure as hell won't be cheap."

"We're willing to pay," Hunze said.

Olo laughed. "Oh, Princess. For that kind of risk, I'll need something far better than coin if I'm going to be putting my neck on the line for that information."

Reluctantly, Hunze pulled back her hood.

"An Ootaki?" Olo said, stunned. "A *free* Ootaki?"

Hunze didn't reply. There was no collar around her neck, and that was answer enough. Slavery had been eradicated.

Mostly, anyway. But it seemed certain power beings were simply too valuable to both sides of the fight to be set free.

She reached up and carefully plucked a single, lengthy hair from her head.

Olo went as pale as a blue man could. "Are you actually *freely* offering me––"

Hunze snapped the hair right at the middle. "Half now. Half later," she said, handing over the incredibly powerful strand.

"Done!" Olo blurted, eyes wide as he took the offered hair, the magic tangible in his fingertips despite his being a non-magical being.

"We will also need supplies," Dukaan added. "Food, and beverage."

"Whatever you want, this more than covers it," the smuggler said, still unable to believe his good fortune.

"You will be cautious, of course?" Dukaan asked, noting the gleam in the man's distracted eyes.

"What? Oh, of course I will," Olo said. "Their eyes may be everywhere, but so are mine." He carefully coiled the golden strand and tucked it into an inner pocket. "Now, this will take some time. What you have asked is not easy. But I will have the information you require within five days."

Hunze and Dukaan shared a look. They knew their time was tight, but they had no choice but to agree.

"In the meantime, I'll give you the name and location of my most trusted supplier. He will outfit you with whatever you need for your journey."

"You won't be coming with to make the introduction?" Dukaan asked.

"I can't be overtly connected to you two from here on out. I'm sure you understand. The attention two offworlders like you are already drawing would spill over to me and make my life difficult. It'll already be hard enough to explain us speaking earlier, but I'll find Azok and buy his cooperation."

"The man you punched?" Hunze asked.

"Yeah. He's a bastard, but he'll forgive my attack for enough coin. And with that, I'll be distanced from you enough to do my work."

He produced a small location skree and handed it over. "Torbin's location is on this. Find him and he'll take care of you. He'll know you're coming."

Rather than share false pleasantries, Hunze and Dukaan rose to leave the man to his task and get on with theirs.

"I'll send word when I have what you need," Olo said. "And if you don't mind, would you please leave by the back door?"

CHAPTER FORTY-SIX

Hunze and Dukaan had taken a circuitous route back to their craft from Olo's place. It had taken a bit longer than they'd anticipated, and the worried AI was overjoyed at their return.

"I didn't know what was going on," Kip said. "I couldn't pick you up on scans, and there were all sorts of snooping people coming around, checking me out. It was all I could do to not say anything."

"But you didn't, and that's what matters, Kip. If these people realized you were a ship that could talk, we'd be in an even deeper pile of trouble than we already are," Dukaan said.

"Trouble? What happened?" the AI asked.

"The Council is apparently no more," Hunze replied, slipping into her seat. "And this new visla who is amassing a fleet is apparently both mysterious and feared."

"So what does that mean for us?" the ship asked.

"It means it is going to be much more difficult to acquire the location of the systems where they have been amassing their craft," Dukaan replied. "Which means it will be harder for us to find a starting point that is within reach of the navigator we are going to be partnering up with."

"Oh, you found one? That's great news!"

"Well, we found a man who knows where to find a power user of sufficient skill and strength to do what we require. But we will still need to have a general idea of where those ships are so we can position ourselves near enough for the navigator to detect the traces of Earth's power flowing through the portal," Hunze said. "It is not ideal."

"No," Dukaan agreed. "No, it is not. But we do possess means to resupply for this journey, thanks to Hunze's selfless sacrifice," he added.

"Sacrifice?"

"It was just a strand of hair, Dukaan," the Ootaki said, downplaying her part in making the deal happen.

"Yes, a strand of hair. The very thing that caused you to be enslaved for nearly your entire life, Hunze. That you were willing to do this is not unnoted."

"It's just a single strand," she said.

"And if you continue to pay for services with them, you could very well wind up bald one day," he replied with a grin. "Let us hope it never comes to that, shall we?"

"A good idea," she replied. "Now, as for those supplies. Kip, we have the location of a resupply facility in another city. We'll need you to take us there."

The little ship was thrilled for the opportunity to do something besides sit around and wait. "Excellent! Point the way, and let's go!"

The city they were directed to was not too far from the one Olosnah resided in, but in that short distance the standards and quality of living conditions as well as overall commerce shifted drastically.

It wasn't rough and horrid like the city where they had fled the arena owner and his lackeys, by any means, but it was not a gleaming beacon of civilization like the one they'd just departed.

It was a workers' city, basically. The place for the lower class to come home to every night after toiling away in the nearby metropolis.

Kip followed the directions Hunze read out for him and easily found the nondescript, low building toward the outskirts of town. It wasn't a typical resupply and logistics station, that much was obvious. In fact, the whole facility had the feel of a converted residential complex.

When they landed just outside and were ushered into the building, they realized they weren't so far from the truth with that assessment.

The outside did indeed look like housing and offices, but past the façade was a vast warehouse space rather than small living and work divisions. The building had been gutted of interior walls for the purpose.

"Olo called by skree and said you would be coming," the man who introduced himself as Torbin the Great said, showing them to his wares. "He also said to fix you up with whatever you need, and I do mean *whatever*."

"We will require rations," Dukaan said. "Our vessel has limited resources, so we will require items that will remain fresh for the span of weeks, if not months, in addition to fluids."

"You want food? I've got food," Torbin said, directing their attention to row after row of packaged and magically sealed delicacies.

There was a robust black market indeed, it seemed. All the more reason for the exchange to be kept quiet, just like their arrangement with Olo. They had plenty of time, seeing as it would be days before the blue smuggler had the intel they needed to move ahead with their plan, so the pair took their time walking the warehouse, carefully picking out the items that might come in handy.

They were all tagged, ready for Torbin's men to bundle up and load onto Kip, when Hunze noticed something in one of the many crates of skrees, slaaps, and other magical weaponry. Most of the items were dented and well-worn. Some even still bore the bloodstains of the previous owner.

But one thing caught her eye. A graceful, yet deadly sword of medium length. Its blade had a slightly blue hue to it, and the grip was designed for ease of use either single or doublehanded. A vespus blade, she somehow knew.

Hunze had been a slave her whole life, so there was no way she could possibly know what it was. In fact, only a select few of the most secretive order of assassins would. But it just so happened she had shared knowledge with just such a man.

It was his memories that flashed through her mind when she picked up the sword and ran her hand across the flat side, feeling the traces of very old magic that still, just barely, lived on inside it, lingering, waiting for the right hands to reawaken it with their touch.

Hundreds of years of misuse by non-magical beings with no idea what they were holding had left it dull, its metal worn and unhoned. But with care, it might be restored. An enchanted sword of the Wampeh Ghalian. One that could power the most arcane of spells in the right hands.

A gift for Bawb, should they survive this ordeal and she ever manage to find him again.

No. I will *find him*, she decided. It was not up to fate. She would make it so, no matter what.

"How about this?" she asked Torbin.

"That beat-up old thing? Hell, it's junk. I can get you a much nicer sword if you like."

"No, this one has caught my eye. It is a most interesting weapon."

"And old and beat-up," the black market trader repeated. "Tell ya what. It's just taking up space, and you're Olo's people, so go ahead and take it. You'll be doing me a favor getting it off my hands. I'll even throw in some cleaning oils and a whetstone too."

Hunze bowed her head slightly, a warm smile of gratitude on her lips. "Thank you, Torbin," she said, sheathing the sword and placing it with their other supplies.

They would have downtime, and now she had something more to do than wait around. She had a gift for her love, just waiting to be brought back to its former glory. And the golden-haired woman felt confident she'd restore it to exactly that, given the time.

And time, for now, time was something they both lacked, yet had, in abundance.

CHAPTER FORTY-SEVEN

It had taken the entire night, and nearly all of the following day before Grundsch and his four-legged companion were finally able to sniff out the visla's daughter's trail. Visanya had taken them straight to the location of the incident just minutes after she had informed Kara's father of the kidnapping, but Bahnjoh could not pick up the scent.

"Magic," Grundsch grumbled, knowing full well his non-magical pet simply did not possess the necessary skills to overcome magical scent masking.

If you wanted something dead, Bahnjoh was the one you wanted. Likewise if you needed to intimidate or otherwise scare a person. And the beast was a fine tracker too, when magic wasn't being deployed against him. Unfortunately, that was the case in this instance.

Word of the issue reached the visla's security team, and they promptly sent out a rather specialized casting team to assist in the hunt. The resource was there, and none of them wanted to disturb their master, especially not while his wife was calming his crackling magical ferocity.

"Multiple spells," a skinny, yellow man named Horkin said

as he read the traces of magic that clung to the fabric of the city in the area of the attack. "Some were crude. Hasty. But one of them seems very well cast. Surprisingly so, in fact."

"That's fine and good, but can you overcome them?" Grundsch asked, his canine associate pacing anxiously at his side.

"It will be difficult," Horkin said. "But I believe with our combined abilities, the others and I should just barely be able to topple the strongest of them. The others will fall in the process."

"That's all I needed to know," Grundsch said, scratching Bahnjoh behind the ears, making the ferocious beast's leg thump involuntarily with pleasure from the sensation.

The spells masking Karasalia's trail fell fairly quickly once the casters got their spells attuned to the flavor of magic that had been used to cast the blocks, and soon they were off, tracking the undisguised scent throughout the city. Bahnjoh led the way, his sensitive nose easily discerning his mistress's scent from the rest of the bustling city.

Well, mostly bustling. When people saw Bahnjoh, Grundsch, and the visla's other men coming their way, and not looking very happy about it, everyone tended to scatter to more friendly climes.

It had been a long night of tracking, then waiting, while the casters dismantled yet another magical block. Whoever had carried out the kidnapping, it was more than just a hasty snatch-and-grab attack. They'd planned this, judging by the quality and quantity of magic used to make their escape. But it was only a matter of time before they were discovered. The visla would make sure of it.

Morning came and passed through to day, yet they had still not found the teen anywhere. Most annoyingly, the trail had looped back on itself several times, a different layer of masking spells concealing the newer trail until they'd already headed off following the older one.

It was a time-stalling tactic, but it was working well. Yet by evening, no ransom demand had reached the high tower. That in and of itself was unusual enough to raise questions, but before they could be voiced, they finally traced the girl's scent to an industrial building on the far side of town.

"Do we call the visla?" Horkin asked, looking exhausted from the lengthy and continued drain of his magic.

"We go in. Now," Grundsch said, slipping a wrist gauntlet onto his arm.

He was not able to cast, but he had no desire to anyway. And this gauntlet was from his own world. A piece of tech that the visla had modified with magic, rendering it inoperable against him or his family and staff. But these kidnappers weren't his, and Grundsch would finally get to have a little fun with his power whip.

And that was how he would use the device once they breached the building, the length of energy spitting out and grabbing the nearest man before he could cast a defensive spell. Grundsch knew he only had a moment to attack if they had konuses or skrees on them, so he wasted no time with pleasantries such as asking for surrender.

Bahnjoh, likewise, simply leapt into the fray, injuring several, while outright killing a few others. The other men swarmed the building as the fight raged, using the distraction to locate Kara and stun the caster who had been guarding her.

It was a lucky spell that had knocked the man out. One that snuck in past his defenses as he was distracted by the enormous beast tearing his lackeys to bits. The other Tslavars soon lay dead or dying, but this one, their leader, it seemed, was taken entirely intact. The visla would be pleased.

Kara was worn out but otherwise unharmed, and Grundsch, despite his gruff nature and the fact he served the visla solely because he wore the man's control collar, nevertheless found himself feeling relieved at the sight of the girl.

She had treated him well, ever since the day he first arrived at their home. And he'd watched her grow into young womanhood, her kindness never faltering, not even where the strange alien tasked with guarding her was concerned.

He carried her exhausted form all the way back home, not once pausing or shifting her load to another of the group, though they did offer.

The visla was beside himself with relief when his servant carried her to her room and laid her on her bed. He quickly cast a general sleep spell to help her recover from the ordeal, then proceeded to cast another spell. One that ensured no harm had been done to her.

"Intact," he said, relieved. She was returned to him unsullied, and for that he was grateful.

Visla Palmarian went to his offices and sat for a moment, sipping a strong drink, centering his thoughts.

"Bring him," he finally called to his guards.

The Tslavar was taken from his temporary cell and ushered into the visla's presence. He expected to be immediately struck and tortured, but the visla merely sat and stared at him, not saying a word. In some ways, that was worse than physical abuse. The wondering what might befall him.

Finally, the visla spoke.

"You took my child from me," he said with a soft, yet menacing growl. "And you are of this place. There is no possibility you did not know whose daughter she was."

The Tslavar remained silent, squirming under the man's intense gaze.

"Now, there are two ways we can go about this," Palmarian continued. "I can ask and you can respond, or you can be stubborn." He paused, fixing his disconcerting stare on the kidnapper. "Trust me when I say, you do not wish to be stubborn."

The Tslavar seemed conflicted, as if he almost feared

something even more than the visla, but then he made a decision.

"Visla Palmarian," he began. "You have to know, I meant no harm to your daughter. It was only at the beh—"

The prisoner suddenly began to choke, and moments later, green blood started pouring from his eyes, his ears, his nose, and his mouth, as he collapsed to the floor.

At that inopportune time, Mareh entered the office. "Dearest, I heard our daughter is back safe. I wanted to—"

She saw the bloody, lifeless man on the ground before her and came to an abrupt stop, spinning away from the sight, her body heaving as she nearly vomited.

Visla Palmarian quickly cast a distortion spell, masking the grisly sight, rushing to his wife's side, his wrath suddenly an afterthought.

"Darling, are you all right? I'm sorry you had to see that."

"What did you do to him?" she asked, horrified.

"I did nothing," he replied. "This was not my doing."

"But the man. His body. It was obviously magic."

"Yes, but not by my hand, I swear."

"If not you, then whom?" Mareh asked, regaining her composure.

"I do not know," the visla replied. "Someone placed a suicide spell on the man. A fail-safe should he be captured, to prevent him from speaking. I'm afraid I won't be learning who employed these men from his lips."

Mareh took his face in her hands and looked deep into her husband's eyes. "Tell me. Tell me truthfully. What's happening, Nikora?"

"I have enemies," he said after a long pause. "There is a power struggle. There always is. And it falls to me to deal with this. And with what has just transpired, there is apparently more urgency than ever. I will have to deal with this sooner than anticipated."

"But what about Kara?"

"She is to stay indoors for the time being," he said, casting a modification to the building's permissions spells. "I've blocked her from leaving the premises," he informed his wife. "All exits will lock, and security will be notified if she tries to leave."

"But isn't that a bit harsh? It wasn't her fault, after all."

"No, but they will use her to get to me. This is for her own good," he replied.

Mareh knew better than to press the matter, but she knew full well that when Kara finally woke, she would not be happy to hear the news. But she was the visla's daughter, and with that distinction also came drawbacks. And at the moment, that drawback was being locked in a tower, unable to escape.

CHAPTER FORTY-EIGHT

Several days had passed since Leila had visited her former home. Captain Sandah had been gracious, not questioning the delay or why his impromptu passenger seemed so moved by a deserted estate untouched for centuries.

Leila had kept her ties to the planet––and her past––to herself, naturally. Time travel would freak out even the most hardy of crews, after all, and these men and women were certainly a tough bunch.

But when Leila quietly rejoined them after her time on the unexpected stopover, the way she carried herself, and the quiet, visceral nature of her reaction to the place they all could sense, had inspired a quiet politeness from the crew when she finally returned to the ship.

If you'd asked any of them why, however, they wouldn't have been able to give a clear answer other than it seemed the right thing to do.

She had left the craft empty-handed, and she returned the same. Or so it seemed. But tucked deep in her most secure pocket was a small tube containing two things. The last note to her from her father, and a small scrap of paper with a few deceptively simple words and a blank space for her name.

Anyone could attempt to use the spell, of course, filling in their name, trying to bond it to themselves. But to do so would achieve nothing. The stone had belonged to Leila's mother, and her mother's before her.

Unlike many of the stones stolen from families over the years, this one had been protected, several generations bolstering the spell, keeping it safe. As a result, the Magus stone was tied to her bloodline, and none but the most powerful and skilled of vislas would even stand the remotest chance of ever breaking that bond.

She had said the words softly as she sat beside her father's grave, reading from the scrap of parchment in a woman's hand and filling her name in the blank. The writing was not her mother's, though. In fact, the little scrap was so old, so delicate, that Leila thought it was likely the same hand-written spell handed down from generation to generation.

Had it been her grandmother who wrote it? Her great-grandmother? Someone even older? Sadly, her family was all long gone, and there would be no answer to that question.

When she finished the spell, Leila prepared herself for whatever the stone would do, the dark green heirloom hanging warmly around her neck. But nothing happened.

Her father's note had said its power would be hers when it sensed she was ready.

"What does that even mean?" she wondered as she sat in the weeds beside her father's bones. "I've been a slave, yet also a queen. I've traveled between galaxies, through time, even, and I've made a life in a new realm powered not by magic, but by tech. And I've fought off invaders on more than one occasion, the Magus stone helping me without my even trying or knowing how. But now? What more does it need for me to be ready?"

The sky and stones had no answers for her as she sat there,

but it was there she remained a good long while regardless. The sun was low in the sky by the time she finally returned to Captain Sandah's ship, at peace, though perhaps a little confused.

"I'm ready to go when you are, Captain," she said, taking one last look at the place she'd known her entire life, so long ago.

"I'll tell the men," he replied. "They've been foraging. Gathering some fresh provisions. The land is fecund and possesses a surprising many edibles, and game is plentiful."

"Yes, it would be," she replied, thinking back to the time when she maintained the visla's animals while her father tended to his gardens. "Please don't rush your men on my behalf. They should enjoy the fresh air as long as you see fit."

The captain nodded, pleased with her considerate answer, leaving the foraging parties to their own devices a bit longer before calling in the last of them with his skree.

It was dark when they finally took to the air once more, gently rising up into the void of space, leaving Visla Maktan's former seat of power to the weeds and dust.

"Still no word?" Leila asked after they'd completed yet another jump to yet another system in search of Eddie and Ripley, but to no avail.

"I'm sorry, Leila, but thus far we have been unable to find even a trace of your friends."

"They were heading to a system where a large fleet of warships had amassed."

"Yes, so you have previously said."

"Well, what about there?" she asked.

"Unfortunately, there has been no word from any of the skree inquiries I've made of other captains throughout the systems. But perhaps we will have better luck when we make planetfall at Oralius. It is a lovely world, and Visla Palmarian is well respected there."

"Let's hope so," Leila said with a pleasant expression on her face.

But inside, she couldn't help but find it odd that Captain Sandah hadn't heard a peep about the mysterious fleet. He was Visla Palmarian's man, after all, and that carried significant weight, from what she'd seen thus far.

They landed in the brightly lit spaceport on Oralius in the early evening. Of course, with the orbital rate and rotation of the planet, evening lasted nearly twenty hours, and a full day was closer to seventy-six.

Captain Sandah made arrangements for her to meet with the most respected captains in the area, and even offered to accompany her personally to ensure her access to them. It was a kind gesture, and she was glad for the presence of the captain and his escort, seeing as she was a stranger on a strange world, yet again.

But as they spoke to the various captains and commanders, she noted an occasional shift in their demeanor when she strayed from the script and asked not about her friends, but rather, the mystery fleet.

All professed no knowledge of such a fleet. However, while several of them said no, their eyes said yes. They also made it clear their lips would remain sealed, no matter who was at her side. It was all most unusual, and more than a little disconcerting.

"I'm afraid I can only continue this pursuit of your friends for a few more days, then I will have to return to the visla's service. He often has tasks for me, and it would not do for me to be absent should he require me for them."

"I understand," Leila said. "And I truly appreciate all of the effort you've put into helping me."

"It is a great honor to be of service," the captain replied.

Leila believed the man. Partly, at least. He seemed a genuinely nice sort, yet something felt off about the whole affair. There was something he was not telling her, but what, exactly, she had no idea. Hopefully, she'd learn before they returned to the visla's base of operations on Slafara.

But at least she had time, though not in the way she would have chosen. Leila had been keeping track despite the odd measure of days in this system. Her window to reach the portal had come and gone, and it had slipped into its weekly schedule for the next several appearances before it would become locked into the sun's burning mass indefinitely.

CHAPTER FORTY-NINE

The *Fujin* was holding up just fine with the stresses of repeated warps so close together. The ship was sturdy as hell and could take far more of a beating than mere warps could produce—even faulty ones that didn't quite take it where it was intended to go.

Rika and Jo, on the other hand, were not handling the stress nearly as well. Frustration at day after day of failure, setting coordinates, warping, then mapping just how far off course they had gone was building.

They'd been making amazing progress, all things considered. It was simply a matter of the nuances of warp travel—and the effects this galaxy had upon the systems that made it possible—were so far out of normal parameters that mapping the anomalies was an epic undertaking.

Even with an accurate star map to their desired destination, they were still having to correct course drastically after every tiny warp. And that was how they had to travel, for to attempt a long warp could throw them so far off course they'd have no chance of getting back on it even with a map.

During one of their first lengthy calculating sessions, Jo had taken the opportunity to utilize the unique characteristics of her cybernetic body and extract the Nasturian shrub she had ingested from her system.

Despite her being an artificial being and having no shyness about her body or its functions, Jo had spared Rika the unpleasantness of witnessing the reclamation process, opting to perform the extraction in the privacy of the ship's head.

Once the spicy meal had been gathered in a receptacle, Jo had then used the equipment in the *Fujin*'s tiny lab space to break the masticated mess into its raw constituent parts. As a result of her labors, they now had a vial of the nasty stuff. Pure Nasturian, and it was all theirs.

Interestingly, Rika said that it did seem there was a naturally occurring magic in the plant residue. They hypothesized it was likely a defensive adaptation the shrub had developed over the years, the magic greatly enhancing the already substantial burning properties of the plant.

Amusingly, that same trait that had protected it for so long was now what put it at greater risk as chefs placed high value on Nasturian, a small portion of the spice used to add heat to a dish costing a pretty penny.

With that realization, the women knew why Jorall had been so persistent once Jo had won the bet. He'd likely spent a good deal of coin just making the dish. Though, to be fair, he likely just used a serving from the batch made up for the other challenger that night. The enormous man who had fled, crying, to the bathrooms after but a few mouthfuls. The one who had failed so miserably where Jo had triumphed.

And that valuable Nasturian was now tucked away for safekeeping, sealed and secure. They didn't know exactly what they'd use it for, but it seemed a useful item to have in any case.

Rika's magically charged tattoos had been back to normal for a few days now, the purple power receded within her. But she had been practicing, and with a little bit of effort, she found she could draw the new magic from the black sun system's rays, bringing the novel power to the surface.

It was tough at first, requiring a fair amount of concentration, but Rika quickly got the hang of it. Part of the ease she had tapping into the dark power was due to her own naturally occurring proclivities for violence.

Long before Malalia had messed with her head, Rika had been known to have something of a temper, and heaven help whoever its blazing gaze was leveled upon.

It was rough going at first when they fled from Jorall and his men. Back then, before she learned to suppress her new magic, the power could flow to the surface without her even noticing at times, the purple making her tattoos glow faintly in the brightly lit craft. It was more than slightly disconcerting to her shipmate, as Jo repeatedly made her aware that a magical discharge in the ship could very well blow them both out into the vacuum. Something neither of them desired.

But then Rika got a feel for the odd new addition to her power. It was a visceral type of magic, and bonded to her system at a cellular level, but Rika had it under control. Enough, at least.

"One more time for shits and giggles," Rika said with a sarcastic grumble as she powered up the warp core.

"Maybe this'll be the lucky one," Jo said.

"Twentieth's the charm," Rika replied, then punched it.

The *Fujin* vanished in a crackling blue flash, then reappeared light years away in a different system. Or more accurately, at the edge of one.

Jo looked at the twin suns and checked the star chart, then checked again.

"What is it, Jo?" Rika asked.

"Gimme a minute, will ya?"

"You're a supercomputer. You don't need a minute, as you keep reminding me," Rika shot back with amusement.

Jo confirmed her readings one final time with the ship's navs and locations logs. "Holy crap. This is it," she said.

"This? I don't remember it looking––" Then Rika remembered exactly how she'd arrived in this system, this *galaxy,* in the first place. Namely, aboard a crashing ship. Not much time for sightseeing under those circumstances.

"We're a pretty far way out," she said, the normally invisible tattoos around her eyes starting to glow a faint white as she surveyed the system laid out before them. "But at least we're finally here. It's just a matter of––"

Her tattoos flashed purple, the fine design around her eyes glowing with menace.

"We're not alone," she said.

"I don't see anyone," Jo replied.

"Shimmer ships. I can see them. All spaced out at random intervals. Or at least, it seems random. Whatever it is they did down on the Balamar Wastelands, it seems they really don't want anyone going down there," Rika said.

Jo rolled her shoulders like a prize fighter before a bout. "Then that's all the more reason to go down there, don'tcha think?"

Rika smiled. "Oh, yeah. Just gimme a minute, okay?"

"All the time you need," Jo said.

Rika focused her magic, sending everything to her eyes that she could. The white glow shifted to purple until the two mixed, leaving her with a strong violet glow. Amazingly, she discovered she could see not only the cloaked ships, but also the spells they'd cast around them. Spells that would allow them to sniff out the Earth girl and her friend.

"Not gonna be easy," she said, eyeing the spells hanging in space.

That was a novel skill, and one no other seemed to possess. The ability to see spells where they lay. Booby traps designed for one purpose. Namely, keep absolutely everyone from going down to the planet's surface. Rika told Jo as much.

"So, what do we do?" the cyborg asked.

Rika smiled. "We sneak down there," she replied. "Right under their noses. Thread the needle between their spells and stay out of visual range until we make atmos. And then we do a slow entry to keep superheating of the hull to a minimum. Should keep us unnoticed all the way from here to the surface," she said cockily.

"Can you do that?" Jo asked.

"I've got a pretty hefty load of magic in my system," Rika said. "I'm pretty sure I can." She rolled her shoulders and gently took hold of the controls. "Okay, I'm gonna thread the needle. Hang on."

CHAPTER FIFTY

It was a lengthy flight, dodging random orbiting debris while carefully staying clear of not only the cloaked ships dotting the system, but also the tripwire spells left as floating magical spacemines, ready to snare any foolish enough to ignore the embargo on traffic to the forbidden planet.

Rika, however, did not have a problem avoiding any of those things with her magically enhanced vision. It was no coincidence that the runic swirls hidden in the flesh around her eyes were different than those of the hunter warriors of the Kalamani people. The shaman had given her a very special gift. One far stronger than any ordinary man or woman could bear.

But Rika was most definitely not ordinary, as he had seen firsthand when she combatted a Tslavar ship and all its men without fear, even when suffering terrible injuries. For that act of selflessness toward his people, she had received her gifts. And now, with the unexpected addition of the strange black sun's pulsing purple magic, she had vision that would put an eagle to shame.

"That ring," she said, pointing to something no one would require enhanced vision to see. "That's where we're going."

It was a perfect circle, fifty miles across. A red sand blot upon an otherwise verdant, green planet. The site of a horrible magic unleashed against a single man, the most powerful visla of his age by far. A man who had likely been Ara's friend, for a time. A man now dead longer than any could remember.

Somewhere down there in the expanse known as the Balamar Wastelands, there would be signs. Clues as to who had taken Rika's old ship, long ago crashed into the planet and left there to the elements before whoever was attacking Earth refitted it with Ootaki hair and a rather nasty set of spells and sent it on its way to the other galaxy.

As they flew low, Rika shuddered a little in spite of her efforts as she remembered the vague instance of her kidnapping. She didn't *remember*, exactly, but Charlie had told her the story of their capture and Shanghai on more than one occasion.

Violence had done against her. Rika's mind had been burned, and this was where her fateful journey had begun. Memories had been lost in that process, stripped from her unceremoniously.

But surprisingly, she was okay with it, for the most part. She'd been remembering a few things here and there, and while she would never fully regain those memories, she was already making good, new ones with her friends.

She wasn't just Rika the space pilot anymore. She was something more, and she didn't know if she'd even want to go back if she could.

"You okay?" Jo asked, noting her silence.

"Yeah, fine. Just thinking," she replied.

Dotting the landscape were piles of stone, some looking like cairns. Rika knew the truth of the structures. Not nature made, but built by man, reduced to rubble when Visla Balamar's home was destroyed.

The shifting of the sands over the years since she'd last been there had entirely buried some of the structural remains, while others that had been beneath the soil when last she was here, had now been uncovered, the same fickle sands that buried some, freeing others.

Up in the distance, something caught her eye. Or her power, to be more precise.

"Do you feel that?" she asked.

"Feel what?" Jo replied.

"Magic. *Familiar* magic. The *Asbrú* was made into a weapon just ahead."

She directed the *Fujin* in close, low and slow, the ship's guns tracking the empty expanse of red soil.

"No signs of anyone," Jo said, reading the scans. "No life signs, and no ships. At least, not that we can see. What's your Supergirl vision telling you?"

"The same. It's empty down there. But this is where she was, I'm sure of it. This is where they launched the *Asbrú* from."

Carefully, she set the *Fujin* down just a little bit away from where she was sensing the magical residue. Better safe than sorry, she figured.

Walking the red soil for the first time in hundreds of years, if you wanted to be literal about it, Rika felt her stomach knotting up ever so slightly as she approached the spot the magic felt the strongest. Yes, this was it. The ship, *her* ship, had rested here for all those centuries until it was taken and turned into a weapon by their enemy. Made into a gateway for invasion.

Opening her senses to the magical remnants, Rika closed her eyes and walked in slow circles, fanning out as she took in the feeling of the magic, trying to discern the unique signatures of the user or users who had designed the Trojan Horse.

"Sonofa––" she blurted, tripping over something in the sand.

She looked down at what appeared to be a gnarled old clump of roots, but she knew there hadn't been proper vegetation here since long before her time. Then she shifted her focus and realized what she'd found.

"Uh, Jo?"

"Yeah?"

"Is that a hand, or am I going nuts over here?"

Jo hurried to her side. "Nope, not going nuts. That's most certainly a hand," the cyborg replied.

The flesh was perfectly intact, the nails close cut, thick callouses visible on the pads of the fingers and palm. Whoever this was, they couldn't have been more than a day in the sand, if that.

"Help me dig him out," Rika said, pulling away the red soil atop the fallen man. "What the hell?" she said, when she reached his torso.

His clothing, it seemed, had almost entirely fallen away, worn thin by countless years exposed to the elements of the wasteland. Only scraps clung to him, but it was enough to preserve his dignity. As much as a frozen man had any, that is.

"He's stasis-locked, Jo," Rika said, pulling him from the dirt and laying him atop it.

She held her hands over him and closed her eyes, tapping into her power to read his body. "He's fine. Just frozen," she said. "Wait, is that another one?"

Rika and Jo quickly rushed to a lump in the soil nearby. Indeed, it was another buried man, frozen in stasis, just like the other.

"What the hell happened here?" Rika asked.

"There's another over here," Jo said. "I think this is a mass stasis spell. And from the look of it, they were pretty indiscriminate who got caught up in it," she said, pointing to a partially buried Tslavar not too far away.

"Friendly fire, huh?" Rika said.

"Yeah, real friendly," her cyborg partner replied with a chuckle.

Rika stood upright, brushing off her hands and resting them on her hips as she surveyed the area. She was beginning to think this was going to be a much more labor-intensive day than she'd anticipated.

Even summoning her magic to help shift the sands, it still took Rika and Jo hours to uncover all of the people buried alive in the red ground, dragging them one by one to a makeshift triage area of sorts outside the dig zone.

They'd found several different species, apparently from opposite sides of a conflict from long ago. One group was composed of a motley assortment of rough-and-tumble sort of men. The others, however, were all Tslavars. And judging by their attire, what was left of it, anyway, they had been Council forces.

The last of the non-Tslavar forces she pulled free from the ground was a fairly tall and particularly well-muscled man with a long scar running from the crown of his head all the way to his collarbone. He was in perfect condition. His clothes, however, were not.

"Oh my," Jo said, noting his shredded pants.

"Uh..." Rika managed to say, then took the pants from a Tslavar roughly the same size––in waist and inseam, at least–– and covered the poor man, though frozen as he was he'd feel neither embarrassment nor the burn from the sun.

"Well, I guess we should separate them into groups now. Tslavars over there, and good guys over here," Rika said.

"How do we know they're the good guys?"

"They were fighting Tslavars," Rika noted. "Good guys in my book."

The two women made quick work of arranging the inert forms, taking care to disarm and bind the hands of the Tslavars, just in case. When they were done, a few dozen frozen survivors lay in the two groups.

"Now what?" Jo asked. "You know how to unfreeze them?"

"Not a clue," Rika replied.

"You think that's all of them?" Jo wondered.

"Lemme check. Hang on a sec," Rika said, her tattoos beginning to glow as she held her bare arms out, feeling into the ground with her magic, just in case they missed one.

No more men were buried there, but there was something else hidden beneath the soil. Big. And metal. A happy smile began to spread across the human spellcaster's face.

"Jo, get the ship and drop me a tow line. There's one more thing we need to retrieve."

CHAPTER FIFTY-ONE

"*Slafara*," Ara said as her eyes fell upon the world as she exited her jump into the tranquil solar system. "*A rather lovely planet. At least, it was, though that was a very, very long time ago. In fact, I haven't been here in nearly eight hundred years, I would have to guess.*"

"*It is a visually pleasing system,*" Bawb agreed. "*Though the riddle seems a bit obvious, does it not?*"

"*So a quick trip to the sun?*" Charlie asked. "*I mean, what else could it be? Some enchanted jewelry belonging to a king is my guess.*"

"*But you know these things are never as simple as that,*" Bawb noted.

"*True. But a guy can hope, can't he?*"

"*Hope can be both a blessing and a curse, my friend,*" the Wampeh replied.

"*Don't I know it,*" Charlie said.

Ara circled the planet once, transcribing a lazy orbit as she and her friends took in the sights. They did not know Visla Palmarian, nor that the capital city was now named for him. What they did note as they flew was that there was a lot of power on that world. Massive, in fact, yet scrambled.

"You guys sense that, right?"

"Yes, Charlie, I smell a strange magic," Ara replied. *"And something else. Something familiar. But it is all so jumbled together."*

"I know. It's almost like it's blocking a proper read, if that's possible," Charlie replied. *"But there's something else. Totally different. And* that *bit's coming from the sun."*

Charlie was right, there was another power signature pulsing out from deep within the burning mass. It was faint, likely masked by the sun itself, but for those as attuned as they were, it was detectable nonetheless. Most would just assume it was the sun's power itself, but knowing what they did, they suspected it was something more than that.

"This has the feeling of a power. Something old. Very old," Ara commented.

"But different than the planet, right?"

"Yes, Charlie. This is something else. But the planetary forces that be can wait. Our quest takes us to this sun, so that must remain our priority."

"What do you suggest we do, Wise One?" Bawb asked as the mighty red dragon drifted just beyond the sun's reach.

"Slafara flames kiss the ring, the guide, the map, to greet the king," she said, reciting the riddle. *"Whatever is inside that sun is what we need."*

"And that would be why no one has been able to get it thus far. It's suicide to fly into the sun. Even for a visla," Charlie noted.

"For some. For most, actually. But for me? Well, I am Zomoki, and old and powerful enough to endure the flames," Ara said.

"You want us to fly into *the sun?"*

"No, Charlie, that would be suicide."

"Thank God, because for a minute there—"

"I will fly into the sun alone," she continued. *"While you and Bawb wait here."*

"I'm sorry, it sounded like you just said Bob and me get to float

around in empty space while you fly directly into a sun," Charlie said.

"That about sums it up," their Zomoki friend agreed. *"I know this system, and I know this sun. It will require effort, but I can protect myself from its heat. For a time, anyway."*

"And if you fail?" Charlie asked.

"Then you are in for an uncomfortable wait until a vessel retrieves you from this place," she replied. *"But let us hope it does not come to that, shall we? Now, free yourselves from your places upon my back and wait here. I will be as quick as I am able."*

Charlie and Bawb, despite their reservations about the whole idea, quickly began unfastening themselves from the harness and were soon drifting free in space. A man and a vampire orbiting a sun, minus the benefit of a ship or planet on which to stand.

"Do hurry back," Bawb said.

"It is my intention," Ara replied, then spun and flew directly toward the faint pull of magic within the sun itself.

Her shape grew smaller and smaller against the burning orb until, finally, they could see her no more.

"So, I guess we'll just wait here, then," Charlie joked over comms.

"It is no wonder what Mandoog said," Bawb mused. "All who would be foolish and greedy enough to attempt this task would certainly perish. The cockiest would assume their magic would protect them, but this is a sun."

"Yeah, kind of beyond the powers even a visla would possess," Charlie noted. "I mean, it's more than just casting. It's in the DNA. I'd imagine that only a Zomoki could stand a chance at surviving, and even then, I bet the younger ones would burst into flames if they tried. Ara's right. Only the oldest, strongest of them would even stand a chance."

"But why would someone hide this relic here? And why something only a Zomoki could retrieve?"

"I don't know, Bob," Charlie said, anxiously watching the pulsing ball of molten plasma for any sign of their friend. "Maybe they trusted Zomoki more than people. I really can't say. But damn. Who would want to hide something in a sun?"

"We did," Bawb pointed out. "The portal."

"Well, yeah. But that was different," Charlie replied.

Movement within the churning sun caught both of their attention as, much to their delight and relief, a glowing red Zomoki pulled her way free of the sun's gravity and flew to her friends.

Ara's scales began to cool to their normal red once she was free from the sun's immediate heat. The specialized harness she'd been wearing, they noted, had been spared from almost all damage.

"I cast a very small, very specific spell on it," Ara said, noting their gazes. "And the equipment still works fine," she added over their comms.

That was when Charlie and Bawb noted what she was carrying. A massive golden band. But it wasn't a control collar. Rather, it was an ancient messaging ring, the secret message it bore in its magically protected core only made visible when exposed to the extreme heat of the sun.

The glowing runic symbols on the superheated band were beginning to fade as it returned to cooler temperatures, but the trio quickly made note of its message.

"Directions," Bawb said. *"And a star chart."*

"Yeah," Charlie grumbled. *"And another freakin' riddle. Ara, you have any ideas?"*

"No, I do not. But seeing as this message is only readable when the ring is immersed in the heat of the sun, I cannot help but wonder if perhaps the person who put it there did not do so on purpose, but rather, perished in the flames while trying to heat it enough to read its message."

It was a valid question, and whose answer they would never

know. All they did know was where they were going next. That, and another riddle. But they'd worry about that when they arrived at the coordinates.

"You going to be okay to jump?" Charlie asked his friend.

"I used a lot of energy just now," she replied. *"I am afraid I will need a little bit of time to recover before attempting a jump."*

"Take your time, Wise One. We do not wish to rush off into the unknown at reduced strength. One can only guess what challenges await us at the next location."

Bawb was right. It could be anything, and if they went there in less than tip-top shape, the chances of failure grew exponentially. Long and short of it, Ara needed to rest.

"Let's find a quiet spot on Slafara where you can recover for a bit, Ara. Once you feel ready, only then will we head on to the next location," Charlie said.

Ara nodded, exhaustion plain to see in her eyes. The two men slid into their seats, and their Zomoki friend quickly flew them to the most remote part of the charming little planet, so tired from her ordeal that she all but ignored the unusual magic on the world, even once she'd landed.

For now, rest was all she wanted, and no sooner had she touched down than she curled herself up and nodded off while her friends stood guard. It would be many hours before she would rise, yet Charlie and Bawb would not let their vigilance slip for a moment.

They did, however, discuss the new riddle, but even by the time she had woken, they were no closer to understanding the cryptic words.

Charlie sighed to himself as they mounted up to begin the next leg of their journey. "Well, I guess we'll find out once we get there."

CHAPTER FIFTY-TWO

Ara had just taken off in the fresh morning air when another person also stepped out on a journey. Only this one's trip was far shorter. Just across town to her best friend's house, in fact.

Visanya had her dull brown hair woven into a long braid that swayed gently as she walked to the front entrance of Visla Palmarian's towering estate. It was a beautiful day, the sun shining bright. As such, she was wearing a sheer, bright outfit that afforded her some comfort in the warm breeze, while complementing her faintly yellow skin.

Given her best friend's inconvenient house arrest-like status, coming to see her at home was their only chance to spend time with one another. With all of the outings they'd planned for the coming month, it was anything but convenient.

"Good morning. I'm here to see Kara," the teen informed the bored security team at the door.

They obviously knew her well over the years, but the formality of checking in was something the visla had insisted upon, no matter who the visitor.

"She's expecting you," the guard said, gesturing to the waiting levitation disc.

"Thanks," she replied brightly, then hopped on and activated the spell that would take her nearly all the way to the top of the building.

"Hey, Vee," Kara said as her friend strode in and dropped her bag on the couch. "I like the outfit."

"Thanks. It was really nice out, so I thought, why not, right?"

"Yeah, it is a gorgeous day," Kara agreed, though she didn't sound terribly thrilled about it.

"And you're stuck in here," her friend commiserated. "But you're looking good. You have some color today," she noted. "You been sleeping better?"

It was true, Kara did seem a bit perkier than usual, the bags under her eyes were fading and her skin seemed a bit less pale.

"Sleep is all right, I guess. It must be all the food Tulagda's been pushing on me. I think Mareh told him to fatten me up while she's gone."

"Ha! Like a sacrificial Bundabist," Vee said with a laugh. "Where is Mareh, anyway?"

"She's off Slafara for the week visiting her friends. And naturally Father is away as well."

"He's always off on business, isn't he?" Vee noted. "He never takes a break."

"I know. There's always something urgent, it seems, and he's the one they call to take care of it."

"Meanwhile, you're locked up here," her friend said.

"It's not fair, Vee. I mean, I get it. He's worried about his daughter. Fine. But I'm not a child anymore, yet he keeps treating me like one," Kara lamented.

"He can't keep you stuck in here forever though. I mean, he'll let you out when he gets back, won't he? We're supposed to be off having adventures and doing fun things, but instead you're stuck indoors."

"Oh, but I still have access to the floating gardens," Kara said sarcastically.

"Forgive me! That makes everything all right, then," Vee said with a laugh. "If Mareh was here, she'd find a way to convince him to let you out. She's cool like that."

"But she isn't, so all I can do for the time being is hang around with you, and maybe bug the heretic once in a while."

"You still talk to her?" Vee asked. "I think she's creepy."

"Maybe, but she's kind of interesting sometimes. And I can't help but wonder what kind of magic she has. I mean, for Father to lock her up like that? There must be something there. And she keeps talking in prophesy riddles."

"Oh?" Vee asked, her curiosity piqued. "Like what?"

"I don't know. Just stuff about me finding a way to be free and fly away. Stuff like that."

"So, things anyone who knows you would be able to say," Vee replied. "You wanting out isn't that big a secret, you know."

"Sure. But it's the way she says it," Kara replied. "Hey, Father is away, and I've still got full access to the *inside* of the building. You wanna go talk to her?"

"Are you serious?"

"Why not?"

"Because she's creepy. I told you," Vee said.

"Oh, don't be a big baby. Let's go talk with her. Maybe she'll even spin a prophesy for you," Kara said, a mischievous look in her eye as she headed for the door. "You coming?"

Reluctantly, Vee followed her friend, opting for the stairs rather than the lift to take them the few levels to the tower's cells. As was the normal state for the magically protected holding facilities, there were no guards on duty. With the visla's layers of spells protecting it, they really weren't necessary.

But if one did happen to come through to make a perfunctory check, the stairs would be the easiest and fastest way to avoid any uncomfortable explanations.

Karasalia walked to the familiar door and knocked, her

knuckles barely making a sound on the thick surface. "Hey, are you awake?" the teen called out in a hushed voice.

Silence greeted her, but then a rustling could be heard through the tiny slot in the door. No words, though. Just the sound of shuffling feet and a body pressing up against the opening.

Kara took a deep breath and calmed her mind, then quietly muttered the words to the negation spell that would allow the heretic to speak. For some reason, it seemed a little bit easier today, and she couldn't help but wonder if it wasn't her father's absence making the spell easier to counteract.

"Did that work? Can you say something now?" she asked.

"Better," a voice croaked from inside the cell.

"Kara, you're casting!" Vee exclaimed. "Like, *really* casting! Does your dad know you can do that?"

"The whole point is him *not* knowing, Vee."

"Well, yeah. But I mean, this is what he's been wanting. To see you show some sign of power."

"Power? He can topple buildings with a few words. This isn't power. This is a party trick," Kara replied. "This is nothing."

"It's not nothing. Do you know how hard it is to counter a visla's spell?"

"He's my dad, Vee. Same blood. I have an unfair advantage."

"Even so, it's not the same as floating a ball or starting a fire or something."

Kara didn't want to let her friend's words give her any hope, but for a brief instant, she couldn't help herself. And after her father's treatment the past several months, the thought of showing him she really could cast was a tempting one.

But not this spell. Not her one true secret.

"Maybe I'll bring it up later," she said, then turned her attention back to the cell. "Hey in there. You know, my father has locked me in the building, so now it seems we're both captives, you and me," Kara said, commiserating with the imprisoned woman.

"Garden. To fly. Get Free, uh. Escape. Rock hides. Dead tree," a crackling voice said.

"What the hell does that even mean?" Vee asked. "Not much of a prophesy. More like random babbling."

"Get free, uh, escape," the woman said.

"Yeah, I wish I was free," Kara said.

"You just told her you were locked in here, Kara. It's obvious that she'd repeat that back to you. The bit about being free. Hell, I could have done that. Everyone knows you want out."

Kara thought about her friend's words, but couldn't help but feel there was nevertheless something more to the prisoner's cryptic comments.

"I guess," she replied. But deep down, Karasalia Palmarian wondered if the mysterious woman might truly know the path to her freedom.

CHAPTER FIFTY-THREE

Visanya had gone home early that afternoon after she and Karasalia had spent a restricted, but nevertheless interesting, morning together high up in the visla's tower. They'd have much preferred heading out to the marketplace at Faloon, or to have taken in a show at the Arcadium, but close as they were, the two made do with their circumstances.

But Vee would be back. Her mother had simply wanted to take her to visit family, but the teens would reconnect that evening for dinner and a sleepover. When under house arrest, one had to make do with whatever possible to stay entertained.

They said their farewells, Vee heading on her way home, while Kara was unable to even walk her out the front doors to say goodbye. When she merely got too close, in fact, a magical barrier stopped her in her tracks, while a rather embarrassing alarm sounded, bringing the security detail running.

Her violet skin deepened a shade as her cheeks felt a hot flush. She understood her father's restrictions, but this was a bit ridiculous, even for him.

As she took the lift platform back up to the recreation level, she found she couldn't get the heretic's words out of her mind. The strange prophesy, if it could really be called that.

"*Garden. To fly. Get Free, uh. Escape. Rock hides. Dead tree,*" the woman had said, but what did it mean? And for that matter, who was she?

"Why did she want to kill my father? And how did she even get in the building in the first place?" Kara wondered. "And from such a high level? It doesn't make any sense."

Something wasn't adding up, and the churning wheel of discontent in her gut told her she had to figure out what exactly that was. The question was, how was she going to do so? The answer was both obvious yet not.

Her father was a very private man, but also a bit predictable in that way. If there was anywhere he'd store important information, such as what he *really* knew about the strange woman who had tried to kill him, those answers would be neatly tucked away in just one place. His offices.

Kara couldn't just walk into them through the doors, though. She knew her father would have placed wards and alarms on them against intruders when he was not present. Even his own family could not enter if he was not in the building. But he had locked the building down, and Kara could not go out.

Or could she?

An idea began to form in her mind. A crazy, unlikely idea, but one that she thought just might work.

Kara made her way to the same level as her father's offices high atop the tower, but instead of approaching the sealed doors, she instead opted for a nice walk outside on the numerous floating gardens magically suspended beside the building. So high up in the air, trespassers were not a concern, and so, the gardens hovered quite near the building. So near, in fact, that her audacious plan might just work.

It was a slightly circuitous route, getting to the verdant garden just outside her father's office window, but after traversing three smaller platforms, easily jumping from one to the other, Kara had arrived just outside his innermost sanctum.

The windows were magical force shields, as all with any true power possessed. No grimy glass to impede the view, but rather, an entirely invisible film of magic.

"We're the same blood," Kara muttered, bringing the window deactivation spell to her mind. "It works in my room, so there's no reason it shouldn't work here," she told herself as she geared up for what would either be a successful, or foolishly stymied attempt.

She began casting the spell, quietly whispering the words as she focused her intent on the window in front of her. Then she started to run.

The thing about growing up with gardens that float so high above the ground is one tends to get over a fear of heights as a result of the frequent contact with those long drops. And one thing Kara did not possess was that commonplace fear. She could walk a narrow beam far up in the air as easily as if it were resting at ground level.

So, jumping across the relatively small gap between the floating garden and her father's office window shouldn't be a problem. At least, she hoped it wouldn't be. Of course, if his windows *were* reinforced with a sturdier magic, there was always the chance she would just bounce right off and rebound right through that gap.

That would be bad.

But Kara was pretty sure there was a safeguard spell in place on all of the visla's gardens to catch any clumsy enough to fall off of them. It was a theory she'd never tested, but it made perfect sense. Having a body splatter outside your residence could sully one's reputation, and when it was so easily avoidable, who wouldn't employ such a simple spell to save face?

As Kara's feet left the safety of the floating platform, carrying her through the air over the horribly long drop to the ground

278

below, a momentary flash of doubt crossed her mind, and in that instant, she briefly knew what it was like to stare death in the face.

Her feet hit the floor of the office with a life-affirming thud, her heart pounding with the adrenaline of fear and risk. She'd made it, but now that she was inside the office, she realized just how risky her maneuver had been.

"Better to regret something you have done than something you haven't," she muttered.

Then she noticed the uncomfortable, *bad* magic feeling where she was standing. Something had happened there. Something decidedly evil, it seemed, though there was no sign of such an event, save the tiniest green discoloration on the floor. Interestingly, she only noticed it due to her particularly strong vision, enhanced by her natural magical abilities, where most wouldn't see a thing.

But with nothing beyond a green smudge to explain the sensation, she quickly put her talent to work on her real reason for being there. Of all the things she was strong in, her vision was the one that seemed to have lived up to her magical potential. And now she was going to put it to use scanning her father's things. Her fingers flipped through the items in plain sight first.

There was nothing on his main work desk of interest. That space was always kept immaculately clean, and she suspected it was merely the place he showed in visitors to give the impression of the man they expected. But Karasalia knew her father. Knew how shrewd he was, and also how secretive.

On the far wall there was a portrait of the visla and his family, mounted to the surface with a simple magical spell. Kara knew he wouldn't be so foolish as to hide anything of value behind a painting like that. It was just too obvious. However, with that realization, she began to pick apart what she knew of her father's thought processes, looking at the room as he would, assuming someone might come snooping around one day.

The painting was the natural decoy choice, and once it was clear there was nothing behind it, an interloper would move on. But wasn't that the best way to then remove suspicion from that entire wall space?

Kara examined the seams of the decorative pattern magically laced into the room's walls. It appeared to be a continuous and solid pattern. But what if...?

She placed her hands against the wall and concentrated, calling up the many spells her father had taught her over the years. They'd never worked for her, but Vee was right, her power did seem to be a little stronger for some reason, so she figured it worth a try.

Surprisingly, she felt a little tug at the corner of her perception. Gently, she backtracked to the spell that had caused the reaction. The spell her father had first used to seal her door when she was a young child to prevent her from wandering.

"Could it be so simple?" she wondered.

But then, they'd been in the building her entire life, and if he had used that spell all those years ago, perhaps complacency had led him to the folly of leaving the same spell in place in his office as well.

Kara repeated the spell, focusing on the wall.

A panel clicked open and slid free, revealing a half-meter square opening. She slid the door all the way open and looked inside.

Not much to speak of, really. An odd, non-magical-feeling heavy wrist bracer thing of strange design. Some stacked documents, and a handful of magical items, though a few appeared to be quite powerful. There was also a thin, but long, braid of golden Ootaki hair, fully charged from what she could sense.

"I didn't know he had that," she mused, touching the braid. It was abhorrent what was done to Ootaki, and though it could very well have been an old braid from many years prior, the fact that her father had the product of so horrible a slavery nevertheless made her uneasy.

There were also a handful of recording discs, the magical devices capable of storing moving images and projecting them at a later time. Only the wealthy could afford ones of this quality, but Karasalia Palmarian was the daughter of the most powerful visla in ages. It was only natural she had been raised with them as a normal part of her existence.

Only later in life did she realize how privileged she had been. It was something that even became a bit of a source of self-consciousness, Kara not wanting to seem like a spoiled rich kid, though, admittedly, she was one, financially, if not in attitude.

Kara picked up the nearest of them and keyed it on with the simple spell her father had taught her as a girl. "*Visus,*" she said.

Images flashed to life above the device, but what she saw was not a record of the heretic or her arrival, but rather, a large fleet of dangerous ships destroying a small moon and the colony upon it.

She felt sick. Tens of thousands of people would have been killed in such an attack, if not more. Quickly, she moved on to the next disc. This one showed a larger mass of vessels targeting and destroying a convoy of smaller ships, taking some for their resources, while leaving the others to the void of space.

Each disc was the same. More and more images of an ever-growing fleet of deadly craft. One recording even showed evidence of several ships going totally invisible. She knew of shimmer spells, but had never actually seen one at work. And to cast with the power to cover an entire ship? And one of that size, no less? Whoever was behind the spells was more powerful than most casters in the colonized systems.

"What are you doing, Father?" she asked the absent man, a

deep sadness filling her gut as she realized he wasn't the man she thought him to be.

She activated the final disc, the one tucked behind the others. Captain Sandah's image sprang to life, standing on the command deck of his ship.

"Visla, I have done as you requested, and we have traveled very far in executing this command. The fleet now numbers in the hundreds, and it possesses many high-level casters ready to do great harm when called upon. I am having this message brought to you by recording disc, as we are beyond range of a long-range skree immediately, for I shall remain here a bit longer. I will see you at once upon my return to Slafara."

"Sandah?" Kara said, stunned. "But I sent Leila––"

Kara didn't know how to process this new information. Not yet, anyway, so she carefully placed everything back as she'd found it and sealed the panel once more, then made her way back out the window with a stress-fueled leap, sealing it behind her as she backtracked through the floating gardens.

Something was going on. Something she needed answers to. None of her father's staff would say a word, and her stepmother was off-world. With whatever he was up to, she thought he'd likely kept her in the dark as well.

"Only one person left," she said, then headed to speak with the prophetic heretic once more.

282

CHAPTER FIFTY-FOUR

As always, visiting the odd prisoner locked away in her father's tower was an unusual experience, to say the least, but Kara had good reason, beyond boredom and novelty, to talk to the prophetic woman this time. Amusing and mysterious small talk was no longer the order of the day. Answers were what she was after.

Unfortunately, she knew they'd come in a cryptic manner.

"I need to talk to you," Kara said as she approached the door.

Casting the spell negating her father's muting magic felt even easier than before. Enough so that she actually noted it in the process of uttering the words that would allow the confined woman to talk. She wondered if the adrenaline from her daring entry to her father's office had caused an uptick in her instinctive casting.

But perhaps something else was happening to her, making her magic stronger. But if that was the case, she had no idea whatsoever what it might be. In any case, she wasn't about to look that gift Zomoki in the mouth.

"Hey, there's something going on. Something big, and no one's talking about it. Not even my father."

"The bad. Gather attack, many. No warp."

Kara had no idea what the woman was talking about this time. "No warp? What does that even mean? And gather for what attack? Is my father raising a force to go to war?"

The heretic didn't answer, but Kara could hear her pacing in her cell, muttering to herself. It was gibberish, but it nevertheless sounded like she was having a conversation with herself. One side of a conversation, at least.

"Who are you talking to?" Kara asked, checking the magical seals on the cell door. They still read the same. One prisoner inside, female. "Hey! I'm talking to you! I need answers."

"Go free, uh. Fly away," the woman said with some urgency. "Help will. Truth. Needs."

"I can't fly away," Kara replied. "I can't even leave the building. My father has sealed off all the exits. I'm stuck in here just like you." She looked at the thick door and regretted her choice of words. "Okay, not exactly like you, but I'm still a prisoner in this tower, and there's simply no way to leave."

"Can leave," the woman said in her croaking rasp.

"No I can't," Kara reiterated. "Literally impossible. If I so much as go near any of the doors downstairs I'll be stopped by my father's spell and trigger his alarms."

"Not down," the heretic said.

"What do you mean, 'not down'?"

"Garden."

"The gardens are all blocked off. I told you, I can't walk out those doors."

"No. Garden up," the raspy voice managed to say over the magical gag restraining her.

"Garden up? What does that even mean?" Kara said, but then the words clicked into place in her head. But that couldn't be what the woman meant, could it? That made no sense.

"You mean the floating gardens?" Kara asked.

"Float," the woman replied.

Sure, the floating gardens were accessible to the teen, but why wouldn't they be? After all, they were dozens of levels above the ground with no way down. To go out onto those magically suspended platforms was the same as standing atop a high roof. She would be outside, but not any closer to freedom.

"Rock," the woman said unprompted.

She sounded unsure at first, as though she didn't want to make the suggestion but had no choice. And given her confinement, that might not have been far from the truth.

"Rock?" Kara repeated. "What rock?"

"Rock. Garden up."

"A rock in the floating gardens? There are plenty of rocks. Now you're just not making any sense at all, and that's saying something, given your usual jumble of words."

The confined woman began arguing with herself in her guttural mumble until finally, she turned her attention back to the slit in the door. "Dead tree," she said. "Rock. Free, uh, fly away. Malibu."

She was making no sense again, and Kara was about to give up on her, but the last word she uttered was familiar. Utterly foreign, but one she'd heard before, and recently.

"Maliboo?" she repeated. "What do you know of Maliboo?" Kara asked, trying to place the word. It was so familiar, right on the tip of her brain, but she couldn't quite recall where from.

"Malibu. Word. Fly free. Home," the voice said.

Home. That was it. The word was familiar because Leila had mentioned it upon first arriving at the visla's tower. Malibu was the name of her home. But how did this heretic assassin know it? Were the two of them somehow connected?

Kara found herself wondering if Leila could possibly be an assassin herself. But even with her giant beast of an animal at her side, Kara simply didn't get that impression from the woman. No, there was a connection, but that wasn't it. If Captain Sandah returned soon, though, she could ask him where exactly he had taken Leila, and if there had been anything unusual about her friends.

If she found them, that is. It was a big galaxy, and her quest, while undertaken with the help of one of the finest captains alive, was nevertheless a difficult one.

"Dead tree," the heretic said again. "Malibu."

"Yes, you said. But there are no dead trees up here. Father is very particular about his people keeping the gardens..." Kara trailed off as a realization hit her.

There actually was *one* garden that had suffered from a bit of a blight. Many of the exotic plants it housed had died off, and there *was* a Yannal growing there that had perished. It wasn't a tree, but rather, a dense growth of grass-like fibers that wove themselves into a solid, towering mass. Kara could see, how it might seem like a tree to someone not familiar with the plant.

And there *was* a rock feature in that garden. And right by the dried out Yannal. But how would the woman know that? It was separated from the other gardens, and all staff were blocked from using it until the groundskeepers had a chance to completely strip it to bare soil and start again from scratch. But that wasn't scheduled to occur for several months.

In the interim, that lone platform was simply kept out of sight, away from the visla's windows, tucked to the other side of the tower near...

"Near the servants's facilities," Kara realized.

The same area the woman had been captured attempting to enter the building. The same area where she buried her sword in the wall as they captured her.

Kara had more questions than she arrived with, but the sound of footsteps reverberating nearby told her she was about to have company. The teen quietly rushed to the stairway and descended on tip-toe, pondering all that had just been revealed to her.

CHAPTER FIFTY-FIVE

Charlie had been contemplating the simple, yet cryptic riddle for the entirety of the lengthy flight from Slafara to the small planet of Nurbec. Ara had never before been there, and the world appeared to have been deserted for hundreds of years, likely due to the instability of the sun it orbited. The locals had abandoned it for safer climes, it seemed.

The planet was a fairly tiny one, bathing in the rays of a brilliant, blue supergiant that cast a strange azure hue on everything from soil, to trees, to the stones of the enormous structure they stood before. The fluctuating power of the sun, however, left them all feeling a little uneasy.

"It is running out of fuel within," Bawb said, looking up at the distant sun. "This is never a good thing."

"Yeah, basic astronomy says when a supergiant dies, instead of collapsing like a regular star, it'll go supernova."

"Supernova? I am not familiar with this word."

"It basically means it's gonna blow up and take out the entire system and anything extra solar nearby. A very big boom," Charlie said.

"Ah, yes. Supernova. Your description is accurate for the

occurrence," Bawb noted. "Though it will likely not happen while we are here on Nurbec, I would very much like to complete this task and be done with this world."

"I, for one, agree," Ara said. "The constantly shifting spectrum of power is making me itch all over."

Charlie felt it too. The sensation of something uncomfortably prickling his skin despite his protective suit. They'd need to be quick about this, because even if the sun wasn't going to blow anytime soon, he had no idea what the radiation from it might do to them, magic or no.

They had followed the star coordinates laid out on the glowing golden ring, down to the exact landing point upon the planet's surface. It was the correct place, all right, of that they were pretty sure, given the massive pyramid-like structure protected by a pair of stone statues dozens of meters high, and powered with a strong and unseen magic.

Whoever had built this place, they had layered much magic into its protection, for to have any hope of reaching the door sealed off behind the statues, one would have to possess immense power. Fortunately, all three of the adventurers standing before it had just that.

"*From within, true power wears mountains into mere stones,*" Charlie said, repeating the riddle they'd retrieved from the glowing ring. "What does that even mean?"

"I am not certain, my friend. However, each of us possesses significant magic," Bawb said.

Charlie looked up at the towering stone statues. They really were something to marvel at, and he hated to destroy them. But they were on a quest, and sometimes you had to break a few eggs to make an omelette. Or, in this case, a couple of statues.

"Well, I don't know if we'll be able to reduce them to little rocks, but we should easily have enough magic to shift these things out of the way," he said. "Shall we?"

The trio focused their attentions on the massive sculptures and began to cast.

Nothing happened.

"Uh, you guys are casting the same spell, right? It'd be silly if we were casting opposing ones and canceling each other out," Charlie said.

"We cast to move the statues aside," Ara said. "The magic is the same, more or less. But for some reason they are as immobile as before. I fear we are going to have to be a bit more forceful."

"Forceful I can do," Charlie said, drawing upon the massive stores of power flowing through him.

He didn't want to overdo it and destroy the entire building, though. Just move the statues out of the way. Using their combined might, it should be a pretty simple affair.

They cast as one, increasing their magical output by several factors, yet the statues and structure remained intact. In fact, it seemed they were even more sturdy than they had been when they had arrived.

"Okay, screw this," Charlie said, unleashing even more of his magic upon the obstacles.

He felt the spell fly true. It was enough to utterly shatter far more than just those statues, despite their size, yet again, nothing happened.

"Guys? What the fuck is going on?"

Ara sniffed the air, a curious look forming on her face as she unraveled the structure's mysteries. "Amazing," she finally said.

"What is?"

"The magic, Charlie. This spell, it is incredibly old. It is also incredibly powerful."

"Yeah, we noticed. But what is it? How can it withstand all three of our spells?"

"Because this magic is designed for one purpose and one purpose alone. To direct any attacking spells and use that power to bolster the building's structure. The harder we push, the more solid it becomes," Ara said.

"Wait, so this thing's like some kind of feedback loop that takes our magic and uses it to protect itself?" Charlie asked.

"It would appear so," Ara replied. "From what I can sense, the former residents of this world would cast against this structure daily. Hundreds of years, if not more, all bolstering its mass. And then the sun began to shift its rays, and that too elicited a magical reaction, rendering the whole thing more or less impregnable."

"So we can't get in?"

"Not by force, it seems."

"Well, that's just great. We jump all the way out here––after you fly into a sun, for cryin' out loud––and for what? A door we can't hope to open. This thing's all feeling like a wild goose chase."

"It was not a deception," Bawb said, walking to the structure and examining the symbols carved into its face. "We simply lack what it takes to overcome the sun's unexpected reinforcement of the spell. I doubt the original caster could have foreseen this eventuality."

Charlie knew he was right, but nevertheless, he couldn't help but wonder if they might have more success if the others were with them too. "Maybe Rika's magic could do it. It's not from this galaxy, so maybe it could overcome it somehow."

"Perhaps," Bawb mused, his fingers tracing the designs in the stone. There were many different subjects carved into the material, but he paused at the image of a tall mountain standing high above the tiny figures rendered at its base.

"Or maybe Hunze could do it," Charlie said. "She draws her power from within. Well, her hair is outside her body, technically, but you know what I mean."

At the mention of her name, Bawb felt a flash of heat in his chest. He'd been quite effectively keeping her from his thoughts as they focused on their task, but now, stuck as they were, he found his mind drifting to his love, wondering if she was all right, missing her comforting presence.

He felt the Ootaki hair wrapped around him, smelling Hunze's scent on it still, embracing its power, not to cast, but to feel the connection he and his Ootaki lover shared.

The stone beneath his hand abruptly shifted, then pushed open and slid aside, then fell to pieces.

"Uh, what did you just do, Bob?" Charlie asked.

"Nothing. I was merely taking a moment to reflect."

"No, you did something."

"I assure you, I did not. I was thinking of Hunze, nothing more."

Ara smiled, her golden eyes flashing with realization. "*From within, true power wears mountains into stones,*" she said. "The riddle was not about breaking down barriers with force. It was a test."

"How so?" Charlie asked.

"One that only a gentle touch from a pure heart could pass," she replied.

"Did you just call Bob a gentle and pure heart?" Charlie chuckled.

"Despite his origins and notoriety, yes," she replied. "And it was not external force that was needed, but proof the person was worthy of the prize."

"So, this whole building is a decoy?" Charlie asked, staring up at the massive structure.

"Likely it served other purposes in the past. But the misdirect was intended for seekers of a specific item. One that is powerful enough to stop this visla," the Zomoki said. "The secret was not in using more force, but in using no force at all."

CHAPTER FIFTY-SIX

Bawb peered into the small space revealed in the structure. "I see something," he said, leaning in to retrieve the item.

He pulled free a sealed box of strong wood, plain in design, lacking any flashy markings or decorations to hint at what might be inside. It had been magically enhanced and remained perfectly sound, even after hundreds upon hundreds of years. He unfastened the latch and carefully opened the lid.

Inside was a whole different story. Where the exterior of the container was plain, the interior possessed enough wards and protections to keep the box whole even if the entire building had fallen upon it. And in the middle, nestled in an enchanted cradle, was what appeared to be an enormous egg.

Only it wasn't an egg. It was magically crafted, that much was obvious. And the stopper on the top made it clear it was a container, not something laid by some strange beast.

"This is it?" Charlie asked, looking at the slightly oblong orb. "It's no bigger than a softball."

"Small things can often contain great power," Ara noted.

"Says the enormous Zomoki," Charlie replied with a grin. "This thing is supposed to be able to stop a visla. I mean, I see the spells etched across the outside, but I don't see how it could possibly be enough. Something's up, and I really don't trust Mandoog."

"Nor I," Ara agreed.

"I as well," Bawb added. "I suggest we see what is inside before we hand over something so heavily guarded to a man of questionable character we have only just met."

"Agreed," Charlie said. "You want to do the honors?"

Bawb grinned. He was no stranger to danger, and opening a simple stopper would be the least dangerous thing he'd done in years. There were no wards on the stopper, only a few simple spells to keep it in place until one wished to open it. The rest of the orb seemed to be designed to hold integrity until it was thrown. A magical hand grenade, of sorts.

Bawb carefully pried the stopper until it pulled free with a pop. The Wampeh leapt backward at the slightest whiff of its contents, his muscles instinctively throwing him to safety before his brain could fully digest what he'd smelled.

"Jesus, what was that?" Charlie asked, adrenaline high, his hands glowing with magic, ready to defend against... Well, he wasn't quite sure about that. At least, not until he was. "Oh. Well, that complicates things," he said, picking up the orb.

Ara sniffed the open container. "Balamar waters?" she said, confused. "And highly potent at that. But not only are these exceedingly rare, they are for healing, to bolster one's magic."

"Unless you're a certain type of Wampeh, that is," Charlie noted, looking at his friend, who now stood at a safe distance. "A splash of this and Bob here would burst into flames like a vampire on holy water."

"But that can only mean one thing," the Wampeh said, quickly collecting himself from the shock.

"Yeah, I know," Charlie said. "It means we'll be up against another Wampeh. One like you. And a visla, no less."

"But this was placed here many hundreds of years ago. Even among my kind, a lifespan that long is an extreme rarity."

"Yes, but the visla who placed this here thought there would be a threat from Wampeh. There was at the time he created this place, so it has to be considered a possibility that a new generation has taken up the mantle," Ara said.

Charlie wedged the stopper back into place and put the orb back into its box, sealing it securely. Gears were already churning in his mind.

"If that's true, then there's something we need to do," he said.

"Not give this to Mandoog," Bawb said.

"Obviously. But more than that. If the waters could give us an edge in combat, then we need to get them to all of our people. And I mean *all* of them. If we could take some through the portal to spread to key forces? Well, it could make all the difference," Charlie said, an inspired gleam in his eye. "Ara, can you get us to the Balamar Wastelands?"

"I can, though it will require many jumps. It is quite a distance from this system."

Bawb could see where Charlie's train of thought was going, and while a sound idea, it made him uncomfortable nevertheless.

"What if it should fall into the wrong hands?" the Wampeh asked. "It might be used against us. To strengthen our enemies, even."

Charlie was ready for that concern. "We booby trap whatever we gather. If we can find any at all, that is. It's been hundreds of years since we were there, and obviously this visla has been to the wastelands too, since they retrieved my old ship from there. But the thing is, the waters would be undetectable if they were still under the sand. Hidden completely without a trace. Unless you knew where to look, it would seem as though there was nothing there but an expanse of dry, red soil and nothing more."

"We will need vessels," Bawb said. "Sturdy, robust ones, capable of withstanding the rigors of space travel, and even combat."

"And we can acquire some on the way there," Charlie said. "It's a long trip, and I'm sure we'll need to stop a few times for Ara to rest and recharge. We can pick them up then." He paused a moment, staring at the structure looming over them. A little smile bent the corners of his mouth. "And what if we use a bit of the visla's trick they employed when building this place on them?"

His Wampeh friend realized what he was saying, and found himself liking the idea. "You mean secure them in a manner that the harder one tries to open them, the more secure they become," Bawb said, admiring the simplicity of the plan. "Of course, it will only work against low-level casters, as we do not have the benefit of centuries of layered casting. But I believe for our purposes that might just work."

Charlie hefted the box and stowed it in the most secure of the containers strapped to Ara's heavy-duty harness. "Well then, it looks like we've got the beginnings of a plan."

CHAPTER FIFTY-SEVEN

It had been a bit of a trek getting to a commerce lane on the bustling world they'd selected to acquire their containers, but the walk had done Charlie and Bawb some good, letting them stretch their legs as they planned the next steps of their ever-changing mission.

As it stood now, they'd be acquiring watertight containers to bring to the Balamar Wastelands, which they'd hopefully fill with the priceless liquid. That is if Charlie could find it again. But he was confident he would find the location of the cistern, it just might take a little time is all. As for the contents, however, there was no telling if any of the waters even remained.

The duo managed to flag down a floating juggernaut on its way into the city and catch a ride. In less than an hour, they were walking the streets of Slafara's capital city.

"Not a bad place to stopover, all things considered," Charlie said as he and Bawb made their way through the industrial part of Palmar. "I mean, it's clean, people seem nice, and the food here's actually pretty decent too."

"And the sizable wilderness area on the outskirts of the city provides Ara a convenient place to lay low while we conduct our business," Bawb added. "Fortunately the outlying planets, while lacking in the supplies we require, did possess adequate game for her to feed upon before coming here."

"Yeah, she's resting well with a full belly, I'm sure," Charlie said. "We got lucky that the route back to the Balamar Wastelands passed this way. I really don't want any more run-ins on shitty little worlds with double-crossing schmucks like Yakatan. You have the address?"

"Yes. The woman at the lading facility said this particular supplier, while a bit out of our way, would be the purveyor of the most reasonably priced containers for our needs," Bawb said.

"Good thing, because while we're rich on magic, we're kinda short on regular old funds."

"We can always trade more antiquities," Bawb noted.

"Yeah, but let's hope what we have to offer will cover it. They may be antiques to these people, but that stuff is our gear, and we might actually need it," Charlie said.

The two were far from the city center and its gleaming towers of the wealthy and powerful, but even so, there was still a lingering *something* odd in the air, just as there had been the last time they'd stopped off on this planet. Only then, Ara had been desperately in need of rest, and Charlie and Bawb had focused their attentions on ensuring her safety as she slept.

But this time there was the opportunity to observe the phenomenon more closely. To try to discern exactly what it was that was going on.

"You sense it, right?" Charlie asked.

"Yes. Indeed, it is unusual, this mix of magic. Someone is attempting to block others from reading their power, and the spell is spilling all over the place, though you wouldn't notice it unless you were actively searching for these magical signatures."

"So someone's keeping those around them in the dark, eh?"

"It would seem. A wise defensive tactic, but one I would not expect on a world such as this," Bawb said. "But the other thing mixed in. It is most odd."

"Right? It's like a lingering trace that feels, I don't know. It feels like home, I could almost say, but shuffled in with all that buzzing feedback from the other user, or users, it just gets lost in the noise. But there's something really familiar about it, ya know?"

"I do. But, as was the case last time, Charlie, we have other things to worry about at the moment."

Bawb was right, of course. They needed to focus and procure the heavy-duty water containers as soon as was reasonable. The portal was on a weekly schedule now, and the clock was ticking away.

"Yes?" a thick-necked man with skin the color of chestnuts and a warm pair of orange eyes asked when he saw the men standing at the door to his warehouse.

"Ilana at the lading company said we should inquire with Donogin about purchasing some large containers," Bawb said. "Might you be him?"

"I am. And who are you?"

"I am Binsala the trader, and this is my associate, Charlie."

"Like the rebel?"

"Oh, um, yes, I was named after him," Charlie said. "Parents were big fans."

Donogin looked him over with coolly assessing eyes. "You'd be wise to not say that too loudly," he said. "Some people still miss the stability of the Council's influence, though it was disbanded long before they were even born. But the idea remains, and some are stupid like that. But that's not what you're here for. Now, tell me what you need these containers for and I will see what I can help you with."

Charlie let Bawb handle the talking. Binsala the trader had a way with these sorts of negotiations.

"We are going to be procuring a sizable quantity of a rather particular spirit. One that we will need to keep perfectly secured and free from any environmental shifts as we transport it. That means the vessels will need to be particularly robust," Bawb said.

"Alcohol? Why not just stack the bottles in a case like everyone else?"

"These spirits are being provided to us at a steep discount, namely due to the lack of such labeling and packaging. By procuring them in bulk as we are, the savings are substantial."

"And you can make knock-off labels yourself and sell it for a profit, am I correct?" Donogin asked.

"You are a shrewd businessman," Bawb replied. "Binsala appreciates a man with a sharp mind in the ways of these things. So, tell me. Can you help us with this?"

Donogin obviously could. That much was clear the moment they'd set foot inside his establishment. Whether he would do so at a price they could pay was the issue at hand.

"I think I may have some items that will suit your needs," the man said. "Come take a look at them and tell me what you think. If they are to your liking, then we shall discuss price."

The containers were essentially what they needed, more or less. And with their new spells layered upon them, they'd more than suffice. To Charlie's surprise, Donogin had been relatively reasonable during the negotiation phase of the purchase, and by the time they'd sealed the deal, he had even agreed to deliver both the goods, as well as their purchasers, to a wooded area on the outskirts of town.

"You sure this is where you want to go?" he asked as they unloaded the containers from his conveyance and stacked them high beneath a copse of trees far outside of town.

"Yes, this is perfect. Our contact will be along shortly to collect both us and our containers for the trip to complete our transaction. But as for us, I believe this concludes our business. Thank you, Donogin, it was a pleasure working with you. And rest assured, if any ask Binsala where to go for such goods on this world, yours will be the first name from his lips."

Donogin liked that reply, as he liked the Wampeh trader. The other one, named after that old rebel long dead, well, he was a decent enough sort, but something about him just rubbed the man the wrong way. But it mattered not. His coffers were filled, his overstock vessels cleared out, and whatever the men planned to do next was none of his business and certainly not his concern.

He drove away, waving as he shrank in the distance.

"A most acceptable assortment," Ara said as she approached a few minutes later once the coast was clear. "I believe these will do just fine."

"I agree, Wise One," Bawb said, switching out of his jovial trader persona.

"Ara, do you smell that?" Charlie asked as they began fastening the large containers to Ara's harness. "Something in this planet's magic. It's familiar. But muddied. You have a far better sense for these things than I do. What do you make of it?"

Ara took a deep whiff of the air, as if tasting a fine wine. "Yes, the same as the last time we were here, though several of the scents are much weaker with the passage of time. It's strange, but one note of this is almost reminiscent of the smells of our home on Earth. There's that, along with a strange and confusing bit of strong magic."

"I noticed that too. Something jumbling it all up. Masking all of the signatures," Charlie said.

"Yes, and I'm afraid I'm unable to determine more because of it," Ara said as they locked the containers into place. "A bit cumbersome, but this should suffice." She spread her wings and shifted around in the harness to ensure things would hold in place as she flew. "I think we may want to come back to properly examine this magic signature if we are able," she said. "But for now, we have a long journey to continue."

The two men finished securing the last of the containers and climbed atop their friend's back into their places. With a mighty flap of her wings, Ara then lunged into the air. Moments later, they jumped, leaving Slafara and its confusing smells behind. At least for the time being.

CHAPTER FIFTY-EIGHT

"How could she know about the Yannal growing out there?" Visanya asked as she sipped her frosty glass of yonda cooler, the fruit's violet juice nearly matching her friend's skin color. "It's not like anyone has access to the gardens, after all."

Kara had been pondering the same thing since she'd heard the woman's prophesy earlier that day. If only Vee had already come over for their slumber party––a party of only two––she would have heard it with her own ears. But there was just no way the heretic could have known, was there?

One thing, however, kept sticking in her mind. A coincidence, perhaps, but then again, maybe not. When she'd been captured breaking into the building, it had been from the servants' section on the topmost floors. Conveniently, the very same area the disused floating garden had been relocated to until such time as it was stripped and replanted.

The woman had somehow made it to that level undetected. A feat in and of itself. But she had come to kill Kara's father. Previously, the teen would have sworn on her life that her father was an upstanding and honest visla, but after what she'd seen in his offices, a sliver of doubt had lodged in her certainty, festering no matter how hard she tried to dismiss it.

"Vee, do you think my father's a good man?" Kara asked her friend, shifting course to the thing weighing so heavily her mind.

"Sure, I guess," Visanya replied. "I mean, he's a visla, and a really powerful one at that, so I'm sure he has to do a lot of stuff that maybe isn't so great. But that's just part of the job, right?"

"I guess," Kara said.

"You don't sound so sure."

Kara hesitated. "If I tell you something, you've got to promise not to repeat it to anyone, okay?"

"Kara, we've been best friends for how long now? Of course you can trust me."

"I know, it's just this could be really bad. Not for me, but for my father."

"What is it?" Vee asked, her curiosity suddenly piqued.

"After you left, I sort of broke into my father's office."

"Why would you do that? And *how* did you do that? Isn't the place totally locked down?"

"Well, it is from the inside, but I went out on the gardens and jumped in through the window," Kara admitted.

"You did what? Kara, you could have been killed, you know."

"But I wasn't."

"Still, what the hell made you do that? Was it being locked in the tower? I mean, I get the cabin fever thing, but that's kind of extreme."

"It wasn't that, really. I mean, yes, it was, but the thing is, after I talked to the heretic, I got to wondering what exactly my father was up to that they'd send an assassin after him. So I got curious and looked through his stuff."

"And what did you find?"

"He had image discs, Vee. Hidden away in a secret compartment."

"If it was so secret, how did you find it?" Visanya asked.

"I just, I don't know, I *felt* it, I guess. And then I tried an old spell my father used to use to seal my door when I was a little girl to keep me from wandering off. I didn't think it would actually work, but he must never have changed it, even after all these years."

"Sloppy," Vee said.

"People get complacent, I guess. But the thing is, there was bad stuff on them. I'm talking really bad, Vee. Like, entire ships full of people being killed, and others taken captive for slaves."

"But that's outlawed in most of the galaxy now," Vee said, nervously twirling her hair. "At least, for most races."

"I know. But I saw it. And Sandah was there."

"Wait, Captain Sandah? But he always seemed like such a nice man."

"I know. It doesn't make sense."

"Oh no," Vee said. "You sent Leila out with Sandah."

"I know," Kara replied grimly. "I can't believe my father would do such a thing, but why else would he be documenting all of that? I need to find out the truth about what's really going on, but I can't do that from in here. But if I could just get out, just for a little while, I could go talk to my Uncle Korbin."

"But your father doesn't have a brother," Vee noted.

"He's not really my uncle, we just call him that. He's been friends with my father since before I was born. If anyone knows what's going on––and will be willing to tell me––Uncle Korbin's the one. And maybe he knows where Sandah really is. I sent Leila with him, Vee. It's my fault."

"But you can't get out. You saw the spells already. And the alarm?"

"Yeah, that was embarrassing, having them come running like that," Kara agreed.

"And don't forget Grundsch always lurking around keeping tabs on you," Vee added.

"But Bahnjoh likes me. I bet he'd let me go."

"Sure, but you can't even get out the doors on the lower levels anymore for that to even be an issue. And like I already said, Grundsch definitely won't let you leave. He wouldn't want to face your father's wrath if he did."

Kara sat quietly a moment, mulling over her very limited options. "There's always the heretic's prophecy."

"That rambling nonsense? What does it even mean? And why would you listen to a madwoman?" Vee asked.

"Because, that mad woman somehow made it to the top of the building undetected, and very nearly got into my father's suites, and fully armed. She may be strange, but I think she's not entirely crazy."

"Denna Palmarian. Visanya. There is food prepared for you awaiting you in the dining hall," a deep voice said from the doorway.

"How long have you been standing there, Grundsch?" Kara asked, surprised.

"I only just arrived, Denna," the huge man said. "Tulagda has made several courses he thinks you will like. I shall inform him you will be coming shortly." The Ra'az then turned and left the way he came.

Kara turned to her friend. "What do you think, Vee? Dinner first, then we get back to this?"

Her best friend grinned. "If we're going to be plotting, we will need our strength," she rationalized.

"Right. Food it is."

The girls rose and headed off to dinner, postponing further discussion of the heretic and her prophecies, at least until their bellies were full.

CHAPTER FIFTY-NINE

It had been days since Hunze and Dukaan had struck up her deal with the blue-skinned smuggler, and the waiting was starting to get to them. They'd loaded Kip with all the supplies they could possibly need, and then a bit more, just in case.

Torbin was more than happy to provide them with anything they could think to want. Olo had apparently put a very sizable amount of coin in his hands for his services––as well as his silence.

In the circles of illicit traders and black market suppliers, secrecy was paramount. For anyone to betray that trust, especially when coin was involved, would mean having their services blacklisted. And word would spread quickly. There would be no restarting on any system remotely nearby.

But even without that hanging over his head, Hunze felt Torbin was genuinely enjoying helping her and Dukaan. Possibly it was because what they needed of him was so simple to procure, and aboveboard. Being paid so handsomely for services that were actually entirely legal was a nice change of pace.

Once that transaction was completed, however, Hunze and

her friends found themselves relegated to waiting. And then more waiting. And then a bit more. They spent so much time sitting around, in fact, that the Ootaki had not only polished the vespus blade to a gleaming blue shine, she had also honed its edge to razor sharpness, then imbued it with some of her Ootaki magic, guaranteeing it would stay sharp even with heavy use.

When Olosnah's messenger finally came to find the offworlders, she did so while Hunze and Dukaan were sampling a local type of dumpling from one of the street vendors. One of the things they had discovered about this world was that while the restaurants were decent enough, it was the little stalls and carts clustered around the city that possessed the truly interesting, and quite delicious, delights.

The girl who found Hunze and Dukaan as they ate couldn't have been more than twelve. A wee thing with bright, multi-colored hair that shifted in the light. The spell had come and gone from fashion so many times over the years that people lost count, but it was always the youth who found new joy from a prior generation's cast-offs.

The girl apologized for bumping into the hooded woman, while surreptitiously pressing a small packet no bigger than one of the dumplings on Hunze's plate into her hand.

She then vanished into the crowd before the Ootaki woman could say anything. Hunze glanced at Dukaan, who quickly finished his last dumpling and settled their bill. The two then made their way back to the nearby landing field where Kip had been waiting.

And for an AI ship as excitable as he was, sitting still for so many days was making him climb the proverbial walls.

"We have news," Dukaan said as they sealed the airlock behind them.

"Oh? What is it? Are we finally going?" Kip asked, more than a little antsy.

"Soon," Hunze said, laying out the contents of the package on the console.

Dukaan picked up a tightly folded parchment with dots and lines on its face. "Can you make sense of this star chart?"

"Hang on," Kip said, scanning the item. "Yeah, I see where we're supposed to go. Just a couple of systems away. This is so close, we should be able to get there without much trouble. Olo did a good job. This even includes waypoints I can use to correct course when our warp throws us the wrong way."

"So you can do it, then?" Hunze asked.

"You betcha I can," the chipper AI replied. "Long warps, we'd be screwed, but this? I got this."

"Good. We are to meet Olo at this address to exchange final payment for the name and specifics of this navigating caster, as well as the other star chart. The one that reveals the fleet's location. Then we leave."

"Great," Kip said.

"For now, however, we are to meet him in thirty minutes," Dukaan said, holding a small scrap of parchment. "Prepare for flight. We shall return shortly."

The Chithiid and his hooded Ootaki friend then stepped out of the ship and headed once more into the seedy depths of the city to seek out the blue-skinned smuggler to complete their deal. Both Dukaan and Hunze were fully armed, each sporting not only blades, but also pulse pistols hidden within their overcloaks.

Olosnah had proven honorable thus far, but they reasoned one could never be too cautious when dealing with men of ill repute. Even those on your side.

"Psst," a voice hissed from the doorway to what appeared to be some sort of medical facility located adjacent a brothel. Given its location, they could only imagine the types of services it provided and ailments treated.

The two stepped inside as casually as possible, then closed

the door behind them. Once it was sealed, Olo turned the lights brighter.

"Good to see you, my friends!" he said, positively radiant in his good mood.

"We are glad to see you are well, Olosnah," Dukaan said.

"I told you, just call me Olo," he replied with a grin. "And thanks to you, I've been able to arrange several very lucrative engagements. Ones I might have been unable to fulfill if not for your most generous payment," he said, referring to the immensely powerful Ootaki hair he now possessed.

"We received the planet's location from your girl. I assume you have the name of the one we seek?" Hunze said, taking the other half of the strand of hair she had offered in trade from her pocket.

"Oh, that I do. His name is Navoon," he said.

Hunze held the neatly coiled, golden hair on her palm, offering it as final payment.

Olo resisted the urge to snatch it from her hand, rather taking it gently and placing his precious in his pocket. In his case, it was because he did not wish to seem overanxious. But others might see an Ootaki and think to take her hair by force. But something about this woman told him that there was more to her than met the eye, and any who attempted so foolish an act would seriously regret doing so.

"Navoon is an incredibly talented, and incredibly powerful navigator. He will be able to get you where you need to go," Olo said, then held out a small disc. "*Visus* is the usual command, but this is dangerous information. The kind that could get all of us killed. So I changed it up. Use the normal spell and it will play a harmless image of pretty landscapes. But if you add *Arganis* to the spell, it will show the details Navoon will need. I'll show you. *Visus arganis*," he cast.

The disc flashed to life, displaying a detailed star chart of an enormous swath of space. He was right, with their malfunctioning warp, they'd never be able to find the coordinates of that system without a navigator, and a talented one at that. He repeated the spell and the disc went dark.

"All yours," he said, handing it to Dukaan, who tucked the device safely in his pocket.

"Thank you, Olo," Hunze said. "We are truly grateful for your assistance."

"My pleasure," Olo said, then retrieved two folded uniforms from the bag at his side. "Here. You'll need these."

Hunze and Dukaan looked at each other, confused.

"Uniforms?" the Chithiid asked.

"Yes, on the house. Navoon lives aboard Emmik Chintsal's personal luxury craft," Olo replied.

"Wait, an *emmik*?" Hunze asked. "We have to retrieve him from an emmik's ship?"

Olo flashed his most charming grin. "I never said it would be easy, Princess," he replied with a wink. "The uniforms are the lowest rank on board. It's a thankless job, and they're always swapping out crew, so you should be able to get in with no problems if you play it right. But don't lose them. It's ridiculously hard to get these things."

Hunze took the offering graciously. "Thank you, Olo. You have gone beyond what we agreed upon."

"For this price, I'm more than happy to help," he replied, patting his pocket happily. "And if you ever need me again, I will always be open to future dealings."

Hunze and Dukaan bid the smuggler farewell, and not twenty minutes later were aloft and on their way to retrieve a navigator in what was sure to be a dangerous attempt.

CHAPTER SIXTY

It took Kip only a dozen small warps to manage to get them close enough to the intended system to allow for conventional approach, albeit at high speeds, but not full warp. Olo's small map had been the crucial element, the waypoints he had laid out had enabled the poor AI to reorient himself after every wayward warp, gradually steering them back on course.

Mostly.

The problem was that while the konus welded to his frame helped him cope with the warp issues somewhat, he simply lacked the casting ability to use it to its full potential. Even with Hunze's attempts at channeling power to it, the AI was still unable to go exactly where he desired.

But finally, they reached their destination. Or got close enough, anyway. And from there they made their approach to the sprawling docking port where the wealthy and powerful kept their craft.

It had been something of a coup, the emmik keeping his luxury ship at the docks rather than at his estate. Either he was not quite so well off as it seemed, or he simply felt no need to have all of his toys cluttering his grounds. Whatever the reason, it would at least make Hunze and Dukaan's infiltration a bit less harrowing.

But not easy, by any means.

Dukaan had modified his uniform as best he could with the equipment Kip had aboard. It wasn't perfect by any stretch, but the sides of the uniform beneath the armpits were now held shut with tactical Velcro, a silent opening material that would allow him to conceal his second set of arms inside the uniform but still push them free if need be for combat and escape.

They both hoped it would not come to that.

"Wow, it *is* a big one," Hunze said of the emmik's ship as Kip flew well past the docking stations of the wealthy and powerful, heading across to the landing zone for the everyday rabble's less opulent craft.

"This Navoon must be a skilled navigator indeed if he is housed aboard so luxurious a vessel," Dukaan mused.

"You know, size isn't everything," Kip chimed in.

"We know, Kip. And you're twice the ship that thing could ever be," Hunze said, playing to the quirky AI's ego.

"More than that," Kip replied smugly. "I set us down as close as I could to the main thoroughfare you'll want to take to the ship. You'll still have a bit of a walk, though. Unless you steal someone's ride, that is."

"Which would bring undue attention upon us," Dukaan said. "No, I think we shall proceed on foot and stay out of sight. Stealth is worth the delay."

Dukaan and Hunze slid loose overcloaks over their uniforms and headed out.

"Not bringing your new sword with?" Kip asked as they headed for the airlock door.

"I think that might draw unwanted attention," Hunze replied. "And besides, we are sneaking in and sneaking out. There should be no need for violence."

"Famous last words," the ship joked.

.   .   .

The trek across the docking and landing area of so many craft took a bit longer than Hunze and Dukaan had anticipated, despite being able to utilize the main thoroughfare. But it wasn't so much as to make them reconsider Kip's suggestion of stealing a conveyance of some sort. They were there to blend in, get who they needed, then vanish.

The long walk also allowed them to assess the luxury ship better as they approached it, taking their time so as to not make a foolish error as they attempted their infiltration. Unlike Bawb, they were not experienced at this sort of thing, and while the knowledge Hunze had received was fairly extensive, it did not include espionage and skulduggery.

Bawb had not thought she would need such a skill set, and thus had not added it to the already large amount of knowledge shared in the neuro-stim. It was something Hunze was finding herself regretting as they looked at the imposing craft before them.

From what they could tell, there were multiple entrances. They would need to select wisely if they hoped to blend in with the lowest ranks of the ship. Of course, that could also help them if they did choose unwisely, allowing them to play it off as the foolish mistake of newbies. But that would draw attention, and they wanted to avoid that if at all possible.

The lowest level rear gangway seemed to be the most logical entry point, and, given the periodic coming and going of crew but none who looked like passengers, they felt that assessment would likely be correct.

"And if not?" Dukaan asked.

"Then we improvise," Hunze replied as they stepped into an alleyway and shed their overcloaks. "How do I look?" she asked.

"Caps seem to be an acceptable part of the uniform,"

Dukaan said. "But I've not seen anyone with a scarf around their head beneath it, such as yours."

"I realize that. But if they see my hair, things could get difficult," Hunze said, the thick mass of her hair separated into smaller braids running through her collar into her uniform and wrapping around her body. The amount of power she could call upon if need be was enormous, but she sincerely hoped she would not require it.

"This is it," she said in a hushed voice as they approached the gangway. "Are you ready, Dukaan?"

"Not much I can do if not at this point, is there?" he said as they set foot on the long ramp and made their way into the ship.

They passed only one other crew member along the way, and judging by her uniform, she was just as new as they were. So far, it seemed, Olo's plan was working. Now they just had to find this Navoon person and secure his services. With what Hunze had to offer, they were confident they could achieve just that.

CHAPTER SIXTY-ONE

"He's a *what*?" Hunze hissed as she and Dukaan hurriedly tucked into a storage compartment to discuss the monkey wrench that had just lodged itself in their plan.

"A slave," Dukaan replied. "A Drook slave, and Emmik Chintsal's favorite, it would seem."

This was not what they'd planned for, and was certainly not what they'd expected. The plan was to locate this Navoon person and buy him out from under the emmik's nose. But if he was a slave, that changed everything.

"Are you sure that's what the man said?" Hunze asked, pacing the room.

"Please, cease your agitated walking. It is unsettling."

"My apologies."

"Now, the man I asked was quite clear when he told me Navoon's location. Level four, rear compartments, with all of the other Drooks."

"What do we do, Dukaan? This changes everything."

"It does, yet it does not. Our goal is still the same. Acquire the services of this man and secret him off of the ship. The only difference is we must now do so in a different manner than we had anticipated. A bribe, as you had planned, will not suffice. But perhaps something else might."

"Such as?" Hunze asked.

"Such as his freedom," Dukaan replied. "From what you have said, it is something most would not even dare dream of, let alone hold out hope for. If we bring him the opportunity to be a free man, he will come with us for that payment alone, I would wager."

Hunze thought about it a moment. He was right. Drooks, like Ootaki, were often kept in slavery their entire lives. To have the chance to be free, it was something that was more precious than coin or even magic.

"Let's find him, then. We need to be quick and quiet. Fortunately, we're not in flight, so he won't be working. Do you think you can lure him away so we may speak to him in private?"

"Lure? My dear Hunze, I am a uniformed crew member of this vessel. I will simply tell him his presence is required and have him follow me."

"Oh, of course," she replied, remembering her own slave mindset of not so long ago.

He was right. Given direction, the man would certainly follow along as commanded, the very thought of independence and freedom long buried and forgotten.

"Let us find a suitable compartment near the Drook lodging area. I will wait for you there. And once you've brought him there, we will free him and make him our ally."

"This is an emmik, though, Hunze. From what you've said, they're powerful magic users in their own right, even if they aren't vislas. Are you sure you can get the collar off of him without anyone knowing?"

Hunze grinned. "*That* is something I am certain of," she replied. "All we need now is to have him separated from the others so we can complete this part of our task."

Dukaan nodded. "Then let us waste no further time discussing. Let us get to work."

Hunze was pacing again. This time in a different compartment on a different level in the emmik's ship. She couldn't help it, though. The waiting for Dukaan and his prize's return was increasing her nervousness by the minute.

What if something went wrong? What if Dukaan was captured?

The door slid open and her friend quickly entered, ushering an older, heavyset Drook with him.

"This isn't the navigation chamber," Navoon said, confused. "Why have you brought me here?"

Hunze stepped from where she'd tucked away when the door opened as a precaution. "You've been brought here because my friend and I are in dire need of a man of your skills," she said. "Please, step over here."

Despite the situation shifting to something very different than what he'd expected when the odd-looking tall man had fetched him, Navoon was accustomed to taking orders and obeyed without even thinking.

Hunze pulled one of the smallest braids of hair from within her uniform and wrapped it around his control collar.

"What are you doing to my collar? If you interfere with it, the emmik will——"

Hunze cast her spell, the magical charge coursing through the little braid, wrapping itself around the collar's magic and snuffing it out, resulting in the collar shattering and falling to the deck in pieces. Navoon, however, hadn't felt a thing. Not so much as a tingle.

She smiled as she tucked the hair back into its hiding place. "There. You are a free man, Navoon. Now, come with us."

"What?" he said, confused. "No, I can't go anywhere."

"You fail to understand, my friend. You are no longer a slave," Dukaan said.

"But this is my home. I don't want to leave my home. The emmik treats me well. And I have a purpose here. I'm respected! I won't go!"

Hunze and Dukaan shared a look. Things had just gotten complicated once again. The Drook was not just a slave, he was institutionalized. So much of his life had been spent doing this one thing that the thought of anything else terrified him.

Now, Dukaan could easily carry the man, especially if Hunze cast a stun spell upon him first, but that would make them the same as his former owner, and that was not how they wanted to gain his services.

"Navoon, listen to me. I was a slave like you once, but now I am free," Hunze said, pulling the scarf from her head, revealing what she was.

"You're Ootaki," he said, shocked. "A *free* Ootaki? But all of your people are slaves."

"I am not," she replied. "Just as you are no longer."

The situation had not changed, but this new revelation had a profound effect on the recalcitrant man's attitude. Suddenly, a new variable had shifted how he viewed the situation.

"If you come with us, you will be your own man. Free to do as you wish," Hunze continued. "But I know how it is. You've spent your entire life driving powerful vessels. What could you possibly want to do besides that?"

The Drook nodded. This woman understood, it seemed.

"But let me tell you a little secret," Hunze said, leaning in close. "Back where we are from, there is a group of free Drooks who power a mighty ship. But they do so not as slaves, but as free crew. Masters of their own destinies flying that ship of their own free will, seeing the galaxy," she said, dangling the carrot in front of the navigator. "You could join them, if you wish," she added, hoping the casual offer might sway the man.

Navoon thought it over silently. It was an opportunity he might have fantasized about in his youth, but he had long ago outgrown such folly. And yet, here it was. A chance to continue living his life the way he wanted to, flying a mighty ship, but doing so as a free man, surrounded by other free Drooks.

It really was the best of both worlds for one so institutionalized as he was. A chance to stay in a familiar, comfortable role, but without a collar around his neck. Slowly, the hope he had so long ago buried started coming back to the surface.

"And you say this ship is a mighty one?"

"Not just a mighty ship," Hunze said. "But a shimmer-cloaked one at that. A vessel the likes of which even you have never seen."

The idea of leaving was still terrifying, but that last little nugget of temptation was enough it seemed.

"Is it far?" Navoon asked.

And at that moment, Hunze knew they had him.

"Not far at all for a man of your skills," she replied. "Guide us to where we need to go and you will be aboard it in no time."

Navoon's demeanor changed ever so slightly as his decision cemented into place. "Very well, then," he said. "Let us go to your vessel. I think I would very much like to see this free Drook ship of which you speak."

CHAPTER SIXTY-TWO

Kara and Vee had spent much of the day lounging around the tower following their sleepover. They'd decided the best possible course of action was to simply act as normal as possible to buy themselves a bit of space later in the day.

So they stayed up late, slept in, and had a hearty late breakfast when Grundsch informed them that once again Tulagda had prepared them something, which would be waiting for them in the dining chamber.

They appeared to be two perfectly normal girls having a perfectly normal day, but the reality was far from it. In fact, the teens had been going over the cryptic words of the heretic assassin all morning, trying to figure out what exactly the strange woman had meant. Finally, they came to a decision. They would have to go investigate themselves.

Come early afternoon, the girls excused themselves to head upstairs.

"What time will you be wanting dinner?" Grundsch asked, somehow knowing to appear just as they were rising to leave. It made Kara even more suspicious that her father had given explicit instructions to spy on them. And that made getting to the bottom of what was really going on all the more pressing.

"I don't know, Grundsch. We had such a late meal, how about we let you know a bit later."

"That would be perfectly acceptable," he replied.

"Great. And now, if you'll excuse us, we're both kind of tired and could really do with a little nap."

"Of course, Denna Palmarian," he replied respectfully as they passed him, heading for the lift platform.

They took the lift all the way up to Karasalia's chambers, where they quickly changed into more outdoorsy adventure wear. They then exited her rooms and closed the door behind them, heading for the stairs rather than the lift platform to take them up a few levels to where the floating garden in question was tethered.

They had picked apart the heretic's cryptic words ad nauseum and come to the conclusion over and over that there was only one place she could have been talking about. The one blighted floating garden. But why, they had no idea. There was one way to find out, though.

Kara and Vee were careful to exit the structure onto one of the gardens that was shielded from view of the tower denizens for the most part. It wouldn't do to have Grundsch or one of the other guards look outside and see them jumping from garden to garden. Sure, those weren't off limits to the teen, but it was the jumping part that she was worried about.

But the only way to reach the sequestered platform was by a less than conventional route, the more direct path blocked by the current placement of the gardens. A configuration that happened to obstruct the path to the blighted garden with more than one water feature.

The girls made their way along the edges of the first of the verdant platforms until they reached the far edge. It was only a two-meter jump, and the adjacent garden was floating just a little lower at that end, making it even easier to reach.

"You sure you're ready for this?" Kara asked as she backed up to get a running start.

"Oh, shut up and go already," Vee replied with a grin.

Kara didn't hesitate, launching into a fast run and hurtling herself through the air. She landed safely on the other platform with plenty of room to spare. Before she could turn to goad her friend on, Vee came tumbling to the ground beside her.

"Lost my footing," she said, rising to her feet and brushing herself off. "Shall we?" she asked, gesturing to the pathway leading to the far edge––the edge from which they would next throw themselves across a deadly gap.

"A whole locked-down building, but Father never thought of this, did he?" Kara laughed. "Come on!"

The two made quick time across the sprawling gardens once they were far from the tower and any possible prying eyes. And the floating garden they were heading toward was the farthest out of them all, making it incredibly unlikely they would be seen.

"I still don't get it," Vee said. "I mean, she talks about flying, but the only flying you'll be doing from up here is to your death. I don't think any safety spells are in place on this platform."

"Probably not," Kara agreed. "It's out of commission, so why waste the magic on it?"

"You sounded like your father just now."

"Just being practical," Kara shot back.

"*Garden. To fly. Get Free, uh. Escape. Rock hides. Dead trees,*" Vee said. "Nope, still makes no sense. And what in the worlds is a *Maliboo*?"

"I don't know. But the rock feature was just meant to be decorative, but it's pretty big and is over by the dead Yannal, so I think that's the best place to have a look around. Maybe there's some sort of clue over there."

"But we have to go around one of the larger rocks to get there," Vee said. "The one up against the edge. And it's a long way down."

"We can do this, Vee. Come on, we'll just take it slow," Kara said, then headed off with or without her friend.

"Ugh. Fine," Vee relented, following her friend to the precipice.

It was indeed a long way down, but there was at least a foot's width of ledge for them to stand on, and the rock, while in their way, did also provide ample handholds as they shimmied along to get to where the Yannal had withered and died.

After such an adrenaline-pumping effort, the end result was something of a letdown.

"There's nothing here, Kara," Vee said. "No one ever came here, even before the garden got the blight in the first place."

Kara looked around the area. It was blocked in by the rocks, a private little patch of formerly lush garden thirty meters across. For all she could see, it looked like Vee was right. There was nothing there.

"Come on, this was a waste of time," Vee said, heading back the way they came.

Kara was about to follow her when something odd caught her eye near the farthest pile of rocks. "Hang on, Vee. Check this out."

"Check what out?"

"Over there," she said, pointing to the rocky cairn. "I thought I saw something."

"What?"

"I don't know. It just looked, *off*, somehow. Just come on, it'll only take a minute."

Reluctantly and with an exasperated sigh, Vee followed her across the dried-out vegetation.

"Ouch!" Kara exclaimed as she bumped into something hard.

Hard, and invisible.

"What in the worlds?" she said, reaching out to feel the substantial shape hidden right in front of her.

"What is it, Kara?" Vee asked, running her hands along the cool, hard surface.

"I don't have the slightest idea. But it's not a shimmer."

"How can you tell?"

"Because there's no magic that I can sense," Kara replied. "And if you touch a shimmer, you can feel its power."

"*Garden. To fly. Get Free, uh. Escape. Rock hides. Dead trees,*" Vee said. "It still doesn't make any sense. There's nothing about an invisible whatever this is."

"Rock hides," Kara said. "This is right by the rocks. And the dead tree. She was giving me directions, I think."

"But fly? Get free? Escape? I don't get it."

"Neither do I," Kara agreed. "And what about that other word. *Maliboo*?"

"Passkey accepted," a quiet voice said in the thin air at the sound of the word. A hiss then escaped the hidden object, followed by a quiet whoosh as an elongated panel slid back, revealing the very much visible interior of what appeared to be a small, elongated cylinder. At least, that's what the inside looked like, though it felt as though it might have small wings on the exterior.

A red glow illuminated the space. A tempting new mystery beckoning them.

"Come on," Kara said, not waiting for a reply as she climbed into the hatch.

CHAPTER SIXTY-THREE

It was a tight fit inside the mysterious craft filled with otherworldly mechanisms and means of illumination. The red light glowed all around, yet there wasn't the faintest whiff of the spell powering it. Likewise, the array of lights illuminated on what appeared to be a control console of some sort had nothing magical powering them.

There were two seats closely mounted, and Kara and Vee cautiously slid into them, the memory foam instantly molding to their bodies, suspending them in utter comfort and security.

The door slid shut silently, cutting them off from the sounds of the outside world. At the same time, the interior illumination shifted from red to regular spectrum light, allowing them to see the full detail of the craft's interior. It was unlike anything either girl had ever seen in their life.

"We're trapped! We're sealed off from the outside!" Vee shrieked.

The walls seemed to blur, then turned transparent, the world around them suddenly visible to them, except for the areas where consoles were mounted.

"Did it just become transparent?" Vee asked.

"I believe it did," Kara replied, the thrill of discovery coursing through her veins.

"What is this thing?" Vee asked, her eyes wide with both delight and confusion.

"I am Pod," the pod said in a pleasant man's voice that seemed to come out of thin air. "And I did not become transparent. I activated the adaptive camouflage nanites and had them give the semblance of transparency."

"Did this device just speak?" Kara wondered aloud.

"Of course I did. I am Pod," the pod repeated.

"What's adaptive camouflage?" Vee asked. "Is it like a shimmer?"

"I do not know what a shimmer is," Pod replied. "Adaptive camouflage, however, is by definition the use of nanotechnology to create a visual representation of the surface behind the object placed before it, thus creating the illusion of invisibility."

"But, this magic does not exist," Kara said.

"Magic? I do not understand," Pod said. "Magic is not real. It is a thing of story books and fairy tales. Nanotechnology and quantum AI, however, are very much real."

"Magic is real," Kara said, calling up a basic illumination spell, brightening the interior. "See?"

"I do not recognize this energy profile, nor the source of the illumination," Pod said. "I will request a data upgrade when my creator returns."

That caught Kara's attention, and she asked a question. One to which she was pretty sure she knew the answer.

"Your creator? Who is your creator? The assassin?"

"Assassin? I do not possess files on an assassin. I am Pod. I am a basic-tier AI transport unit. My files are limited due to my size constraints."

"But why?" Kara asked.

"Proper processing and storage for an AI intelligence normally requires more space than is available within my airframe. This iteration of my design did not have the capacity to house more without compromising flight and life support functions."

"Whatever that means," Vee said. "But if you don't know the heretic assassin, then who created you?"

"Daisy," Pod replied. "I am her latest project. I was not due for atmospheric flight for another moon, but something happened and I was launched early."

"What happened?" Kara asked.

"Unknown," Pod replied. "I found myself adrift as I powered up. But where is Daisy?"

"I think he means the heretic," Kara said.

"I kinda gathered," Vee replied.

"Uh, Daisy tried to kill my father," Kara informed the tiny craft. "She's imprisoned in my father's tower now."

"Daisy is imprisoned? What does this mean?" Pod asked, sounding almost like a toddler in his uncertainty.

"Look, we really should go," Kara said. "I need to go talk to my uncle about all of this."

"Okay. Where are we going?" Pod asked as a low hum rumbled through the vessel as flight systems displays flashed to life on his consoles. "My navs tether signal has been severed. I am on my own, just sitting here, waiting."

"Hang on. We?" Vee said. "I don't see any Drooks here, so how do you plan on flying?"

"The same way I always do," Pod replied. "And what is a Drook?"

"The casters who power craft for flight," she replied.

"I fly utilizing a basic fusion arc reactor. There is no 'Drook' power on this vessel. I am not designed for warp travel, however, so any longer distances would need to be covered aboard my home ship."

"Home ship?"

"Yes. Freya. Where I was residing until this occurred."

"Is Freya another talking craft like you?" Vee asked.

"Oh, no. Not like me."

"There's a relief," Vee said. "The thought of more talking ships was making my head—"

"She is much smarter than me. A class of her own, top tier stealth AI with full nanotech complement and upgraded armor nanites of her own design."

"Oh."

Kara was astounded by the discovery, and it was one that could change everything. The heretic, Daisy, was not an assassin. At least, not so far as her strange craft was aware. And she had built this thing. Built a self-propelled vessel with an intelligence of its own. It was horrifying, yet exhilarating at the same time.

But why would someone so brilliant and advanced have tried to kill her father? It made no sense.

"We need answers, Vee," Kara said. "Pod, you say you can fly?"

"Of course."

"Then let's fly. Show us what you can do."

The scene shown on the screens around them shifted as the little craft lifted up into the sky and flew away from the visla's tower.

Its adaptive camouflage was rippling now that it was in motion due to it only truly functioning at its peak when stationary. The result was a strange shape that some people caught a glimpse of out of the corner of their eye, but when they looked up, they simply couldn't identify what they saw.

"Where are we going, Kara?" Vee said, clutching the arms of her seat tightly as they glided over the city.

"I don't know, Vee. We need to warn Leila that something is up."

"But she's long gone."

"Yeah, but Captain Sandah flies one of my father's ships, and they all have a secret tag spell so he can keep track of them."

"So we just follow that. You do know how to follow that, don't you?" Vee asked.

"Well, yes and no. Yes, I've seen him cast the spell to zero in on his craft plenty of times, but the problem is, I'm pretty sure we need to be within a few systems distance for it to work."

"In other words, it won't help us," Vee said.

"Not at the moment, no. But my uncle may be able to help," Kara said. "In any case, I'm free for now, and we've at least got to try. My father is up to something, Vee, and we need to find out what."

The teen then gave Pod basic directions to her uncle's estate. It was clear across the planet, but the unusual vessel assured her it could make the flight without issue.

"This is it, Vee," Kara said. "We're finally going on an adventure."

CHAPTER SIXTY-FOUR

Navoon had never left Emmik Chintsal's ship as a free man in his lifetime. In fact, he couldn't even remember the age when he wasn't bound by a control collar.

Interestingly, his lengthy service under the emmik made him one of the faces the crew didn't question. He'd always been there, and always would. So when he was walking down the corridor with a pair of new crew members, no one thought twice of it.

That he had a coat with a collar that covered much of his neck was of no consequence to them. However, that same article of clothing conveniently hid the absence of his control collar, just in case any should take a second look as he passed.

Leaving the ship was a far more unusual occurrence for him, or any Drook for that matter. But again, being accompanied by members of the emmik's crew, none thought to stop and ask what they were doing. It was akin to the ancient Earth adage about how wearing a hardhat could get you into any building. So it was for a Drook leaving the ship. So long as he was with "official" crew, none paid any heed.

The Drook had been reticent when they first departed the

innermost chambers of the emmik's ship, the whole freedom and fleeing thing not quite sinking in as anything more than an abstract at that point, and a scary one at that. But once they'd gotten over the terrifying hump of exiting the gangplank and blending into the city, a new vitality seemed to have burst from within him. It was as if all those years of captivity-induced restraint had been suddenly shed, leaving the man free to take in the world with fresh eyes.

"These clothes, are they what is the fashion of the day?" he asked as they tucked into the alleyway they'd stashed their non-crew attire in.

Naturally, they'd brought a few things that would fit just about any sized man as well. Fortunately, Navoon wasn't that large of a fellow.

"I believe it is," Hunze said, slipping from her uniform, revealing the form-fitting outfit she'd been wearing beneath it all along. She slid her overcloak back on, quickly pulling the hood over her golden hair as the others changed.

"You...you have four arms!" Navoon said, gawking as Dukaan pulled off his uniform, letting his second set of arms free.

"Yes, I do," the Chithiid replied with an amused grin. "And I have these as well," he added, turning and pulling off the cap, revealing the second set of eyes on the back of his head.

"I-I've never seen anything like it," Navoon said.

"I would suspect not. You see, I am not from around here. In fact, I come from very, *very* far away."

"And is it there you wish me to help you return?" the Drook asked as he fastened his new attire in place.

"Yes, in a manner of speaking. Our destination will allow us to return home. You'll see when we get there. I'm certain you will find it a most fascinating and rewarding voyage."

Hunze pulled out her comms and signaled their AI friend. "Kip, we have him and are on our way to you."

"It's about time," the ship replied. "We've been on this planet too long as it is. I'm getting antsy."

"I understand. We'll try to hurry back," Hunze said, then tucked the device back in her pocket.

"We should go," Dukaan said, turning for the street. "Kip is right, time is ticking, and the longer we delay, the more likely our new friend's escape will be noted."

"I am eager to meet this other friend of yours," Navoon said. "And once we have fled this world, might we stop somewhere, anywhere, that I can walk the streets without fear of recapture? It is a sensation my newfound freedom has found me unexpectedly desiring."

Hunze and Dukaan shared a smile. They hadn't been sure about this mission, but now that Navoon was out in the world, uncollared and free, the pure joy he was experiencing made it all worthwhile.

Of course, his being able to get them to the portal wasn't so bad either.

The walk back to their waiting ship was longer than they'd have preferred, but there was simply no way he could drop down in the middle of the thoroughfare and pick them up. The roadways were far too narrow, and the scene it would cause, well, it was simply unacceptable.

So, back to the open space of the landing field it would have to be.

Fortunately, they did not encounter any problems along the way, and were even able to pause for a moment to buy a fried dough pastry for their new friend. There was no line, and it only took a minute, and the look of delight on the man's face as he bit into it made the pause well worth their time.

"Thank you, my new friends," he said, chewing happily as they stepped into the wider landing field area. "I think I am going to enjoy free life very much indeed."

Kip was just up ahead, his airlock door already cycling open as soon as he saw his friends in the crowd. Dukaan hurried ahead, making sure the path was clear, while Hunze and Navoon followed, the Drook safely behind her, just in case anyone might happen to look more closely at the man.

"Everything good?" Kip asked as Dukaan stepped aboard.

"Yes, Kip. And I think you'll like our new navigator. He seems a fine fellow."

Hunze had just stepped up into the ship when a cry from behind her made her spin. A masked man had seized Navoon and was pulling him back, five of his friends covering his retreat. Without thinking, Hunze grabbed the newly restored Vespus Blade, still safe in its sheath, and leapt from the ship.

A powerful spell blasted out as soon as her feet hit the soil, sealing Kip in a force field, unable to take off or even fire his weapons. And Dukaan was still aboard, just as trapped as his AI friend.

Hunze didn't hesitate, quickly charging the men, bashing them with the sheathed weapon, not wanting to draw blood in this public place, but also needing very much to rescue the poor Drook from the men's clutches.

Navoon, for his part, was suddenly inspired by his new freedom and lashed out against his captors. But it quickly became apparent that the poor man was not their target at all when a dagger was unceremoniously plunged into his chest, dropping him to the ground, dead, leaving the men with free hands with which to capture the Ootaki woman.

It was a trap. A trap for Hunze. Kip had been right. They'd stayed in one place too long, but it wasn't that they'd been observed. It was the hidden tracker spell that had led the very pricey and very elite hit team to capture the golden-haired woman.

Emmik Hunstra had been humiliated in front of his arena. Now his hired goons would remedy that situation.

Hunze's soft nature cried out at the death of the gentle

333

Drook, but Bawb's Wampeh Ghalian spirit took over, sending her into motion without even realizing it, her body moving on instinct alone.

The attackers swarmed her, but Hunze's skill shone through, and in moments four of them lay on the ground, broken and unconscious, or very much wishing they were. But they had not come alone, she noted.

A tall, pale man watched her fight with interest, then nodded to what had seemed like average bystanders just moments before.

The men shed their disguises and charged her, a seven-on-one fight. It wasn't even close to fair. Not with Hunze possessing Bawb's knowledge and skill.

Like their companions, those men were quickly dispatched as well.

The remaining man smiled, his pointed teeth flashing in the sunlight, and Hunze could feel his power as he moved closer. A Wampeh. And one like Bawb. He could take another's power, and it seemed this one had fed recently and was full up with magical potential.

Hunze smiled back at him, a trace of Bawb's defiant nature showing on his love's face.

The Wampeh quickly cast a stun spell, but Hunze was ready, easily blocking it with her own magic. This actually startled the man, and she could see the gears suddenly spinning behind his eyes.

An Ootaki who could cast? Oh, this was not going to be nearly as easy as he thought.

His smile started to grow, and Hunze knew full well what was going through his mind. This man could drink the power from a user and make it his own, but Ootaki power was always tied to their hair, rendering them useless to the Wampeh. But Hunze was different. She was connected to that magic, and if he could lay his fangs upon her neck, that power would be his.

He had been contracted quite handsomely to bring her back to the emmik, but if she arrived a little drained, it wouldn't make a difference and he'd be paid just the same.

The Wampeh flung several spells at Hunze as he charged her, which she blocked and countered easily. But his intent was not to stop her with magic, but to overpower her with his superior fighting skills.

The man moved in a blur, his mix of magic and combatives a flowing ballet of death and power. Hunze's body was not trained to the degree Bawb's was, but she was nevertheless extremely fit as the result of working hard to become so after so many years as a slave. As a result, she was quite capable of matching the man's attack. For the time being, at least.

The Wampeh seemed surprised, yet simultaneously pleased to have an actual challenge for once. It had been so long, he almost forgot what it felt like to have to not hold back.

They exchanged spells and blows, faster and faster, but much to the Wampeh's dismay, each one was a perfect counter for the other. This in and of itself wouldn't be a concern, but for the fact he was now utilizing secret spells and attacks of the Wampeh Ghalian. He was just wrapping his head around the impossibility of the situation when Hunze drew a series of arcane spells from deep within Bawb's memories.

She unleashed a flurry of blows, followed by the secret magic. The sheer force of it, backed by her Ootaki power, forced the Wampeh to draw upon every last ounce of the magic he had so recently stolen from his powerful victim. And even then, it was just barely enough to halt the onslaught.

In the heat of battle, Hunze had unintentionally called upon a spell that was only to be used in the most dire of circumstances. And even then, but a mere handful of men and women in the entire galaxy knew this spell and its counter. The man she was battling just so happened to be one of them.

The Wampeh seemed drained, his energy flagging from his

defense, but then he abruptly lunged forward, drawing a long blade from the sheath hidden on his back.

Hunze reacted instantly, drawing the Vespus Blade in kind, the blued metal ringing out as it drew from her internal magic, its own enchantment flashing briefly as it checked the Wampeh's attack and sent him tumbling backward.

"Parlay!" the man blurted. "By the tenets of Gorzkin, I request parlay!"

Hunze didn't know what that meant, but Bawb's essence flowing through her did, and something deep within told her to lower her blade.

The Wampeh, likewise, ceased combatives and lowered his weapon, though he kept it at the ready.

"What would you say to me?" Hunze demanded. "Your lackeys killed an innocent man just now. There is no honor in that."

"No, there is not, and had you not handled them yourself, I would have made an example of the local help to show what happens to those who disobey my commands. You were the target. The Drook was not to be harmed, and for that, I apologize."

There was something familiar about the way the man spoke. How he acted. And Hunze was pretty sure she knew why.

"You are skilled," she said.

"As are you," the man replied. "Far more than any I have ever encountered, in fact. Your techniques are...*unusual*," he said, hinting at something far more than that.

"I learned from the best," Hunze replied. "In a place he was not bound by certain *constraints*," she said, hinting at the oath that Bawb said no longer applied, as they were in an entirely different galaxy.

"Perhaps," the man said. "But you know the ways of the Wampeh Ghalian, yet you are Ootaki. And a magic-wielding one at that. And you not only possess a Vespus Blade, you also know how to utilize its enchantment. That should be impossible. Who of my kind did you kill to claim such power?"

"I killed no one," she replied. "Like I said, I was trained by the best."

"Impossible. These are skills known only to the highest of the Wampeh Ghalian, and none would part with them willingly."

"My love did," she replied.

"Your love?" the Wampeh said, confused.

"The man who saved me. Who taught me," she replied. "You would know him as the Geist," Hunze added, savoring the look of shock on the man's face.

While others would doubt that a centuries-dead man was her boyfriend, this particular Wampeh sensed something about her that made him believe her claim.

"*Orphalla nictus,*" he said, casting a secret greeting of the highest ranks of his order.

"*Nictus sorallia makta,*" she replied with Bawb's knowledge, the spells merging with each other in a covert greeting known to the most select few.

"I am Kort," he said, sheathing his weapon, his physical demeanor shifting to one showing no threat. "*Torvalius oompa,*" he cast, releasing the force field from around Kip. "Go," he said, turning to the bystanders. A half dozen of them blended into the crowd and vanished while the real bystanders merely looked on in shock.

"You had more friends, I see," Hunze noted.

"As you have just become," he replied. "On my honor and that of the order of the Wampeh Ghalian, I guarantee no harm shall come to you from my hand or those of my people. But tell me your name, strange Ootaki who casts Ghalian magic and wields a Ghalian sword."

"I am called Hunze," she said.

"Well, Hunze, it appears we have much to discuss."

CHAPTER SIXTY-FIVE

Charlie and Bawb were tired. Tired of sitting atop their Zomoki friend as she jumped from system to system, pausing to rest on habitable planets periodically, then resuming their trek. It was a fair distance to reach the Balamar Wastelands, and Ara was wasting no time getting there.

The portal was on a weekly cycle now, and they only had a few more chances before it would close to them permanently. At this moment, the three magic-wielding beings found themselves regretting not keeping someone behind as a backstop for their safety plan.

But they'd never expected their forces to be scattered and themselves tasked with facing and unmasking their deadly opponent on their own. But what had started out as an intelligence gathering mission and quickly morphed into a relic quest, and now a retrieval and dispersal mission.

They were going to find whatever was left of the Balamar waters and get them to the forces waiting on the other side of the portal. So bolstered, their people might just stand a better chance against what appeared to be a Wampeh visla leading the enemy fleet. And an incredibly powerful one at that.

Yet something as simple as those magical waters could spell the difference between victory and failure. *If* they could find them, that is.

Charlie hadn't been to the desert plain since their battle against Visla Maktan and the Council of Twenty. It hadn't been that long ago in his memory, but when one travels in time, memory can be fallible.

Things would be different, and the wasteland itself might have even been overgrown, reclaimed by the planet itself, though Ara was quite confident the killing spell that had ended Visla Balamar in the first place was so violent and potent that it would take millennia rather than centuries for plant life to slowly creep back into the empty wasteland.

"The next jump will take us there," Ara said as her friends loaded back onto her back.

They'd been resting the better part of the afternoon on a warm planet with abundant water and game, both of which the dragon had taken great pleasure in, recharging her energy as she filled her belly.

"You feeling ready to jump?" Charlie asked, not wanting to unnecessarily drain his friend's magic with too frequent casting.

"Yes. The final jump is not far and will not require much magic," she replied.

"Okay, then. Let's hit up the wastelands and see if we can't find ourselves the last dregs of Visla Balamar's wonderful waters," Charlie said.

Ara flapped her wings and took to the air, heading straight for space. Free of the atmosphere, she drew upon her Zomoki magic and jumped, the spell taking them the rest of the way to their destination.

They arrived just outside of orbit, immediately descending into the atmosphere. The giant ring of desolate, red soil acted as a sort of bullseye from that height, rendering further navigation pointless. They knew where they were heading, and didn't need any magic to find it.

The area seemed pretty much as it had been hundreds of years ago when they'd last seen it. Empty of life, the stone remnants of structures dotting the landscape like geological formations. But the sands had shifted over time, and nothing was as it had appeared on their prior visit.

Ara touched down in what she believed was the general area they'd been before. But in a vast desert like this, it was easy to miss your mark by miles, if not more. Charlie and Bawb hopped down, walking the sands, scanning for any signs of their prior visit so many years ago. But the Council would have retrieved the wreckage of their ships, so no such easy landmarks were laid out for them in the sands.

Without warning, violent magic blasted the air and ground around them, their constantly cast protective spells deflecting the assault.

"We're under attack!" Charlie yelled, spinning to see who was shooting at them.

Several fair-sized ships were bearing down on them from above, apparently having followed them in from space. More magic was cast, this time from below, the forces appearing to have come at them from the edges of the wasteland where they'd set up near the lush forests surrounding the red sands.

"There appear to be forces on the ground as well," Bawb noted, reinforcing their magical shielding. "I believe our adversary has stationed a garrison here after utilizing your old ship for the portal, Charlie."

"Just in case we came back," the Earthman grumbled. "Just our frigging luck."

Ara immediately took to the air, casting powerful spells at the attacking ships. Charlie and Bawb likewise drew upon their magic and unleashed their power against the craft as they swooped in lower in an attempt to flatten them with their spells.

Ara banked hard, locking in on the tail of one of the ships and spraying it with her most powerful magical flames. The ship, however, appeared unscathed. Charlie and Bawb also cast violent attacks, all of which flew true, but which were also deflected and absorbed by the ships' shielding.

"Uh, Bob? What's going on?" Charlie asked as he cast another attack against the ground forces rapidly approaching. Those, at least, seemed more vulnerable to his magic. But the ships in the air? That was a whole other problem.

Bawb unleashed a blast from his wand. *That* seemed to have an impact, though why a single strand embedded in that Earth wood would be more effective than the mass of hair he wore was unknown.

"It would seem that the visla who positioned these ships here did so with an incredible amount of defensive power backing them. It's unlike any I've ever seen."

Despite the enormous power Charlie and his friends possessed, there was suddenly the very real possibility they might not be able to overcome this opponent. Given the immense magic they each possessed, that was a very disconcerting notion.

Of course, they had been expending power since arriving in this galaxy, and minus the Earth's sun to so quickly recharge them, they were not operating at full capacity. The Ootaki hair Bawb wore was still incredibly potent, but nowhere near as much as when it was soaking up the magic from the other galaxy.

In this one, vislas and emmiks would spend years channeling power into their Ootaki, charging their hair over time. It wasn't like that in the other galaxy, however, and they'd become so accustomed to the rapid recharges that the very real possibility they could drain their magic in this one hadn't really occurred to them until this moment.

Ara, likewise, was having a difficult time of it in the air. Her magical defenses were keeping her from any serious harm––so far, anyway––but her attacks were having little to no effect on the enemy ships.

"We cannot continue like this," she sent down to her friends.

"I know," Charlie replied. *"Can you get to us? We're gonna have to make a run for it."*

"I do not know if I can get past these ships. They're blocking me from reaching you. And I see forces approaching you from both sides."

"Well, that's just fucking great," Charlie grumbled. *"Stay safe, Ara. Bob and I will take care of ourselves."*

He turned to his friend, realizing this might very well be their last stand.

"Better to go out using it all than leave anything on the table, right?" he said to his friend.

Bawb knew what Charlie meant. They would cast together, using every last drop of magic they possessed in hopes of at least taking as many of their enemy with them as possible. If they were going to go, it was going to be in a blaze of glory.

"It has been an honor, Charlie," Bawb said, locking eyes with his friend.

"Me too," Charlie replied, already pulling deep from within, calling up the most potent of his magic.

But for some reason, Charlie paused.

"Bob? Do you feel that?"

The Wampeh reached out with his senses, but it wasn't just magic in the air. There was a rumbling shaking the ground, and it was getting closer.

Without warning the spell Bawb cast flew right through the enemy shielding, tearing into the smaller craft that had been hectoring them from above. The shattered wreckage fell to the ground hundreds of meters away. There would be no survivors.

The two men looked at one another, confused. Then Charlie's eyes focused on a rapidly approaching shape.

The man who had been sucked through a wormhole,

befriended a dragon, and traveled through time, found himself at a loss as his brain processed what he saw. Finally, he found his tongue.

"What the hell?" he said, a happy, yet confused smile growing on his face.

This was unexpected. Unexpected, but very welcome.

CHAPTER SIXTY-SIX

"Ara, we have company!" Charlie sent to his airborne friend.

"I see. But is that—?"

"Yeah, it is. How, I don't know, but it is."

The ships above didn't know how to react to their shielding suddenly weakening. They'd been so confident in the magic protecting them that when it faltered they hesitated, unsure. Something new was in play, and it was knocking down their shields as fast as they could cast them, despite the visla's stored magic bolstering their efforts.

An odd, purple glow illuminated the red sands despite the orange light of the planet's two suns. And it was growing near at a very fast pace. But it wasn't the glow that was shaking the ground and sending the enemy into a panicked scramble. It was *what* was glowing. For Charlie, it was a sight for sore eyes.

The giant mech had been buried in the sands of the wasteland for centuries, safely protected from the harsh elements on the surface, tucked away like an Easter egg waiting to be found. And what a deadly one it was at that.

Rika's magic was flowing through the machine, powering it effortlessly as only an Earth mage space pilot could. Her strange mix of power from both galaxies had melded and transformed into something new. New and potent.

She unleashed her magic again, targeting the craft above. The spell flew true, disabling the enemy's shielding enough for Ara's flaming attacks to penetrate. In moments, several of the ships were aflame. The amount of damage being done was uncertain at that early stage, but one thing was for sure. The tide had just turned.

A spray of pulse blasts tore into the ground forces that were rapidly approaching. A second later, the *Fujin* blasted past them with a sonic boom, the cyborg at the controls targeting the terrestrial troops before pulling up hard and unleashing a stream of rail gun sabots, the hypersonic projectiles perforating the enemy ships where their shields had failed, sending several crashing to the ground.

"You guys just gonna stand there gawking, or are you gonna fight?" Rika's voice boomed out over the mech's loudspeakers.

Charlie snapped out of his shock and began casting again in earnest. They weren't making a last stand after all. Not today.

"Let's go, Bob!" he shouted, charging into the fray once again, but this time his spells were not impotently deflected. This time, they were flying true and strong.

The enemy ships finally changed their tactics, dropping down low to allow their own ground troops to make a hasty jump to the sands to join the forces already advancing on the two men and the moving statue that had disrupted what should have been a slaughter. Their deadly contents disgorged onto the ground, the ships then lurched skyward once more, trying to target the troublesome Zomoki and its incredibly fast companion.

Jo was having the time of her life piloting the *Fujin*, and given the odds against them, she felt she was justified in using every last bit of weaponry at her disposal in this drastically outnumbered fight.

The poor magic users didn't know what to make of the impossible craft that was hurtling balls of energy and rods of metal at them. It was unlike any foe they'd ever faced, and their tactics were sadly lacking for it.

On the ground, however, a more traditional type of fighting was taking place. While magic was being cast fast and furious, the Tslavar horde charging the men on the ground were also wielding sharp and deadly weapons, anxious to plunge them into the hearts of their enemies.

There were simply too many to keep picking off one at a time, and while Rika was able to target individual ships or pockets of magically protected troops, numbers were simply not on their side.

Something had to be done, and fast.

"Rika!" Charlie called out over his comms as he rushed toward the giant mech. "We can't keep chipping away at them like this. We don't have the numbers or the power."

"I know, Charlie," she shot back. "But I'm doing all I can."

"I can see that," he said. "But we need to do more."

"What more can I do?" the woman with the glowing tattoos asked. "I'm just figuring this stuff out, ya know? There's no guide manual for it."

"I know, and I need you to trust me."

"To the end," she said.

"Let's not take it that far," Charlie said.

"What do you want me to do?" Rika asked as she targeted and disabled another ship's shielding.

The shields were down long enough for Ara to swoop in and rip into it with her claws, tearing open the hull and providing her an opening into which she sprayed a deadly stream of magical flames. Hundreds would perish as the craft exploded in mid-air, and Charlie found he didn't feel the slightest pity for them.

They'd invaded his home, attacked his friends, and now were at it all again. Enough was enough.

"Pick me up," he said to his mech-driving friend. "I need to be near you if there's any chance this will work."

Rika bent down and reached out the mech's giant hand for Charlie to jump onto, the towering machine easily moving under her expert guidance. While Charlie had known the basics of mech piloting, Rika had always been the pro, and, apparently, whatever Malalia and the Tslavars had done to her mind, that bit of knowledge was very much intact.

Lifting him high in the air, Rika had the mech position her friend right next to her shielded cockpit.

"Now what?" she asked.

"Now I want you to open yourself to your power. Let it flow freely, then reach out for the only other thing from our world and latch on."

"But there's nothing here, Charlie."

"I'm here. Focus on me. Focus on the only other human in this galaxy."

A strange sensation began tickling Charlie's magic. His own power was tied to Ara and Bawb, a mixture of Zomoki and Ootaki magic that wanted to flare up and fight this foreign magic, but Charlie pushed the defensive reaction down, reaching out to embrace the human caster's power.

A jolt of pain flashed through his body as they linked. Rika's power was so strong. So different from any he'd ever felt. But it was also familiar. She was from his galaxy, and, together, they could do what no one else could.

"When I count to three, I want you to cast that shield disrupting spell you've been using as hard and as wide as you can."

"At what?" she asked.

"Not at anything at all," Charlie replied. "Just let the power flow as strong as you can. I'll do the rest."

Rika trusted Charlie with her life, and given what they were up against, that could very well be the price today if they failed.

"You ready?" he asked.

"Good to go," she said, already feeling the power within her building to a crescendo.

"Okay. Here we go. One. Two. Three!"

Rika pulsed out her magic with all her might. The sheer force was staggering once she relaxed her tentative control over it, letting Charlie take up the slack. It was that trust and willing subjugation to his control that let the magic *truly* flow for the first time, and it was far more than she had ever realized she possessed.

Charlie took what she offered and mixed it with his own magic, layering Zomoki, Ootaki, and Human magic all together into one. He found he did not need any casting words at all to use this magic. The intent alone sent it to do his bidding.

As a whole, every enemy ship in the system's shielding failed, opening them up wide to the subsequent layer of his attack.

A moment later, every last Tslavar within the spell's reach dropped dead.

It wasn't a violent end, but merely an end. Where in the past he had stunned and frozen his enemy, this was different. Their enemy was vast, and they were on hostile ground. They were fighting for their very survival, and no quarter could be given.

Charlie would have plenty of time to regret his actions later. But for now, his friends and loved ones depended on him for their lives, and he would shoulder the burden of that responsibility, whatever the cost.

The massive pulse of magic slowly dissipated, leaving the surviving ships aimlessly hovering in place, their Drook contingents untouched by the spell. Only Tslavars had been targeted, as was apparent by the scores of dead green men littering the red soil.

It had been magic the likes of which had never been

witnessed in the galaxy, and the effect on the very magical power binding the systems together was tangible across them all.

Far, far away, in a distant system, a mighty and terrible visla felt the strange shift in power viscerally, like a sharp knife in the gut. *This* was new. This was something they'd never felt before. Even more so than the earlier disturbance caused by what, impossibly, had felt like Ootaki and Wampeh magic combined, this new magic was *different*. And it contained a power not of this galaxy.

And for the first time in the years since they'd begun amassing power, the visla actually felt a hot flash of worry.

CHAPTER SIXTY-SEVEN

"You actually got it salvaged and working," Charlie said, admiring the fully functioning mech now that the fighting had ceased.

Rika grinned brightly. "You have no idea how stoked I was when I found it. I mean, it was buried pretty deep, but with a combination of magic and the *Fujin* helping me pull it free, I was able to get it to the surface. From there it was just a matter of some basic repairs. Well, repairs, and figuring out how to power it, since the power cells were nowhere to be found."

"Yeah, about that," Charlie said. "I kind of had to jury rig something with Bob's Drookonus way back when. But I took that with when we cut out. How did you get it operational?"

"Something about my new magic just connected with it. Maybe it's because I've spent so much time in it from design, to testing, to the final systems checks. And it wasn't the magic from our world that did it. Not entirely," she said.

"Yeah, I saw that. You used to glow white. But now you were purple. What in the world was that?"

"Jo and I wound up in a black sun solar system when we first arrived. Something about that ultraviolet power meshed with the pigments the Kalamani put in my skin. It just soaked it up like a sponge. Only, I wasn't quite sure how to use it. Not until today, anyway."

"Well, you made one hell of a good showing," Charlie said. "And nice job on the mech. If you found that, then you must've been near the site of the *Asbrú*'s crash. Were there any traces left of what they did to her before sending her to our galaxy left?"

"None," Rika said. "But there was something else I think you'll want to see."

"Oh?"

"Yeah," she replied with a knowing smile. "Hop on, I'll take you there."

Charlie climbed atop the mech, while Rika slid into the cockpit. "Hey, Bob. Ara. We're going to go check out the old crash site. You wanna come?"

"We will join you momentarily," Ara replied. "Bawb and I are first going to double-check the field of battle to ensure there are no survivors left to threaten us."

"Trust me," Charlie said, recalling the terrible spell he'd cast. "There aren't."

Jo was already waiting for them when Rika arrived at the excavation site. Ara had actually been fairly close when she landed and was only off by about four miles, which, given the size of the area, really wasn't that much.

As the mech slowed its lumbering run and settled down to the ground, Charlie couldn't believe what he saw.

"Are those––?"

"Yep. A bunch of mostly naked dudes, and a bunch of less-naked Tslavars. I guess their clothes were made of hardier stuff," she said. "We found them here, buried just below the surface. Looks like the same sort of spell we encountered back on Earth. Stasis of some sort, and a damn powerful spell at that."

Charlie knew it well, recalling the day he'd so narrowly avoided being struck by it and left to the deep red sands.

"Holy shit. Marban!" he exclaimed when he spied his dear friend among the frozen bodies.

"You know this guy?"

"I know many of them," Charlie replied. "Space pirates who helped us fight off the Council. This was before you were picked up by Malalia, so you'd have no recollection of it."

"So he's a buddy of yours?" she asked as she gave the strapping man with the long scar on his head another look.

"He captured me, actually," Charlie said. "But I don't hold that against him. In fact, we became good friends. More than friends, really. He's like a brother, in many ways. Taught me all I know about piracy."

"Charming," Rika said. "So what do we do with all of these frozen men? I tried to cancel the stasis spell, but I was really just shooting in the dark. I haven't the faintest idea how to negate it."

"I do," Charlie said, having cast a rather massive one himself not so long ago. "Let me see what I can manage."

"Wait. What about the Tslavars? We bound them all, but we should have the others stand guard just in case."

"Don't worry about them," Charlie said, a shadow briefly crossing his otherwise cheery demeanor. "When I cast with you, I killed *all* the Tslavars in the system."

"Even the ones in stasis?"

"I think so," he replied, horrified at what he'd done in the heat of battle. Just how far he'd taken it.

"Damn, Charlie, that's cold-blooded," Rika said. "But given the situation, entirely warranted."

Her words didn't make everything okay, but they did lessen the sting of what he'd done that day. "Okay, stand back. They were frozen in the heat of battle, so they may be a little jumpy when they wake," he said, then focused his power on the frozen men.

The spell that had locked them in stasis was a Council spell, and quite different from the one Charlie had cast against the

Tslavars and their control-collared Uroks when they were attacking Earth, but the principle was the same. All he needed was to find the right form of the spell and they should awaken.

The fierce battle cries and looks of shock on the men's faces as they lunged to their feet, desperately searching for the weapons that had just been in their hands a moment ago––hundreds of years in the past––were more than enough to tell them the reversal spell had worked.

The Tslavars, as Charlie had expected, remained motionless. No longer frozen in stasis, but never to move again.

Marban lurched to his feet, quickly regaining his wits as he surveyed the scene. Dead Tslavars littered the red soil.

"We are victorious!" he bellowed with glee, then abruptly stopped and looked down. "Where are my pants?" he asked. "Why am I wearing Tslavar pants?"

"Uh, that was me," Rika said. "Sorry about that, but yours had fallen apart, and those were all that was around that would fit your, uh, measurements."

Marban was a pirate and had seen many fierce battles in his day, but something about the way the strange, inked woman's eyes crinkled with amusement when she said that made him blush nevertheless.

"Oh, well, I, uh, I thank you, then. But who are you, exactly?" he said before spotting Charlie. "Little Brother! You survived the engagement!" he said, giving his friend a massive bear hug.

Ara and Bawb touched down beside them, watching the confused pirates take in the scenery that had so drastically changed from what they'd been fighting in just moments ago.

"Uh, wasn't your Zomoki frozen to stone?" Marban asked, looking around. "And wasn't there a large ship crashed just over there?"

"Yeah, the thing is, some stuff happened since then."

"Since? It's been mere moments."

There was no easy way to tell someone everyone they knew was long dead but to just do it.

"You were hit with a stasis spell, Marban. You and the others, you've been frozen beneath the sands here for hundreds of years."

A look of pain flashed across his face, but Marban, ever the stoic warrior, hid it behind his jovial mask an instant later. But Rika had seen it, and she knew full well the pain he was feeling, despite his outward appearance. It was the same kind of hurt of realizing your life would never be the same that she had faced. And it had taken her quite some time to get over.

"So, were we victorious?" the pirate finally asked.

"Yes and no," Charlie replied. "There's way too much to fill you in on, but the short version is, yes, we won, no, it didn't end there, but what happened here started a revolution across the colonized systems. The Council was broken up, its members scattered to the winds."

"Then we are safe!"

"Not exactly," Charlie said. "Sorry to be the bearer of more bad news, but there's a new visla amassing a huge fleet of powerful ships. And our forces got their asses kicked and had to flee back."

"Back?"

"To my galaxy," Charlie replied. "Like I said, there's a lot to fill you in on."

Marban nodded once. "There is fighting to be done, and no matter if it's hundreds of years later, we're still with you, Charlie."

"We have a space pirate army now," Charlie said with a grin. "Of course, the *Fujin* can't possibly carry them all."

"What is a *Fujin*?"

"It's Rika's ship," Charlie replied, nodding to his pilot friend.

"Ah, the divine, glowing creature," Marban said, his eyes lingering a moment longer on the inked warrior woman before returning his gaze to his friend. "We will make do. Does the *Rixana* still fly?"

"I honestly don't know, Marban. I haven't heard word of her since we returned to this galaxy."

"Hey, fellas," Rika said. "You do realize you don't need to go searching for your old ship, right?"

"But yours is not nearly large enough to hold but a handful of us," Marban noted.

"No, it isn't. But y'all are forgetting, Charlie just killed all the Tslavars in the system."

"You did *what*?" Marban said, looking at Charlie with an expression of pure shock.

"It's a magic thing," Charlie said. "I'll explain later. But I see where Rika's going with this. The spell killed the Tslavars but spared their ships and the Drooks on board. We have a bunch of Tslavar warships just floating around, waiting to be used."

"Magnificent!" Marban exclaimed. "An excellent pillage, Charlie! Worthy of a man of the *Rixana*, if I do say so myself. We can divide our numbers and skeleton crew these ships until we can gather more able-bodied fighters to join our ranks."

Charlie and Rika shared a smile.

"It looks like we've got ourselves the beginning of our own pirate fleet," Charlie said.

"We shall take control of them at once!"

"Hang on a minute, Marban. You and the guys take a minute to gather yourselves. You've been frozen a long time, and there's one thing I need to do." He turned to his Zomoki friend and inspected the containers strapped to her harness. All appeared to be intact. "Ara? You ready?"

"Indeed."

"Then let's go do this."

CHAPTER SIXTY-EIGHT

With Rika's excavation of the mech and frozen combatants, Charlie had lucked into something of a road map. Without the fruits of her labors marking a definitive starting point, he realized they'd have had a snowball's chance in hell of finding the hidden cistern that once contained the priceless magical waters.

Not only did the rocky remains of the buildings that dotted the landscape look like nothing more than naturally occurring stone cairns, the hundreds of years that had passed since they were last on this world had seen the shifting sands effectively change the landscape to something entirely new.

Where there had been dunes before, the land was now flat, and where the red sand had been blown free of rocky ruins, those same remnants were now mostly buried.

Fortunately, Charlie knew the rough distance from the wreck of his ship to the hidden chamber. While there was no longer a debris trail and deep red gouge in the soil from his ship's crash landing to act as a compass, Rika had provided him with something just as good.

"The Tslavars were where, exactly?" he had asked.

"Just over there. And these other guys were buried right here, with the mech," she had replied.

It was all he needed to orient himself. The wreck of the *Asbrú* would have been directly behind the pirates, meaning if he departed at a forty-five-degree angle, in approximately two miles he should hit the secret cistern.

Ara lurched into the air and made the hop in no time, dropping down when Charlie spotted the slightest sign of stones poking through the red sand.

"Down there. I think that might be it," he said.

"And if not?"

"There weren't too many of these piles out here, so now that we know the general area, hopefully we'll be able to track it down relatively quickly. But I think this is it."

"On the first try?" she asked. "That would be good luck, Charlie."

"Yeah, and I think we're about due some, don't you?"

"Indeed," the dragon replied.

Charlie set to work clearing the sand from the buried ruins, but unlike his last visit to this planet, he no longer needed to dig with his hands and a scrap of wreckage. Instead, he let his magic do the work, shifting the soil with a spell rather than manual labor.

He had cleared down nearly ten feet of the red sand when he came across dampness. *Felt* it, more like. With renewed vigor, he quickly forced the remaining soil back from the long-buried stone. The angular piece of ruin had been buried for centuries, yet Charlie recognized it just as if it were yesterday.

"That's it," he said. "That's the entrance to the tunnel that leads to the cistern."

The edges were damp, he noted. That was unusual, given the arid climate, but seeing as it had been buried, perhaps that allowed a bit of condensation to gather from the temperature shift to the humid chamber inside.

This time around, Charlie used a simple spell to slide the stone aside rather than straining his back and arms. He almost jumped back when a slosh of water gushed out, splashing his legs.

The water soaked through the material in an instant, and a blissful wave of power flowed through his body. It had been so long since he'd taken a swim in these waters, and now, somehow, they had not only been preserved, but the long-hidden chamber had flooded with the stuff as the centuries passed.

"Ara, what happened?" Charlie asked as he sank to his knees and brought a cupped handful of the water to his mouth. His magic flashed bright and alive as the fluid slid down into his welcoming stomach. "Sorry, you should get in here and have some of this," he said, stepping aside so his Zomoki friend could drink her fill.

Ara's nostril's flared at the welcome smell. "It has grown stronger, Charlie," she said, lowering her head and carefully drinking the magical liquid.

This time, she was going slow, not wanting to have a repeat of the phoenix-like event the last time she'd imbibed the Balamar waters. Just enough to sate her thirst and fuel her magic. Finally, she raised her head, her eyes and scales brilliant beneath the twin suns.

"I had heard tale that perhaps the visla's secret cistern was merely a holding vessel for his true source. One that would produce concentrated waters long after his passing. It would appear, judging by the current levels, that was more than just legend."

Charlie was astonished. A tiny vial of the water would fetch a fortune anywhere in the galaxy, and here they were, drinking it. Bathing in it. More than any would believe possibly existed.

He unfastened the containers and filled each to the brim easily, not having to trek down into the subterranean chamber and then lug them back out, though he'd have just used magic to carry them.

In short order, all were filled to capacity, sealed and magically reinforced to ensure no dangerous leakage might splash their Wampeh friend.

Of course, he would be safe while wearing his space suit, but Charlie had no desire to risk Bawb's combustion.

Ara landed among the gathered pirates looking absolutely radiant. Bawb knew that look, but to the others, it seemed as if a minor miracle had occurred.

"Okay you all, gather around," Charlie said. "We've got something here. Something priceless. Something people kill for across this galaxy. And we're going to give it to all of you."

That got the group's attention, and even the more seriously injured hobbled closer to hear what he had to say.

"In these containers are special waters. Healing waters that will give you strength and cure what ails you. In addition, it will, for a short while, at least, render you somewhat more resistant to magical attacks. Trust me on this, it can make a killing spell feel like a nasty stun. But let's not try that one out on one another, okay?"

The men laughed, their spirits rising with the pep talk.

"Now, this part is *very* important," Charlie said. "This water will kill you if you drink it. I'm not playing around here. Stone dead is what you'll be if that happens, so whatever you do, make sure not to get it in your mouths."

"But how do we use it, then?" a wounded pirate asked.

"It absorbs through your skin," Marban said, stepping forward in front of his men. "Charlie poured some on me just before we went into battle," he said. "Well, it was hundreds of years ago, apparently, but as you all know, it's as good as just a few hours ago to us. In any case, you'll feel it immediately, kind of a pleasant refreshing sensation as your aches flee your body. And it is safe, so long as you do as Charlie instructed. You know me, and you all have my word on that."

"So, I need you all to line up, and we'll give you each a good wet down," Charlie said. "Marban, you good to handle that?"

"You bet, Little Brother," he said, then turned to Rika with his trademark grin. "Ladies first," he offered.

"Oh, I'm good," she replied, holding up a smaller container Charlie had handed her. "No wet T-shirt contest for you, I'm afraid. I'm like Charlie. Not from your galaxy, you see. We're the only ones who can drink it and live."

"Well, Ara too," Charlie added.

"Oh, I didn't know that," Rika said.

"Yeah, you were kind of a brainwashed slave when that all went down. Sorry."

At the words brainwashed and slave, Marban's bright smile faltered a moment. It seemed this strong woman had something of a darker past. Yet she had come through in fine form. It only made her more intriguing.

But for now, there was work to be done.

CHAPTER SIXTY-NINE

Marban had the men line up and began carefully spraying them down with the healing waters, getting an extra helping himself in the process from the runoff. Bawb, however, was standing with Jo, very, very far from the process.

"Why don't you apply some to your flesh?" he asked the cyborg.

"I'm not really human. It won't do anything for me," she replied.

"You cannot know that. From what I understand, your flesh aspect is integrally tied to your mechanical one. Yes, you can live without it, but you cannot deny there is a bond between the two. I think it would be wise, given the enemy we face, if you were to bathe in the waters."

Jo looked at the Wampeh a moment, contemplating his words. She could do a quick wet-down, she supposed. And she could even drink some, storing it for later in one of her internal storage compartments.

"Okay, Bawb. Your point is well taken," she said, heading over to get in line for a spraying.

Rika and Charlie watched from a little distance as the weary and injured men were healed by the waters one by one, emerging from the impromptu shower wet, healthy, and ready to rumble.

"There's so much more water than before," Charlie said. "With the right equipment, we could easily dose a huge fighting force and still have plenty to spare."

"If we can get home, that is," Rika noted.

"Well, yeah. There is that," he replied. "In any case, I'll refill the containers when they're done, then bury the cistern good and deep. After a day of this sun and wind, no one will be able to see any trace of my excavation."

"Good," Rika said, opening the bottle and taking a much-needed swig.

A flash of something jolted her, shaking Charlie to the core as well.

"Did you feel that?" she asked. "Are we still linked?"

"I think so," he replied, a slightly panicked look in his eye.

"It's like when I reached out, Charlie. When you told me to share my power."

"I know," he said, not knowing what the hell to make of what just happened. But the feeling was undeniable. "The link to your power. You opened it up to the only other one of us out here. Oh, shit."

"Does this mean what I think it means?" Rika asked, uneasily.

"I'm pretty sure it does," he replied. "It means somehow, somewhere in this galaxy, there's another human. And they just got a dose of your magic too."

Astonishing as that was, the clock was still ticking, and Charlie realized that whatever this meant, they had more pressing matters at hand.

Through unexpected good luck, they'd not only won the day, but armed themselves with both the waters that could apparently destroy the visla, as well as a new fleet of ships, crewed by their very own space pirates.

Things were looking up for Charlie and his friends. And if Lady Luck continued to smile upon them, they might just reconnect with the rest of their team and make it out in one piece.

"Charlie!" Bawb called out. "Quickly, over here!"

Charlie took off at a run, sprinting across the red soil to his friend's side.

"What is it, Bob?"

"This man," he replied, pointing to a Tslavar who was miraculously still clinging to life.

"How can that be?"

"He's a half-breed," Bawb said. "You can see in his ears. Not full Tslavar. He is gravely wounded, but the spell did not kill him outright."

"And we can get some answers," Charlie said, turning his attention on the dying man. "Who are you working for? Who controls your fleet?"

The green man coughed in pain. "I shall not betray my visla," he replied.

"You are dying," Bawb interjected. "And there is nothing we, or your visla, can do to stop that."

A look of fear flashed across the Tslavar's face, replaced with an unconvincing stoic calmness. "So I die," he said, plainly.

Charlie and Bawb didn't buy it for a second. He was scared.

"Listen, friend. We are not asking you to betray your visla. We do not ask for secrets, merely the visla's name."

"Why would I give you that?" the man asked.

"Because the spell that wounded you is going to turn your insides to liquid. But it will do so very slowly over the next several days until you shit out the slush that was your organs and finally die. Trust me when I say, it is not a pleasant way to pass, and you will be awake and in excruciating pain the entire time," Bawb said.

Charlie flashed him a look. *"That's not what it'll do,"* he said silently in Bawb's head.

"You and I know that, but he does not," the Wampeh replied.

"Tell us this one thing, and I promise you, we will help you pass quickly and painlessly. You will die with honor, having served your visla, and their name is all that is required. Surely that is something you can do to spare yourself such a fate."

The green man winced as the little spell Bawb was quietly casting twisted his gut sharply. It was a cheap trick, but they were limited on options.

"Dominus," the man finally said. "Visla Dominus."

He then stiffened and fell silent, never to speak again.

"You kill him?" Charlie asked.

"No. That was your spell running its course. But he spoke, and just in time, as well."

"Visla Dominus," Charlie said. "Obviously a pseudonym."

"Yes," Bawb agreed. "But it is a start. Let us gather our troops. We have a long flight ahead of us."

Rika collapsed her mech for travel and had it loaded onto one of the seized Tslavar craft, as the giant metal robot was too big to fit on the *Fujin*, then joined Jo aboard the alien ship, the *Fujin* anchored to the vessel's hull for the time being.

Charlie and Bawb suited up and climbed atop Ara, while Marban and his band of survivors loaded into the Tslavar ship brought to the ground to transport them to the rest of their pillaged vessels.

Then the newly formed fleet of humans, pirates, and their vampire and dragon friend, took to the skies, ready to face a new day, and their new enemy.

EPILOGUE

Sitting in the silence of her cell, Daisy Swarthmore, woman of Earth, paced back and forth. It was something she'd done often since they'd zapped her with whatever the hell kind of weird stun weapon they'd used on her when she'd tried to break in to end whoever it was who was threatening her home.

But this? This was different. And it didn't feel like it came from the bastards who had captured her. Or the teenage girl who kept visiting her. No, she was pretty sure this was something new. And disconcerting.

The fact of the matter was, her body was glowing purple. Ever so slightly, but glowing nonetheless. And Daisy had absolutely no idea why.

Uh, Sarah? You seeing this? she asked the neural clone of her formerly dead sister now living in her head.

"*See it? You're fucking glowing, Daze. How could I miss it?*"

But what happened? I mean, the kid hasn't been around today, and neither has anyone else, for that matter. You think they spiked my food with some kind of hallucinogen or something?

"*I'd be able to tell,*" Sarah said. "*Nope, this is something totally different. And I can feel it in here too. Like, you know how I can't tap into your body and control it? Well this is different. This I can actually wrap my hands around."*

You don't have any hands, Sis. You're riding shotgun in my head.

"Ha-ha. You know what I mean, ass."

Daisy chuckled. These little internal conversations with her sister were the only thing keeping her sane in this place.

The glow slowly began to fade, but the sensation of its presence remained even after her body appeared to return to normal. But a persistent tingle lingered, just at the edge of her awareness.

"Oh, great. Now what?" she grumbled, her voice no longer raspy and broken.

"Uh, Daze?"

"Yeah, what?"

"You can talk out loud again," Sarah pointed out. *"Whatever just happened to you, it broke whatever weird-ass tech they were using to keep you from talking."*

"Holy crap, you're right," Daisy said. "Hell yeah! But I think I'd better keep this to myself for now, don't you think?"

"Damn right. The way things have been looking, we'll need every little advantage we can get," Sarah said.

Daisy flopped down on her low bed and looked around the featureless cell. Weeks she'd been there, and she was still none the wiser as to what was really going on. It had all been such a whirlwind rush. One minute she and Freya were popping out of warp back at Earth, looking forward to taking in the view after finally finishing their latest inter-system survey for new life.

The next minute, they were tossed through some kind of vortex into troubled space. The kind that made Freya's warp engines totally unreliable.

That would have been bad enough, but the massive fleet of ships that opened fire on them with some totally bizarre weapons systems they couldn't even track had forced them to perform an emergency warp. But they'd be back to kick ass, that was for sure. Once they figured out who the hell was attacking them, that is.

It wasn't the Ra'az Hok, that much they knew, and the Chithiid were allies now. So who could this new threat possibly be? A quick warp back for a little intelligence gathering with her stealth ship was in order.

Only the warp went terribly awry.

Repeatedly.

Freya didn't know what to do, which is disconcerting for one of the greatest AI minds ever to live. The poor ship had been beside herself with distress when every single attempt to backtrack instead sent them to some strange new system, totally off course from her intended destination.

Daisy had made the most of the situation presented them when they stumbled upon what appeared to be one of the fleet's ships by blind luck following yet another bad warp.

Freya's stealth tech didn't seem to be working against whatever systems these aliens were using, and she had no idea if her adaptive camouflage might also be compromised, so she was forced to stay far, far back, scanning with her most powerful equipment to just barely keep the hostile ship in sight.

When a smaller craft departed from it, Daisy had followed, temporarily parting ways with her ship, each tracking a vessel, and both hoping to get some answers. And in Daisy's case, maybe a little payback.

And that, ultimately, had led her to this place, though she'd made her initial landing thanks to Pod. And then things went tits up, resulting in Stabby, her genetically engineered, ultra-strong bone sword, being stuck in a wall, and Daisy being stuck in a cell.

"You think the kid figured it out?" she wondered aloud.

"*I hope so,*" Sarah replied. "*She seems like a smart kid, after all. Though she does keep insisting on calling you a heretic, which is really not cool. And that gibberish you've been spouting? She calls it a prophesy."*

"Hey, I was just trying to get a few words past that silencing tech they used on me. But if she wants to call it a prophesy? Fine by me. People hear what they want to hear, anyway. But if she did figure it out and managed to find Pod, maybe, just maybe, that little AI will have the sense to call Freya. We have to catch a break eventually, right?"

"Let's hope. Heretic."

"Shut up. You're supposed to be on my side."

"I am. I wouldn't want to be on a heretic's bad side, after all," Sarah said with a laugh.

Daisy leaned back, staring at the walls that had held her for so many weeks. Illumination with no visible source, restraints that she couldn't see. It was not how she'd envisioned making first contact with a new race.

"This planet? It's a messed up place, Sis," she sighed.

"Yeah, but if the kid listened, we might stand a chance."

"Time will tell," Daisy said, allowing herself the tiniest glimmer of hope. "Time will tell."

BUT WAIT, THERE'S MORE!

Follow Charlie on his continuing adventures in the fifth book of
the Dragon Mage series:
Rebel Mage Charlie

ALSO BY SCOTT BARON

Standalone Novels

Living the Good Death

The Clockwork Chimera Series

Daisy's Run

Pushing Daisy

Daisy's Gambit

Chasing Daisy

Daisy's War

The Dragon Mage Series

Bad Luck Charlie

Space Pirate Charlie

Dragon King Charlie

Magic Man Charlie

Star Fighter Charlie

Portal Thief Charlie

Rebel Mage Charlie

Odd and Unusual Short Stories:

The Best Laid Plans of Mice: An Anthology

Snow White's Walk of Shame

The Tin Foil Hat Club

Lawyers vs. Demons

The Queen of the Nutters

Lost & Found

ABOUT THE AUTHOR

A native Californian, Scott Baron was born in Hollywood, which he claims may be the reason for his rather off-kilter sense of humor.

Before taking up residence in Venice Beach, Scott first spent a few years abroad in Florence, Italy before returning home to Los Angeles and settling into the film and television industry, where he has worked as an on-set medic for many years.

Aside from mending boo-boos and owies, and penning books and screenplays, Scott is also involved in indie film and theater scene both in the U.S. and abroad.

Made in United States
North Haven, CT
29 October 2024

59557095R00232